S.C. Defiant

Timothy Diamond

Copyright © 2019 Timothy Diamond

National Library of Australia Cataloguing-in-Publication
entry

Creator: Diamond, Timothy author.

Title: S.C. Defiant / Timothy Diamond.

ISBN: (paperback)   978-0-6487364-0-0
ISBN: (EBook) ASIN: B07WR5Q8GJ

Subjects: Science Fiction.
Action/Adventure - Fiction
War - Fiction.
General Fiction.

Dewey Number:

About the Author:

"Timothy Diamond" is a pseudonym for my real name.

I Started writing between 1988 and 1994 I wrote multiple articles and reports on recreational diving that were published in Scuba Diver Magazine and the Gold Coast Bulletin. I also wrote the feature article 'The Round Trip' for Yachting Australia magazine in 2009.

My first foray into writing full length novels was in 2014 with the Catalyst Trilogy, which was loosely based around my own experiences.

Other books written are:

Playing With Fire: Catalyst Book 1
Divine Retribution: Catalyst Book 2
Last Man Standing: Catalyst Book 3
The Other Side of the Coin: a companion book to the Catalyst Trilogy
Ocean Gold
Chasing The Sun
The Tale of the MV Eagle Star
Kingdoms Bounty
The Ultimate Gamble
Rebellion!

Acknowledgements.

Ralf B: My friend for more than 30 years. To change Spock's dialogue a little, "you have been, and always will be, my 'best' friend."

All my Family and friends who enjoy the books.

LJ Kidd: Keep up the good work with the writing and illustrating.

William (Doc) Brose: Thanks Bill for collaboration, all your hard and frustrating work was appreciated, I couldn't have done it without you. Cheers from your mate in Australia.

Star Charts.

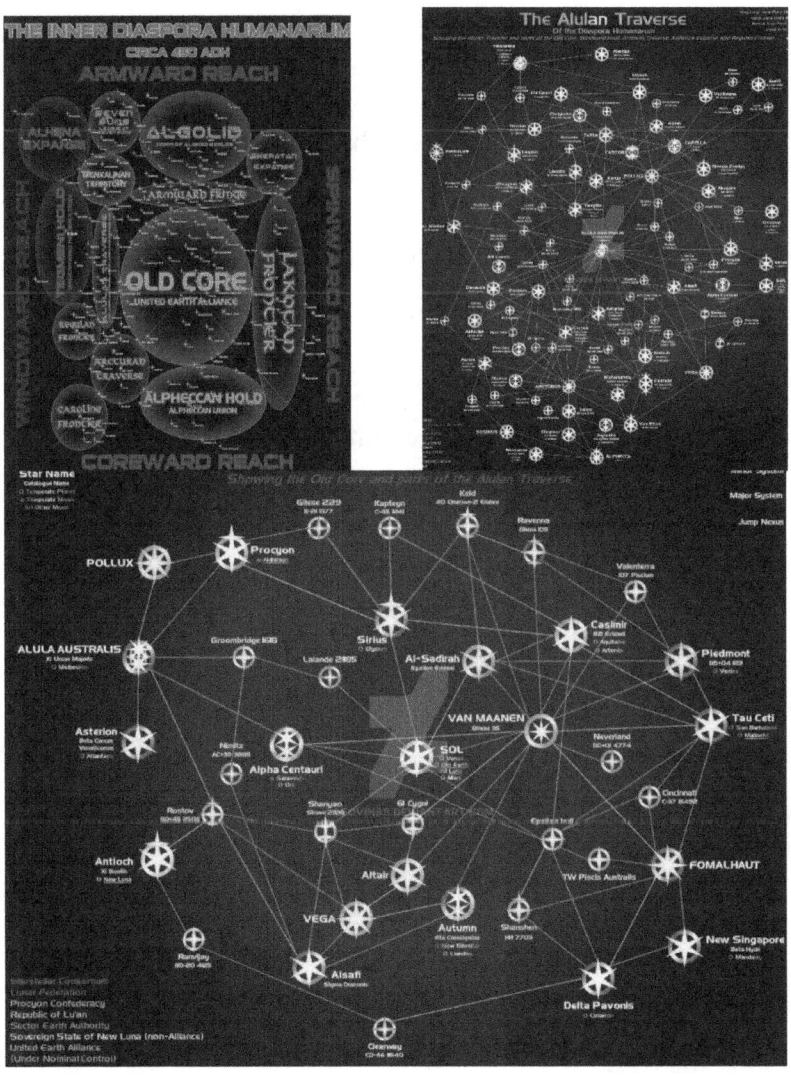

Note to Readers, from the Author.

Dear Readers, those of you that read my novels would know, I usually don't write science fiction books. Well, all that is about to change, I have had the idea for this book genre in my head for some time now and have finally decided to put it down on paper to see where the story takes me.

If I think it good enough to publish, that's what I'll do, if not, well at least it's now out of my head, and I can concentrate on my normal novels.

In explanation, Distance and Speed: A parsec is a unit of measure for distance and speed on universally standard star charts, showing from one-part section of a chart to another, hence the use of the name parsec. As to regard speed, 1 Parsec is equal to 3.26 light years.

A ship cruising with a speed of warp 20 in hyper-space, could cross the distance of a light year (6 Trillion miles) in one hour, or 31 parsecs an hour.

To put this in perspective, a ship traveling to Earth from the edge of the milky way galaxy (a distance of 60,000 light years), it would only take 30 minutes including coming out of hyper-space and establishing orbit of the planet.

As you can see, the story came together rather well, and I have decided to publish it, please let me know what you think of it, as I welcome the feedback and as usual, I hope you enjoy the read.

Yours Sincerely,
Tim Diamond

Prelude

In the year 2410, the central government of Earth sent emissaries to all the known worlds with invitations for ambassadors to attend a three-month conference on Earth. The main topic on the conference agenda was to establish an alliance of all the known planets.

The conference started during the second week of January 2411 in the newly built united council auditorium in San Francisco. All the ambassadors were given translation pins so that each group would be able to hear and speak in their own language and be able to understand each other. This device had been invented by Ivan Dyerson a university professor and would soon become known as the universal translation device.

When the conference ended three months later not only was the new alliance named, but there were many new reforms listed, that would be made to each and every planet within the alliance. All the conditions of entry to the alliance were read over every broadcasting device throughout the universe, on small and large planets, and colonies, even those on the Outer Rim, so that everyone not yet aligned with bigger planets would know how to join the new United Planetary Alliance. After the new reforms were spoken of in their entirety, then all the present ambassadors at the conference added their signature to the main document, that each off-world ambassador would receive a copy of, to take to their homeworld.

Some of the major reforms from that of the conference are listed below:
1/ That all worlds within the alliance would share and exchange knowledge and technologies freely with each other.
2/ Free trade of goods and services to all worlds within the alliance.
3/ To deal with defence of the alliance, a naval academy be established on Earth open to all persons wishing to crew military starships of Alliance Fleet Command from all allied worlds.
Training academies would be established on Alpha Centauri for pilots and technicians joining Alliance Fighter Command.
And a training academy for those willing to join as normal ground troops on Sirius, that wished to become members of the Alliance Mobile Infantry.
4/ Each world would establish law and order offices and a judiciary system in each town and village so that alliance law and order rules would be maintained.
5/ Any unallied planet or system could be invited to join the alliance should it reach, and could prove, maturity and technological advancement and adhere to the rules of the alliance.
6/ All alliance planets and systems would adopt the universal Earth calendar for the chronological telling

of time and known as stardate.

i.e. 2411.03.31.1500, the year, point, month, point, day, point, time (in 24hr time), was when the Alliance conference concluded. If no time is reported the point and last four digits are removed, i.e. stardate 2411point 3 point 31 is the date without time recorded.

Stardate 2503.02.10:
This was the day that the Alliance was attacked by armed forces from the planet Zytronos.

This was the first anyone had encountered them, and the Alliance knew absolutely nothing about them. However, after the capture of some of their robotic soldiers, which were called Zytrons, a picture and knowledge of them and their homeworld quickly emerged and sent throughout the Alliance.

Zytronos was a machine world, ruled by sophisticated computers, but they also had a command structure much like those of humans, and the reason they attacked the Alliance was because it was deemed to be a threat to their existence.

During the war, the Alliance left all of the Outer Rim Planets to their own devices to deal with the Zytrons, preferring to protect only worlds that were part of the Alliance, but they did transmit all the

intelligence gathered to the Outer Rim Planets to help them fight the Zytrons. Despite repeated appeals to the Alliance for their help, the Outer Rim Planets were refused any help in their fight.
This refusal by the Alliance eventually would become the source of its demise.

The war with Zytronos raged for seven years before the Alliance hit back with massive counter attacks, and this was only after one of the Alliance planets, Duros Major, came under attack and was obliterated entirely, though many of the Outer Rim Planets had been destroyed in this same manner.
The Zytrons made use of many terrible bombs they had at their disposal, the worst being a Quantum bomb, just one of these bombs could destroy an entire planet, turning it into nothing but floating rubble. Before the Alliance struck back, they pleaded with all Outer Rim Planets to help in the strike back, by way of ships, troops and supplies.

During a meeting held on Zeta Australis by all the heads of government of all the Outer Rim Planets, it was decided that,
1/ the rim worlds would form their own alliance and it was called the Federation of Outer Rim Planets and Systems, and,
2/ the Federation would refuse any help to the Alliance, due to the Alliance's refusal to come to the aid of the Outer Rim when it was so desperately required at the start of the war with the Zytrons.

This answer was conveyed to the Alliance chairman, not via an ambassador (as required by protocol), but by a coded video message from the elected chairman of the Federation.

The counter strikes by the Alliance lasted for another three years (perhaps this would have been shortened if the Outer Rim Federation had joined with the Alliance, but who is to know). The Alliance counter strikes forced the Zytrons from all their bases on different worlds between the quadrant of space from the alliance worlds all the way back to Zytronos itself.
Having captured a few of the Zytron Quantum Bombs on their march to Zytronos, the task force commander of the Alliance decided to end the war for all time and ordered one of these quantum bombs be dropped on the Zytron homeworld, thus destroying all forms of life, and turning the planet itself into dust.

The war with Zytronos came to an end at stardate 2513.11.15.1105.

Chapter 1.

Stardate 2505. 02. 02:
Since arriving at the Alliance Fleet Academy yesterday, all of my fellow inductees and I were hoping to become flight officers, having been encouraged to begin keeping a personal journal. Most of our first day was taken up with orientation classes and being issued with all manner of flight uniforms, communication devices, including this journal tablet, blasters and holsters, and personal assault weapons.

Having been assigned my quarters, I squared away all my personal items I'd brought from home, weapons, and hanging up my uniforms, changing into a set of general duty clothes, because I don't start my first class until tomorrow, I have sat down with the tablet to start my personal journal.

My name is Clayton Davis and I was born on Vega 13, an Outer Rim world, fifteen years ago. My father is a mining engineer, and mother a teacher. My physical features clearly show I'm an offworlder, I have dark brown short hair, and stand five feet seven, which is shorter than most Terrans because my homeworld has a heavier atmosphere than here on Earth, but my body is perfectly muscled and formed for my homeworld. On Earth, with a lighter atmosphere I'm stronger and faster than any terran here. My intellect has been tested and rated at

196, which is above the normal Terran rate of 150 (perhaps that's why I have no problems with learning new things, and I can recall anything I've seen, read or heard from my head instantly), but I keep this fact to myself as much as possible.

Stardate2506.06.02.1210:
Today I have been given the callsign Hunter after my simulation fighter combat run, due to my ability to track and hunt down all the enemy ships and destroying them which gave me a perfect score.

Stardate 2508.04.05:
I have been at the Academy for three years now and as a senior cadet, I now hold the rank of lieutenant junior grade.

I have a lot of those that I met as fellow inductees as friends, only two of my original group have dropped out of the training. We were advised on our first day, that not all of us would graduate the Academy due to the pressure of the training.

After classes, training scenarios, and flight simulations where we would each be assigned different roles to play within the large bridge simulators, we would all get together at the Academy tavern and discuss the day or the scenario we'd been involved in and wonder what we would face next.

It was during one of these decompression sessions
from a difficult simulation scenario that I first heard
of one training scenario we would all face during
our third year, this came from Thad Norman,
a native of Earth, as he said, "I've been talking to a
couple of the cadets in the year above us and was
told that during this year, we all have to go through
a scenario in the simulator that is a no-win situation,
where everyone dies!"

His announcement brought all talk to silence, as we
looked at him, as he went on. "It's the truth, I learnt
about it yesterday during the lunch break."
As we all took in his statement there was quiet at
our table, until I scoffed, "Well, I don't believe in
that sort of situation, there is always a way!"

Later that night while I was alone in my quarters, I
recalled a statement one of our lecturers had
hypothesized, "How we died could be construed as a
reflection of how we had lived." I fell asleep as I
pondered over his hypothesis, when I awoke the
next day, all thought of it had left my mind, not that
I had forgotten it though.

A week later, we all filed into our lecture room in
the morning, and an instructor announced that we
would be in the Diligent Bridge Simulator most of
the day, looking at his tablet to assign our roles for
the scenario that he kept secret, as he read out,
"Davis you'll be the Captain," as he went on

assigning roles, I was chuffed, this was the first time I'd been given the role of captain, I was usually assigned to a junior role. The best I'd ever drawn was Executive Officer. When all of us had been assigned our roles, we made towards the main Simulator building, and all filed into our assigned station chairs in the large Bridge Simulator.

During the next hour, things went routinely, but fifteen minutes into the second hour, my starship went into battle on two separate occasions with the result that my ship had suffered minor battle damage but destroyed our attackers.

Five minutes later, Lara a native of Tau Ceti, announced from her communication station, "Captain, I'm receiving a faint distress call from the Centari, carrying crew and refugees over one hundred souls. They say they're being sucked into a gravity well near beacon 120, their shields are buckled and failing. They need immediate help Sir!"

"Very well Tara. Alert fleet command!"

She answered shortly, "Fleet replies ours is the closest ship and they're aware of our battle damage sir."

"Alright. Fastest speed Mister Tolliver."

"Aye sir," he replied from his helm station, "Arrival

in four minutes captain."

"Main screen, Tara," I ordered, as I focused on the viewer.

Then Olga, seated next to John Tolliver at her scanning console, excitedly exclaimed, "Three Zytron destroyers in the close proximity Captain!"

"Shields up! Tara, hail the destroyers, tell them we have no wish to fight and are here only to rescue the Centari."

Thad Norman, my Exec said, "Sir, they will most likely attack us anyway."

We arrived onsite and, thinking quickly, I issued my orders, "Return fire only if we're fired upon. Tractor beam?"

"Out of range Captain."

"Transporters?"

"Also out of range Captain."

Resignedly, I ordered, "Take us into transport range John, even if we enter the gravity well. Our engines are more powerful than the freighter. They should pull us out in time."

Then I heard from the weapons station as I watched the viewer, "Destroyers opening fire sir!"

"Fire the phaser cannons," I ordered as we started taking hits to our shields.

From my command chair, I was thinking quickly that if we didn't get into transporter range in time the effects of the gravity well and fire from the Zytrons, I could very well lose my starship.

My Exec announced, "Shields down to sixty percent with one minute until transporter range Captain."

I was nervously moving about in my chair, and screaming in my head, *come on, come on!* Then weapons announced, "Phaser banks offline Captain!

"Torpedoes!"

As Norman said, "Shields at twenty percent, but the transporters are operating."

"Fine," once the transporters have everyone John, get us the hell out of here!"

"Shields down!" yelled Norman.

Then the simulator rocked massively as the bridge was hit by an explosion, and most of my command crew fell over killed or injured, then I heard over the comms, "Engineering to bridge, they've got the engines!"

All I could do was sit stunned in my chair, thinking, *shit, shit, shit!*

As the lights came up and the doors opened our instructor ordered, "Alright! Everyone back to the lecture room. Move!"

I was still sat in my seat stunned at the result of the Simulation, as my fellow team-mates passed me by, with looks of sadness and compassion on their faces, I was the last person to get up and leave the Simulator, with a dejected look on my face, because I still couldn't believe what had happened.

Back in the lecture hall, I was the last one to enter, my head was bowed, and I felt utterly dejected, but I still noticed the looks of concern and sympathy from the rest of my class.

As I sat down our instructor said, "That, ladies and gentlemen, is the Do or Die scenario. It epitomizes decisions that a captain of a fleet vessel must face every day he commands one of our ships. Every one of you will have this scenario sometime during this year of your training, think it over each time you are not in the Captain's chair, think what you can do differently. Mister Davis, please stand."

As I stood all eyes were turned toward me as our instructor continued, "Hunter, I'm sorry that you were the first to undergo this scenario, rest assured that your orders and actions rank as one of the best attempts I've ever seen performed during thc Do or Die. Do you have any questions?"

Pulling my shoulders back into place, and raising my head to look at him, "Yes sir, may I take the test again?"

He smiled, "I'll see what I can do to arrange it, but if I can it won't be until all your classmates have their turn."

I smiled back, "Thank you Sir!" As I sat down again.

Stardate 2508.10.05:
Today is the day I get to have another go at the Do or Die scenario. After going through it countless times with other classmates as the captain, I was hoping to find the flaw in the scenario program, and I think I had found it. The scenario proceeded through the earlier part and came to the distress call.

This time, the enemy ships did not open fire. After rescuing all the crew and refugees from the Centari, we exited the gravity well with our shields still intact, but only at a bare twenty percent.
That's when the enemy destroyers opened fire on us.

We could not pull far enough away in time, and the ship was pounded by the enemy. As we lost shield power altogether, our weapons banks were destroyed along with the engine compartments, I had failed again!

As our instructor entered the Simulator he said, "That was another good try Mister Davis, but as you saw another failure."

"Sir is it at all possible to try again?"

He looked at me doubtfully, "I'll see what I can do, but no cadet has ever asked for a third try, don't get your hopes up because no one's ever done it, the instructional staff may not allow it, I can only try. Do you have a valid reason as to why you should be allowed to take the test again, remembering that this is a scenario is to gauge your reactions in the face of certain death?"

The rest of my class were waiting with bated breaths as I answered his query, "Yes sir I do, I think there is a flaw in the program that I wish to investigate and try yet again."

He thought for a couple of minutes, "Very well, I'll see that your argument is heard by the instructional staff."

As he finished speaking, my communicator chirped

announcing "Lieutenant Davis, please report to the Chancellor's office urgently!"

Hearing the communiqué our instructor said, "Very well Hunter, you best report. The rest of you back to the classroom, now!"

Chapter 2.

I entered the Chancellor's office, gave my name at reception, and was directed to take a seat.
Ten minutes later a door opened, and I was facing the Chancellor, Admiral Neil McManus. He came over to me, "Well Mister Davis, come in please." He escorted into his office and directed me to take the seat in front of his desk, and I waited for the Admiral to be seated before I sat down in the designated chair.

"I see that you are into your third year Davis and it looks like you are getting excellent grades from what I see here, how you are finding the academy?"

"Very good sir, I'm learning a lot and have only found one problem."

He looked directly at me, sighed, "Alright, we'll talk about that in a minute, but there's something you need to know, and there's no good way of saying this, so I'll just go ahead and tell you. A short time ago I received word the Zytrons have attacked your home world of Vega 13 and bombed it with one of their quantum bombs. There are no survivors as the planet was completely destroyed... I'm sorry to give you this news Clayton, your entire family is dead, and I grieve with you for their loss. Are there any other relatives you have close by? I can give you a fortnight's leave on compassionate grounds if you would like."

It took me a moment to process the news I'd been given, then lifted my head looked directly at him, "No sir, that won't be necessary, I'd rather stay here and continue my training."

He looked at me, as if trying to read my thoughts, "Hmm, very well, now tell me about this problem."

I told him all about my Do or Die scenarios and how I thought I had found a flaw in the programming and about the results in my attempt to have a third try, he listened to me interestingly. When I had finished, he said, "I see, well we usually will grant most cadets a second chance of taking that particular scenario, but you have valid reasoning behind your request for a third try, so I'm going to instruct the instructing committee to let you have another chance. You go ahead and do your investigating and let's see if you're right, that will be all Mister Davis."

Having been dismissed I stood, saluted, and made my way out of his office as he lifted a comms unit.

Making my way from the Chancellor's office to the tavern where I knew my friends would be waiting, I was in a rage and annoyed that I had nowhere to vent my anger.

My friends were instantly aware that there was

something wrong as I joined them with two glasses full to the brim with the whiskey, I had found I liked on Earth. As I joined them, I placed one glass on the table and drained the one in my hand in one long drink. Nothing was said until I had drained the glass, then Tara found the courage to say, "Well Clay, it looks like your meeting with the Chancellor didn't go well."

I looked at them with a sad expression, before I answered, "Well, yes and no, he called me there to tell me my homeworld has been obliterated by a Zytron planet killer, so my family are all dead."

The girls all came and embraced me, as the guys all expressed their condolences, I thanked them all, "He also told me he could have given me leave, but I'd have nowhere to go anyway. So I elected to stay here, but he did say he was going to make sure I get another go at the Do or Die scenario. I just hope this war is still going when we graduate, because right now all I want to do is kill Zytrons!"

They were all both happy and sad about the loss of my family, and my third chance at having another go at the scenario. After our decompression session, we all headed to the mess hall for dinner.

After that I left them to go my quarters. I started work on writing a subroutine on my personal log tablet, I was now more than ever was committed to try to bring the no-win scenario to one that had a successful conclusion.

The subroutine I wrote, and hoped, to insert into the computer programming of the Do or Die scenario would be triggered to run only for me after a set of key words spoken during the scenario.

Stardate 2508.10.07.0800:
The previous day, I had been allowed to view the routines of the computer scenario coding for the Do or Die program by my instructor, while the rest of my class went through routine away team scenarios in the Simulator (so-called because the team is away from the ship).

I was successfully able to secretively insert my subroutine into the scenario programming, but continued to peruse the coding for another hour before my instructor came into the room and asked, "Well Hunter have you found anything to help?"

"Yes sir, and I'm now ready to give it another go."

"Very well. Tomorrow morning at zero nine hundred, but I will warn you the entire instructional committee will be there to view your last chance, along with the Chancellor himself."

The next morning, my friends and I gathered in the mess hall for breakfast before reporting to our classroom, as their joking comments were expressed due to my wearing of my command uniform for the scenario.

At 0830 we filed into our classroom to find our instructor waiting our arrival, once we were seated, he said, "Right, you all know what we're doing today, your role assignments will be the same as Hunter's last two attempts, this time however when it becomes your time to die, please do it with a bit of reality, I want to hear screams of pain, not you just folding over quietly, do you have something to add Mister Davis?"

This last question was directed at me because I was sitting back with my hands folded behind my head smiling.

I instantly came to attention, "Yes sir," looking around the classroom at my friends and with a smile continued saying, "Don't worry girls and boys, no one dies today!"

Our instructor scoffed and ordered, "Right, everyone to the Simulation building. I hope for your sake Hunter, that you are right."

We all entered the 'Diligent' Simulator and took our places as the doors were shut and locked. As we waited for the lighting to change that let us know that the scenario had started.

As it did, I reached for the ships log and said, "Ships log AFC Diligent, stardate 2508.10.09.0900, Captain Davis reporting, we have been ordered by fleet command on a routine patrol of the gamma quadrant."

Having used the ships log, the ships name, mine, plus gamma, triggered the subroutine I had inserted the day before and I sat back and smiled.

Everything went as before, then Lara announced the distress call, I became all business as I ordered the message sent to fleet command.

Then she said, "Fleet replies ours and the Saratoga are the only ships in the quadrant with ours the closest ship and they're aware of our battle damage sir."

"Alright. Fastest speed Mister Tolliver."

"Aye sir," he replied from his helm station, "arrival in four minutes Captain."

"Main screen Tara, long range scans Olga," I ordered, as I focused on the viewer.

Then Olga, seated next to John Tolliver at her scanning console excitedly exclaimed, "Three Zytron destroyers in the close proximity Captain!"

"Main screen Olga, John adjust course to exit warp behind them, and we'll run past their portside at full impulse power." As I saw they were in Line Ahead Formation.

John replied, "Aye sir."

Then I ordered, "Weapons have all starboard phaser cannon and torpedoes ready to fire as we exit warp."

"Weapons aye sir," came the reply.

Thad Norman said inquisitively, "Shields Captain?"

"Not yet number one, we'll raise them as we enter the gravity well and close to transporter range, beam them all aboard, then get the hell out of there. Lara make (send) to Saratoga; we require urgent assistance have her commander come on screen."

As the screen wavered, a screen shot of the Chancellor came on, "What do you need Hunter?"

I communicated the reason for help and my intentions in full, then the screen shot nodded, "Understood Hunter, we're making fastest warp and are five minutes behind you, we'll mop up the Zytrons for you and keep them off your back, Saratoga out."

I looked around the bridge, "Now you all know what

we're going to do. All I ask is that you all just do your jobs, Lara viewer to starboard view please."

Then Tolliver said, "Coming out of warp captain, reducing to full impulse power."

"Thank you, John," I replied watching the viewer we had come out of warp just where we needed to be, as we closed with the destroyers port sides, I ordered, "Weapons fire the broadside and keep firing!"

"Aye sir," was the reply as our guns opened up, they must have had their shields down, as all our guns opened up, because the first destroyer we passed exploded without firing a shot, the next two in line were pounded by our fire power, as we inflicted heavy damage to both of them as we passed them.

After noting the damage, "Viewer to front. Secure from battle stations. Mister Norman, be ready to start beaming as soon as we're in range. Reduce to half impulse, John be ready to pour on the power to get us out of here when we have everyone aboard. Lara send our battle results to the Saratoga."

As we turned, to get out of the gravity well, and went to full impulse power, I saw the Saratoga arrive and start firing on the remaining two Zytron Destroyers. Both exploded a few minutes later.

Then the viewer wavered as the Admiral came on, "Well you didn't leave us much sport Hunter, but thank you all the same, we'll stay in the quadrant while you make for home."

"Thank you Captain, we caught them with their shields down, good hunting, Diligent out."

As the screen went back to forward view, I ordered, "John set course for home, maximum warp please."

He had time to reply, "Aye sir," before the lights changed, and the doors unlocked.

I saw the Chancellor make his way into the Simulator first, and ordered as I came to attention, "Attention! Admiral on deck!"

All the class rose and snapped to attention and saluted, the Chancellor returned the salutes, as all the instructors followed and fanned out around the bridge as he said, "Well done Mister Davis, you'll receive a commendation for this, gentlemen and ladies you are all looking at the first person to ever defeat the Do or Die scenario, in the ten years we've used it. And dare I say it the only one into the future.

It seems you found that flaw you mentioned Davis, unfortunate that it came at a time of great sorrow to you. I wish to see you in my office first thing tomorrow, but for now you, and your classmates

deserve the rest of the day off, go on off you go."
We all came to attention again, saluted, and I
said, "Thank you Sir."

We headed toward the tavern, all talking smiling,
and laughing. For the rest of that day I never paid
for a drink or for any lunch. Each of them only
wanted to know how I had done it, but my only
reply was, "You all heard me the day before
yesterday when I told the instructor that I had
discovered a possible flaw in the system, and I was
right, plus this morning you all heard me say, no one
was going to die."

Thad Norman replied, "Yeah, but how did you do
it?"

Lifting my beer, I leaned back, smiled, "Why don't
you ask for another try at it, and do it the same way I
did… are you game enough?" I challenged.

Chapter 3.

The following morning, I arrived at the Chancellor's office at 0830, and I was shown into his office straight away. After inviting me to take a seat, he got down to the matter in hand, asking, "Alright Clayton, how did you do it?

"Well sir, remember my saying that I thought there was a flaw in the program. There is and I used that to my advantage allowing me to win because I don't believe in a no-win situation sir."

"But how? All the instructors and the person who wrote that scenario, have gone through it meticulously and have not found a fault or flaw!"

I smiled, "That's because they all think it's foolproof, and haven't looked for the most obvious thing of all sir."

"Alright, I give up, tell me what you did, so that it can't happen again."

I smiled once more, "Yes sir, all I did was write a subroutine that allowed me and me alone, along with certain words to access what I had written. Of course you also had to know the passwords. This allowed my subroutine to invade the scenario and produce the result I required. Then all I had to do was get access to the computer program itself and insert it into the program from my personal log tablet. Even if it's found no one else can use it but me because of my wording and triggering system, so you have no worries as to whether it can be used again, but you may wish to think about embedding an encrypted password to allowing access into the program sir."

He had started chuckling halfway through my explanation and that turned into full laughter as I finished. After his laughter he said, "Well damn me that serves me right, I was the one that allowed you that access, this goes no further than this room Davis."

I just replied and agreed with one word, "Sir."

"Alright, as I told you yesterday, you will be given a commendation for your actions and it will be for gallantry and ingenuity. I've scheduled a full Academy presentation for Monday morning next week. Full dress uniform Mister Davis, that is all."

Being dismissed, I stood, saluted, and made my way to the door of his office, and went back to the classroom where a lecture was taking place. The instructor told me to come in, be seated, and that I could be caught up by my fellow students later. The lecture was about ground assault firearms and we were all going to be taken to the firing range after we had collected our personal weapons at the end of the lecture.

During our trip to the firing range I told the rest of the class about the following Monday morning parade, and they caught me up with what I had missed while I'd been with the Chancellor.

The following Monday all cadets were gathered in the quadrangle according to the length of their time at the academy with the newest years intake at the front and the last year being at the back. On the podium there were several dignitaries, according to rank, sitting each side of the Chancellor, and the senior instructors seated one row behind them.

The Chancellor took the lectern, his voice rang out around the quad, "Most of you cadets may not know why we're here at this time during a workday, so let me tell you, it is very rare that a cadet receives a commendation whilst still here at the academy. There is one person that has just had that said honour awarded to him. The award is for gallantry and ingenuity and has been awarded for being the first person to ever win and defeat the Do or Die simulator scenario, Lieutenant Clayton Davis report to the podium."

With my cap in place I took one step forward, turned right and marched to the end of our row where I turned left and marched up the centre between the rows, after taking the two steps up onto the podium I faced the Admiral and saluted.

The Admiral leaned forward pinned the commendation medal onto my dress uniform and presented me with the box and scroll. Transferring it to my left hand so that I could shake the Admiral's hand. I took a step back and we saluted each other. After that I had to shake hands with all the dignitaries and instructors before marching back to my place in the formation. Then the parade was dismissed.

Back in my quarters I changed into standard work clothes and headed to our lecture room, where our instructor was ready to continue our training, after the parade.

Stardate 2510.11.30:
Today is our graduation day after five long years of endless lectures, simulator scenarios, and various other duties, that as fleet officers, we could be called upon to perform. Even though we graduate today, we still have to remain at the academy for one additional week to receive our duty assignments telling us which fleet ship we will be posted to, our duty on that ship, and where and when we will board.

Since our third year at the Academy, the relationship between Lara and I had developed from good friends to casual lovers. Lara's parent's and family had been killed in a Zytron raid on her homeworld early in our fourth year and we became kindred spirits.

Our affair started halfway during the fourth year when we faced choices of what to do over the holiday break. Due to my homeworld's destruction, I made the decision to visit different locations on Earth, so Lara had decided to come with me.

Now that graduation was approaching there was the possibility of being posted to different ships. We decided to spend our holiday break together on Earth, if there was time before boarding our assigned ships. We also spent every night prior to graduation in bed together.

I reflected on this as I changed into my dress uniform, with a smile I had to admit to myself that I was fond of her and would miss spending our nights together. Once in my uniform I looked at myself in the mirror, I grabbed my cap and donned it. I checked to see if everything was in place and noted how good my uniform looked with the new commendation medal on it, smiling I thought to myself, *the first of many, I hope.*

Satisfied with my appearance, I left my quarters, and made towards the exit of our building to join my friends.

We lost another classmate during our fourth year after she was recalled home, but my core friends remained the same. Joining them at the doorway, we had to wait for John Tolliver and Olga Checkenco, when they joined us, we all made our way to the parade quad.

The graduation ceremony was for just the graduating class so there weren't other of the Academy's other years present. The quad had been set up with chairs for the class and their families and friends attending the graduation. When we arrived at the quad, I patted both my pants pocket to once again reassure myself that I had my speech. I was the 2505 intake class valedictorian. (The valedictorian was always kept secret, but the chief instructor passed the news onto the winner, due to the duty to give a speech to the assembly during the graduation ceremony, but to be kept secret).

We had thirty minutes before the ceremony started, so we were all introduced to the families and friends of our core friends. We were all having a good time until one of Thad's friends asked me, "So Clayton are you going to introduce your family to us?"

At the comment, all the smiles disappeared from my friends faces as they bowed their heads and silence descended as the smile disappeared from my face, to be replaced with a stern look, Thad looked at me, and I could see his embarrassment.

I turned to the speaker replying, "I'm afraid not sir, they're only here in spirit, as they were killed when Vega 13 was bombed." With that, I about faced and walked away from the group, as Thad started to berate his friend. Lara joined me and we went to sit down in the front row of seats.

As Lara and I were holding hands and talking to each other. I noticed all the instructors we had had during our years at the academy walk onto the podium and take their seats, the ceremony was about to start. Then the Admiral came on stage and arranged his speech on the lectern, as all present started taking seats for the ceremony.

The Admiral tapped the microphone, "Ladies and gentlemen, family and friends, it gives me great honour to welcome you here for the graduation of the 2505 intake class. As you know these graduates have been here for five long years to reach this point in their career, and I dare say they all thought it to be indeed gruelling."

He paused for laughter and applause, then continued, "But before we go on, there is the matter of electing this intake's class valedictorian, which is voted upon by the instructing faculty and is considered by us as a high honour. Here at the Academy, the valedictorian is promoted to First Lieutenant in the fleet ranking system. Therefore, he or she must be worthy of the honour. It is usually a tight race, but this year there is a clear outstanding winner of this honour, he has a one hundred percent average over all his exams and field exercises, his intellect and capability are beyond question, ladies and gentlemen the class valedictorian for 2510 and gallantry medal winner, 1st Lieutenant Clayton Davis!"

As I rose and made my way to the podium there was resounding applause and whistles especially from my inner circle. When I reached the podium, the Chief Instructor came forward, we saluted each other with a smile he removed the cadet insignia from my shoulder and replaced them with my First Lieutenant bars. Then we shook hands, saluted each other once more. As I stepped to the lectern the Admiral faced me, we saluted, then he shook my hand as he gave up his place at the lectern.

Withdrawing my speech from my pocket I placed it on the lectern and faced the assembly, "To the Chancellor and faculty of the Allied Fleet Command Academy, I thank you for this great honour bestowed upon me. To the classmates who had to endure me during the past five years, thank you for your trust and being able to put up with me.

Now as we are about to embark upon our future careers in fleet command savour the time and fun we've had here as friends, smile as you recall the time John crashed his ship into another and the ribbing, we gave him. Or your failure in the Do or Die scenario, because tomorrow we may never see each other again.

I know some of you, like me are itching to just get into this war, but remember I have personal reasons for this, don't make them yours, cherish your families if you still have them unlike a couple of us.

Also, don't whine or bitch if you get what you may consider a shit ship allocation. Some of us may not end up on a ship that goes into battle and end up getting a supply ship or less. Just think about this for a minute. Every ship in the fleet is in the fleet for a reason, that means it's needed, and it requires command crew, so do your best wherever you end up, remember what you were taught here because you are all Fleet Command Officers. I thank you."

I was given a rousing applause coming from my classmates as well as the faculty and families. As I moved away from the lectern and back to my seat, the Admiral moved back to the lectern still applauding my speech.

"Thank you, Clayton for that inspiring speech."
He continued by saying, "Now ladies and gentlemen Here are the graduates of 2510…"
He went on to announce each of the names in our class. As he did, each person went to the podium, saluted, shook his hand and was handed a

graduation scroll by one of our instructors. One more salute and the recipient left the podium and went back to their seat.

The ceremony ended forty-five minutes later.

Chapter 4.

Stardate 2510.12.02.1100:
While Lara and I were luxuriating in bed after making love, our clothes were still on the floor after a late night at the tavern, my shirt communicator chirped, retrieving my shirt and tapping the communicator, "This is Lieutenant Davis," it was answered by a request for me to report to the chancellor's office main reception to collect my orders and travel warrants, "Copy that on my way."

This was immediately followed by Lara's communicator chirping, and I handed her, her shirt. As I closed out mine. Her message was the same, so we both got dressed and walked to the office.

Once there we both went to the main receptionist, "Lieutenants Davis and Kemplar reporting as requested."

She replied, "Ah yes the Admiral is waiting to see you both please take a seat."

We had no sooner sat, when the Admiral's office door opened, and he beckoned us in and invited us to take seats. We waited to salute him before sitting across the desk from him. He returned the salutes and had us sit down, "Now you two, you are both going to the destroyer AFC Scimitar. Hunter, you as the executive officer, and you as the communication officer Growler (which was Lara's callsign). It will dock with its Battle Group next week at the Skyring, but you two don't report until next month. You can both keep your quarters here because we won't need them until February. I suggest you take some leave time." He passed our orders packets to each of us. "You'll find some blank travel warrants in your packets. That's all, thank you."

We both stood, saluted, I let Lara proceed me to the door. We both returned to my quarters and opened up our orders. To go with them were a travel warrant each for our transfer by the academy shuttle depot to the Skyring, and an accommodation warrant at the fleet quarters on the Skyring for one night. There were also four blank travel warrants available for worldwide travel on Earth, and one blank accommodation warrant.

Deciding that we would both like to visit Switzerland and do some skiing, we put aside one accommodation warrant for that because the warrant covered the room and meals but did not state number of occupant's until we filled it out. Which gave us a spare warrant to stay somewhere else. With that sorted out we made our way to the tavern to join our friends for a pub lunch.

There were only three of my core friends circle left at the academy now, Thad Norman, John Tolliver, and Olga Checkenco. When they heard our news about being on the same ship and that it was a destroyer, they were happy for us and asked when we were leaving. We told them about joining the ship next month, and our plans to travel and ski in Switzerland as well as telling them we were allowed to keep our quarters at the academy until we left for the Skyring. Just as we finished filling them in what we were going to do, their communicators chirped calling them to reception, as they left for the office, I ordered lunch for Lara and me.

Shortly after we finished our meals, our friends returned talking amongst themselves and smiling as Olga said, "We've really got some news for you two, but we'll order some lunch and drinks first, then come back and tell you."

When they returned, we both looked at them inquisitively. John said, "Well we've all been posted to the Sabretooth, which is the Admirals flagship for Battle Group Three. The same battlegroup that the Scimitar is part of."

Lara and I both laughed and congratulated them, then Olga said, "The chancellor has done the same for us as he did for you, so now we can all go to Switzerland together!"

Stardate 2511.01.04:
Early this morning, Lara, and I said our sad farewells to our friends and took the transit shuttle

to the Scimitar. Reporting to Captain Edgar Miller, he took us into his ready room for privacy. He told us to sit, as he brought our fleet records onto his viewer, "It says here that you two are suspected of being in a relationship?"

I replied, "Yes sir we are, but that in no way effects our duties."

He smiled, "Very well, I'll assign you married quarters. Now Davis you're to be my Executive Officer, and I see that they sent me one of their best. You already have earned a commendation for gallantry, and even that you defeated the Do or Die scenario! You must be damned good; I failed that one both times. Alright Hunter, as my exec, you must be available for duty 24 hours along with your normal bridge day watch. Growler... that's a hell of a callsign, but I'll not ask the obvious, you'll be on the day watch also and my head communications officer. I hope you can speak different languages."

Lara answered, "Aye sir, all known Alliance and Outer Rim languages, also Zytron, and my callsign is because I growl as I fire weapons sir."

He laughed, "Alright, now to business, our mission. We are part of the protection screen for Battle Group Three led by Admiral Kalashian, an Outer Rim native, we are part of the Alliance revenge and fightback in conjunction with Battle Groups One and Two. The Admiral will be sweeping clear every planet of Zytrons, from here to the border of the sector and beyond, until we reach those bastards' homeworld. Sometimes we will provide away teams as spotters for the infantry but not always, any questions?"

I asked, When do we start sir?"

He half smiled, "As we're in dock, settle into your quarters, take a tour and meet your fellow officers, lunch is at midday, and dinner at seven in the wardroom. You'll both be seated at my head table as senior officers along with the chief engineer, weapons, helm, navigation, and security. Come back to the bridge when you're ready to take a tour and I'll assign someone to take you. You start your bridge watch at eight tomorrow. Right, that's all."

We rose without saluting, that was not done aboard ship. As we passed out of the day cabin, a yeoman was waiting for us. She came to attention saying, "I'm to show you to your quarters sirs."

We gathered up our duffle's and followed her. After we had settled into our spacious cabin, we both changed into our rank coloured shirts, with our officers bars in place as well as our communicators. Lara was wearing a red shirt while mine was blue. Then we made our way to the bridge, where the captain assigned a lieutenant 4th grade to show us around the ship. After he introduced us to the senior officers on the bridge. During our tour, we met the chief engineer in Engineering, and Lara was introduced to her subordinates in the main communication section. Our tour finished at the same time as lunch in the officers wardroom, and the captain introduced us to all the other officers, before we sat down to eat.

Stardate 2511.02.01:
We have reached Gamma Virginis and established a low orbit ringing the first planet in our sweep to drive the Zytrons from the sector. Two weeks earlier all Captains and First Officers were beamed aboard the Sabretooth where the Admiral outlined his strategy: Two fighter squadrons would stay in orbit of the planet, while four squadrons attacked all the Zytron bases known about from resistance forces. If any Zytron ship made it into space, it would be destroyed by the two squadrons waiting. After the initial air attacks, the mobile infantry would move into to assault the bases with the fighters in support.

Lara announced from comms, "Fighters leaving the Sabretooth Captain."

The captain sitting in his command chair, while I was seated on his right, "Thank you Growler. On the main viewer please."

We were on station behind the Sabretooth in case of

attack and had a good view of the fighters leaving the carrier, as I ordered, "Nav, keep your long-range scans going, we don't want any surprises."

The Captain turned to me, "Good thinking Number One."

Then two Zytron ships left the planet and the fighters sped off after them, I ordered, "Nav, quickly follow the pursuit on your scanners."

Two minutes later as we watched the infantry drop from the personnel carriers, the Nav officer announced, "Both bogeys nailed sir!"

"Thank you nav," I replied.

Two days later, the operation came to an end. A fleet wide announcement was issued from the flagship, saying our first operation had been extremely successful, and to get ready to break orbit and head to Beta Virginis our next target.

For the next two years, we pursued our clean sweep against the Zytrons repeating the same tactics for each new world we came across. We had left our quadrant of space behind and were now in the void between the Alliance and on our final push toward the Zytron homeworlds.

Sometimes our fleet was attacked during our travels,

but we didn't lose any ships due to our defensive formations and having the fighter carrier able to get our Lancet fighters into almost immediate battle. While these attacks usually resulted in the loss of most Zytron attackers if not all.

Stardate 2513. 03.21:
Scouting ahead of the fleet, I had the con whilst the captain was in his ready room. Nav reported, "Sir, I'm getting a signal on long range scans indicating a Zytron base on that distant planetoid!"

"Thanks Terry," and tapped my communicator. "Captain to bridge!" I switched chairs, so he could sit.

"What's up Clay?" When I told him about the scans, he ordered, "Lara, pass that along to the flagship."

"Aye sir."

Shortly after she said, "Captain, we've been ordered to investigate when we're in beaming range."

"Acknowledged, I'll lead this one Clay, can't have you having all the fun, you have the con. Lara, Security, you and a full squad with me."
As they left the bridge for the transporters, I returned to the captain's chair, and a replacement for Lara took her station at comms.

Shortly after the away team had beamed down, a full flight of Lancet attack fighters flew past heading for the planet, which was followed by mobile infantry landing craft. Turning to comms, I asked, "Comms have you had any chatter as to what's happening?"

"Yes sir, the away team has been talking directly to the flagship."

I angrily replied, "And you didn't think to inform me? Damn it! Do your job properly those are our people down there! Next time think. Now play back what you have on speaker."

"Yes Sir, sorry sir," she replied.

Then I listened to the playback along with the entire bridge crew. The tape had a lot of static interference, but the communique was audible, and we heard: "Growler to Sabretooth, we need immediate help at our position, our Captain is down, and we're pinned down by enemy troops. Taking heavy fire. Aargh, (the message went silent for a moment then resumed, I listened while on the edge of my seat), medic! Damnit! Snake to flagship, Growler down, we need help now! Get fighters and backup now damnit!"

I pushed a button on my chair asking, "Transport can you beam our away team up?"

"Negative sir, there's too much interference and they're moving around too much."

I was furious, and I needed a target, rounding on the comms, 1 looked her in the eye and vented my fury.

"Damn you! You didn't think that important enough to tell me, those are your bloody shipmates, get your supervisor, and get the hell off my bridge!"

Chapter 5.

I was still fuming as I sat back in my chair. I looked around the bridge noting the change of personnel at the comms station. The junior operator left the bridge silently crying. Whilst I looked at the main screen viewer, my mind was thinking all manner of scenarios that had happened on the planet when my communicator chirped with, "Snake to Hunter."

I tapped the communicator, "Hunter to Snake report." (Only callsigns were used on open communication).

"Sir, we beamed into a shit storm and were hit by enemy ground patrols. Turbo and one of my men are dead the rest of us need medical attention and will be transported to the flagship after the mop up. Growler's in a bad way but still alive, she took the most of a grenade blast. Luckily the fighters arrived before we were all KIA (killed in action), we're about to depart on the boat now. Snake out."

Everyone had heard the report and knew that the captain was dead. This meant I was now the captain, unless Miller was replaced with another captain by the Admiral. I looked around at comms, "Request permission for me to beam aboard the flagship Linda."

"Aye sir."

I watched Guy Anderson on the helm, remembering he was next in the structure of command, as Linda from the comms station announced, "Permission granted Captain." I nodded at her use of my new position.

Then said as I stood, "Guy you have the con."

Making my way to the transporter, I gave my destination to the technician. I waited for the tingling sensation of the transport beam and arrived aboard the Sabretooth.

A security person was waiting, and I asked him to take me to the medical bay, where I was met by the surgeon. "I'm afraid your comms officer died of her wounds shortly after lift-off from the planet Captain Davis. She, your Captain, and the three dead security men have been taken to storage for burial back home. The rest of your crew have been patched up and are able to return to your ship. You can see them if you like"

I nodded, "Yes please, then I wish to see the dead."

As he showed me to the survivors of the ill-fated away team, he said, "I'll arrange for your escort to take you to the dead after you leave here."

I thanked him, then as I approached Snake and his remaining two men, Snake called, "Attention!"

I waved them back to sitting again and said with a smile, "Well, good news boys, the doc says you're fit enough to go back aboard the Scimitar, so make your way back when you're ready."

Inclining a small head gesture to Snake, he joined me in the anti-room. "I'm terribly sorry about Lara sir, I thought that she was going to make it."

I nodded, "Thank you Mister Torf (who was a Cragoid with only one name), I appreciate what you did for her. Before you head back to the Scimitar, on my authority, collect replacements for your section, and I'll see you back there. After viewing our losses, I have to report to the Admiral."

"Very well, thank you sir."

I left the med bay and took the long walk to cold storage where the bodies were lying on tables, covered with sheets. There was a tag with name, rank, and serial number attached to the big toe on the right foot of each body. I looked at each of them; my eyes taking note of their wounds before I replaced the cover. Looking at Captain Miller and the photon gun wound to his chest, I knew he hadn't stood a chance. Finally I looked at the body of my lover. Before taking in her wounds, I gave her face a tender loving caress. She had taken two blaster wounds, but the most significant damage was from the grenade, it had torn her beautiful body terribly.

Before replacing the sheet, I gave her face another soft caress down the side of her face and cheek. Then sadly, I replaced the cover.

Leaving cold storage, I addressed my escort with a nod, "Right, take me to the Admiral please."

Nodding as we moved off his eyes displayed sadness for my loss, then we headed back through the ship.

The Admirals large office was situated behind the bridge. It was also the place where he held officers conferences. As we approached the office door my escort knocked and opened it. Taking a step forward, I heard my escort say, "Acting Captain Davis of the Scimitar, sir."

I entered as I heard, "Good, show him in please."

As I stepped into Admiral Kalashian's office I took in the large conference table and saw him coming forward to shake my hand. We shook hands as he said, "Come sit down, I thought I'd have seen you before."

I replied, as I sat, "I went to see my crewmen sir, both living and dead."

"Ah yes, quite right too, and the mark of a good officer. Such a sad business for which I take responsibility. I can only apologize for taking such a rash decision I'm afraid Davis," he said with a sorrowful look.

"Thank you sir."

He nodded then asked, "Tell me Clayton is it?"

"Yes sir, Though I'm usually called Clay or by my callsign, Hunter, sir."

"Very well Clay, did your security officer tell you what occurred? Here's his debriefing statement by the way."

I took the proffered tablet and read Torf's statement before answering. I passed back the tablet, "That's a good deal more than the abridged version I got from him. I would like to recommend Mister Torf get a commendation for his actions, sir."

He nodded, "Already being taken care of son. Now, down to business. I can't spare another captain, so I'm promoting you to full Captain Clay, and have already logged it in the Fleet Command Journal."

He flipped a switch on his desk, "I've just switched off the recording monitors because what I say next is just between you and me. It doesn't go past this room. I know you were born in the Outer Rim. However, I need to know where exactly your allegiances lie… with the Alliance, or the Federation of The Outer Rim?"

This question was out of the blue, and one I hadn't considered. "It's a question I haven't considered before sir, but to tell you the truth, I was pretty pissed off when the Alliance didn't aid our worlds and colonies. When the Zytrons invaded, I was at the Academy when they blew my family and homeworld to bits. Though there were fleet ships in the vicinity, they didn't help when they should have."

The Admiral nodded, thought for a moment then said, "Well Clay, I'm going to give you something to think about. When we return to Earth after this war, I'm going to be resigning my commission with Fleet Command. I will make my way to the Federation capital on Zeta Australis to join their forces because my allegiancies lie with the Federation of the Outer Rim.

Here's something else to ponder, from what I've heard, what's going on back there, is that another war is brewing. But this time it will be a civil war between the Alliance and the Federation, as an Outer Rimmer, I wouldn't like to be caught alive in Alliance space no matter what position I held. Otherwise, I'd likely be arrested and killed. Please think carefully Captain Davis."

Then he leaned forward, switched the recorders back

on, as he said, "You may draw some command shirts from supply before you head back to the Scimitar Captain Davis. That is all and…thank you."

Being dismissed, I stood, came to attention, then turned and exited the room. My escort was standing there waiting. I made eye contact, "I need to go to supply."

"Yes sir," and he guided me to supply.

I collected a dozen command shirts with captains bars already sewn in place. I turned and faced my escort "Ok back to the transporters please."

Back on the Scimitar, I changed into the pale yellow, coloured command shirt and pinned my communicator to it. I then went through my quarters boxing up Lara's personal possessions which as a fleet officer were few and far between. I realised that she had no immediate family to send them to, so I put them in a drawer to be packed with my things. I put all her clothing into the box instead. These would go back to our shipboard supply store.

As I walked onto the bridge, I saw that Torf was back at his duty station. I took my seat and said, "Mister Torf, please arrange to have Captain Millers quarters cleared and my stuff transferred into it please."

"Aye sir," he replied.

I picked up the ships log from its slot, dictating into it, "Ships log, stardate 2513.03.21.1405: having assumed command after I have been officially promoted by Admiral Kalashian to Captain of AFC Scimitar upon the deaths of Captain Edgar Miller and 1st Lieutenant Lara Kemplar earlier today, I hereby promote 2nd lieutenant Guy Anderson callsign Boxer, to 1st lieutenant and my executive Number One officer, also 2nd lieutenant Linda Coslow, callsign Blondie, to 1st lieutenant and comms chief forthwith. Linda, send a copy to the flagship and Fleet Command please."

"Aye sir, thank you Captain."

"Yeoman Pierce, I haven't had lunch yet," I asked, "can you see if the galley can rustle me up some sandwiches please?"

"Aye Captain," she replied and scurried off.

Stardate 2513.10.02.1310:
Our Battle Group arrived at the rendezvous point where we are to meet both Battle Groups One and Two before the final push onto Zytronos homeworld, our Battle Group has arrived fifteen minutes ahead of schedule, and so we've been ordered to station keeping while the fighters patrol to keep the fleet protected. Battle Group Two

arrived over on our port side, shortly after Battle Group One arrived out further on the portside of Battle Group Two, and the massed fleets were certainly a sight to behold, more fighters flew into space from Battle Groups one and two, to help our pilots protect all three fleets.

We were surrounded by fighters flying by constantly. The main screen was off, but ships filled the forward viewing window, as I thought to myself, *OH LARA, YOU WOULD HAVE LOVED TO HAVE SEEN THIS SIGHT!*

Stardate 2513.11.02.0800:
We remained at station keeping the rest of yesterday and last night, this morning we've been ordered to advance toward Zytronos at half impulse power with the other two fleets.

Fighters are still buzzing all around the massed fleet, looking for a chance enemy target. I ordered Terry on Nav, "Terry keep watching the long-range scanners as we move ahead, don't worry about anything close. The fighters will take care of that area."

Now that we had entered the Zytronos home system, any planet we came across during our advance would be bombed out of existence by the Zytrons own quantum bombs. Then when we reached Zytronos itself Battle Group One's fighters stayed in space, while all of Groups Two and Three's fighters went to refuel and rearmed with missiles, and when ready Battle Group Two's fighters launched in four waves each five minutes apart toward the planet to find any targets of opportunity and fire upon them. Ten minutes after that, our Battle Group Three fighters were launched. After our last fighters launched down to the planet. Group Number One's fighters went home to rearm and refuel.

There are only six planets left in this sector. Once the fighters return to their carriers, we heard over the comms that our group and Number Two are each given three planets to destroy. Battle Group One is to remain in orbit around Zytronos.

Stardate 2513.13.11.1320:
Our battle group received the co-ordinates for three targets, and we were ordered to into battle group formation with our ship as the lead scout ship. When we are clear of Zytronos itself we are ordered to proceed at our best warp speed to target one.

Chapter 6.

As the forward scouting ship, we dropped out of warp first, and I ordered, "All scans Terry."

He reported, "Long range has picked up six, no ten, fighters leaving the planet sir."

"Shields," I ordered, "Battle stations. Intercept course. Full impulse Mister Braydon (Max Braydon had become senior helm officer after I promoted Guy to my exec). Guns we need all you have ready to fire!" It is ironic that our weapons officer John Lawson's callsign was in fact Guns.

"Aye sir," came the reply.

Terry announced, "Captain, the flagship has arrived and is launching fighters."

Noting the time, I quickly calculated our speed and that of the fighters, "They won't arrive in time. We'll be engaging the enemy before they get here. Open fire as they bear, Guns."

"Opening fire sir."

Our opening salvo of defensive fire destroyed two of the enemy fighters as they broke formation to attack. But to fire we needed to lower the shields which left us vulnerable. Just then Terry announced, "Our fighters have arrived captain!"

It was with relief that I nodded, "Very good Terry. Shields back up Guns."

Our fighters destroyed all the enemy ships. But they remained on station, as our fleet moved into a high orbit of the planet designated target one. The enemy sent more fighters to attack us, but by now all our fighters had launched from the flagship. The attackers were grossly outnumbered and destroyed. Then three squadrons of our fighters were ordered to attack the planet bases.

Stardate 2513.13.11.1745:
All fighters have been recalled after repeated attacks on the planet, and a huge bomber was launched from the flagship, as the admiral ordered all ships to raise their shields. I ordered all viewers to be turned to the fleet channel.

The Admiral came onto the viewer, "Officers and all crewmembers of the fleet, as you are aware, we have now pushed our enemy back to its own sector in space. A few short hours ago we arrived at their homeworld. It was decided at our previous command meeting to cleanse the entire sector of Zytron influence and end this war forever. There are only six planets left in this sector beside the homeworld, we have been assigned three of those planets, Battle Group Two have been assigned the other three. During our counter attacks to clear the Zytron menace from Alliance space, a number of Quantum Bombs were recovered. As you will remember they used these bombs devastatingly on a large number of the Outer Rim Planets. Now we're going to send one back to them! I hope the members from those Outer Rim Planets and Colonies rejoice in our vengeance, please continue watching, thank you."

Then the screen showed a quantum bomb being loaded into one of our bombers. It was as big as four fuel cannisters lashed together in diameter. Taking up the entire payload area of the bomber. The screen showed the bomber being launched, flashed to the bomber itself as it made its way to above the planet. The bomber communications were being monitored, the pilot announced, "Ugly Duckling in drop position with the bomb armed command."

"Command to Ugly Duckling drop when ready."

"Ugly Duckling to command releasing in five, four, three, two, Now! Let's get the hell out of here Baker!"

The cameras followed the bomb dropping until a flash was seen far below on the planet. Small at first, the flash began spreading right around the planet as it exploded. The shockwave that followed shortly

after was immense. Even with our shields at one hundred percent my ship was thrown around violently, and I was thrown out of my chair.
In mild shock, I re-seated myself and stared at the screen in horror. I thanked my lucky stars that none of the fleet ships had been in close proximity to my ship or each other. Then thought to myself, *Bloody hell! That's what happened to my homeworld! At least my family died quickly.*

I was still staring at the screen in horror as the replay was on the screen, When the Admiral came back onto the viewer, looking a little dishevelled and shocked as he said, "That is exactly what happened to many Outer Rim planets and Duros Major in the Alliance. I hope you will carry the memory of what you have seen here today with you always. The work you have done during our assignment is critical to the Alliance and I thank you for your service to the fleet. We will remain at station keeping until tomorrow, when your Captains will receive their orders, goodnight."

The viewer flickered and went back to the forward view it was set for, as I slowly said, "Linda, give me a view of the planet, please."

"Aye sir," she replied, The viewer flickered once again, and we were looking back where a planet once existed. There was no planet now, just a slowly dissipating dust cloud where it had been.

Stardate 2513.14.11.0730:
Scimitar has been ordered into the scouting position
again as the Admiral ordered us into warp enroute to
our next target planet number 2. While we were in
warp, I ordered, "Terry, same as yesterday all
scanners up as we drop out of warp. Guns, you too,
weapons and shields. Battle Stations Mister
Anderson."

Because target two was so close by, we came out of
warp after only ten minutes of travel. Everything
happened as it did the afternoon before, with just a
couple of minor changes. I sent the results of our
scans to the flagship. There were about twenty
fighters or more coming to attack us, and we didn't
have to fire a shot. Our fighters flew past us at full
burn to engage the enemy fighters.

As our fleet established high orbit, fighters were sent
down toward the planet. A message started coming
in at comms. Linda said, "Captain, the Admiral
wishes to speak to you via secure video link!"

Standing up, "Copy that, I'll take it in my ready
room. Guy you have the con."

I entered my ready room and began to sit at my desk
the computer screen popped up, began chirping and
flickered to life. The Admiral appeared on the
screen and began speaking. "Ah, Hunter, I have a
job for you son."

"Yes sir."

The Admiral smiled, "Today is going to be a little different. I want to be out of here in an hour, or as close to as possible, so here's what's going to happen, a bomber is going to drop from a higher orbit and hightail it back here. Then I'm going to order the fleet into warp before the bomb explodes, but I want your ship to stick around until it explodes. Then make warp to our third target where the fleet will be. You can appraise me of the results of the drop when you join us."

"That won't be a problem Admiral."

He smiled again, "Good, but here's the kicker son. You will have to wait for the dust cloud to dissipate to see if the bomb did all of the job. Hopefully it will go as well as yesterday, but that's for you to find out. If it didn't, we'll have to return and blow the hell out of what's left. Do you understand what I'm saying son?"

With a wry smile, "Yes sir I fully understand what you're saying."

"Very well Captain, and good luck. Deadbeat out," I had a small laugh at his callsign.

Leaving my ready room I moved to my seat on the bridge. "Linda, keep an ear on the fleet bomber channels, and let me know when the bomb has been dropped please."

"Yes Captain."

A while later Linda announced the bomb had been dropped. "Alright girls and boys, It's time to strap in!"

Buckling my seat straps, I watched the fleet disappear into warp. Setting the viewer to display the planet, we saw the bomb explode with the same devastating effect we saw the day before. We all braced for the shockwave we knew was coming. Being in high orbit didn't lessen the shockwave to any degree. After it had passed, I said to Guy, my exec, "Check for any damage Number One. Linda, keep the screen on where the planet was." I stared intensely at the screen wishing the dust to clear.

We waited and waited for the dust to clear. After an hour, I asked, "Terry, anything on the scanners?"

"Nothing sir. Switching to intense close scan, I've got a large rock about asteroid size Captain."

"Guns, target that rock and pulverize it."

"Target destroyed Captain," Guns replied.

"Nothing on intense scan sir." Terry acknowledged.

I asked, "Does anyone have any suggestion how we can blow this dust cover away, short of flying into it?"

No one did, so I made a decision, "Alright, take us into the cloud at quarter impulse. Max, Terry, intense close scans."

We crisscrossed the dust cloud where the planet had been a number of times and found nothing. There was only dust particles hanging in space. I decided that we had spent enough time searching, and had Max take us to warp to join the fleet at target three. Once we joined the fleet, I had Linda ask permission for me to transport to the flagship.

"Permission granted Captain," I told Guy he had the con and made for the transporters.

When I exited the transporter, my escort was waiting. "Take me to the Admiral please."

"Ah Captain Davis, let's go to my office,"

We left the bridge and headed toward the Admiral's office. The two of us entered while my escort waited outside. The Admiral closed the door behind us, and we headed toward his desk. He held a finger up to his lips for silence. He went to his desk, switched off the recorders, "Well Clay, how did it go?"

I told him that I thought he would like my report in person, which he assured me was correct. I told him everything that I had done, and the steps I took to try and discover if there were any remnants of the planet left then he said, "Hmm, sounds like the results are the same and we can assume that the targets have all been destroyed. I wonder what it would be like to have torpedoes with that sort of firepower? Even if they had a much smaller yield, they could be used to blast ships to bits even with their shields up. Interesting thought don't you agree?"

"It is indeed sir."

"While you're here Clay, have you given any thought to what we discussed when we last met here?"

"I have sir," especially over the last couple of days, but I was going to leave it to when we are on the way home to really think it over. I want to go through my crew list to find out if any other Outer Rimmers besides Torf that maybe interested in your idea as well. If you had an address where they could go for help that would be of use. Back to the Quantum Bombs that we have been discussing sir, what's to stop the Alliance from using them against the Outer Rim?"

While he was listening, he had written an address on

Zeta Australis down for me, he passed it across to me saying, "Get them to go there. They'll help you and any others. Your idea about looking for Outer Rimmers in your crew is also a solid one, do that. Now, even though it took us a long time to get here, even moving at fastest warp it's going to take at least three to four months to get back to Alliance territory. We better wrap this up. Call me if you have any other questions. Also, by the way, I'm recommending you for a couple of medals, you earned them. Now let's get out of here quietly."

I thanked him for the medal recommendations before he switched the recorders back on and we silently left his office. I put the address he had given me in my pants pocket as my escort took me to the transporters.

Back aboard my ship, I returned to the bridge to await the orders to return to Zytronos. They came half an hour later.

Chapter 7.

Stardate 2513.11.15.1050:
Our fleet arrived back at Zytronos yesterday afternoon and joined Battle Group One in high orbit, Battle Group Two returned early this morning. While we had been away, Battle Group One's fighters were pulverizing the planet, but had suspended operations late yesterday, and had been returning from their last action to the carrier as our fleet joined Group One. I was in my ready room going through fleet records of my crew and found six people including Torf who were natives of the Outer Rim Worlds and Colonies.

The comm screen flickered indicating an incoming message and automatically acquired the fleet communique. "For those of you who don't know me I am Vice Admiral Blane, assistant to the fleet command chairman and presently your taskforce commander. Very shortly our war with the Zytrons is going to come to a permanent end. We are going to drop one of their own quantum bombs on their homeworld, thus extinguishing their race forever. Battle Groups Two and Three have been away recently, blasting out of existence, all of the planets in this entire sector. Now it is time to deal with Zytronos. Let me remind you how this war began in the first place. The Zytrons attacked us without provocation or declaration of war and it cost us many, many lives. They started at the Outer Rim

Worlds and Colonies destroying anything and everything in their path. Today we are going to give them an example of our vengeance. That is all."

His speech ended but the screen remained opened on the fleet channel to show the bomb dropping. Having no wish to face the horror of what that bomb could do, I turned away and returned to the bridge. Turning to my crew, "Here we go again, strap in tight boys and girls." I fastened my seat straps and said, "Raise shields to their maximum Guns."

"Shields up sir," Guns reported.

I did not want to see the devastation and tried to look away, but I couldn't seem to take my eyes off the screen as the path of the bomb was followed to the impacting flash on the planet surface. Then the viewer flickered and returned to its normal screen just before the shockwave of the blast reached us.

After the effects of the shockwave passed, comms reported, "Captain, the Task Force Flagship has ordered all three Battle Groups to return home. Departing at fifteen-minute intervals after Battle Group One, with orders to return at a set speed of warp factor seven."

"Thank you, Linda." I turned to the crew, "Well that means we will probably leave in group order. That gives us thirty minutes at least before we depart the system for home. Guy, you have the con. I'll be in my ready room."

"Aye sir," he replied as I headed to my office, where I resumed my search of personnel records.

I finished my search twenty minutes later and switched off all recorders in the ready room. I placed the list in one of the desk drawers and casually walked back to the bridge. I had only just sat down in my chair, when Linda said, "The Admiral has just ordered the fleet to return to Earth at warp factor seven sir."

"Copy that Linda. Terry lay in the course. Max you heard the speed, go." As he set the engine speed control.

Once the ship was at warp it increased quickly to factor seven, and as Max announced, "Warp factor seven sir,"

I smiled, "Terry how long before we reach home?"

Terry replied, "Four months and six days sir."

Laughing, "Well you all heard that boys and girls, just a spin around the park." My comment was followed by laughter from the bridge crew. "…so we can all relax on the way home. Once we are home let's hope that we won't be going out straight away. That will mean shore leave for everyone. You have the con Number One!"

"Aye sir," Guy replied, as I stood and went to the security station, "Mister Torf would you join me in the ready room please"

In my ready room I invited him to take the seat across from me. "Torf, this may sound strange, but I'm going to ask, where do your loyalties lie in regard to the Alliance and the Outer Rim worlds?"

"Sir, as you know I'm a Cragoid and we don't lie. Should the tension between the Alliance and the Outer Rim Federation escalate, my allegiancies lie first to my homeworld, and secondly the Federation, Cragon is a member world."

"Alright, this is hypothetical now, what if it came to war between them, what would you do?"

He paused briefly and thought for a moment, "Sir, if I had enough time and warning, I would leave Fleet Command and make my way to the Federation. If not, I would probably be arrested or killed, but even that would not stop me trying to escape."

I nodded, "Thank you for being honest with me Torf."

He replied with his own question, "Sir if you don't

mind, why have you asked these questions?"

Thinking for a minute, "To be honest with you Torf, I'm not sure. It's mainly because I'm not sure what I'm going to do myself yet, but it is something that all of us from the Outer Rim need to consider. I have some news from back home that was told to me by Admiral Kalashian and I think it should be given to all from the Outer Rim so they can make their own minds up about it. Also, I wanted to see where your loyalties lie because I have a job for you."

"Thank you for being candid with me sir, what do you want me to do?"

Opening my desk drawer, I removed the list of names and passed it to him. "I wish to see all of these crew members in the officers wardroom at ten hundred tomorrow please."

He thought for a moment, "They'll be there sir."

"Good. You can start making them aware of my request as soon as you leave. Don't return to your station before it's done please."

"Aye, sir." He stood and left the room. After he had departed, I turned the recorders back on and returned to my seat on the bridge.

Stardate 2513.11.16.0950:

I was on the bridge early the next morning. I knew I had that meeting at ten hundred this morning and I kept checking the clock. Finally I said, "You've got the con Number One. I've got a couple of things I need to do." I made my way off the bridge and towards the wardroom. It was a little early, but I needed to move. Once inside the wardroom, I looked around and decided it wasn't private enough. I waited until all of the invited crewmembers had assembled. "Right, follow me."

I led them to an emergency airlock large enough to accommodate all of us, opened the inner door, and led them in. I had Torf remain just outside the partially opened hatch of the inner airlock to hear, but also keep an eye out for anyone entering the area.

I began by telling them first the news from home and then where the information had come from. I told them what I had decided to do and then asked, "So, what you each have to do now is choose whether to stay with the Alliance and face arrest, or desert and head for the Federation. Even though this ship is now my only home since Vega 13 was bombed, my loyalties, lie with the Federation.
If it happens, I will be resigning my commission and heading to an address the admiral gave me on Zeta Australis.

Once there I hope to enlist in the Federation Navy.

But that's just what I'm going to do. Torf will give you all copies of the address later. Each of you has to decide for yourself; there will not be any further meetings like this one. That is all ladies and gentlemen, thank you for listening." Torf opened the door, and we both headed back to the bridge.

Stardate 2514.03.21:
We dropped out of warp and went to impulse power at the outer system marker. As we approached our home base. I told Linda to put me on the bridge speakers and open a channel to Fleet Command at the Skyring. "Fleet Command, this is Captain Davis of the Scimitar. Our ETA your position in one hour, over."

"Welcome home Scimitar. We have you cleared for docking in Bay 24. Captain, your ship's crew will stand down for three months shore leave except for you and Lieutenant Torf. Both of you are to attend a special parade, followed by a reception at the Academy. Accommodation passes for the Academy and shuttle passes to the planet are waiting at HQ for each of you. A skeleton crew will board once you dock, Fleet out."

I smiled and turned to see what Torf's reaction was. "It looks like you and I don't get shore leave straight away, but everyone else does. Linda, pipe me throughout the ship please. Attention all hands, this is the captain. After we dock, a skeleton crew will be coming aboard while all crew are stood down for three months shore leave. Well done everyone, and welcome home. Captain out."

Stardate 2514.03.22:
After we said our goodbyes to all of the bridge officers yesterday, Torf and I went to the Fleet Command office to receive our passes. Carrying our belongings with us we headed to the Academy. After we checked in, we were shown to our quarters in the visiting dignitaries' wing. After hanging my dress uniform and unpacking my essentials, at eleven I made my way to the Academy tavern.

The place was packed, but my eyes were drawn to a girl sitting at a table all by herself over by the windows facing out towards the main thoroughfare. Even at this distance, I could tell she was a Vegan from the Outer Rim because her features matched my own, except that her hair was black, where mine is dark brown. I headed to the bar and ordered a double scotch. Standing there, taking the first sip of my double, I continued looking around the room, but the only thing I saw was her. She was stunning, and I HAD to meet her.

I started in her direction and as I got closer, I saw the Squadron Leader ranking on her Fleet Air uniform. She looked to be in her early 20's, a year or two younger than me, and becoming a Squadron Leader at her age really impressed me. Knowing that fighter command only promoted people on merit, she would have had to earn each and every one of her promotions. Oh, right, and yes, I think I now believe in love at first sight.

I walked toward her table. As I reached it, "Do you mind if I sit, Squadron Leader?"

She looked up at me, and with a small smile, "As a fellow Outer Rim native and especially a Vegan, Captain be my guest."

I smiled, "Thanks, I'm Clay Davis," as I held out my hand.

She shook it. "Pleased to meet you Clay. I'm Karen, Karen Kirkland. They call me KK, what about you?

I smiled, "Hunter." Just that little touch when we shook hands had thrilled me, sending shivers down my spine.

She smiled and asked, "Where do you live in the rim Hunter?"

I grimaced, "Nowhere now I guess, I was from Vega 13."

"So was I!" her voice just above a whisper. As she

looked at me, I could see a tear forming in her left eye. She slowly lowered her eyes, reached for her drink, and took a long, slow sip.

Changing the subject to lighten the moment, "So, what do you think about the chances of us two people from the same homeworld, meeting in a place like this?" As she took a sip of her drink.

She burst out laughing, almost choking on her drink, "Oh, about a trillion to one I would think. Nice pickup line though."

The magnetic attraction was instantaneous for a moment, smiling and gazing into each other's eyes. She broke the moment by asking, "Tell me about yourself Clay, if that's your real name?"

I laughed again. "Well, it's not. It's Clayton, but most call me Clay or Hunter..." I then went on to tell her more about me than I had ever told anyone before. I even told her about my thoughts regarding the horror I felt when I saw the quantum bombs being used. I told her about the current political situation and how I intended to solve it for me should I ever have to.

"I'm going to use my shore leave first. Then, if I have to, I'll resign my commission and make my way to Zeta Australis. I plan to enlist with the Federation Navy, if there is one."

I looked up and took a brief, introspective pause. Agitated, I exclaimed, "Bloody hell! I've never told anyone that much about myself. How come you've affected me this way?"

She had unconsciously leaned in and lightly placed her hand on my leg and was listening intently and staring at me the whole time. It was as if she could read, not just my mind, but my very being. Her facial expressions underwent changes as she listened to me. When I finished, she leaned back and then leaned back in again automatically replacing her hand.

"Oh, I feel so sorry for you Clay. You saw four of those bombs dropped, but I only saw the one, and that one was enough. It left me in tears. Thank the stars I was watching the screen in my quarters at the time.

Chapter 8.

As she told me this, she had laid her hand on my arm tenderly, and my heart skipped a beat. I noticed that her drink was getting low, so I asked her what she was drinking. She said she was drinking scotch whiskey, the same as me, but her's was mixed with soda. Looking at her tenderly as I stood, I offered to buy drinks. "I'll get us another round of drinks, back in a minute."

She smiled, "Thank you Clay."

When I returned with our drinks, I sat opposite her on my seat, then passed her drink to her. As she reached for the glass, I felt that spark of electricity again as our fingers touched. I looked directly at her and found her staring intently back at me. We smiled at each. I raised my glass saying, "A toast."

Karen broke our eye contact and, lowering her eyes asked. "What shall we toast?"

My smile gets even bigger, "To us, and our future life together."

Karen returned her gaze to me, raised her glass toward mine, "To us, and everything yet to come."

We clinked our glasses together, take sips, then we both started to giggle. The giggles soon became laughter. For the next twenty minutes there was a lot of sipping our drinks, smiling, laughing, and eye contact. Then I remarked, "Well Karen, you know about me, now it's your turn."

While she told me about herself her hand returned to resting on my arm. She was in fact twenty-two, two years younger than I was, and had left Vega 13, for the Fighter Command Academy on Alpha Centauri, only a month before Vega 13 was destroyed. She too had been contemplating leaving the Alliance for the Federation, and even had her own small ship, originally a shuttle, she had converted it into a mobile home of sorts. She had replaced the old impulse engine with an updated twin impulse warp engine that could reach warp five. She also had a shield generator, but no defensive weapons. She seemed quite fond of her ship that she called Serenity. I equally admired the work she had done and about her owning it in the first place. I wondered why I had never thought of doing anything like that, buying my own ship that is, but then I hadn't had the time.

Karen and I stayed together for the rest of the day, holding hands quite naturally and it seemed normal for us to do so. When we moved from the tavern to the mess for dinner, our hands were linked and as we walked together afterward. We only separated them when we reached her quarters, and I gave her a kiss good night. She in turn, wrapped her arms around me and pulled me in tight, turning my kiss into a long lingering lovers kiss. We both enjoyed that, and it could have gone further. However, I did the gentlemanly thing, by wishing her a goodnight, then waited while she shut her door. I was overjoyed at how things had gone between us and carried a smile on my face all the way to my own quarters.

The following morning I showered, shaved, and slowly got ready to attend the parade, I had just finished polishing my boots when my communicator chirped, I tapped it, "Captain Davis."

It was Karen, "How are you this lovely morning Clayton?"

"Much happier for hearing from you, how are you?"

"Oh, that's smooth, I feel wonderous. I'm just getting ready for the parade. Would you like to get together before the parade. I'll be ready in an hour."

With a smile on my face, "I'd love to, I'll be at your door in an hour. How's that?"

"Perfect! See you then, Kirkland out."

Fifty minutes later I put on the jacket of my dress uniform, looked the mirror to see if everything was ship shape and walked out the door. I walked to

Karen's quarters and pressed the call button. I could see a big smile on her face as the door opened. She stepped out and closed the door behind her. Linking hands we walked to the turbo lift to take us to the ground floor.

Outside the building, she asked, "We've got an hour before the parade. This is your Academy. Is there somewhere we can walk to before we have to head for the parade?"

Smiling, "There most certainly is my dear, come."

I pointed out the boardwalk and we headed that way. We walked to my favourite spot by the lake. From there we could see the large, ornamental fountain in the middle and Karen exclaimed how beautiful it was. As we walked around the boardwalk, she said, "Clay, you know how yesterday you said you'd never told anyone that much about yourself, and how come I'd affected you that much. Well, I feel the same way, it's as if I feel that I've known you my whole life. I can honestly tell you anything, so here's something you don't know. When you came to the table yesterday and I saw you, it's as if I fell in love with you straight away, if you believe in that sort of thing."

I smiled, inwardly I was shouting, *Yes, oh yes, she feels the same way I do.* "Karen, to tell you the truth, I never believed in love at first sight. That is, until I saw you yesterday."

She stopped, pulled me to her, wrapped her arms around my neck, and kissed me. It was one of those long lovers kisses and whispered in my ear, "Thank you."

"For what my love?"

She smiled lovingly, "For feeling the same way about me. I tossed and turned thinking about you last night until I realized that I had fallen in love with you. After I came to that conclusion, I slept like a kitten. This morning I wondered if you felt the same way about me and now that I know, I'm deliriously happy."

We continued our walk as we headed to the quad.

Stardate 2514.03.23.1130:
The parade quad was set out with chairs for officers and the public. There was even a broadcasting unit. That was televising the event.

Karen and I walked hand in hand to seats in the front row. We watched the dignitaries assemble on stage and then sit is specific chairs. In the centre of the first row was the Chairman of the Alliance Council, Chancellor Bortov. To his immediate left was the Fleet First Lord. To his left were Vice Admiral Grice, Vice Admiral Blane, Admiral Pierce, and finally Admiral Kalashian. We would have to salute and shake hands with each of them as we went up on the podium. Earlier I had learned the ceremony was to publicize medal winners during the counter attacks on the Zytrons.

Admiral Neil McManus, acting as MC for the proceedings, rose and approached the lectern. Adjusting the microphone, he greeted everyone, "Ladies and gentlemen, Chancellor Bortov, Fleet First Lord Admiral Grice, and other dignitaries, we are here today to recognize and pay homage to some of our heroes of the Zytron War.

All of the officers you see seated in the front row are to receive their awards from Chairman of the Alliance Council, Chancellor Bortov himself. Each will also receive a Gold Zytron Service Medal. Everyone else that receive these service medals will only get normal silver. So, without further ado, our first recipient is First Lieutenant Torf.
…Lieutenant Torf is receiving the Alliance Meritorious Bravery Medal for his actions whilst leading an away team during our counter offensive on stardate 2513.03.21"

Applauding Torf I watched as he saluted and shook hands with each of the admirals as he moved down the line. Finally he was directly in front of Chancellor Bortov where he snapped an extra crisp salute and then shook hands with the Chancellor.

The Chancellor spoke to Torf as he pinned each of the metals to Torf's chest. One final salute and Torf exited the stage to the right only to return to his seat a few minutes later from the left side so as to not interfere with the ceremony for the other recipients.

Karen received her awards next. "I call to the front, Fighter Squadron Leader Karen Kirkland. ...Squadron Leader Kirkland is receiving the Distinguished Flying Cross for her actions on Zytronos. Single handedly she destroyed a rocket launch facility aimed at our fleet and flagship above.

Two more officers were called up and received their awards before my name was called.

Admiral McManus called out, " Captain Clayton Davis please come to the front... Captain Davis is receiving two awards today, the Alliance Meritorious Bravery Medal and the Fleet Command Bravery Cross. The Alliance Meritorious Bravery Medal is being awarded for his actions during an away team landing on stardate 2513.01.20: His second award, the Fleet Command Bravery Cross has been awarded for his actions as he led his ship against superior forces on stardate 2513.11.13:"

While the announcement was going on, I saluted and shook hands with each of the officers in the line. When I got to Kalashian, I whispered, "I thought you were bugging out."

"See me at the reception, I've got news," he whispered back.

There were three more presentations after mine. When everyone had received their awards and returned to their place on stage, McManus said, "Thank you ladies and gentlemen for attending today's program. Now that homage has been paid, this concludes our award ceremony. Please join us at the reception in the Academy Ballroom where you meet each of our awardees and express your appreciation for their exemplary service personally.

As soon as the ceremony ended Karen embraced and kissed me. I wanted it to last longer, much longer, but we had to find Torf. We found him on the way to the ballroom. I introduced Karen to Torf, "Torf, have you worked out what you are going to do about what we talked about?"

"Yes sir, I have. I have decided to take your advice to resign and make my way home during our leave period."

I nodded, "Well don't do anything yet. Admiral Kalashian has some news. Join us at the reception when you see me join him."

He nodded back, "I shall sir, thank you."

During the reception Karen and I kept our eyes on

Kalashian to see when he was free and whilst having our third dance together the moment came. He must have been watching me too, because he inclined his head outside to the garden, and I nodded. As we left the dance floor Torf joined us as we went outside to the garden. Joining Kalashian, I introduced Karen and Torf, telling him they were doing the same thing as he planned.

"Good, the more the merrier. The Federation has a good-sized navy, all fighter pilots and fleet officers are more than welcome. Now my contacts have appraised me that things have gotten a whole lot worse than when we left, a declaration of war is imminent. Turning to Torf, "My best advice to you, Torf, would be to go directly to that address on Zeta Australis, and don't take too long. Remember, time is of the essence. Get out within the next week if you can. That advice applies to all of you. I hope to see you all again soon. Now, go and enjoy yourselves."

The reception finished at 1400, then Karen and I made our way to a little shop that I knew, inside I asked the owner if he could mount all my medals onto one bar.

He replied, "Of course I can Hunter, and I'll also make you up a ribbon bar, and what about the little lady?"

Karen nodded, "Yes hers too, when will they be ready Zeke?"

Zeke replied, just before midday tomorrow, cost you sixty credits, how's that sound Hunter?"

"Fine Zeke, I'll pay you when we pick them up."

We had had enough food during the reception, so we walked to the tavern for some drinks. Karen grabbed a table as I went to the bar for drinks. Then joined her at the table with our drinks. We sat side by side, holding each other's hand, we took sips of our drinks after saluting each other with our glasses. Then we talked quietly as we planned what else we needed to do. First, we had to write our resignations. Secondly, find a ship headed to Alpha Centauri, and book a cabin. Thirdly, pickup our medals, and four, I had to hand in my resignation. Karen would do that at Fighter Command on Alpha Centauri when we picked up her ship.

While we were having our drinks, we were playing with each other's hands, and I was studying her fingers. I slipped off my academy class ring and slipped it onto her left ring finger, it fitted snugly, I remarked, "Well what do you know, we have the same finger size. Pity you don't have a class ring; we could swap them and be a real couple."

She laughed, "Oh I can fix that," she reached into

her pocket and brought out her own class ring and placed it onto my left ring finger, "There now, we're a married couple. I want you to know I couldn't be happier, I'm in love with you Captain Clay Davis."

"I love you too, Squadron Leader Karen Davis. Hmm has a nice ring to it, pun intended, though your ring is a tad light on my finger. After we've had dinner, we can start our honeymoon."

Smiling coyly she replied, "Oh, definitely yes please."

Stardate 2514.03.24:
Last night after we both printed out letters of resignation for our respective fleets, we spent the night in my quarters making love to each other. From what I observed and moans she made, and what she told me, I was well more than able to fulfil her sexually speaking.

Today, I will be handing in my resignation. Picking up our medals from Zeke. Though I hadn't told Karen, I was going to find an engagement ring and two wedding bands. While Karen went off to find a ship going to Alpha Centauri, leaving this week.

Going to the Chancellors office, I requested to see the Admiral. I waited for ten minutes, then his door opened, and he ushered me in.

He asked what he could do for me. I passed across my letter of resignation, saying, "I was wondering if you could pass my letter of resignation onto Fleet Command sir."

In shock he leaned back and exclaimed, "My god, son, what are you doing?"

Chapter 9.

I pondered his question briefly, then answered him, "Sir, I realize what I'm giving up. After seeing the results of our bombing of the Zytronos sector, and the horror of what those bombs can do, I realized that I don't want to see them used again. With the growing political unrest, I think that a civil war could unfold. My loyalty lies with the Outer Rim, especially if the Alliance uses those quantum bombs against planets of the Outer Rim again like the Zytrons did. Quite frankly Admiral, I think they should be outlawed, and there's nothing you can say that would convince me the Alliance isn't already studying the bomb's technology to produce more."

He gave a heavy sigh, "I fear you may be right Clay on all counts, but to give up your commission? It seems such a waste of your talent... Then again being arrested if a war did breakout would be too. I'll pass your letter onto fleet, and good luck son with whatever you do. I'll surely miss our chats."

He had a sad expression on his face as I stood up. We saluted each other and shook hands for what I thought would be our final time. I left his office and didn't look back.

My next stop was at a jewellery shop where I bought for Karen an exquisite set of engagement and wedding rings made of white gold. For me, I bought a heavy wide white gold ring with a blued titanium stripe down the centre. The rings were perfect, but they were all a little too large. The jeweller said he could resize them for me immediately and I could pick them up in an hour.

Even though I was early, I went to see if Zeke had finished mounting our medals. He had finished both sets and had made ribbon bars for each of us as well. Thanking him, I flashed my ID over his machine to transfer the credits to him. He called, "Good luck," as I left.

Returning to the jewellers to pick up the wedding rings. I decided on one more special gift. I bought a thick gold chain necklace with two hearts intertwined with a diamond set in the middle. I collected our rings, transferred credits for everything, and was on my way to meet Karen.

We had arranged to meet at the tavern for a drink and debrief before heading to the mess for lunch. Karen was already there when I arrived. I saw that she had two drinks waiting. I joined her at the table and after a long kiss, passed across her mounted medals and ribbon bar. "They are perfect," she said, and pinned the ribbon bar to her uniform shirt. I liked the way mine looked too, once I finished pinning them on.

"I've found a ship, It's a fleet transport taking

supplies and personnel to our Alpha Centauri Base. It's leaving from the Skyring at 1800 and I was able to get a cabin assigned to us. How about you? How'd you get along with the Admiral?"

As I took a sip of my drink, "Well it began pretty well..." and recounted our entire meeting to her, filling in all the details and finished with, "There's only one thing, I've been feeling lopsided all morning. I've missed the weight of my class ring. Let's swap them back, but first I need to ask, 'Will you marry me?'"

I pulled out the jeweller's box containing her engagement band and presented it to her. She opened the box, looked into my eyes, "Yes, with all my heart. Of course, I will."

After she took off my class ring, I took the engagement ring from the box and placed it on her finger. Then we traded back our class rings. I returned mine to its normal place and she put hers on her other hand. She was admiring her engagement ring, "There's a proviso to our engagement though."

She looked at me in surprise before I could continue. "I'd like it to be short, because I would like us to be married today." With relief showing on her face, "Oh yes, that can't come soon enough darling, as far as I'm concerned."

Stardate 2514.03.25.1605:
After lunch we went to our quarters to pack our belongings. From there we went to pick up shuttle passes for the Skyring from the quarters office staff.

At the Skyring we boarded the transport to Alpha Centauri. Once comfortably on board I asked to see the captain. We were shown to the Captain's ready room and our escort knocked on the door.

The door opened and there stood Julie Morris, one of my inner core friends from the Academy. We both laughed and embraced as she invited us into her office. I introduced Karen to Julie as my fiancé. She returned to her desk and nodding to the two chairs in front of her as we all sat down. She looked across the desk and took in our battle ribbons. "Well, it looks like the two of you have seen some action. Damn it Clay! I didn't think you'd be talking about me in that valedictory address, but anyway I am a Captain now. What can I do for you?"

I smiled. "Julie, Karen and I want to get married. Now… by you!"

She arched her eyebrows inquisitively, "Hmm, sounds like you are both expecting to go back into action soon. She paused only briefly, "Ok, I'd love to."

She tapped her communicator and asked her exec

and comms officers to join us in the ready room. We all stood when they arrived, and she reached for the ship's Bible. Looking directly at her officers she said, "I've called you both in here to be witnesses to the marriage of Squadron Leader Karen Kirkland to Captain Clayton Davis."

I passed the rings to Julie. She lay them on the Bible and began the ceremony. When we got to the part where we said our vows, Julie handed me Karen's ring. She said, "Clayton, repeat after me. I, Clayton Davis, take you, Karen Kirkland, to be my lawfully wedded wife. I present you this ring as a token of my love."

I placed the ring on Karen's finger in front of her engagement ring. They both looked good together. The ceremony continued as Karen said her vows and presented me with my ring. Julie said, "By the power vested in me as Captain under Fleet Regulation 475, I now pronounce you husband and wife. Clay, you may kiss the bride."

We kissed as Julie and the two officers applauded us. Then the exec and comms officers exited the room. Julie turned toward us and, with a twinkle in her eye, said, "Now, I've got to get my ship ready for departure. Is there anything else I can do for you Captain and Mrs. Davis?"

"No thank you Captain, we'll let you get to it."

She smiled, "Congratulations you two, now get the hell out of here."

Back in our cabin, Karen told me how much she adored her rings and mine.

"Nothing but the best for my wife, Missus Davis. Oh, but I do have one more thing, your wedding present."

I presented her with the necklace laid out in the presentation box. To say she loved it would be an understatement as she jumped into my arms and kissed me.

The ship left the Skyring and quickly jumped into hyperspace. Soon there was a knock at the door. There was a yeoman standing in front of the door, as I opened it, holding a silver tray. On it was a large plate of finger foods, two champagne flutes, and a bottle of one-hundred-year-old Bollinger champagne. As the yeoman passed me the tray she said, "Compliments of the captain sir."

I thanked her and turned with the tray, shutting the door with my foot, and headed back to my bride. After consuming the champagne and nibbles, we happily consummated our marriage another way for the remainder of the evening before drifting off to sleep in each other's arms.

Stardate 2514.03.26:
We arrived at the fighter command base this
morning and were farewelled by Julie and her crew
as we left her ship. We walked from Julie's
transporter in the base cargo receiving area. Karen
wanted me to see the Serenity, so we went to inspect
her ship.

Ten minutes later I was looking at the Serenity. She
was in an auxiliary hangar, at the start of a row of
fighter hangars that faced the main runways.
She was really sleek. Just sitting there on the pad,
she looked fast, but Karen had already told me she
could only do warp 5, even with the new engines.
Karen escorted me in and guided me to the bridge
where she showed me around. Then we explored the
balance of the ship. When we finally got to her
quarters, we deposited our belongings. On our way
out she asked her flight chief to get the Serenity
ready for launch and we headed to the base tavern.
She left me there, briefly, while she went to make
changes in her personnel file to her married name
and to change her callsign. Then she would rewrite
her letter of resignation using her new name and
hand it to the Fleet Commander.

I checked out the room. The decorations were
minimal; mostly photographs of various craft and a
couple of spaceports. On one wall was the
Federation medallion. I ordered a scotch from the
bar. I then sat at a table where Karen would see me

when she returned. As I sat there, I saw that a group of men were becoming animated and pointing in my direction. I guessed that they were intent on giving me grief about a naval person being in their bar. One of them got up and as one came toward my table. He started belligerently to say, "What's a naval swabbie doing in a man's…"

That was as far as he got before I stood up and he saw my rank. He swiftly stood to attention and saluted. Seeing by his shoulder bars that he was only a cadet. "I suggest you learn some manners cadet…Cadet who?"

"Mawson sir." He was still standing in his salute.

I barked with authority, "Cadet Mawson! As I was saying about manners, it would be prudent to determine the rank of your intended victim. My name is Captain Clayton Davis, callsign Hunter. Go look it up and report back to me here. Now move!" as I returned the salute.

He scuttled away with his fellow cadets following him, as I went back to my drink. Ten minutes later, Mawson and his group returned. He marched over to my table and saluted. I returned the salute with a wave of my hand.

"Sir, I wish to humbly apologize for my earlier demeanour, and would like the honour of buying you a drink please sir?"

I smiled, "Very well cadet Mawson I accept your offer. I'll have two large scotches, one with soda, thank you."

I saw Karen come in and while Mawson was at the bar, she joined me at the table. She leaned over and asked, "Something going on dear?"

I innocently replied, "No love, just a cadet offering to buy me a drink. Ah, here he comes now."

Mawson placed the two glasses down in front of me. I took one of the glasses and placed in front of Karen, "Thank you cadet Mawson."

He snapped to attention, "My pleasure Captain, Squadron Leader ma'am."

Karen looked at me enquiringly as Mawson moved away. She began to sip her scotch as I told her the whole story. She laughed, "Good to see you put him in his place. Honestly some of these upstart rookies are a pain. They think they're tough and know it all."

We had lunch in the tavern with our drinks. Karen told me how her meetings had gone with everything. She was now officially Karen Davis, and her new callsign was KD.

The Fleet Commander tried to persuade her to stay but she told him exactly what I had told McManus and he finally agreed to submit her resignation. We finished our drinks and made our way back to the Serenity. Meeting us at the hangar entrance, the flight chief wished us good luck and moved outside to watch our take off. He had done an excellent job and Serenity was prepared and ready to go with engines running.

As soon as we settled in our seats on the bridge, Karen requested clearance to taxi. Once on our way, permission to take off was granted. We took off on impulse power and I computed the course to Zeta Australis. We were quickly in clear space and Karen took us to warp five. It would take us three days to reach the planet. Leaving the ship to fly itself, we moved into the captain's quarters, put our belongings away, and restarted our honeymoon. Because the two of us were the only ones on board, neither of us thought it was important to get dressed. We had no use for clothing, even when moving about the ship. Besides, I will never grow tired of watching her beautiful, lithe body as she moved.

Stardate 2514.03.29:
We finally had to put our clothes on again as we neared Zeta Australis. As soon as we began our approach, Karen requested a hangar at the Onworld Spaceport. We were cleared to land at Hangar 12. After lowering the landing gear, Karen directed the

Serenity to Hangar 12 and set her down gently. Wearing our Fleet uniforms, and carrying our belongings in our duffle bags, we went through the customs formalities. Outside the spaceport, we took an aircab to the address I'd been given.

We presented our ID's to security when we arrived. We declared that we were there to join the Federation military forces. We had to answer a number of questions and surrender our blasters and communicators. Then we were shown around the building and assigned to married quarters. Our guide explained that quarters were in a temporary facility where those switching sides could congregate safely. We were told that eventually we would each be interviewed by government hierarchy agents, and once cleared, would be moved to another location for additional interviews by a more official military tribunal.

Our quarters were spacious. Although rather utilitarian in design. They were clean, well-maintained, and very functional. We stored our belongings, hung up our dress uniforms and a couple of normal, everyday uniforms. Since we had to turn in our blasters with our communicators our holsters looked rather strange without weapons in them, we left them in our kit bags and headed to the mess for drinks. The door to our quarters was operated by biometrics and, once programmed, would only open for Karen or me.

Chapter 10.

In the mess, we stood near the door adjusting our eyes to the room, and surveyed it looking for anyone we knew. Torf was there with a couple of the Scimitar crew. Karen noted a couple of acquaintances but no one she actually knew. Getting our drinks, we moved to where Torf was sitting and I asked, "Do you have any room for an old shipmate and his wife?"

Everyone stood and I waved them down as Karen and I took seats, Torf asked, Captain, when did you get here?"

"Just a while ago, and it's not captain anymore Torf. I resigned my commission before I left so I'm plain old Clay Davis now and Karen is just Karen Davis. She resigned too. So, how have you all been, and when did you get here?"

"We're all fine, captain. I got here two days ago, and Jim and Yagi got here the day before me."

"Have you seen anyone else from the ship?"

Yagi spoke, "Aye sir, all the rest from the ship were leaving here as I arrived, so everyone's safe sir."

A feeling of relief fell over me, "Well let's hope we're not here for long, Karen and I have been out of touch recently, so what's the latest political news?"

Torf replied, "Crisis talks between the Alliance and the Federation have broken down, but at present the delegation is still on Earth sir, so the talks may resume. However, if the delegation returns, my father being one of them, we can assume that a declaration of war will be made."

"Hmm," I responded, "Not a pretty picture then, by the sound of it. Looks like we got out just in time."

"Aye sir," Jim mumbled.

Stardate 2514.04.02:
Today before breakfast a staff member came to our quarters to tell us that we were to make ourselves available for questioning by government agents at ten hundred hours in private offices. Later that morning we made our way to our appointment at reception. We were separated as soon as we passed through the door, each of us was met by a different agent, I was taken to a small window-less room for a private interview. He began the questioning by asking where on Vega 13 I was born and what I remembered of my home planet. The agent asked, about my childhood and then about my life at the Academy and about my military history. I was permitted to ask questions, so I asked about our communicators and weapons. I was told we would

be issued new communicators, with the universal translators built in.

"That's great, but, what about our weapons? I want my old weapon back. I know it. I like it; and it's saved my life more than once."

The agent looked surprised, but then smiled, "I understand. I'd want mine back too if it were me. Yes, you will both get back your weapons."

"When?" At this point I wanted to know how long this next phase of the procedure would take. The reply was rather innocuous. I was told it would all depend upon how easily my answers were corroborated.

A week later, Karen and I were each issued new communicators and told where we could pick up our old weapons. That meant we had passed the government background checks. We were in!

Stardate 2514.04.17:
This morning my communicator chirped, "Captain and Squadron Leader Davis, please pack your belongings. A vehicle will be sent to pick you both up at zero nine thirty. Please be waiting at reception."

Karen and I both dressed and packed up our stuff, but we left our duffels in the room and headed down to breakfast. We were in the mess eating breakfast when Torf appeared and joined us at the table. He wanted us to know that he, Jim, and Yagi had a vehicle coming for them at eleven hundred.

"Well Torf, looks like we're on the move." I offered my hand. "Good luck."

"To you too sir. It's been a pleasure serving with you." Torf turned toward Karen, "Ma'am... I don't know if I should salute, shake hands, or give you a hug." Smiling, shook hands, and then gave Karen a hug before he moved away.

"He's a good man Clay, and I'm glad to have met him."

"Aye, that he is darling."

We were waiting, bags in hand, as an aircar came to rest in front of the building. After showing our ID's we were asked to stow our bags and then to enter the vehicle. It took us to a high block tower and entered through a port built in one of its sides.

"You may leave your bags sir, ma'am. I will be your driver today. Please let me show you to the conference room."

After following him down a labyrinth of corridors,

we stopped at one of the unmarked doors. He knocked on the door, opened it, and let us pass. Then he sat by it. Karen and I were directed to take seats at the table.

As we looked around, we quickly determined that we were in, what appeared to be, a courtroom. Directly in front of us was a long, tall bench; and behind the bench were five very tall chairs. The chairs were occupied by high military officers representing the navy, air command, and mobile infantry. We looked at the officers and realized that they were looking at us.

The officer in the centre spoke first. "Welcome to Zeta Australis. I am Admiral Robert Kalmus, chairman of this tribunal and we have some questions for each of you this morning. If either of you have questions of your own during the proceedings, please address them through me and we'll answer the best we can. Let's start shall we, Captain Davis, when did you two marry and why?"

I smiled, gave them my answer, and finished by saying, "I admit our marriage may seem sudden to you, but we *love* each other. It's as if we already have known one another forever. To put it in perspective, I already know more about my wife in this short time than what others take ten or twenty years to find out." Out of the corner of my eye I could see that Karen was smiling at me as I spoke.

She leaned over, cupped her hand to my ear, and whispered, "Nicely put dear."

The chairman erupted, "Please! Do not talk to each other during these proceedings. Squadron Leader Davis, please tell the tribunal what you said to your husband."

Karen told them proudly, receiving smiles all around. Even the Admiral was smiling.

"Squadron Leader Davis," asked the air command marshal, "Tell us how you met your husband, in detail please." Karen told them in detail, right up to our marriage.

The admiral presented the next question to both of us, "So, are we to believe that each of you has the same view regarding a potential war as well as the use of the quantum bomb?"

We answered at the same time, "Yes Sir," Then I continued alone, "You may think these quantum bombs are a figment of someone's imagination but go ask inhabitants of the outer rim planets that have been destroyed. Oh, that's right; you can't, because they're not here anymore! Go ask Admiral Kalashian about them. We dropped three of the bloody things and had to watch a 4th being dropped. They should be bloody well outlawed!" I do not remember when I stood up while I was speaking, but there I was, standing in front of the bench, waving and pointing. My voice must have risen because I was agitated. It took me a second to realize the admiral was banging his gavel and motioning for me to sit down.

"Alright let's move to something else, How come you suddenly changed your allegiancies Captain?"

"It didn't happen suddenly sir. I was born on Vega13 a rim planet. When tensions started between the Alliance and Federation over no aid to the Outer Rim, I wasn't happy, but I had my studies and exams to complete. Because there is no Fleet Academy in the Outer Rim. I had no choice but to go to Earth. Otherwise, I would have stayed in the Outer Rim. After graduation and receiving my commission, I was obligated to the Alliance. As a fleet officer I had no choice. It was the use of that quantum bomb that caused me to rethink my obligations. My allegiance is, first and foremost, to the Outer Rim Worlds and Colonies. That's why I am here before you today."

The chairman replied, "I see, very well. Squadron Leader answer the same question please."

Karen answered in her own way, but it was clear to everyone in the room that we were in total agreement.

The air command marshal said, "Very well put Squadron Leader."

The chairman said, "Now let's move to your military exploits. It says here you defeated the Academy Do or Die Scenario. That has never been done before. How did you do that?"

I told them the truth, and the results. When I had finished my answer there was laughter from the tribunal members. Even Karen was laughing.

The Admiral then asked, "Please explain what you did, once your ship entered the Zytronos system during the war."

I explained how I attacked the Zytron fighters at the first target and went on explaining everything up to leaving the system for home.

Finally they asked me to tell how we got to Zeta Australis. I told them the story of our resignations, mine and Karen's, and continued with the story all the way to us arriving at the processing centre.

They seemed satisfied with by answers but had one final question that took me by surprise. "Will you have any qualms about firing on alliance ships, considering you may have friends aboard said ships?"

I considered my answer for a minute, "Qualms yes, but would I hesitate? No, they would be enemy vessels, and would do the same to my ship in a war situation."

My answers apparently satisfied them, and they turned to question Karen. Her answers to some of their questions were given with anger, but in the main they were satisfied.

They conferred for almost ten minutes before the chairman spoke up, "Captain please stand. You are hereby raised in rank to Flotilla Commander. You will command the destroyer escorts of Battle Group One based on Beta Australis, where our main military strength is located. You will report to the Admiral in Command aboard his flagship the Vega 13. Some of our ships have been named in honour of planets destroyed, your ship will be the Trion. When you reach base, you will be issued Federation uniforms and anything else you may need.

Squadron Leader, please stand, "We usually like to keep married couples together, however in this case we cannot do that. You are promoted to Group Captain and posted aboard the Vega13. As such, that's the best we can for both of you, but at least you will be in the same Battle Group. When you leave, your escort will take you to transport leaving for Beta Australis tonight."

Karen and I looked at each other. Before he could bang down the gavel, "WAIT! Mr. Chairman!"

"You have a question, Flotilla Commander?"

"As you have heard during our testimonies, we have our own ship available. Seeing that Beta Australis is the main base of operations for Battle Group One, is it possible for us to fly there in our own ship and hangar it on base?"

The tribunal conferred, and the Admiral replied, " Granted. A hangar will be made available to your ship indefinitely. You may leave from the spaceport and your fees at the spaceport will be taken care of, but you both must report to the Vega13 by zero nine hundred the day after tomorrow. Your driver will now take you to the spaceport. That is all."

We found our aircar waiting outside. We got in and the driver gave us our orders and supply issue chits for our uniforms and whatever else we needed. He dropped us off at the space depot and made his way to the administration office, while we made for our hangar and Serenity. We settled into our seats on the bridge. I computed the course to Beta Australis and determined that if we only used warp three it would take until ten hundred hours tomorrow to reach Beta Australis. Karen retracted the gear, while I asked for and received clearance for take-off. Once we made warp, I turned on the autopilot and let the ship fly herself. We had a little bite to eat, drank a little scotch, and retired to the bedroom.

The following morning, we decelerated to impulse power, I tapped my communicator and announced, "Flotilla Commander and Group Captain Davis aboard the Serenity to Federation Naval Base. Request permission to land at our hangar please."

The reply was immediate, "Naval Base Akron to Serenity, permission granted sirs. Please use hangar ten."

Smiling at Karen, "Copy that Akron, landing in five."

When we landed a four-man maintenance crew was waiting, as we left the ship, they saluted and the crew chief greeted us, "Welcome aboard the Akron Ma'am, Sir, is there anything we can do for you?"

We returned the salutes and Karen spoke up, "A cover over the ship when she cools down would be nice sergeant. We intend to sleep aboard her tonight."

I saw the sergeant press a button on his control tablet as he replied, "Easily fixed ma'am, and we'll attach the power cables. If you will follow me, I'll get your biometrics scanned in. This tablet controls everything in the hanger; and it has a map of the base built in as well." As he was speaking, the two-foot-thick blast doors slid silently closed. There was a loud clang when they slotted together. Now that our biometrics had been scanned, the sergeant presented each of us a tablet.

At the door to the hangar we separated, after he had said, "Only my maintenance crew, and you two have access to this hangar now sir, ma'am, now I have other duties, so I'm afraid you're on your own." He saluted, returning his salute he moved off with his men.

Chapter 11.

Stardate 2514.04.19.0855:
We used the tablet base map, to make our way to the Quartermasters store. There, we were issued a dozen sets of uniforms in our command colours with our shoulder rank bars already sewn on. We both opted for new pull-on boots as well as a couple of new dress uniforms. Karen added new flying boots and a lined flight jacket as well. We were issued the new Phaser pistols with the variable power setting feature that could range from stun to kill. We also got holsters for the new pistols. All of our stuff was placed in brand new gear bags.

We returned to Serenity to change into our new uniforms. The new shirts were a pale purple and looked quite sharp with our service ribbon bars pinned on over the left pocket and our new communicators below them. Then we packed the new duffle bags. Finally, we stowed our old bags away.

Dressed in our new uniforms we headed for the officers mess for a drink before lunch. In the mess we encountered quite a few people we knew. I came across a couple of classmates I knew from the Academy and a few from my days as Captain of the Scimitar, Karen recognized a number of the pilots she had flown with. As we moved through the room, they came up to greet us and to introduce us to many of the officers present.

After lunch we set off to tour the base and found the flagship carrier we had to report to the following day. That night we decided that when we return to base, we would spend our time on the Serenity instead of using base quarters. That way we could get away from everything and spend time together the way we wished.

Now we are both standing at attention, facing Admiral Kalashian once again, and are presenting our orders to him. He smiled, "It's good to have you both aboard. Congratulations on your recent marriage. Now it's time to get to work; let's go back to my office."

We followed him to his ready room. He invited us to sit as he went to his desk. "By the rings of Cragon, it's good to see you both and with my battle group too. It's good to see those pen pushers at command are finally taking notice of my suggestions. Now then to business; firstly, you Karen, you'll be under the direction of my executive wing commander. I'll leave you two to work out each other's duties. Your office will be on the flight deck along with a briefing room. You know the drill, so I don't have to tell you too much. I've assigned you married quarters as due your rank, That way Clay can visit whenever we're not on a war footing or engaged in operations. My security people already know this, so you don't have to ask permission to beam over Clay. Karen, we do have one squadron leader that is experienced the rest are newly promoted. There are a lot of new hotshot pilots, so it will be up to you to whip them into shape. Any questions?"

"No sir, seems pretty straight forward."

"Now Clay, as Flotilla Commander, you have responsibility for all twelve of my fleet destroyers. I don't need to tell you how important their job is. Different to Alliance operations, the Federation fleets have two supply ships that accompany each Battle Group on operations. In a battle situation they lay back away from the action, but they will need protection.

Federation ships have a new type of shielding, more powerful than Alliance ships, and they allow us to fire and launch fighters through our shields. This could be a deciding factor in our favour during a battle. Please don't ask me how they work, As far as I know it has something to do with the shield modulation, but I do know that there are still a few slight bugs in the system that show up periodically. All I can suggest is that you both read the tech specs in your ship manuals. Any questions?"

"Yes sir, how long before the fleet moves from base?

He smiled, "We're still waiting for our final crewing numbers to be made up, but I hope to launch to practice fleet operations a week from today. That should give you plenty of time to familiarize yourself with your ships and crews.

I've assigned a yeoman to show you both to Karen's quarters to drop off your gear, and then around my ship, so you'll know where you're going, and finally back to Karen's quarters. That is all, you are both dismissed."

We picked up our bags and followed the yeoman to Karen's new quarters. Karen left her bag and I hung a spare uniform set in the wardrobe. I carried my bag as we toured the ship. After the tour we said goodbye with hugs and kisses, and I promised to join Karen on her ship at the end of the workday. I now knew my way around the flagship without an escort which would make life so much easier for me.

My ship, the Trion, was next the flagship on the starboard side. I went aboard and was met by my executive officer Lt. Commander Arras, a Tritonian humanoid. Our ship was named after her destroyed homeworld, so I think she now considered this ship her home, which in fact it is. She showed me to the bridge, From there we went to the ready room which connected to a conference room containing a long table. Behind the ready room were my large living quarters. Leaving my bag in my quarters, we returned to the bridge.

Back in my office Arras told me, "Sir, in case you notice the heavier atmosphere, all Federation ships have a living atmosphere of Earth plus two."

"That won't be a problem Arras, Our flagship is named after my homeworld where the atmosphere was Earth plus three."

She smiled and nodded. The Trion bridge had less command personnel than Alliance ships, The only stations were comms, weapons, security, with a combined helm and nav. Entering the bridge, the first thing you see are the three command chairs on a raised platform near the centre. To the right of the captain's chair sits the exec, while the seat to the captain's left is unassigned. To the immediate left of the command chairs is comms; the far left is guns; the immediate right – security; and the far right – engineering. Directly forward of the captain's chair is nav/helm.

All the command staff is humanoid. Arras went around the room introducing them to me: at comms - Mary Tarrant, a Uslyssian; guns - Theta Baron, an Australis native; security - Tark, a Cragoid; and at nav/helm - Jonas Major, a Zetian.

I went to the command chair and sat in it for the first time. Reaching for the ship's log tablet I recorded,

"Stardate 2514.04.19.1130: Ships log, Federation of the Outer Rim destroyer Trion, I, Flotilla Commander Clayton Davis, callsign Hunter, have now taken command of the Trion, and all of the destroyer fleet of Battle Group One, Hunter out."

"Comms, copy that and send it to all of our group ships. Also, order all destroyer Captains to a conference aboard this ship at fourteen hundred,"

"Aye sir," she replied.

"Number one, schedule an all crew parade outside the ship tomorrow at zero nine hundred."

My exec quickly responded, "Aye sir."

"Alright Arras," I sighed, "Now you can take me to the wardroom to meet all the officers, and then we can have some lunch, I'm famished."

In the wardroom I was introduced to my final senior officer, Chief Engineer Zarkan, an Arcadian refugee. Then Arras introduced me to each officer in the room, one by one. After all the introductions had been made, we went to the command table to be served lunch.

Later that afternoon I met with all my new captains. There was only one face that I knew, that of Torf, who had been promoted to captain by the tribunal and given command of the Draga. I moved to the head of the table and directed everyone to find a seat. "Now then," I began, "Our first order of business. Should the Trion be disabled, and I'm still alive, I will transfer to another ship and take command from there. However, if I'm dead there must be someone to take over command of the flotilla. So which of you has served on destroyers before?"

Only one person's hand went up, Torf's, so I asked, "Out of all of you, put your hand up if this is your first command." Every officer in the room raised a hand... except Torf.

Sighing, I placed my elbows on the table and lowered my head into palms in exasperation. Then I leaned back in my chair and scanned the room, "Very well Captain Torf, you will be my second in command of the flotilla. So, apart from Torf and myself, who knows what tactics we use in battle?"

All hands went up. I muttered under my breath, "Well at least that's something I guess." Looking at them all, "Now we'll go around the table, and I want you to list any defects your ship may have, starting with you Torrence."

None of the ships had any defects that they were aware of, which was good news. Then I told them what the admiral had told me about the shields maybe having some bugs in them. I ordered them all to study their ship manuals to the point of memorization, so that they knew what to do if a problem arose.

"Lastly, our Battle Group will be launching next week. Now our order of flight: I will be to starboard of the flagship, Hammer you'll be on the Admiral's port, Torf, you and Meeker will be the supply ships escort. Jantine, you'll be forward scout, and Collis, rear echelon. The rest of you will be spread around the group, in-line-ahead formation, any questions?... Good, thank you, you're all dismissed!"

At the end of the day, I joined Karen on the flagship, and we went to the wardroom for drinks. We sat together and complained to each other about the day we just had. After dinner we went back to her quarters and relaxed in each other's arms on the couch watching an old Earth science fiction movie about a Martian invasion that had us laughing.

After breakfast the next morning I left her at her office on the flight deck and went back to my ship.

Stardate 2514.05.02.0900:
This morning all senior officers have been summoned to the flagship for a command briefing by the Admiral.

He told us the fleet is going to launch tomorrow morning for Wolf sector 835. We can expect a month of movement and battle tactics exercises. Once the Admiral had finished with his briefing he asked if there were any questions.

I raised my hand and stood. After being acknowledged, "Admiral, during our exercise will I have time to train my destroyer captains to practice these manoeuvres in real life? All their experience comes from simulations."

The Admiral smiled, "I can appreciate the problems you, and all the other battle-hardened veterans, are facing Hunter. The answer to your question is yes! That's why we're going out and staying away for so long. Any other questions?... Alright thank you, you are all dismissed!"

Ship's log Stardate 2514.05.03.0700:
I have come aboard early this morning to have breakfast in the wardroom before the fleet launches at zero nine hundred, My destroyers would follow my lead as the first ships to launch, followed by the flagship and infantry carrier, and lastly the two supply ships.

Stardate 2514.05.03.0900:
Everyone on the bridge heard the command coming from the squawk box, "Trion, you are cleared for take-off."

Having been given clearance for take-off, I ordered, "Alright Jonas, thrusters to full power." As soon as we reached twenty thousand feet, I said, "One quarter impulse, shut off the thrusters, get the nose up Jonas."

Once in space, we orbited the planet waiting for the other ships to lift off one by one and join us. "Jonas, keep an eye on the scanners and let me know when the last ship has lifted off. Mary, all destroyers to follow our orbit, we'll move into our stations as the last ship is up."

"Aye sir message relayed."

Jonas said, "Last ship leaving the planet now sir."

"Thank you, mister Major. On viewer please Mary, make to destroyers. All ships assume your assigned stations."

Jonas directed our ship into its position on the starboard side of the flagship. When all ships were on station, the flagship ordered us to warp 9.

Chapter 12

Stardate 2514.06.13.1200:
We stayed in this sector for longer than what was really necessary. After five solid weeks of training all of the new officers, pilots, and ship captains needed some relaxation time.

Today, at midday, the United Planetary Alliance declared war against the Federation of Outer Rim Planets and Systems. Thirty minutes after war had been declared, the Admiral ordered us back to Beta Australis at fastest warp speed. Coming out of warp two days later, we entered a low orbit of Beta Australis and remained at station keeping. We sent our dummy exercise munitions back to the planet and received a full supply of live armaments in return. Our food supplies were also returned to full capacity. All of the supply ships were maxed out with additional weapons, munitions, and food rations, by a continual stream of supply vessels. Now that we were on a war footing, all officers wore their phaser pistols, but only at the lowest stun setting while onboard ship.

Taking the time for a Captains Conference while our supplies were being loaded, I ordered all my captains to beam aboard the Trion. They all stood as I entered the room and moved to the head of the conference table. "Well, ladies and gentlemen, this is why I have been driving you hard during your recent training. All I can say is remember what I have tried to teach you. Do your duty as best you can, and hopefully we will come out of the other side of this war without too many casualties. That is all, thank you."

The following morning, I was ordered to beam aboard the flagship for a briefing. At the conference table I sat beside my wife, and as we waited for the Admiral, we held hands. The Captains of all the other vessels were seated with us as well as Karen's boss, Wing Commander Morcombe. As Kalashian came into the room we all stood until he had taken his seat, then returned to being seated.

He started proceedings, "Well finally, ladies and gentlemen we've come down to it. Now that all the politicking is done, we move to war. Whether we win or lose will be determined by the amount of damage done to each other. Just remember this is not about an alien race invading, you'll be fighting fellow humans in a Civil War. Our grievances are just, but they think otherwise, so be it. This Battle Group has been ordered to the Armward Region of the Outer Rim Sector with only one aim: to prevent any Alliance assaults in that sector and to protect those planets, any questions?"

Captain Tor Wensall of the mobile infantry carrier asked, "For how long Admiral?"

"For however long it takes, or until we're relieved by another Battle Group, any other questions?"

"When do we leave Admiral?" Asked one of the supply ship captains, "My ship is still being loaded."

Kalashian smiled, "I've been assured all the loading of supplies will be finished by midnight. So, the fleet leaves at zero eight hundred tomorrow, you can all set your course for Altair. We'll move at warp ten to get there and start our patrolling of the sector from there. Any more questions?"

The second supply ship captain asked, "What do we do if the fleet goes into action Admiral, we are fighting men also?"

"And so, you are! But two of Commander Davis's destroyers will be your escorts and will try to protect you as best as possible. However, you may be needed to aid their efforts if we encounter a large force."

The Wing Commander piped up, "Besides the two destroyers, Group Captain Davis will lead a flight of twelve Rapiers to your position."

I growled, "It would have been nice to have a heads up. Thanks for letting me know Morcombe. My destroyers would have opened fire on them!"

"Well, I'm letting you know now commander!"

Kalashian intervened in our dispute. "Enough! The Flotilla Commander is right Morcombe, he should have been told. The last thing we need is our ships shooting on friendlies. Do not keep these sort of matters to yourself! I should have been told, at the very least, and this is the first time I've heard of your decision. Don't make that mistake again! Commander Davis please inform your shield ship's captains."

"Aye sir."

Kalashian nodded, "Well that's it, any other questions?... Dismissed people!"

As we left the briefing, I had time to talk to Karen and asked her about the fighter cover for the supply ships, "How long have you known about this, love?"

"Since yesterday, and I argued with him to inform command, but the fool thought he'd keep it as a surprise, I'm sorry darling, but I'm dealing with an idiot."

I sighed and nodded, "At least I know you'll be safely away from the flagship should something terrible happen."

She smiled sweetly, "I love you too, but now you

have work to do, I'll see you soon," and we kissed each other goodbye.

Back aboard Trion I went to the bridge, "Mary, make to all Captains, the fleet leaves tomorrow at 0800 bound for Altair, also be aware that any ships guarding the supply ships, should we go into battle anytime, there will be a flight of Rapiers joining them, led by Group Captain Davis callsign KD."

Stardate 2514.06.20:
We arrived at Altair and established a high orbit of the planet, and I was summoned to the flagship. Once onboard the Vega13, I was met at the transporters by the Admiral, Karen, his Comms officer, and a security team. The admiral told me that we were beaming down to the council chambers on the planet. After beaming down outside the chambers, we were then escorted into the council chambers.

The Admiral addressed the council saying, "Good morning to you councillors, I am Admiral Kalashian from the Federation of Outer Rim Planets, I have come to inform you that my fleet will be patrolling in this sector for your protection against the Alliance. My comms officer here will give you our fleet communication frequency and the emergency frequency so that we can come to your aid quickly should your world be attacked while my fleet is out patrolling. I would also like to introduce my destroyer Flotilla Commander Clayton Davis, and my fighter Group Captain Karen Davis."

While the Chief Councillor was welcoming us, someone with a tablet joined our comms officer, and they began conversing. After the introductions were complete all of the council members moved forward to greet us and shake hands. We were invited to a civic reception, but the Admiral declined, "I'm sorry councillors but at present our duties must take priority, but we will be back from time to time. Perhaps next time, right now we must return to our mission, thank you all the same."

Once the diplomacy was finished, we left the building and at Kalashian's order were beamed aboard the flagship. Back aboard the admiral addressed the group, "That's the first of many times we will have to do this. I chose to have you with me Karen instead of that fool Morcombe remember to keep me informed of what he's up to and hopefully, you'll give me grounds to stand him down. Now say your goodbyes to Clay. We will be getting under way shortly."

We said our goodbyes, and I beamed back aboard the Trion. Ten minutes later our fleet was under way to the next planet.

Stardate 2514.07.04:
The fleet was just getting ready to orbit Chi Chantria

the fifteenth planet in the sector when Captain Collis of the Martique, the rear echelon position, radioed openly "Alliance fleet coming out of warp on our port rear quarter!"

I ordered quickly, "Shields up! Mary, make to our captains, assume battle positions. Draga and Baracolla, take your supply ships into a low orbit on the other side of the planet. Guns, charge all weapons and load photon torpedoes!"

Mary on comms called out, "All ships have signalled compliance with your orders sir."

Weapons barked, "Shields up, guns armed, and torpedoes ready sir."

I smiled as I thought, *are you lot in for a surprise when we open fire with our shields up!* Still smiling I saw a flight of fighters launch from the flagship, and head after the supply ships, thinking, *Go look after them sweetheart.* Then more fighters launched from the flagship heading into space. "Mary, main screen on port view."

"Aye sir," the screen flickered and changed to the view towards the inbound enemy fleet.

Two flights of our fighters engaged the incoming Alliance fighters while two more headed to engage the enemy fleet.

Collis on the Martique was the first of my destroyers into action as he closed with two Alliance destroyers passing between them. He fired broadsides on both of them simultaneously. Catching them with their shields down, his broadsides created havoc and serious damage to them both, and they had to withdraw. Coming about, Collis drew away two more destroyers, that chased his ship. He led them into an ambush as Hammer's Calista and Taggart's Phorus opened fire.

Because of the work of these three destroyers the Alliance lost two more of their destroyers when they were blown into space junk.

Calling one the other destroyers to take my position, I turned Trion into the attack. Four of my ships that were not yet engaged followed me. I ordered them into line astern of my ship. Then ordered Collis's ship to lead Calista, and Phorus, into another line astern formation. Ordering, "Collis take the port side of the enemy flagship, I'll take the starboard and we'll give them continual broadsides that they won't recover from."

One of the fighter Squadron Leaders had his entire squadron join up with us to form a protective screen and began blasting away at anything in our way. Our ships closed in on both sides of their flagship. I gave the command to fire, and our ships raked both sides of their flagship from stem to stern with phaser, photon cannons, and torpedoes. As the Martique and my ship cleared their flagship, we came about, and watched as the rest of my destroyers, punished the flagship as their guns came to bear. We watched the severely crippled flagship blow-up internally, as chunks from the once menacing ship drifted slowly off into space.

Then I led my ships, to engage the Alliance mobile infantry vessel and it's escort. While I engaged the escort, my ships blew the troop carrier apart.

Ten minutes later, my ship was hailed, "Federation Destroyer Trion, this is Captain Anderson of the Alliance ship Scimitar, we surrender, do you copy?"

Shocked and surprised to hear my old Alliance ship's name I ordered, "All ships cease fire immediately! Mary, put him on screen and patch it to the flagship as well."

"Aye sir, on viewer now."

"This is Flotilla Commander Clayton Davis of the Trion, What can I do for you Guy?"

He looked in shock as he saw me, "Anderson to Davis, my god Clay, thank the stars it's truly you. We surrender! There's only four of our ships left and even those are damaged severely, so we surrender. Please let us look for survivors, over."

I nodded and sighed, "Trion to Scimitar, very well

Guy, I will give you an hour to search for survivors then you will leave this sector. If you don't the ship's I leave guarding you will blow your remaining ships to bits. Oh, and Guy, I'm sorry it had to come to this."

"So am Clay, so am I, Scimitar out."

"Trion out."

"Mary, patch me to all of our destroyers. Well done boys, I owe you all drinks. Collis and Hammer, stay on station here and make sure the Scimitar and the other Alliance vessels depart within the hour. Your orders are to destroy any Alliance ships that don't go. Then you both are to join back up with us after the Alliance vessels leave. The rest of you are to head back to your normal fleet positions. " Their replies came in over the comms.

"Alright Jonas take us back."

"Aye sir," and the ship started to move.

Chapter 13.

After all our ships joined the fleet and the fighters were hangered, I was summoned to the flagship. In the Admirals office, I was seated opposite him.

"Clay, what's the name of the first destroyer captain who went into action and the two that joined him. I'm putting them up for commendations."

Smiling, "The first one was Captain Archie Collis, and the other two were John Hammer and Mark Taggert sir."

"Noted, thank you, NOW what the blue suns did you think you were doing, leading an attack like that on their flagship! Hell man, you could've been killed, and I would have lost my flotilla commander, damn it!"

Sitting back, I replied calmly, "No sir, you wouldn't have sir, Captain Torf knows to take my place as commander should that ever eventuate, and he was safely on the other side of the planet. As for me dying, that wasn't going to happen either sir. We had them cold and vulnerable. I think the fact we could fire with shields up really dealt them a shock, one that they couldn't recover from Admiral."

He smiled, "I think you're right Clay. Their morale seemed to really take a beating. I saw the look in young Anderson's face while he was on the viewer talking to you. By the way you handled that with extreme mercy, I can only hope that other captains in this war do the same for each other. How bad are our casualties?"

"Our casualties were nil, sir. The Alliance lost the crews of eight destroyers, their entire flagship and fighter pilots, and their infantry carrier. Those ships were all destroyed. But that's not taking into account the survivors that were found. Of their destroyers that are returning, all are severely damaged, and one may not survive the jump into or out of hyperspace. Sir."

"Thank you, Clay, a precise report as always." Standing up, he continued. "Your wife and our security detail are waiting for us. I was about to send for you when the battle started. We've still got to do that diplomatic thing on the surface."

In the transporter room, Karen, the comms officer, and a security detail were waiting. We all stepped onto the pads and were instantly transported to the planet's surface, near the Council's chamber.

During the reception that followed our meeting, we were congratulated on our victory over the Alliance fleet. Most of the planet's inhabitants were able to watch the battle on viewers. I was singled out for congratulations over my audacious attack on their flagship.

The battle we fought was the first battle in the Civil War. Three months went by before the Alliance would strike again, this time in another sector. Our fight is now being hailed as the Battle of Chi Chantria.

Stardate 2515.01.20:
We having been patrolling this sector for six months now, and morale is low because we've had no action since Chi Chantria. Everything is a boring repetition of the day before. I have taken to spending more time in my office during the day and more time at night with Karen aboard our flagship.

Months ago, I rotated the supply ships escorts. Torf and Jantine were now assigned to outer screen duty. Collis was switched to forward scout, while Meeker became rear echelon.

I was getting set to go to my ready room when Mary called out, "Captain you've been summoned to the flagship."

"Very well, tell them I'm on the way, Arras you have the con." Already standing, I changed direction, and made my way to the transporters.

The Admiral's conference room was beginning to

fill when I entered and sat down. The captains from two of the supply ships and the mobile infantry carrier were already there. We were soon joined by Karen, who sat beside me, and Morcombe, the Wing Commander. Kalashian entered and we all rose until he was seated.

He went straight to business without any preliminaries, "Right, I am aware that moral in the fleet is at a low point due to the inactivity; but here's something that should perk everyone up. Our relief fleet has arrived at Altair. Therefore, after we rendezvous with them and a short presentation, we will head for our home base. Once home, all personnel will be stood down for three months shore leave. That news should perk moral up. Now on to the state of the war: whenever an incursion has been made by the Alliance, we have met them with our forces, and they have been soundly defeated in every situation. As you have learned from Chi Chantria, the ability to fire through our shields will win us this war. We will leave our patrol at sixteen hundred and make the jump to Altair. Any questions?... Good you are all dismissed

As we all rose to leave, Kalashian drew me aside, "Clay, stay behind please."

When we were alone, "I'm giving you a heads up. That presentation I talked about will be at ten hundred tomorrow and it concerns you, and captains

Collis, Hammer, and Taggart. There will be a ceremony on the flight deck of the Flagship Corinthia. All command crews will attend in dress uniform. Hammer and Taggart are to be presented with the Federation Gallantry star, Collis will receive the Gallantry Star and Federation Navy Cross for heroism, and you will receive the Gallantry Star, Navy Cross, and the Federation Humanitarian Medal."

I started to protest, but Kalashian held his hand up to stop me, "You earned each one of those awards, so don't argue Clay. Now get out of here and let an old man get some work done."

Knowing the old man reference to be untrue, we were both chuckling as I left the room. Without being able to see Karen, I returned to the Trion.

As soon as I was back on the bridge, I called out, "Mary, make to all captains summon them to a briefing aboard our ship now please, you too Arras, come with me."

"Aye sir," Mary replied.

Arras turned control of the con over to Jonas and followed me into the briefing room. I sat at the head of the table with Arras at my right.

They all entered one or two at a time. When

everyone was assembled I had them sit without the usual formalities. I waited until I had everyone's attention before I began. "There are only four items on the agenda today guys and girls: 1/ At sixteen hundred hours we will cease our patrol duties and make for Altair. Once there, we will join with our relief Fleet Number Four, under command of the Cragoid, Admiral Tarkas. 2/At ten hundred tomorrow there will a presentation ceremony on the flight deck of his Flagship Corinthia. The command crews from all ships are to attend, in dress uniform! 3/ both Captains Hammer and Taggart will be presented with the Federation Gallantry Star, and Captain Collis will be presented with the Gallantry Star, and Federation Navy Cross, so you lot better brush up on your saluting. 4/ After the presentations tomorrow, and things settle down a bit, we will be making for home base and three months shore leave! This item you can share with your crews."

As excited murmurs went around the room, I interjected, "Now I know I said there were only four items, but I just remembered something, 5/ I still owe you all a drink. Arras, bring out the booze and glasses please."

Our celebrations continued for an hour before I dismissed everyone. Our fleet came out of hyperspace at nineteen hundred hours above Altair and took station behind Fleet Four, our relief fleet.

The next morning at zero nine hundred, we were all in our dress uniforms with our comms units pinned on, and in my case, my medal bar as well. We assembled in the transporter room and beamed aboard the Corinthian and made our way to the flight deck. Even though only the command crews were present, it was still a large number, and more were arriving all the time. Karen joined me and was introduced to my crew as we waited for the proceedings to start.

At ten hundred to the dot, Admiral Tarkas spoke into the microphone, "Assembled officers of the Federation for the Outer Rim's Navy and Air Force. Having newly arrived in the sector with news from the Federation Council, Admiral Kalashian and I are taking this opportunity to fulfil the council's orders. On stardate 2514.07.04: the Battle of Chi Chantria took place. During that engagement, many officers did us proud, and today we honour their exploits. Therefore, as the outgoing fleet Commander, Admiral Kalashian will have the pleasure of awarding the recipients their commendations. First the fighter pilots…"

Tarkas then went on to name the award winners and why they were receiving each award. There were five pilots, one of whom I was glad to see her get the recognition she deserved. She was the Squadron Leader that had brought her men to aid my attack on the enemy flagship. Then it came to Captain

Hammer followed by Taggart and Collis. Collis is receiving the Navy Cross for heroism by simultaneously attacking two enemy destroyers with broadsides, single handedly.

Then I was called up to receive medals for actions taken when I attacked the enemy flagship, and the Federation Humanitarian Medal, for mercy shown to the survivors of the battle. After my awards, the ceremony came to a close and drinks were brought out to the assembly.

Stardate 2515.01.21.1400:
The ceremony gathering lasted until midday, when we all returned to our ships for lunch. After lunch we got ready to depart the sector for our homebase.

With our course laid in for Beta Australis, Admiral Kalashian gave the order for the fleet to go to warp ten. Our journey home would take four days.

Once home, Karen and I took the Serenity off base. We spent our leave time at the crystal lakes on the moon of Nu Indi. With no one else in the area, we had a wonderful, relaxing time together and spent much of it naked. That is, except for the times we used towels after swimming. Our time together was lovely, and it came as a surprise to us that our leave ended so quickly. One day I was checking the calendar and exclaimed, "Shit!"

"What's the matter darling?"

When I told her that we only had a week left of our leave, she couldn't believe it either, "No, surely not!" then got up, checked for herself, and continued "Bloody shit, by the moons of Rigel sweetheart, we have to pack up and head back."

Having been granted permission to land in our hangar, we touched down shortly thereafter. We changed into our uniforms before heading to the Vega 13. I left Karen there and beamed back aboard the Trion.

Some of the crew had returned early, but we still had a day before our leave ended. I did a careful inspection of the Trion and found everything to be shipshape. Later that day I returned to the Vega 13 and headed for Karen's quarters. She joined me shortly afterward bearing news, "It seems we have a new commander darling, an Admiral Treach. He's a Uslyssian. Apparently Kalashian has been moved up to fleet command, I just hope we'll be able to share my quarters like Kalashian let us, guess we'll know tomorrow."

Stardate 2515.04.22.1000:
The following morning, I was on the Trion bridge at zero seven hundred. After Arras informed me that all our crew had reported for duty, I gave a sigh of relief.

Normally, after such a long shore leave, there would always be one or two crewmen that failed to report for duty. While we were having breakfast, I shared the news about our new Admiral. We returned to the bridge, and were making way to our seats, when Mary told us what she knew about Treach.

According to her, Treach graduated from the Alliance Academy and was captain of the first Alliance ship the Zytrons destroyed. He rose to the rank of Flotilla Commander before he joined the Federation navy and was eventually promoted to Admiral. Reportedly, he is an old school tactician, and according to rumour, wasn't thought highly of by the Federation hierarchy.

I will soon have the opportunity to form my own judgement of Admiral Treach. Mary interrupted my thoughts, "Your presence is requested aboard the flagship for an officers conference sir."

"Thank you, Mary. Arras, you have the con. I'll let you know what he's like when I get back."

Chapter 14.

I entered the conference room, sat beside Karen, and waited for the mobile infantry carrier's captain to arrive. He joined us just as the Admiral came into the room. Wensall drew out the vacant chair beside me, and I heard him mutter, "Shit, not this idiot again."

Treach glared at Wensall, and barked, "You took your own sweet time getting here Captain!"

"Yes sir, well you see Admiral, it's such a lovely day, I decided to walk."

Most of us lowered our faces to hide our smirks. I wondered why Wensall was being so disrespectful, he was never like this normally.

Treach's face turned bright red, "Don't you realize I can charge you with disrespect?"

"Aye that you can try, but if you remember me at all, I'm not in your navy."

Wensall's statement seemed to deflate the situation and Treach just sat there looking at him. Then recognition dawned on him, and looking around, he cleared his throat, "Right, ladies and gentlemen, I am your new Fleet Commander, Admiral Roger Treach. So, to get to know one another, we'll go around the table. You sir, who are you?"

Each person told the Admiral his name and rank and what he or she did. Karen introduced herself, and then it came to me, "Flotilla Commander Clayton Davis sir, I command your destroyer escorts."

"Are you any relation to the Group Captain sir," he wanted to know.

I replied with a smile, "Yes sir, Karen is my wife."

"Well, I don't know what that fool Kalashian allowed you to do, but there will be no fraternizing while I am in charge. You hear me Commander?"

Hearing him call Kalashian a fool rankled me. I could not hide the edge in my reply, "*Admiral* Kalashian is a fair man. and he allowed us to share my wife's quarters when not on active duty, and that's the only time we *do* fraternize, sir."

"Commander, THAT WILL STOP, now that I am in charge."

He paused briefly before continuing, "Right, now *that* matter has been cleared up, let's proceed with the briefing. In three days, this fleet will launch for the Charbois system at eleven hundred hours where we patrol for three months before being relieved. After which we will return here, to await our next mission. Any questions? ... Right, dismissed."

After arranging to meet Karen that night aboard Serenity, I met up with Wensall as we walked back to our individual ships. On the way, I asked Wensall, "Do you know this piece of knark's dung?"

"Aye Clay, unfortunately I do. Do yourself a solid my friend and record this entire mission and get your captains to do the same. This heap of shit is a coward Clay and he won't fight, so be careful my friend."

We didn't get many steps further along before I wanted to know, "Will you be recording the entire mission too, Tor?"

"Too right I will Clay, he got off cowardice charges last time, by only the skin of his teeth. Then the bastard counter charged me. Luckily, I got off, after a rollicking of course."

"Thanks for the warning Tor."

Back aboard my ship, I asked Mary if she had recorded the briefing from my communicator. She said she had, and she also recorded my conversation with Tor Wensall.

"Good, keep them on file, and make a back-up copy

as well; just to be on the safe side. I want to record the entire mission too, just as Captain Wensall suggested, with audio *and* video."

"Aye, Captain. Do you want all captains sir?"

"Yes please, Mary." Moving toward the briefing room I added, "You too, Arras."

Once all my captains were present, I gave them a rundown of the meeting and added my own opinion of Treach. I asked all of them to record the entire mission and then gave them the mission details. After the briefing adjourned, we moved to the wardroom for drinks and dinner.

Following dinner, I went to meet Karen on the Serenity. We arrived at the same time, and after she told about how shutoff she was with the new admiral, I told her what I'd learnt from Wensall. "So please be careful dear, especially if we get into a fight."

"I will honey, now let's go to bed, we'll have to be up early."

Stardate 2515.04.25.1115:
All my destroyers are up, orbiting the planet, the flagship and troop carrier are up and we're just waiting the supply ships. They arrived, and my screening force moved into place, As a unit we

moved away from the planet on impulse. The Admiral ordered us to jump into hyperspace at warp eight, which will place us in the Charbois system six days from now.

Stardate 2514.05.01:
We came out of hyperspace and slowed to half impulse. The Admiral ordered us into orbit around Charbois One. He gathered his small team and beamed down to the planet. He decided that he could handle the diplomacy with just the comms officer and a security team, so this small group were the only ones to beam down. While the Admiral and his team were on the planet, I sent the Martique out on a scouting mission. I ordered him to keep his shields up, just in case. When he arrived back aboard the flagship, Treach announced his intension to stay in orbit until morning.

We were eating lunch in the wardroom when I was paged via my communicator, by Mary's relief officer, "Captain I'm picking up a distress call from the Martique sir!"

Halfway through my lunch, I stood, yelled "Command crew!" and started running.

When I reached the bridge I barked, "On speaker."

Mary switched into her seat. As we all heard,

"Martique to Trion, our position is …we are under heavy attack an enemy fleet is hiding on the rim of the Quasar, … our shields are draining from a combined attack of fighters and four destroyers… We need help now!"

Collis, get the hell out of there!" I tapped my communicator, "Snake, take three ships, go help Collis immediately; full impulse, but don't get into a dogfight. Get him back here!" Then I tapped again, "Trion to flagship, Admiral, the fleet needs to move now! I've got a scout ship under attack on the rim of the Quasar!"

As I awaited the Admiral's reply, I nervously paced around the bridge. Finally, the speakers came to life, "Vega 13 to Trion, the fleet stays here. You are denied permission to intervene. We are not ready for battle. Flagship out."

"Admiral at least send the fighters out to help," I pleaded.

"Admiral to Hunter, we are not, I repeat NOT interfering. For all I know, your scout ship may have initiated this attack, I order you to stand down!"

"But sir, I have already sent ships to help, before your order."

"Then order them back, now Commander!"

Furious, I took out my anger by throwing my ship's log at the viewing screen, "NO SIR, I WILL NOT RECALL MY SHIPS, AND I WILL NOT STAND DOWN! LET THE RECORD STATE, I'M CHARGING ADMIRAL TREACH WITH COWARDICE IN THE FACE OF THE ENEMY. All destroyers except the supply escorts, follow me with shields up at flank impulse,"

I nodded at Jonas, "Make it so Jonas."

As my ships pulled away from the fleet, the speakers came alive again, and we heard a pained voice, "Martique to Trion, I am transmitting recordings to you. Our shields are completely drained, and my ship is severely damaged. My command crew are dead, but I'm going down fighting, sir… It has been an hon…"

The speakers went silent. The screen shimmered and we got a view of what happened to the Martique. It was Torf's voice we heard next over the speakers, "The Martique is gone sir."

"Thank you Snake, remain where you are until we get there. Then we're going to take those bastards down!"

When all my ships had gathered, I asked Mary to patch me into all ships, "Alright boys and girls, we are outnumbered. I have analysed their attacks and believe they will try to get each of us alone and then attack with two, three, or even four of their ships at the same time. Be alert.

When we attack, we will go in fast using our V-formation. That way our ships are protecting one another. We will only attack their destroyers. Once they are down, we'll take on their carriers. Do not give them any quarter. We go in hard and fast, flank impulse; and no single engagements… except to finish them off. Let's go!"

As we started moving, the speakers crackled, "KD to Trion, I've got every fighter I could get. What's the attack plan Hunter?"

I smiled, "You'll all get arrested for this KD, but glad to have you with us. Just keep their fighters off our backs. We're going to hit their destroyers first; then worry about the carriers, if we survive. Hunter out."

Then we heard, "You heard the man ladies, **let's go to work!**"

Flight upon flight of Karen's fighters lit up the darkness of space as they passed us with their burners on. There were hundreds of them! The opening pass of my destroyers killed four of their ships. Then, as my ship blew another one apart, I muttered, "Good now we're even."

I ordered us about for another pass and three more were destroyed. As we came about for a third pass, I ordered, "Alright, break formation and take them on. Remember don't get caught alone!"

I saw over Mary's shoulder that she was looking at her small viewer screen and I saw that Karen's fighters had all but cleared the sky of fighters, pouncing on any flight that tried to leave the flagship. They were doing a great job softening up the defences of their carriers for us.

Of the ships in my fleet, Hammer's had been destroyed. However, just prior to the final explosion, he beamed off to Torf's Draga. Three more of my ships were down, with two of them totally destroyed, but by this time the enemy only had two destroyers left in action. All of my ships converged on them and, firing at will, blew them apart in short order.

"Alright everyone, they are gone. Now it's time to take care of their flagship; then we'll visit their troop carrier. All fighters disengage. We are about to do our thing."

Their flagship didn't stand a chance. It took less than two minutes for my four remaining destroyers to systematically tear it apart. Then we did the same thing to their troop carrier.

After the battle, I ordered to all ships, "Well done folks, chalk up another victory. Now let's return to the fleet at quarter impulse. Draga, have Captain Hammer beam over please. My actions are bound to have ramifications, which means I could be arrested. If that is the case, Captain Torf will assume command of the flotilla. Every one of you are to say that you were following my orders as your Commanding officer. Let the axe fall on me alone, that is an order! It has been an honour serving with every one of you. Thank you, Trion out."

Karen piped in almost immediately, "KD to all pilots, Flotilla Commander Davis is not going down alone. You are to lay the blame on my shoulders for ordering you into action when the Admiral ordered otherwise. You were just following my orders as your Group Captain, and as Hunter said, this is an order, even if it's the last one I give you, KD out."

I asked Mary for the data tapes that Collis transmitted. Hammer arrived on the bridge and I took his tapes as well.

"Mister Tark please find appropriate quarters for Captain Hammer. John you are to take command of this ship if I get arrested."

He nodded, "It would be an honour sir."

Mary opened a communication channel with the

flagship, "Trion to Vega 13."

"Go ahead, Trion."

"Admiral, I wish to report complete destruction of the Alliance fleet."

Treach replied, "And I have pleasure in saying to you, YOU are under arrest for insubordination and failure to obey orders from your superior officer. You will be taken into custody to face a Captain's Mast tomorrow,"

As he finished speaking there was a shimmering on the bridge and four security officers materialized. They took me into custody, and we were beamed back to the flagship."

Chapter 15.

Stardate 2514.5.1.1640:
Karen and I were placed in separate cells of the flagship's brig, but we were able to converse with each other. She told me that she loved me and would cover my back even if we were to go to prison.

"What do think will happen at the Captain's Mast Clay?"

"Well, what usually happens is the charges are read out, and then the accused are asked how they plead, guilty or not guilty. If you plead guilty, a sentence is imposed immediately. The charges we face are serious ones and have serious consequences. I'm charged with Insubordination, and Failure to Obey Orders from my superior officer, so in both our cases it's better to plead not guilty and ask for a full court martial to hear the charges."

Karen replied, "Looks like we're in the same boat. My charges are the same, what happens if we plead not guilty?"

"Well then it's up to him, *He* can't sentence us to anything, but he can return us to our cells or confine us to quarters until we're called before a full court martial. Because we are very senior officers, I think he'll confine us to quarters. I'm also quite certain I won't be allowed to share your quarters because of his no fraternization rule. I'll be sent back to my quarters on Trion I would think."

She laughed weakly, "Well I guess that's better than being locked up down here, even if we don't get to see each other."

Next morning, we were escorted by two security personnel each, to stand outside the Admiral's office. I was escorted in first, to find the Admiral and four senior Captains, one of whom was Tor Wensall.

I stood in front of his desk, a guard standing on each side of me. The Admiral said, "Captain's Mast Stardate 2514.05.02.0915: Flotilla Commander Clayton Davis, you are hereby charged with two counts: The first is Insubordination, and the second - Failure to Obey Your Superior Officer. Do you understand the charges against you?"

"Yes sir, I do."

"How do you plead to the charges, guilty or not guilty?"

"Not Guilty; and request to face a Full Courts Martial, sir!"

"Very well, you have that right. You will be returned to the cells until a court martial can be convened."

Tor jumped to his feet, "I protest! As a senior officer, Commander Davis should be afforded the courtesy to being confined to his quarters!"

I saw by the expression on his face that the Admiral knew he wasn't on firm legal ground, "Very well, we'll put it to a vote. Those for cells raise your hand." His was the only hand to go up. He growled, "Flotilla Commander Davis, you will be confined to your quarters aboard the Trion until a general court martial can be convened. Remove the accused please."

I smiled as I was led out of the room, and passing Karen, I whispered, "Quarters."

Ten minutes later, I was aboard the Trion sitting at my desk. There was a security guard outside the door, but she was one of my ship's security officers. That meant anyone could see me if they wished.

Half an hour later Captain Wensall came in to see me. After shaking hands, he said, "I hope you have done as I asked Clay and recorded everything."

I smiled, "Yes Tor, I have. Not only me, but all of my ships captains too. I will be speaking with Admiral Kalashian soon about charging Treach with Cowardice. How about Karen, is she in her quarters?"

He laughed, "Certainly is Sport. Treach didn't even dare try for the cells again. Mind you, he would've failed again if he had tried."

Pouring us both a drink, I asked, "I take it each of us can call on you as a witness at our court martials."

"Too bloody right man, but if you can get him charged, try to get his case heard before both of yours. That way they'll be summarily dismissed. anyway, best be off, just wanted to reassure meself is all, ta for the drink, see you laddie," and then he left.

I began reviewing all of the video and audio files. After an hour or so there was a knock on my door. "Come," I responded.

Mary entered and handed me a video/audio file. She said the comms officer on the flagship sent it to her for me to see, "It's a recording of the bridge yesterday *and* the Captain's Mast this morning."

We watched the video carefully and listened to what was said. The surprise came *after* Treach gave me the order to stand down. Treach had said openly, "That'll force that Vegan mongrel to disobey me, then I can charge the bastard and get rid of him, the bloody upstart."

Mary was shocked, but I was smiling.

Before she left, I asked her to get a very secure and encrypted line to Admiral Kalashian at Federation Fleet Command. "Put it through to my computer Mary. No one is to know about this, especially the flagship, is that understood?"

"Yes sir, you can rely on me."

After she left my screen flickered, and I was staring at Admiral Kalashian. "This must be important Clay, why all the security measures?"

I sent him the files as I spoke, "Sir, I'm sending you a lot of files, both audio and video. Are you receiving them?"

"Yes, I am, now what's this all about?"

I told him everything about the events of yesterday and the Captain's Mast this morning, finishing with, "So, I wish to charge Treach with Dereliction of Duty, and Cowardice in the Face of the Enemy."

His face went white, "Those are very serious charges Clay. Do you have the evidence to prove these claims?"

"Yes sir, apart from the files I sent you, I have others, and witnesses that are willing to give testimony to his actions."

"All right, I'll review what you've sent me and get back to you the same way. It may take a while, because I may have to show some of them to other people."

"That's fine sir, as long as he doesn't get wind of this. Otherwise I might disappear, if you hear what I'm saying."

The Admiral sounded shocked "Surely he wouldn't dare!"

"Sir, I wouldn't put anything past this piece of shit. He's got a lot to lose when he's found guilty, so another charge added certainly wouldn't bother him. Just look at everything and you'll see what I mean. Hunter out."

I sat back thinking, *Well Clay, there's no going back now, it's sink or swim!* I was taken from my reverie by a knock on the door. It was my guard telling me that she would escort me to lunch in the wardroom, or I could have it in my quarters. Preferring to have it in the wardroom, I stood and headed to lunch. My guard followed me there and took up a position along the wall opposite the head table.

The buzz of conversation died when I entered the wardroom and sat down. Looking around the room

I spoke out, "Well I'll be blowed. I can't get anything past you lot, even getting confined to quarters. Carry on." The room burst into laughter at my remark, and everything went back to normal.

After lunch I returned to my office to make copies of all the audio and video files. I hid the originals in my quarters for safe keeping. I put the copies into my gear bag; in my shaving case. That way they wouldn't be separated from me if and when I had a change of quarters. I went back to my desk and made a list of potential witnesses for Treach's trial. The list included my entire bridge crew, the entire command crew of Vega 13, all of my surviving captains, Tor Wensall, and my wife. The list completed, I named it 'wits', saved it on my computer, and then backed it up on a flash drive.

Stardate 2514.05.03:
After breakfast, I returned to imprisonment in my quarters. I was sitting at my desk reading a book when my screen flickered and Admiral Kalashian came on the viewer, "Sorry I've been this long getting back to you Clay, but I've been in discussion with the Federation Advocate General's chief prosecutor. He has authorized me to tell you that he *is* going to formally charge Treach with both counts on your behalf. I'm sending to your tablet the nullification of your arrest. The same goes for Karen. What he wants from you now is a list, so start…"

Holding my hand up, I interrupted him, "Already ahead of you Admiral, it should be on your computer now."

He started laughing, "Your fleet will receive orders soon to return to base. There will also be separate orders for you and Karen. After you land at base, you are to make your way here to Fleet HQ. Your quarters have been arranged, as well as a hanger for your ship. I'll see you both when you get here, Deadbeat out."

Chuckling I picked up my tablet on the way to my door, opened it, and called, "Security Chief Tark, if you please."

Tark arrived with a quizzical look on his face. I passed him my tablet without saying a word and gave him time to read everything. His expression changed when he got to the part about the nullification order signed by the Chief Fleet Commander.

Tark smiled and turned to the guard, "Flotilla Commander Davis is freed and resuming command! You may return to normal duty."

"Aye sir," replied the guard, with a nod and a smile to each of us as he walked off.

Moving to my seat on the bridge I noticed everyone

smiling. Smiling in return, I called out, "Mary, call all my officers aboard for a briefing, please." Then I tapped my communicator "Hunter to KD, look at your tablet."

With her comms unit back on air, she said, "What? How? Oh, well done Hunter. You did it! ...resumed to normal duty, but how? Oh, thank you Hunter, KD out." Karen's confusion as to how I had managed to pull off this miracle was evident in her response.

Pointing upward, Mary caught my gesture and put me on speakers, I said, "Trion to Vega 13, Flotilla Commander Davis returning to normal duties. Trion out."

Admiral Treach's response was immediate, "Davis, what are you doing? You are committing mutiny!"

Smiling, "No, I am not, Admiral. You should read your tablet communiques more often. Davis out."

Seated around the table were all of my remaining captains and Arras. I addressed the group, "Right, girls and boys, the fleet will soon be ordered to return to our homebase. All of you will also be ordered to attend the court martial of Admiral Treach as witnesses for the prosecution. Please take all of your audio and video files with you when you go. Captain Torf, I am resuming command of the flotilla. Right, that's all. Any questions?"

Of course, there were many. Everyone wanted to see my tablet, so I passed it around the table. Once the tablet had made the rounds, everyone came over to shake my hand and congratulate me. After they left, Arras took the con, and I went back to my office. I tapped my comms unit and asked Mary to get Wensall on a secure channel.

He was laughing as he came on, "Well done boyo! I just heard, so I guess this means the trial is a go."

"Yes, it does Tor, when we get back to homebase, be ready for orders to report to Fleet Headquarters as a witness for the prosecution... and bring your audio and video recordings."

He was overjoyed and smiling. "Now, what about this returning to homebase, what do you know, you scoundrel?"

I smiled, "Tor, trust me, the fleet will be returning home before the end of the day, Hunter out."

Back out on the bridge, I tapped my comms unit, "Flotilla Commander Davis to Vega 13, request permission to come aboard."

The reply took a while. I was about to repeat my call when it was answered, "Permission granted

Commander."

Telling Arras, she had the con, I went to the transporters and told them I wanted to be beamed directly to the bridge of the flagship.

As soon as I was on the bridge of Vega 13, their comms officer spoke up, "Sir, I have orders for you from fleet command."

Chapter 16.

I smiled, "In a minute lieutenant."

She was insistent "No sir, I really think you need to see them now!"

Reading them, my eyebrows raised, "Has he seen these?"

"No sir... He's in his office."

I looked around, then ordered, "Have Captain Hammer join me here on the bridge please. Tell him I will return shortly and ask him to wait for me."

"Yes Sir *Admiral,*" she replied with a smile.

Making my way to the security chief, I had him look at the orders, then he looked at me, tapped his comms unit, "Security team to the bridge."

Two security men were there instantly and followed the chief and me to the Admiral's office, I knocked and opened the door at his command. I strode to the desk with the security chief, and stood there until he looked up growling, "What the devil are you doing here Davis?"

I thrust the orders at him, "Read!"

His face went white, because the orders said for me to relieve him of command and assume command myself. The orders also stated that he was to be placed under arrest for Cowardice, and Dereliction of Duty. Also, the fleet was to return to homebase immediately.

"On your feet Admiral. Take him away to the cells Chief." Treach was taken out of his office roughly and marched away, security guards on either side, all the way to the brig.

I returned to the bridge and found John waiting for me. You could see from the expression on his face he didn't know what was going on. I passed him the orders and gave him time to digest what he was seeing, "You will take command of the Trion please."

He nodded, "Aye Admiral," and tapped his comms unit, "One to beam to the bridge please."

After Hammer beamed out, I said to the comms officer, "To all ships and internal this one please comms."

"Aye sir," she replied, "You're on Sir."

"To all ships, this is *Acting Admiral* Clayton Davis, in my hand are orders to relieve Admiral Treach and to assume command of the fleet. I was ordered to arrest Admiral Treach on charges of Cowardice in the Face of the Enemy, and Gross Dereliction of Duty. He has been placed in a cell. The fleet has been ordered to return to homebase immediately. Therefore, all ships set your course, and make the jump into hyperspace at warp ten, Vega 13 out. Make it so, Nav."

"Aye sir," came the reply.

"Comms, summon Group Captain Davis to the Admiral's… my office please. You have the con Number One."

I went to the office and waited for Karen to arrive. I was pouring drinks for each of us when she arrived. I handed her one as we sat down and filled her in on everything. When I finished, our drinks were too. "Well! No wonder you were smiling when you told me 'quarters' as you were being dragged away."

Still smiling, I refilled our glasses, "Yep, but I was only able to do it because I was on my own ship, and I have a very loyal crew. Oh, and by the way, that fraternization law is now rescinded, I'll be in your bed tonight baby."

Stardate 2515.05.07.2050:
We have arrived back at Beta Australis and landed. During the journey back I beamed aboard the Trion

to retrieve all of my possessions and uniforms and turn the Captain's quarters over to John Hammer. I took everything to the Vega 13 and Karen's quarters. During dinner in the wardroom that evening I told Karen it would be too late when we landed to start another journey, so we would stay aboard Vega 13 overnight and take off for Zeta Australis in the morning.

Stardate 2515.05.08:
Our landing bay was atop the Fleet Command building, and Kalashian was there to meet us after we landed the Serenity. He took us down to our new quarters, an apartment on the one hundredth floor. He explained that only the first fifty floors of the building were used for fleet administration, and the rest of the floors were used for quarters. "You two settle in, then come to my office on level forty-six at eleven hundred. We have things to discuss."

We arrived at the Admiral's outer office at eleven hundred and were ushered in by his assistant captain. After taking seats, Mark Kalashian wasted no time and got down to business. "First off tomorrow, at a civic reception on the third floor, you two will be officially promoted; to full One Star Admiral in your case Clay, and Karen, you to Wing Commander.

What isn't generally known is that I'm giving you a new fleet, not as big as our normal fleets, however.

Instead of a carrier, I'm giving you command of our newest super cruiser, so new it's not finished being built. You will only have five destroyer escorts, but you will have provision for over one hundred fighters. Here are the details of the ship," and passed across a thick book, which I left sitting on the desk.

He continued, "You'll also have your pick of crew members. The screens in your quarters have complete dossiers of all navy personnel. Karen, you can study personnel files and make your requests for your fighter personnel from your screens too since all their files are also loaded, any questions?"

"You say I have the pick of who I want. In that case I want all my former command crew from the Trion, with Arras promoted to Captain. For my destroyer escorts I want all my surviving captains, with Torf promoted to Flotilla Commander; and I want Karen as my executive wing commander, for a start. I'll make further requests later, sir."

Then Karen said, "I have one for you Admiral, that Squadron Leader Tuckett be promoted to Group Captain and assigned to the new ship."

Kalashian smiled as he replied, "So far, I can grant all of your picks. But Clay, you'll need to pick another officer for your command crew because, on your new ship, weapons is a separate console, whereas helm and nav stations, like the simulators you had at the Academy, are together. You'll also need an Engineering Chief."

"Copy that sir, and noted, thank you."

He smiled and got up, "Right now let's go to the senior officers mess for lunch. After that you can go down to supply and get your new uniforms."

As I moved from the desk, I picked up the book relating to my new ship for memorizing later. We went up to the senior mess on the fiftieth floor for lunch. Only Flotilla Commanders and above were permitted to enter so we were quite pleased when we were not questioned as we went in.

We went to the bar and Kalashian ordered drinks for all of us. He handed each of us a drink, picked up his own, and raised it in a toast, "To you both on your promotions, Admiral and Wing Commander Davis, my two-favourite people!"

During our fine lunch, I asked Kalashian, "Sir, at twenty-five, doesn't that make me the youngest Admiral ever?"

He leaned back and laughed, "I'm afraid not Clay. I made admiral when I was twenty-four, but that was back when the Alliance was being formed. Like you, I rose quickly in rank through battle during the wars, but I do see a lot of my former self in you. Perhaps that's why I like you so much but look at me now. Once all the wars ended, I'm still an admiral, so don't expect many promotions from here onward."

"That's fine by me sir."

He smiled again saying, "Enough of the sir now, we're the same rank so call me Mark. By the way, after tomorrow you two better expect to make time for Dal Arkin, the chief prosecutor over at the Federation Advocate General's office.

"Will do si...Mark."

After lunch, Mark got off the elevator on the forty-sixth floor and went to his office, while we continued down to supply on the ground floor. We each picked up new daily and dress uniforms and replenished assorted toiletries. With all of these items we were also supplied with a solid, wheeled suitcase to pack them in. No more duffle's for the Davis'.

We went back up to our apartment to change into our new uniforms and change our ribbon bars over to the new uniforms. My new uniform shirts were white, while Karen's were a pale blue.

Stardate 2515.05.09:
Karen and I arrived at the reception area an hour before the ceremony was due to start. Karen took me

over to meet newly promoted Group Captain Reece Tuckett, callsign Bucket. While we were talking, I noticed my captains arrive together. Getting their attention, I waved them over. Torf was in his new uniform, just as we were. I made introductions and we were soon having a grand time reliving battles, as military people tend to do. Before we knew it, the ceremony was about to begin.

The Chief of Fleet Command took the stage and addressed the crowd, "Ladies and gentlemen, officers of all the military branches, it gives me great honour to announce that barely a week ago Federation forces engaged the Alliance in the battle for the Charbois Quasar. What would have been a defeat, was turned to a victory by a few who had the courage to disobey orders and engage the enemy. Some of those brave warriors paid the ultimate sacrifice and have been honoured posthumusly. Some of the survivors of that engagement are here today to be honoured by you. Many of them are to be awarded the highest honour we can bestow. So, without further ado, I call newly promoted Group Captain Reece Tuckett, to receive the Distinguished Flying Cross and Bar, and the Federation Medal of Honour."

After Tuckett, Karen was called up to receive the Distinguished Flying Cross and bar (the bar represents that this is a second such medal won), and the Medal of Honour. Torf, John Hammer, Mark

Meeker, Rose Jantine, and Jill Torrence were all presented with Medals of Honour and then it was my turn. I was called up to receive the Gallantry Star and Bar, the Navy Cross and Bar, and the Medal of Honour.

After the ceremony there was a reception that went on for another two hours. We all had to endure a lot of small talk. Never before had there been so many Federation Medal of Honour recipients in one place.

After the reception, Karen and I went down to supply where we saw the quartermaster to arrange our new medals and ribbon bars. He whistled in amazement at all of our high honours, "We should have them ready for you the day after tomorrow sirs."

Back in our apartment, Karen asked for my advice in picking her pilots. I said, "I don't know about you darling, but I'm going to be looking for medal winners, which shows their bravery and dedication to their work."

She came over and kissed me, "Wonderful idea honey, thank you," and went back to her study of fighter command pilots. Once she had her list of names, she sorted them by rank not wishing to demote anyone. After hours of work she had sorted them into the four squadrons, which would be the new ship's compliment of fighter pilots.

While she was using the screens, I couldn't use them, so I started learning about my new ship from the top-secret, authorized, eyes-only book. The new ship would be named the Star Cruiser Defiant.

She was a radically new ship design, powered by a trans warp drive engine that could cruise at warp 20. At that speed we could travel a light year in one hour! The Defiant's top speed was warp 28, if needed. At Impulse power she could be cloaked, making her invisible to normal vision and scans. Her shielding was fifty times more powerful than current Federation ships, and still had the capability to fire even if the shields were up. Fighters could land and take off with the shields up. Each of the hundred and twenty Javelin class fighters had their own individual shielding that could be fired through as well, something never available to fighters before! I marked the page to show Karen later.

The Defiant's firepower consisted of phasers; phaser and photon cannons; and two types torpedoes; the regular photon ones and the new SK type. I had not heard of the SK torpedoes, so I looked for them in the manual index and went searching for more information about this new type of torpedo.

Invented by engineer Sirtis, the SK, which stood for Ship Killer, could be fired at a ship with their shields up and the concussive blast could blow the ship apart, depending upon the strength of their shields. Testing data indicated that the shielding on current Alliance vessels was incapable of withstanding the force of the SK, and would be destroyed completely. Ships with Federation rated shielding would be severely crippled. I thought as I read this, *Bloody hell, this is like a quantum bomb, only on a smaller scale.*

Chapter 17.

The following morning, while we were in the senior officers mess for breakfast, my comms unit chirped. It was the chief prosecutor's office calling Karen and me to a meeting with him at ten hundred. He said we would be picked up on the roof by an aircar at zero nine forty-five.

Back in our apartment, we gathered up all our audio and video files, placed them in a bag, and took them with us. I picked up the Defiant's manual and we went to the roof port. While we waited for the aircar, I showed Karen the section of the Defiant's manual I had marked and watched her as she read it.

Her face clearly showed her emotions, "Oh Wow, I've just *got* to try these babies out! Do you think there's a possibility of actually talking to their designer anytime?"

I smiled my reply, "I think it may be possible, he's on Alpha Cor Six, where the Defiant is being made ready. By the way, see if you can find another twenty pilots and add them to your list."

"Why's that darling."

Before I could answer our ride arrived. After we got into the aircar, I answered, "Look at this honey," and showed her the manual again. "Each of the 5 destroyer escorts carry four fighters, in addition to their regular armaments."

She laughed, "In that case, I'll find *my Admiral* his additional pilots then."

We spent most of the day with Dal Arkin, the chief Prosecutor, and some of his subordinates. They sifted through all our files picking the sections they wanted to use as evidence. Karen and I went over practice testimonies with him. We also talked about my witnesses and the chief prosecutor said he wanted to talk to all of them. He set up appointments to meet each of them individually over the next day or two. He was hoping to take Treach to Court Martial the following week, but we would be informed of the specific date at a later time. By seventeen hundred we were fairly flagged out and were glad to get back to the apartment. We took time to freshen up a bit and then headed out for drinks and dinner.

Throughout the following day I found time to go through some of the appendices in the Defiant's manual. I found out that my five new destroyer escorts had the same engines as the Defiant and were capable of the same speed as my new ship. The have the same shielding as the Defiant does too. In addition to the four fighters they each carry; they still have the same armaments, but upgraded and heavier versions, than their old destroyers had. Going through the manual I noticed that most of the engineering was designed by engineer Sirtis. Since Sirtis was in the navy, I decided to look him up sometime in fleet records.

After breakfast, Karen was going to see Kalashian to give him her revised list of pilots she wanted. It now included the twenty additional pilots I had suggested. While she was doing that, I went back to the apartment to use our screens, now that they were free, to develop my crew list.

For my extra command crew, I selected another Cragoid, Gort, as the second nav and scanner officer. To accomplish this, Gort needed to be promoted to 1st lieutenant. I found Sirtis in the naval records and was surprised to find out he was only 30 years old. He was married to Mahria, also an engineer, and they were both Valdivlians. That was significant because married Valdivlians have a psychic link to each other. I chose them both; Sirtis, as chief engineer final member of my command crew; and Mahria, as chief of my engine room crew. Both needed promotions for their new assignments. Then I continued choosing the rest of my officers and crew.

Karen returned, gave me a kiss, and started reading the manual Kalashian had given her concerning the new Javelin class fighters. Every now and then she would read aloud to me about their features. The most significant of these was that they were launched from turbo tubes on a sled, very much akin to a slingshot. To land, they returned to the sled using their vertical thrusters. The sleds were then withdrawn back into the carrier ship.

While I listened to Karen, I checked the Defiant's manual and found that she was equipped with said launch tubes, fifty on each side. I wondered about the time factor involved with fighter retrieval. According to the manual it took less time than having them fly into a runway port because all of them could land at the same time. I thought, *That makes perfect sense, it's a wonder this hasn't been thought of before.*

I returned to my perusal of the Fleet Command personnel records. Almost everyone on my list had received commendations for their work and bravery. An hour later I was finished with my crew list, and shutdown the screens I was using.

By then, it was approaching lunch time, so Karen and I went down to the mess. As we left the apartment, my comms unit chirped, It was the quartermaster letting me know that our medal and ribbon bars were ready for pick up. I told him we'd be there after lunch.

In the mess, we were joined by Kalashian for a premeal drink. He asked me if I had finished my pick of personnel.

I laughed, "You must be a mind reader Mark, I just finished before we came down, but I left the list back in our quarters, otherwise I'd give it to you."

He returned the smile, "That's alright Clay, in fact, I didn't think you'd be finished this quickly. Relax and finish your meal. Bring it down after lunch and we'll discuss it. Karen, your crewing list has been passed on to fighter command. They are acting on it immediately so I should be able to let you know who you have by the end of the week."

Karen thanked him, then I said, "Mark, I'm just about finished with the Defiant manual, so I'll bring that back to you, but can I have the manual on my destroyer escorts please?"

He smiled saying, "Of course son, but keep it, and I'll have the destroyer ones ready for when you come down. Now let's go and eat."

After lunch, we rode the elevator with Mark down to his office level, and then continued down to the ground floor. In the quartermaster's office I was given back two of my original medals, but Karen was only given one of her's back. The expression on her face was quizzical and charming all at the same time. The quartermaster jumped in to tell her that original medals were superseded by the ones with bars. The mountings were perfect. Karen's bar had one row while mine had two. Thanking the quartermaster for his fine work, we returned to the apartment.

Karen sat back down with her manual while I picked up the Defiant crew list and headed back to Mark's office.

He passed over six copies of the destroyer manual, then he looked over my crew list. He laughed, "I thought you'd grab up Sirtis and his wife, that's why I kept them available to you. So, it's a yes on the command crew. The rest I'll have to see, I'll keep you informed. I was speaking with Dal Arkin earlier and it looks as if the court martial of Treach will start Monday morning, but he'll confirm that with you. Now, unless there's anything else, get out of here while I start on your crew list."

Back in the apartment, I pinned on my Federation Medal Bar below the Alliance one on my dress uniform and pinned on the ribbon bar to my work shirt.

I tapped the comms unit, "Admiral Davis to comms."

Receiving the reply, I asked them to have all my destroyer captains report to my apartment giving the quarters address.

Half an hour later, all of them were sitting around the kitchen table, except for Torrence, who was with the Judge Advocate prosecutors. I placed copies of the destroyer manual on the table, "Alright, I can now give you the lowdown on your new ships, and I think you'll be quite impressed. They are each named after a moon; Torf, you have the Titan; Hammer, the Callista; Jantine, the Triton; Jill gets the Oberon; and Meeker, you've got Europa."

"Now here's something new for you, your ships will have a cloaking ability making them invisible to eyesight and scanning, and you'll each have four fighters aboard! Your top speed will be warp factor 28, with cruising at 20, and your shields are fifty times more powerful than Federation normal, with the same abilities. Also, you will have two types of torpedoes onboard at your disposal. You will have a full complement of the torpedoes you have used in the past, as well as a full complement of the new SK model. The SK is amazing, but you'll have to read your manuals to find out what it's capable of. That's it, that is your manual. I am sorry, but you will have to study it here; and I suggest you go through it very carefully."

To say they were impressed would be an understatement. It was only because I was speaking that they didn't interrupt with questions.

I appreciated their show of respect.

They all dug into their manuals, but Torf was the first to speak, "Listen to this…"

There were long periods of absolute silence; it appeared they couldn't read fast enough. The stillness in the room was interspersed with bursts of 'Wow, I can't believe it!' and "Hey, everybody, check out Appendix B" and other exclamations as they discovered what their destroyers could do. They stayed around the table, exploring different sections of the manual until sixteen hundred, when I collected their manuals and dismissed them. As they got up to leave, Rose Jantine declared, "Those ships are incredible Sir, and I, for one, am glad for your faith in us to request us as your protective screen."

"Thank you Jantine, and all of you. Fill in Torrence on what you've seen and heard but protect the information from everyone else. I will see you all at the court martial." Each of them shook hands with me as they exited and then Karen and I made our way to the mess for drinks, and eventually dinner.

Stardate 2515.05.18:
Today, the Court Martial of Admiral Treach began. A court martial, being a trial without jury, has a panel of peers, the same rank as the accused. Since Treach was an Admiral, the panel was comprised of

all Admirals. Witnesses are allowed to sit in the courtroom and watch the trial, as opposed to a civilian law matter where they have to remain outside until called to give evidence.

Prior to the trial beginning, the panel of admirals elected a chairman to preside over the Courts Martial. When the trial began, the Chairman asked Treach's legal consul to stand, and stated, "Because this is not a civilian court Mister Blair, I will explain the rules to you what you can and cannot say or do."

Once all the legal rules had been explained, the chairman asked if the defence consul understood. Mister Blair said that he did.

Then Treach and Blair stood as the charges were read, "Admiral Treach, you are charged that on Stardate 2515.05.01: You showed Gross Dereliction Of Duty in a time of war. How do you plead, guilty or not guilty?"

Treach replied, "Not Guilty!"

"You are further charged that on Stardate 2515.05.01 you displayed Cowardice In The Face of The Enemy. How do you plead to that charge, guilty or not guilty?"

Treach again replied, "Not Guilty!"

The chairman continued once more, "You are further charged with Conspiracy, in that on Stardate 2515.05.01 you conspired to remove a senior officer from the Performance Of His Duties. How do you plead guilty or not guilty?"

The defence consul interjected, "Mister Chairman, I must protest. This is the first time I have been made aware of this charge and therefore it should be stricken from the record as inadmissible!"

The Admiral said, "Mister Blair, I told you beforehand the rules of this court martial. The charge at hand has been added by the prosecution, as it came to light during their investigation, and *is* admissible. Your client will answer the charge!"

After looking at his lawyer, who nodded, Treach replied, "Not Guilty!"

"Very well, you may sit," said the Admiral,

"Colonel Arkin, you may proceed, call your first witness."

Dal Arkin stood, "I call Captain Tor Wensall to the stand, mister Chairman."

After Tor had given evidence, his audio and video logs were played. Blair stood to cross examine Tor but was unable to trip him up on his testimony, nor call into question the audio and video tapes.

And so, it went for the next four days. All of my command officers, except Mary Tarrant from comms, were called, one after the other. Arkin decided to save Mary's testimony until later. Next, he went through the audio, video, and personal testimony with Torf and the rest of my captains.

Being late on Friday afternoon, the Chairman banged his gavel a couple of times to get everyone's attention, "I think we can leave further witness testimony until after the weekend. We will reconvene at zero nine hundred Monday morning. Court is adjourned," and he banged his gavel again to close the proceedings.

That meant there were only three witnesses to go: Mary Tarrant, Karen, and me. Making our way through the Fleet Command building we wondered why Arkin was holding Mary's testimony back. Guessing that Karen's testimony would only take a half day and mine, perhaps, a full day, we wondered if Mary would go first or last. Entering the turbo lift, we went up to the mess for drinks.

Chapter 18.

On Monday morning Mary gave her testimony and her audio and video files, then Arkin asked her if she had any other material in relation to the charges? Blair was halfway out of his seat to object when Mary said, "Yes Sir, I do!'

Everyone began to smile and Blair, caught in the middle of rising, froze, and stayed that way, in total surprise. Dal Arkin had definitely schooled Mary properly. He then went on to ask Mary what else she had. Mary produced the audio and video logs of the bridge conversation from the Vega 13. They were played while all members of the panel and court looked and listened to what was said. They paid particular attention to that portion of what was said *after* giving me the order to stand down. They heard Treach say in his own voice, "That'll force that Vegan mongrel to disobey me, then I can charge the bastard and get rid of him, the bloody upstart." Finally, the tapes of the Captain's Mast were played.

Arkin asked Mary, "From whom and when did you get possession of these tapes?"

Mary replied, "That same afternoon, from LT Mann the chief communication officer onboard the Vega 13, Sir."

After Mary's cross examination, the chairman

adjourned for the lunch break, "We will reconvene here at fourteen hundred hours. Court adjourned," and banged his gavel.

Karen and I went up in the turbo lift to the mess and had lunch. Because the court martial was being tele recorded, every screen had on the court martial. They were all presenting different portions of the trial and we heard on the screen closest to us the newsreader saying, "Now just to recap, the trial of Admiral Treach has adjourned for the lunch break. On day six…" Karen and I weren't listening very carefully because we were experiencing it first-hand, "… of this momentous trial, and court will resume at fourteen hundred hours. Stay tuned."

While we ate, I said, "Well, Mary's last tape nailed him on the conspiracy charge well and truly. Looks like you'll be up next, darling."

"Hmm, yes dear," she replied, lost in thought, "I wonder why Dal Arkin didn't tell us he was going to add the third charge?"

I thought for a moment before replying, "Probably because he didn't think he had enough evidence, but the way he set it up was brilliant. The members of the panel will certainly remember it now, because the trial's almost over."

After the lunch break, there was a surprise witness,

the command comms officer of the Vega 13. Lieutenant Mann was called up and the tapes were played again. She was asked to explain how and when the recordings were made. Her recording and answers corroborated what Mary had already presented. She verified that she sent a copy of the recordings to Mary.

Then it was time for Karen to take the stand. Her time on the stand went well and she stuck to the facts. In his cross examination, Blair pushed the point that we knew we were disobeying direct orders. He even tried to hang her out to dry with her own cockpit recordings: we heard Karen say, "KD to all pilots, Flotilla Commander Davis, is not doing down alone, you are to lay the blame on my shoulders for ordering you into action, when the Admiral ordered otherwise, you were just following my orders as your Group Captain, and as Hunter said, this is an order, even if it's the last I give you, KD out."

Blair asked, "Yes or no, is that your voice Wing Commander?"

Arkin objected on the grounds the question had been asked and answered and was sustained.

The chairman growled, "You're trying my patience and badgering the Wing Commander, that will stop now, unless you have other questions that you haven't asked already. I'm going to excuse the witness. Wing Commander, you are excused, with our thanks."

Noting the time, the Admiral said, "Now's a good time to adjourn. We will reconvene at zero nine hundred tomorrow," and banged down his gavel.

The next morning it was my turn to testify. Arkin began the session by saying, "Now Admiral Davis, we have all seen the tapes numerous times. I just need you to clear up a few points for us if you will. You clearly knew you were outnumbered, when did you realize that and how?

"I knew that because of the way I had stationed my Flotilla, I had to leave two destroyers behind to guard our supply ships. The flagship and troop carrier have more than enough guns and firepower to repel an attack until the destroyer escorts can get to the enemy. I had already sent out Martique as the scout ship, so I was down three ships to start with and we were attacking a fleet which usually numbers twelve destroyers plus we would also be facing the guns of the two carriers. I was attacking fourteen ships with only nine. Plus, the enemy had their compliment of fighters, which would attack us too."

Arkin interjected to ask, "Would it then be fair to say that when Group Captain Davis led her fighters to aid you, it was fortunate indeed?"

"Yes sir, without them or our flagship and carrier, we would have been defeated, without the fighters and my fast speed attack, we wouldn't be here today, and probably dishonoured as well."

Blair was instantly on his feet, yelling, "Objection!"

The chairman banged his gavel, "Sustained, please don't surmise Admiral."

"Yes, Mister Chairman," I replied contritely.

Arkin asked, "How many enemy ships did you destroy in your attack?"

"Four on the first pass. We tore through them at well above battle speed, turned around, and got another three on the return pass. Then we split formation and took them out one by one. During the destroyer battles our fighters were attacking their fighters and drawing fire from their carriers away from my destroyers. We did lose two ships to their guns sir."

How many of your ships did you lose in that engagement Admiral?"

"Six sir."

"How many would have been saved, if the flagship

and troop carrier had engaged with you?"

There was an objection about speculation from Blair, but it was overruled by the chairman telling him that I was a seasoned veteran and my speculation would be based on my experience, and I was directed to answer the question.

"How many would have been saved, if your flagship and troop carrier had engaged with you?"

"Four, perhaps five out of the six could have been saved. They would have been severely damaged, but they would have survived."

"Thank you, Admiral that is all. Do you have any other evidence you would like to present, Sir?" Arkin asked.

Being wary of Arkin's tactics, Blair was slow to his feet. But he pressured me again and again on whether I knew I was disobeying Treach's orders.

"You've seen and heard me numerous times on the tapes through this trial, where I acknowledged that fact, so the answer is yes!"

The Chairman, intervened, "Mister Blair, you have been warned about badgering the witness. Why do you persist in this baseless charge?"

Arkin was on his feet, and interjected, "Perhaps I can shine some light on that Mister Chairman!"

"Go on Colonel."

Arkin said, "Thank you sir, I expect that Admiral Treach is trying to cover his debacle by having all the evidence you've seen and heard thrown out. He has made counter charges against both Wing Commander and Admiral Davis. Both of them are charged with the serious offence of Disobeying a Direct Order. This has been a source of concern to the Judge Advocates Office. I wish to say that should Admiral Treach try to bring these charges up in retribution to Admiral and Wing Commander Davis. The prosecution will not be presenting any evidence on this matter, and I ask that the charges are summarily dismissed."

"I see," said the Admiral, "Do you have any witnesses for the defence mister Blair?"

Blair knew he was utterly defeated, and replied, "No, mister Chairman."

"Very well," he said. "The panel will now rise to consider our verdict. We will reconvene at zero nine hundred tomorrow. Court is adjourned," and banged his gavel down.

Stardate 2515.05.27:

Today is the last day of Admiral Treach's court martial. Everyone stood as the panel took their seats. The chairman banged the gavel, and we all sat as the chairman began, "The Courts Martial of Admiral Roger Treach is reconvened. The panel members have reviewed the evidence presented and have considered all the testimonies; the accused will stand to receive our verdict."

Admiral Treach and his attorney rose together. The Chairman looked at both of them and then addressed Treach directly, "Admiral Roger Treach on the charge of Conspiring to Remove a Senior Officer from Performing his Duties, you are found Guilty and sentenced to five years hard labour at a military prison world.

On the charge of Gross Dereliction of Duty in a time of war, you are found Guilty, and sentenced to a prison term of ten years hard labour at a military prison world and stripped of all rank and privileges.

On the charge of Cowardice in the Face of the Enemy, there is only one sentence, you will be hanged from the neck until dead, after your prison terms have been served. Prison terms are conclusive and without parole. We further order that any charges brought by you to Wing Commander and Admiral Davis are to be summarily dismissed. Escorts, take the prisoner away."

Two guards stepped forward and stripped Treach of his uniform coat and shirt, leaving them on the floor and he was dragged out of the courtroom.

The chairman addressed everyone present, "That concludes this Courts Martial!" and banged the gavel once.

Outside the courtroom, everyone wanted to congratulate me. My hand was shaken by all of my captains and every member of my crew. I raised my hand and addressed everyone gathered, "Well... It's finally over! We will see you all on Alpha Cor Six in the near future. "

Going back up to our apartment, we collapsed onto the bed relieved, the trouble was now behind us and we could relax at last.

Over the next week, Karen and I toured the capital at will, just relaxing from the strain and rigors of the whole incident. We took in the sights both in and out of the capital, enjoying each other's company.

Our mini vacation was cut short though, when we were summoned to Admiral Kalashian's office the following morning at zero nine hundred. When we arrived, we found my destroyer captains and Karen's new group captain waiting for us.

Kalashian came out of his office, "Good you are all

here, follow me. Captain, you too please." The last was directed at his assistant.

We followed him into a room behind his assistant's desk. It was a large conference room with room for twenty people around the large table. Mark moved to the head chair and we all sat down. Then he proceeded to give us a bit of a history lesson.

"When the planets of the Outer Rim were first attacked by the Zytrons, the Federation chose a planet where they could build attack ships to hit back. The planet they chose was perfect: it was out of normal space lanes; it was an M-1 class planet, with no sun to light it; and it had no atmosphere. Therefore, all work had to be done in spacesuits, until the ships being built could be pressurized. This is why our shields are much stronger than the Alliance ships.

When the war with the Alliance was declared, it was still an ideal place to build our navy, but now it is an untenable proposition, and there are moves to have our ship building done back on Beta Australis, which I for one support.

Now, most of you are probably wondering what this all has to do with you. Here's your answer; the ships of your fleet, which by the way, is a clandestine one, will only be referred to as the Ghost Fleet. As I was saying your ships and fighters are being built there and are almost complete. It will be your job to take those ships to Beta Australis with only your command crews, the rest of your crews and pilots will join you at Akron Base, and as a matter of fact, there, you will not land on the normal ground runways large deep bunker hangars have been built to house your ships in a restricted and secure area of the base. Your ships will land inside those bunkers.

Admiral Davis you will report to Alpha Cor Six at your earliest convenience. You are to report back to me when your ships are ready to move. If the remaining work can be completed at Akron, so much the better, that's up to you to determine, but let me know when the ships can be moved, and I'll have all your command crews sent to Alpha Cor Six."

"Aye Sir."

After that, Mark ended the briefing, but he joined the post conference small talk amongst us all.

Chapter 19.

Stardate 2515.06.09:
Karen and I flew the Serenity to Alpha Cor Six. We landed directly in a hanger that closed over us as soon as we touched down. We had to wait until the hangar was pressurized before we were cleared to leave our ship.

Leaving the ship, we were first escorted to the main building and then to our large, married quarters. We took time to relax for a bit, check out our new quarters, take showers, and get some food.
I requested base control for an escort to take us to the main administration offices. Once there, we were assigned two adjoining office spaces. As soon as we settled in, I sent for Sirtis and his wife.

They joined us, introductions and pleasantries were exchanged, and we were all seated, "Now then, are both of you aware that once we leave here, that you will both be coming with us as crew members?"

"Yes sir," Sirtis was quick to reply, "I, as Chief Engineer in the Command Crew, and Maharia, as Chief Engine Officer."

Perplexed, I looked at his wife, "I'm confused, I thought your name was Mahria?"

Sirtis and Maharia both started laughing. Sirtis

replied, "It's Maharia. Maharia asks that you beg her indulgence Sir, but the fools at Fleet have always misspelled it. They mispronounce it too."

I grimaced, Karen laughed, "Yes, we can understand that, but now that I'm aware of this, *I will* take steps to have it rectified. Would you like me to do that Maharia, with your authority of course?"

Maharia smiled, but it was Sirtis who replied, "She would like that very much Admiral; and she likes you."

"Just don't tell my wife that." Karen, Sirtis, and Maharia all laughed, they both knew that Karen was my wife.

Then Maharia herself spoke up, "Or my husband, Admiral."

We all laughed again, a little shocked, "Please excuse me Maharia, I thought you didn't speak at all."

"I am quite shy at first, Admiral," she explained, "But, when I have to order those numb-bat workers around, they hear me, loud and clear!"

Karen and I chuckled, "Alright in that case, whenever we're out of earshot of other people, I'm Clay, and my wife is Karen. Now let's get down to business, Sirtis when will my ships be ready?"

"Clay, all the fighters and destroyers are ready to leave. The fighters are in their tubes on the destroyers and the cruiser. There are twenty spare fighters in the hangar deck on Defiant. All work on the cruiser will be finished by the end of the month. All the armaments are onboard. All craft are loaded with fifty photon and one hundred SK torpedoes. The cruiser is waiting for an additional hundred SK torpedoes to be loaded, which will be completed by week's end."

I nodded, as Karen asked, "Will there be enough room for us to store our personal ship aboard the cruiser?"

Sirtis answered, "I'm not sure Karen, we'd need to have a look at it."

"That's easily fixed, let's go to the hangar and look her over, she's in Bay 10."

We all got up and made our way to the hangar. We entered and Sirtis gave Serenity a quick once over.

"Nice. Got any guns? What about shielding?"

Karen told him that the Serenity did not have any weapons, but she did have a small shield generator. Going inside, we went to the propulsion deck. Sirtis checked out the system and looked carefully at the drive, but it was Maharia who asked, "What's your top speed?" When Karen told her it was warp 5, Maharia said, "Hmm, seems like you need an overhaul. Do you mind if I tinker with it, out of work hours?"

Karen laughed, "Be my guest, do what you want. I want to show you the shield generator too, it's been playing up lately."

"Oh, I can fix that," Maharia quickly replied, "If you can imprint my biometrics into your lock panel, I'll start later."

Back outside Sirtis said, "Well Karen, there is plenty of room in the hangar for your ship alongside ours."

"You have your own ship too?"

Maharia laughed, "Oh yes of course, we know better than to rely on fleet transports. It's in Bay 12, come and have a look."

Maharia's biometrics were added to ours and we went to take a look at their ship. I whistled in appreciation. She was a Nubian, passenger-only, transport ship fitted out much like the Serenity.

On our way back to the office, they showed us the mess area. It was divided into two distinct areas; the wet mess area, and the eating area. Maharia told Karen that she and her work crew would be finished in the engine compartments of the cruiser in a couple of days, so her work on the Serenity would be enhanced by her whole work crew after that.

Back in the office, Sirtis went over the blueprints of the Defiant and answered every one of the questions either Karen or I asked. Hers were mainly to do with the fighter launch systems and the fighters themselves. I asked Sirtis to make arrangements with the base chief pilot to run Karen and me through orientation and training flights in the new Javelin class fighters. After that I let them go back to their duties.

Karen and I talked for a while about our first encounter with Valdivlians. "If I were you Clay, I wouldn't play cards with Sirtis. Did you notice his face really doesn't express any emotion, whereas Maharia can be read like a book? She did, however, have a weird, secretive expression when she was talking about the work on the Serenity."

We both laughed. I nodded, "Hmm, I *did* notice that. It could be that she was communicating with Sirtis at the same time. What do you think?"

"Yes, I suppose that could be the answer. I guess we'll have to watch them closely next time to find out. Ok, what's next dear heart?"

"Well, I suppose I better make my work schedule report to Mark. What about you?"

"I think I'll go find the chief pilot. See you soon lover," and kissed me on her way out of the office.

I tapped my comms unit, "Admiral Davis to comms, please set up a secure, encrypted video call to Admiral Kalashian at Fleet Command on Zeta Australis."

"Yes sir. I will transfer the call to your screen as soon as I have him on the line sir."

"Thank you, Hunter out."

After a ten-minute wait, the screen flickered and Mark came online, "Well hello Hunter, nice to hear from you, how are things going?"

"Hello to you too, Deadbeat. Work here is ahead of schedule, in fact you may despatch that cargo you mentioned earlier to this locale and send everyone else to you know where. The big one will be ready before the end of the month to join her family."

"Oh, that is great news indeed, but can the mother move beforehand?"

"Negative on that, must be in this locale."

"Alright. Can't be helped I suppose. Let me know when you're ready to re-join the family, Deadbeat out."

"Hunter out," The screen flickered again and resumed its normal screen. I sat back thinking, *Well now, Kalashian knew to send the transport with all the command crews to Alpha Cor Six, and when the Defiant would be leaving here. He also knows that the finishing work needs to be done here and not on Beta Australis. I wonder if Karen found out if the chief pilot here can be moved to Akron to checkout her other pilots? There's only one way to find out, I guess.*

I tapped my communicator, "Hunter to KD."

"Copy Hunter," came the reply.

"KD, can you confirm status of chief pilot, is he coming back to Akron with us? Over."

"*She* will be. Our father obviously anticipated us and sent her orders. Squadron Leader Matra, callsign Needle, is one of my pilots and will leave on the first ship going, but she will run us through the Javelin tomorrow at ten hundred, over."

"Copy that, Hunter out."

"KD out."

My next call was to Fleet Records and arranged for Maharia's records to be changed to her correct name and new credentials be sent on the transport bringing my crews.

Stardate 2515.06.20:
The transport ship with all of the crew members arrived yesterday. Arriving around noon, the crews got the balance of the day off. That wasn't true for Group Captain Tuckett however; he spent the afternoon with Needle getting checked out in the Javelin fighters.

During the time we were waiting for the transport ship, Karen and I got checked out in the Javelin fighter. This took us the entire day, mainly because I didn't want my solo to end. Karen and I tore off the planet and enjoyed a game of catch amongst some asteroids. Our flights were over far too quickly for my mind, as I enjoyed every exhilarating minute of the fighter's speed and manoeuvrability.

The day before the transport arrived, Maharia came to my office. She asked both of us to follow her to the Serenity hangar. When I saw the ship, I noticed something a little odd, but until I mentioned it, Karen hadn't seen it. We both looked questioningly at Maharia, who said, "I have modified her a little, adding Phaser banks and four Photon cannons for defence. If you'll follow me, I'll show you the engines."

On the engineering level, I whistled in appreciation as I spotted the new warp drive engines and a much larger shield generator. Maharia said, "I put in the new warp drive engines from our spares. She's not quite as fast as your new ship Clay, but she will reach warp 25, I would suggest keep it at warp 20 if cruising. Your impulse drive is three times that of Federation normal. The shielding engine, also an old test spare, is twenty times Federation normal.

Karen was amazed, "Wow! Thank you Maharia, *oh thank you*. Do you think we can try it out?"

Maharia replied, "I thought you'd never ask, Let's go!"

We got in and went up to the command module. I took the left seat, Karen the right, and Maharia sat behind me. I requested take-off clearance from Command. As the pressured doors unsealed, the roof opened, and Karen fired up the new engines. We didn't make it to warp, but we certainly tried the new impulse drive. Karen and I took turns flying and found that the Serenity was almost as good as a fighter. Maharia showed us the weapons control system and we blasted a few meteors trying out the guns. Smiling, I only said one word, "Perfect!"

Maharia suggested, "There is enough room for me to install two torpedo tubes on each side, and if you look at the weapons console, there's enough room for the switches and firing buttons. But it's only a suggestion, it'll only take my crew another two days to do it."

Turning toward me, Karen looked deeply into my eyes with 'that' look. A plaintive smile began to creep into her expression, and if I didn't know better, batted her eyes, "Can we get them darling?"

"It's up to you love," is what I said, but I was thinking… *Yes, oh yes, say you want them Karen; I sure do!*

She turned to Maharia, and said, "Yes please."

Maharia and I both nodded, and then we headed back to Alpha Cor Six. With only the shields up, we had meteors bouncing away like balls of rubber.

Maharia added, "Just remember, you can only use the cloaking device on impulse power, just like the rest of your ships."

Back in the hangar, after the doors were shut, we waited the five minutes it took to pressurize the hangar before exiting. Her work crew came in and Maharia told them to get four torpedo tubes and order four more SK's.

Today I gave my briefing to all the command crews and escort captains, "Alright now, all the destroyers are going to be flown to Beta Australis, take-off at zero nine hundred tomorrow. When you ask permission to land at Akron, remember to declare that you have to land in the Ghost Fleet restricted area.

Commander Torf, you'll have two passengers with you, Group Captain Tuckett, and Squadron leader Matra. They both will be checking out all pilots on the Javelins, any questions?... Good, dismissed."

Chapter 20.

Stardate 2515.07.12:
After the group briefing, I had the command crew of the Defiant move to my office. I contacted Sirtis and asked him to join us. I had a quick chat with the flotilla captains before they left with a few last-minute instructions, one of which was to have Torf contact me after he had checked out our new base. I wanted his honest assessment of the base quarters, our ships bunkers, and the messing areas. I didn't want my crews traipsing all over for food or drink.

When I got to the office and saw that everyone was there, I introduced Sirtis to them as the last addition to the command crew. After everyone was seated, I filled them in on the ready date for Defiant to launch.

Sirtis stood after being acknowledged, "Sir, I've been working on a new navigation computer that uses artificial intelligence to compute courses, and I would like to test it out on our trip to Akron Base. It'll mean liaising with nav quite a deal, but if I can perfect it, we'll have the most advanced navigation system in the universe, without using star charts."

I nodded, "Very well Sirtis, permission granted, but keep the watch officer, me or captain Arras informed of your progress. As everyone can see Sirtis is an inventor, and in fact, our whole ship's design and systems were invented by him, and don't you dare refer to him as an egghead. If you need something clarified, Sirtis is the man to ask."

Arras stood, "There is one item I'd like to address sir. This new cloaking device, what exactly does it do?"

Sirtis smiled and was quick with the answer, "In effect, it actually deflects signals away from our ship rather than allowing them to return to the sending device, making us invisible. The only drawback – it is only effective when we are using our impulse engines; otherwise, the masking effect is torn away at the high warp speeds our ship can achieve."

Arras answered, "So, what your saying is that, we could literally sit in the middle of an enemy fleet and they wouldn't know we were there."

"Exactly, Captain," Sirtis replied, still smiling.

Knowing her expressions by now after serving with her, I could tell she was impressed. Arras continued, "Can it be used like our shields, so we can fire or transport people while it's operating?"

"Yes, Captain," replied Sirtis, still smiling.

By this time, Arras was smiling too, "Thank you, Chief."

Still standing I looked around the room, "Are there any other questions? Anyone?" Hearing none, I continued, "Right, in that case, you are all to follow the chief, he will give you a tour of your stations on the bridge."

Everyone followed Sirtis, so I was able to return to my desk. On it, I found an envelope addressed to me. Inside the envelope I found all of Maharia's new ID's displaying her correct name. I put them in my pocket and headed to our hangar where she was working on the Serenity. I saw her talking to one of her work crew. Sensing my presence, she turned with a smile, and said, "Ah Admiral, you're just in time. We are just finishing up installing four torpedo tubes on your ship. You now have four SK's sitting in their tubes ready to fire."

I smiled, "Thank you Maharia, you can stand your men down for the rest of the day as a reward for work well done. The reason I'm here is to give you these, throw your old ones away." I handed her all her new ID's then I told her all her records had now been corrected as well.

She thanked me by saying, "If there is one thing about you I've learned, you are a man of your word. Thank you again."

All the work on the Defiant was finished ahead of time and preparations were made for a launch the following morning. Our launch went without any mishap then I ordered for the first time, "Warp 20 Mister Major."

Less than a minute later, he turned to me smiling, "Warp 20, Admiral."

We arrived above Beta Australis in a third of the time it would normally take. Just to give the command crew an idea of how good our cloak was, I ordered us cloaked as soon as we came out of hyperspace. Then I had Mary call Akron for permission to land. Akron's reply was in the form of a question, "How far away are you? You are not showing on our screens yet."

Laughing, I ordered, "Decloak please, Theta."

Everyone on the bridge heard the gasps and murmurs of amazement coming over the speakers. Ten minutes later, Defiant was in her hangar.

After landing I sent Mark a coded report letting him know that the Ghost Fleet was together at homebase.

Over the following couple of days I was kept busy. First there was a general parade where I addressed the entire fleet compliment, instilling in them how top secret our fleet was. I wanted them to know that each of them was handpicked for the job, because they were the best of the best, by Karen in the case of the pilots, or by me. Next, I went over the new features of our ships and fighters, comparing them to the ships they already knew. I told them they should go to their new assignments to check out their onboard quarters and workstations.

The crew was told that tomorrow they each would receive a new, ghost-shaped comms unit and would be required to turn in their old unit. I smiled, then continued, "I must say, they look really, really good. Made out of gold, they still have all the functions of your old comms units, plus a personal locator beacon function… and perhaps, a few other special features you will learn about later."

I went on to explain why we must have our own restricted area on the base, and that entry and exit will be strictly controlled by special security teams; exit by written pass only. Once the parade was dismissed, I gathered my captains and senior fighter officers together back in my office, to develop a number of battle scenarios and tactics.

By the end of the third day at our new base, Karen told me that all pilots had been checked out and signed off in their new, Javelin class fighters. It was at this point I finally felt that the Ghost Fleet was battle ready. We found our cloaking abilities to be outstanding, the crew liked their onboard quarters, and everyone was checked out at their new workstations. Karen and I were just finishing breakfast when my comms unit chirped. It was Base Control calling to tell me I had an incoming secure message from Fleet Command.

I told them I would be in my office within seven minutes, and to patch it through to me there.

After decoding, the message from Mark read: Bring your fleet to Zeta Australis at once. Remain in high orbit, using Ghost Protocol. Contact me when you arrive, use a secure channel. You and your senior officers are to beam down to the following co-ordinates. The co-ordinates were then specified.

I pressed the base intercom button, "Now hear this, now hear this, all fleet personnel, man your ships, lift-off in fifteen, I repeat, all fleet personnel, man your ships!"

I had myself beamed aboard the Defiant's bridge. Captain Arras reported, "All crew and pilots accounted for Admiral."

"Thank you, Captain. Mary, to all ships, on speakers please."

After Mary responded, I addressed the officers and crew, "This is Admiral Davis, we are to make for Zeta Australis. When we come out of warp at the outer marker, we will cloak and establish an orbit, At that time, all captains will beam aboard Defiant.

That is all, Hunter out."

Mary announced, "All ships report ready for lift-off sir."

"Very well comms, all ships on my mark; Launch!"

The Defiant bridge had screens around all the walls. Due to the 360-degree panoramic display I was able to see what was going on all around my ship. Swivelling my chair around I was able to watch every ship in the fleet launch. As we made space, I said, "All ships warp 20, Engage!"

An hour later, we were cloaked and in orbit around the planet. I pointed up and around, Mary patched me into all ships as well as the Defiant's internal speakers, "KD and Bucket, please report to the transporters, all captains beam aboard the Defiant now. Arras, you're with me. Jonas you have the con."

"Aye sir," He replied.

Arras joined them all and stepped onto a transport pad as I gave the chief the co-ordinates, and he energized the pads. We materialized in the Fleet Commander's briefing room. Kalashian entered the room, went to the bottom of the table, leaving the head of the table for the Commander. The seven of us took seats to Kalashian's left, then waited for the rest of the officers take places on his right which put them on left side the Fleet Commander at the head of the table. The Fleet Commander nodded, and Mark announced, "Ladies and gentlemen, allow me to make introductions. Around the table, starting at my immediate left: Admiral Davis; Flotilla Commander Torf; Captains Arras, Hammer, Meeker, Jantine, and Torrence; Wing Commander Davis' and Group Captain Tuckett; all from Ghost Fleet." We each inclined our heads as we were introduced.

The Fleet Commander began, "Welcome ladies and gentlemen. Here is the situation, four days ago the Alliance, using quantum bombs, destroyed all four planets of the Charbois system. We think, Admiral Davis, this was in retaliation for your destruction of their fleet during the battle for the Charbois Quasar. By our own protocol, Hunter there are no restraints placed on your fleet, because you are ghosts. You are able to come and go wherever, and whenever you wish. The only order I can give you is the Ghost Fleet goes to war. Now!

We are unable to tell you if the Alliance ships stayed in the Charbois system or not. If they didn't, they are probably staying close to the Alliance bases at Eridani or Procyon.

Hunter to you I say, you can freely destroy enemy

fleets wherever to find them. We believe that, with your protocols, you will be capable of destroying their fleets in their own territory. We believe this will demoralize the Alliance completely. But I haven't said that; you are not here; you are ghosts. Take the fight to them, good luck to all of you, and happy hunting."

We got up and moved away from the table. Mark came and shook my hand, which I acknowledged with a nod. I tapped my comms unit, "Beam us all up." As Karen, Arras, Reece, and I left the pads, I turned and made eye contact with my captains, "You heard the man, we make for the Charbois system, warp 20."

Stardate 2515.07.22:
The last time we went to the Charbois system it took six days, this time it only took two. We arrived at the co-ordinates of what was once Charbois One; now there was only empty space. I gave the order to cloak the fleet, and then I had Torf send out two scouts to comb the system, looking for the Alliance fleet responsible for the destruction and genocide of the Charbois people. If the scouts found the Alliance fleet, they were to report their position, and keep station. We would attack them as a battle group. When they cleared a sector they would report back to the fleet. While we waited for the reports from the scouts, Arras had the con and I was in my office. I heard a knock at the door and said, "Come."

Sirtis came in to report the success of the new navigational system he invented. It was even more precise that he had calculated, and his calculations were based on the best navigational star charts available. After congratulating him on his work, I wanted to know, "How long will it take you to install it into our navigational systems?"

Sirtis thought before answering, "A day, or maybe a little more, but I'll need Maharia to help me."

I nodded, "How many do you have ready?"

"Just this one Admiral."

I shook my head, "That won't work Sirtis, if we're going to connect it to our navigational systems, I've got to have one for the Defiant as well as one for each of our destroyers. When you have them *all* made, let me know. You need to make six more, that way there's a spare."

Smiling he replied, "Very good Admiral, I'll let you know, and thank you for letting me test it."

During dinner, Karen and I were exploring the possibilities that the Alliance fleet was still in the area. When my comms unit chirped, I tapped it, "Hunter here."

I heard Torf's voice, "Hunter this is Snake. The

Europa has found the enemy fleet. It's still here and close to the Echo Sector boundary. What are your orders Sir."

I thought fast, "Have Europa stay cloaked on station. The fleet will hold position tonight, and we'll move to back up Europa in the morning, Hunter out."

I smiled at Karen, "Well that answers your question dear."

Later that night, Karen and I made love. This had become a ritual with us. We would always make love on the eve of a battle, just in case one of us was killed in the fight. But then again, any reason is better than none I guess, and I'm certain it's something we aren't going to stop anytime soon.

After breakfast the next morning, I called for battle stations and we headed to the Europa's co-ordinates. On the way, I ordered the forward screen to maximum magnification, so that we could watch them. *Well, that's a bit careless, and a tempting target. Their flagship and troop carrier are too close together.*

My battle plan thought out, I hailed all destroyers, "This is Hunter, Europa found their fleet, so to Mark goes the glory. Here's the battle plan; Mark, I want you to fire an SK into the port side of their flagship. Hopefully, the bang will take out their troop carrier as well. Once the SK is away, all ships are to decloak. We will let the fighters soften them up a bit before we move in. Alright, whenever you're ready Captain Meeker."

Chapter 21.

We all watched the screens, as a torpedo seemed to launch out of nowhere. Our eyes followed the track of the torpedo all the way to impact. I watched it strike the enemy flagship exactly where I wanted it to. There was an initial flash that was followed immediately by another, much more intensive flash that outshone the first.

The shock wave caused by the blast made our screens go offline temporarily. I hoped none of our ships were in close proximity as the Defiant was literally thrown around. As things started to settle down, I yelled, "Damage report!"

The screens came back online one by one. Mary, her face white with shock, saw me point up and put me on coms, "Medics to the bridge."

I looked at the screen where the enemy fleet had once been. There was nothing! I tapped my comm, "Defiant to Titan, if you have no damage, make a search for enemy survivors."

His shocked "Aye sir," reply came from the speakers.

When I heard the speakers click off, I turned to Sirtis, asking, "What the hell! Was that the SK?"

His mouth opened and closed without a sound. He was unable to speak. Finally, he got the words out, "No sir, that wasn't our torpedo. Perhaps they still had a quantum bomb aboard that exploded."

Arras jumped in, "Damage report Admiral, no ship damage, all personnel injured have been transferred to the med bay, one seriously."

I nodded turning to Sirtis again, "Thank the stars you built our shields strong, otherwise we'd all be dead now!"

The hailing speakers activated, "Titan to Defiant, sir we have found one life pod and are beaming it aboard, please standby."

Five minutes later, we were hailed again, "Titan to Defiant, the lone survivor is the Captain of the troop carrier sir. What would you like me to do with him sir?"

I looked at Tark and gestured for him to move while I was replying to the Titan, "Torf, beam him directly to the brig on the Defiant please. Tark!"

"On it, Sir," and he left the bridge.

I pointed to the speakers, "Return to the fleet, Titan." I pointed up again and waived my hand, "To all ships and internal speakers please. To all ships and crewmembers, for those that are unaware; that shockwave was not caused by our SK torpedo. That was the results of a quantum bomb explosion. You should all thank your lucky stars that our shielding was built to withstand hits over fifty times greater than Federation normal. Otherwise like the enemy fleet, we'd all be dead now. We will stay on station here for the next day, to give our injured time to heal, Hunter out."

I handed over the con to Arras and went I went to have a talk with the survivor. Because it was covered by security protocols, I was accompanied by Tark. I interviewed the prisoner using the cell holding screens and found out that the enemy fleet had come from their base on Eridani. He also told me there was a fifty-mile zone around the entire base meaning civilian areas were excluded.
But the most important fact I gleaned was there were two more fleets based there. Satisfied with what information I had gained, I told him he would be returned to Alliance territory at a future date, and we left.

Tark and I returned to the bridge and he returned to his station. I didn't, I took Mary with me to my office We sat in a pair of comfortable chairs, away from my desk, "Alright Mary, it's time you and I had a chat. Because you are my comms officer, you need to know these signals from me. I showed her some new signals I wanted to use and what each signal meant. "Just add them to the list of the ones we already use. They will save us both from speaking unnecessarily." Then, as she was about to leave, I added, "Please inform all Captains, Karen, and Reece, there will be a conference in my office at thirteen thirty hours today."

"Yes sir." She said she would relay the message and went out the door.

A plan was beginning to take shape in my head, but to confirm that it would work I called up maps of Eridani, and the Alliance maps we had on record of their military base. The more I saw, the firmer my plan became.

During lunch I told Karen what I had in mind. She was all for the idea. She said she would get together with Reece after lunch and start working out an attack plan. The first part of my plan involved stealing a shuttle transport ship, and for that, I need Tark. I found him and let him know that he was to be a part of the conference after lunch.

There was enough room and casual chairs in my office for all those invited to the conference. I sat back, resting on the front of my desk, looking at all of the screens in the room. One displayed an aerial view of the perimeter around the base. Two screens showed different views of Eridani, and another displayed a close-up view of only the base itself.

As soon as everyone had assembled, I began, "Well girls and boys, seeing as our job here was done for us by Mark with only one shot." Laughter interrupted my thought, but it didn't matter. Everyone got the point. "By the way Mark, it was just where I wanted it. Well done, but you can't take all the credit for the result." Laughter filled the room again.

"Alright, now to business. That fleet came from this base on Eridani." I pointed out the base on the closest screen and continued, "I was also told that there are two more fleets stationed there to patrol the sector. We are going to destroy that base.

This has to be a surgical strike in two steps. We have to destroy their ability to communicate first. I want no messages getting out about the attack. We have identified this," pointing at a specific building on the close-up image of the base, "As their comms building. Once they are unable to communicate, I will lead a ground assault with the intention of stealing two troop transports. Now, here's how we're going to do it…"

I went on to outline my strategy; Torf is to position his ship so that his guns can destroy all main buildings *after* the SK levels the comms building. Following that, the fighters from the Defiant will attack in force. Then I turned the briefing over to Karen to outline the fighter attack.

When Karen finished, I went back to the base close-up and pointed to another area on the screen, "Now this is the transport area. This is where Arras, Tark, myself, and one hundred of his men will be, once we've beamed everyone down. When we're ready, I will give the order, 'Execute!'

When you hear that, Torf will open fire and the fighters will launch. The rest of the destroyers will be covering the Defiant. With any luck, we will not only destroy the base, but two more fleets as well. Any questions?"

Torf asked, "What if we encounter a patrolling fleet before we reach the planet, sir?"

"As soon as we come out of warp on the edge of the sector, we'll immediately cloak. In fact, that will be our number one Standard of Procedure (SOP). Whenever we come out of warp from here on, we will cloak immediately after coming out of warp. But as to your question Torf, we will bypass them, attack the base, and then go back and kill them."

Jantine asked, "Sir, why are we bothering about stealing transports?"

"Because Rose, we're not murderers, Once the base has been levelled and the fighters withdraw, Torf will land all his security personnel assault troops. On a base this size, there's bound to be survivors.

They will be given the opportunity to surrender, and we'll use those transports to house and transport any prisoners. Any other questions?"

There weren't any, so Karen stood. Grinning, she faced Torf "Please don't hit any of my fighters Torf, or I'll be most annoyed."

Her comment relieved the tension in the room, and also drew chuckles from the group, and a smile from me, "Ok, that's all girls and boys, you each know what you have to do, dismissed."

Once they all trooped out, I went through to our quarters and retrieved my phaser pistol and holster. I used my comms unit to call Arras and Tark to my office. They entered at my command and took seats. I detailed the entire attack plan to Arras and explained the rolls she and I would take. Then I turned to Tark, "Tark, we will need photon rifles in addition to our normal phaser side arms. Sort out your best fighters and brief them about our attack." Using the close-up screen of the base, I pointed out where we'd beam down, and then the perimeter guards his troops would need to silence.

Stardate 2515.07.28:
We arrived in orbit above Eridani two days later. The patrolling fleet we bypassed whilst in warp was just outside the Alliance territories and Gort noted their position and course for a later time. Our scans

of the planet determined that there were two entire fleets on the ground at the base we were going to attack. When I heard that, I thought: *Hmm, that means the fleet we bypassed are from elsewhere. We might just track them to their base as well. Two attacks inside Alliance territory will certainly cause consternation in the Council!* I sat there, on the bridge in the Captain's chair, smiling at my thoughts.

I left the bridge and went down to Karen's office on the flight deck, "You all set darling?"

She nodded saying, "Yes dear, everyone's been briefed and will move to their fighters soon. You be careful down there, sweetie." She leaned in and kissed me.

I smiled, "You know me honey, I'm always that."

She scoffed laughing, "That's what I'm worried about." We were both smiling as I headed back to the bridge.

Back on the bridge, I pulled out my phaser and adjusted it to the kill setting. Arras was doing the same thing. "Titan to Defiant," suddenly was heard over all speakers on the bridge, "In prime position above base, no sign that our presence is being detected, out."

It was Arras who spoke next, "You have the con mister Major!" Arras and I rushed from the bridge and headed to the transporters. Somewhere along the way, Tark joined us. He half-passed, half-threw photon rifles at each of us while we made for the transporters.

We were the last to beam down. By the time we materialized on the ground, the advance teams had already eliminated all of the patrolling security guards. Scanning the base, I spotted three transporters standing on the tarmac, not 300 yards away.

I whispered, "Ok, we will form around those three. Find any convenient cover." When all ground forces were in place, I tapped my comms unit, "Execute!"

A large explosion followed my command. Torf had destroyed the comms building. Then the sound of phaser and cannon fire closely followed. Armed men started running from the buildings near our position, and my troops opened fire. Then the first flight of fighters zoomed in firing at the buildings, causing explosions and general mayhem. They continued deeper into the base complex with continual fire from their cannon and phasers.

Wave after wave of fighters followed creating their own mayhem as they flew over the base firing. My troops added to the general mayhem as we defended the area around the three ships I had selected. Then above the noise of explosions and firing, the external speakers of Titan announced, "This base is now under Federation control. You survivors have the choice to surrender to our troops or die!"

The surviving troops that had been firing upon my forces, started rising from their positions, throwing down their rifles, and placing their arms into the air.

I shouted, "Cease Fire," not that I needed to, my men were already moving to the five surviving defenders. Silence followed. I tapped my comms, "Hunter to all attack groups, report!"

Torf was the first to answer, "Snake to Hunter, the base and both fleets have been destroyed, all buildings are rubble, my ground troops are sweeping for any survivors, and heading toward your position Snake out."

"KD to Hunter, all fighters are returning to the ship, no casualties, KD out."

"Copy that all. Defiant, beam down Brains to my position please." Giving Sirtis a callsign.

"On my way Hunter," Sirtis answered, knowing I meant him.

Sirtis materialized beside me. I asked him how many of the transports would fit aboard the Defiant. He replied that two would be all that the ship could fit in.

I smiled, "Good, can you reach Maharia telepathically from here?

He smiled, "Yes sir, would you like her down here?"

"Yes please. Now you can check out fleet wreckage and buildings, Find those Q bombs."

I tapped comms, "Hunter to all ships, land at the base, but stay cloaked.

After Maharia materialized, I told her what I wanted done, and she scuttled off to get it done.

Chapter 22.

Maharia had done as I requested and painted a ghost figure on the two transport shuttles we were going to keep. She was busy removing the warp engines from the third one as our security forces converged on my position. They were herding a group of fifty odd survivors from other parts of the base, all with their hands on their heads. My own force placed their prisoners with the main group, and they were all kept covered by both forces.

I turned to Tark, "Can you arrange to have our previous prisoner brought along to this lot please."

He nodded and walked off tapping his comms pin.

Maharia had finished her work and returned, "Admiral, I've taken out the warp engines and beamed them aboard the Defiant. The impulse engines work fine and will get them to Earth sir."

I smiled, "Good, now when these two transports are aboard Defiant, I need you to install the same shielding as our ships, and cloaking. Don't change the paintwork, we may use them as scout ships."

"It's lucky I grabbed everything in store from Alpha Cor Six sir." Smiling, she continued, "They'll be ready with the conversions in three days sir."

"Good, you and Sirtis fly them aboard Defiant now please."

Prior to leaving, Sirtis found two Quantum bombs aboard one of their flagships. He disarmed them both and made their component materials unusable by dissolving them in acid baths.

Tark brought the captain that had been in the brig forward, "Now then Captain, I said you would be released. You will take that transport, and all these other prisoners, back to Earth." Handing him the two video files I recorded earlier. I continued, "You will deliver these to Fleet Command and the Alliance Council."

Both video files contained the same message: "This is Admiral Clayton Davis of the Federation of the Outer Rim Planets. My fleet is responsible for the destruction of the fleet you sent to obliterate the four planets of the Charbois system. Our response for your actions was to destroy your base on Eridani. We have also destroyed the two fleets based there and captured the remaining quantum bombs. Unless you agree to peace and end this war, I will make Earth one of the targets of said bombs. My abhorrence to the use of these bombs is on record with Fleet Command, but I WILL NOT HESITATE to use them if I must. I leave the decision to your Council and Fleet Command, out."
The message was a huge bluff, but with Sirtis

finding the bombs, it was now a bluff with substance. Fleet Command knew there were at least two more bombs on Eridani, so my video claim could be substantiated. Turning to Tark, "Would you get the ship ready for departure, and the prisoners loaded please mister Tark, but don't touch the navigational systems!"

"Aye sir," and he walked off.

Then I faced the captain once more, "Your course has been plotted, and once you take off, the explosives connected to the navigation system will arm. If you try to alter your course, the ship will blow-up. The same holds true if you try to stop anywhere. Anything you do other than pilot and land the ship will result in the same thing, do you understand, Captain?" *This was another bluff on my part. Nothing had been done, but he didn't know that.*

Looking defeated he replied, "Aye, I do Sir."

"Good, I'm glad we understand each other. Now one more thing, your warp drive has been removed, you've only impulse power, so I suggest you make a start. Go on, off you go."

He walked toward the transport, and once there lifted off, I ordered all our personnel back to our ships. In accordance with my earlier orders, our ships did not decloak until *after* the survivor ship had departed.

Back on my bridge, I gave Mary the signal for what I wanted. She nodded and I addressed the crews, "This is Admiral Davis to all fleet personnel, this was a job well done by everyone. My thanks go to each of you. We have made our first strike into Alliance territory a success, and when that transport arrives on Earth, the Alliance should be shitting themselves. But now we are going back to work. On the way here, we passed a patrolling fleet just outside the border. We are going back to find it and do our duty. All captains and chief fighter officers, please join me after we are back in space and cloaked, at full impulse, thank you all, Davis out," and I gave Mary the signal to cut.

Turning to my crew on the bridge, I ordered, "Find that fleet mister Gort. Mister Major, full impulse."

Their responses were simultaneous, "Aye sir."

As I left the bridge, I undid my pistol holster and said, "Arras, you have the con."

In my office I hung my holster and phaser pistol on the wall hook behind my desk. I went to the liquor cabinet, opened it, and began placing bottles of alcohol and ale on the tray atop the cabinet. Then I set out a tray full of glasses. Karen and Bucket came in just as I was sitting down at my desk after pouring myself a drink. I just nodded and waved to the drinks.

Karen was pouring herself a drink when I asked, "So, how's morale with the pilots?"

She laughed as Bucket answered, "Couldn't be better Boss. They really enjoyed getting into the action, and certainly made a mess of those grounded ships."

I was still smiling when the rest of the captains joined us, even Arras. Every one of them was smiling and joking as they poured drinks and sank into chairs. Then I stood and raised my glass, "A toast, to our first official successful attack in Alliance territory. Well done to you all!"

They all raised their glasses and cheered. Then they settled down and partied. Sometime into the celebration I told them about the bluff I made about the quantum bombs in the message I sent to the Council. "Sirtis did find *two* of them. Thank goodness they didn't detonate during the attack; otherwise some of us wouldn't be sitting here. He was able to disarm them and destroy the ingredients in acid. But this shows how dangerous it will be if we attack any more bases. Anyway, I'll show you what was sent. Computer, show latest video file." After they saw what I had sent, Hammer exclaimed,

"That's telling them Clay! That should put the wind up 'em."

I nodded and then reminded everyone how concerned I was about the bombs. When we attack other fleets, or bases, we will not know if there are quantum bombs present. I stopped there and asked for suggestions.

Meeker suggested that we torpedo all the destroyers and troop carriers; then board the flagship and take it by force of arms. I told him his idea did have some merit, but it didn't allow the fighters to come into play, which would not do the pilots' morale any good.

Arras suggested fighting their destroyers and troop ship conventionally, then give the flagship a chance to surrender. Jantine replied that the flagship should be the first target in any engagement, because doing that shuts off their chain of command.

Torf suggested using the transports we'd stolen and infiltrate their flagship, getting the Admiral alone, and kidnapping him. Again, another possibility, but not practicable since many of us would be recognizable from our medal presentations broadcasts or as Outer Rimmers.

I called an end the discussion, "Ok that's enough. There is really only one way to do this, which is how we did it last time. Fire an SK into their flagship while we're cloaked, then attack the rest of the fleet afterward. We don't get too close, that way if there is a quantum bomb aboard, we'll be ready for the shockwave."

When I finished, I looked around the room. Although their faces were sombre, every single one of them was nodding support.

"Alright, we're all agreed. I'll launch the SK, then if nothing happens, we go with Attack Plan Bravo. Everyone agree?"

They all voiced their agreement, so I continued "Ok, you all know what we're going to do. Now I have to send a report of our actions to Fleet."

They finished their drinks and made their way out. I spoke out, "Computer, ship's report to Admiral Kalashian at Fleet Headquarters." As I spoke, the words appeared on the screen. My report took an hour to dictate, attach the video file sent to the Alliance Council, and encrypt. After I checked it, I said, "Produce file."

The file popped out, and I took it with me. In the wardroom I gave the file to Mary and asked her to send it to Kalashian after dinner.

Karen and I were resting in bed when internal

comms hailed me, "Admiral, we've caught up with the enemy fleet."

"Very well, reduce to match their speed and shadow them until further notice. Pass that to all ships, out."

Karen said, "Well, we better some sleep, it's going to be a busy day tomorrow Dear. Lights out," and we snuggled into each other and went to sleep.

After breakfast the next morning, Karen and I went out the wardroom door together, but we were heading in different directions. "It's time to go to work Honey, take care out there." She smiled and headed to the flight deck to brief her pilots, while I went to the bridge, and gave Mary the signal. She nodded and I began, "Defiant to all Captains, move to your attack positions, then wait for my order, Hunter out."

Looking at Guns, I nodded, "Launch Theta."

She announced, "Torpedo away sir."

We followed the track of the torpedo. As it approached the target, I said to the command crew. "Ok, brace yourselves."

The torpedo hit their flagship and exploded without any further explosions. I ordered, "Decloak! All fighters away. Torf attack!"

Their flagship was destroyed by the torpedo, and serious damage had been done to their troop carrier. Then Torf led the flotilla into action, first with an initial broadside. Next the fighters joined in and helped with the destruction of all but two of their destroyers.

The two remaining Alliance destroyers were seriously damaged and quickly surrendered. When the search for survivors began, I got on the viewer and spoke to the senior enemy captain who announced their surrender.

"Captain Rogers this is Admiral Davis, status report please." I wanted to ascertain their damaged conditions.

He reported that both destroyers were trying to ascertain structural damage and repair their engines.

"Where is your base, Rogers?" I wanted to know, "And will you be able to make it home?"

Before he answered, Mary interrupted, "Admiral, all fighters are back aboard, and Commander Torf reports that forty-three survivors have been found."

I nodded, "Thank you Mary. As you just heard Captain, forty-three survivors have been found, so please answer my questions. Can you accommodate that number aboard your ships for the return to your base?"

Rogers told me that they could accommodate all the survivors and that they would be able to make it home. He told me they were stationed on Xi Bootis at a small, one-fleet base near the edge of the Alliance zone.

"Very well Captain, we will beam the survivors aboard your ship and you can be on your way. But I can assure you that I intend to take over your base, so I would recommend that you inform your base commander to surrender to us when we arrive. I do not need to tell you how many lives this will save."

He acknowledged that fact and told me he'd do his best to convince his base commander to surrender.

"Very well Captain. Now one more thing, do you have any quantum bombs held on base?"

"Yes sir, not that I agree with them. I was with Battle Group Two during the war with the Zytrons and saw their effects. We have one in store on the base, use it and be damned."

"Brave words Captain, I was with Battle Group Three, so I know what they are like. I don't intend to use it, I intend to destroy it! My Fleet will be following you even though you won't see us. Should you require any help, just hail, good day Captain Rogers."

"Callista," I ordered, "Cloak now, and follow them to their base. Jam all Alliance communications from his ship now and the base as soon as you are able."

Chapter 23.

The Fleet arrived above the Xi Bootis base twelve hours after Hammer reported in. He reported he had been station keeping since he arrived. Because it was still dark, I had all ships land, but to remain cloaked.

On the bridge the next morning I took my seat and asked for a status report. Arras told me we were on the ground not far from the base and still cloaked. Looking at Mary, I signalled, and I waited for her nod before hailing, "Xi Bootis Base, this is Admiral Clayton Davis of the Federation of Outer Rim Planets. I am here to demand your surrender to my fleet, over."

The reply was almost instantaneous, the screen flickered, and I was eye to eye with my counterpart. She said, "Well, it's been quite a while since we've seen each other back at the Academy, Clay. I hear you're still a ruthless fighter, but with some compassion. I will surrender the base to you, as long as you give me your word that none of my personnel will be harmed."

"Yes, it *has* been awhile Erin. I give you my word no one will be harmed. You will all be incarcerated in the detention cells for the time we are here, then you will be freed to make your way back to Earth, because I am going to destroy your base. Also, Erin if you are prepared to give me your parole (officer's word of honour), you need not be placed in the cells."

Erin Masters replied, "Very well, I accept and give you my parole. I will await you outside the main offices Clay."

"Alright Erin, I'll beam over in a tick with my officers and a security force naturally." I switched Erin off, and addressed my crews, "All ships decloak, all senior officers beam to the main offices. Tark, a security force please, Davis out,"
And then I switched back, "On my way Erin." The screen went blank, and I ordered, "Tark, I want an escort with Admiral Masters at all times. Sirtis you, and Maharia are with me. Arras you have the con."

A minute later, I stood with my captains, Karen, Sirtis and Maharia and a force of one hundred security personnel. We were facing Admiral Masters, her senior officers, and Captain Rogers. Erin and I strode forward and saluted each other, then we embraced as old friends. She leaned in, whispered in my ear, "I heard about Lara, Clay and I'm sorry," and then stepped back.

She introduced me to her officers, and I did the same for her. She arched her eyebrows as she was introduced to Karen but said nothing. After the pleasantries, she formally said, "Admiral Davis I surrender this base over to you and have asked all personnel to muster in the detention area. If you will follow me, please."

Following her and her officers, she led the way to the detention block, where her officers joined the rest of the base personnel. My security people checked all the entries and exits, securing them properly. After the headcount to make sure all base personnel were present, Tark nodded to me, indicating the block was secure. I said, "Ladies and gentlemen, Admiral Masters has surrendered your base to me. Once we do what we came here to do, you will be given transportation to Earth. If you adhere to the orders to stay put and not try to interfere with what we are doing, our job will probably be done by tomorrow. The longer it takes, the longer you're all here, so please behave. Thank you."

Erin accompanied me and some of the guards outside. Four of them took up posts with their rifles. Erin said, "That was a nice little speech Clay, thank you for reassuring them. Shall we go to my office?"

"In a minute," I replied, "Sirtis, find and disarm that bomb. Maharia find a ship for this lot and do what you did last time please. Also scrounge for anything you want. Tark, start setting the demolition charges. This entire base and contents is to be turned into rubble."

Before Sirtis left, I whispered in his ear, he looked at me in shock, then smiled. "Now Erin, let's go to your office. Hammer, Meeker, Torrence find the comms office. You know what I want done. After you, Erin."

As Karen, Torf, Jantine, and I sat in the comfy chairs, Erin poured drinks and handed them out. "Well now, hello again Torf, have you been with this scoundrel the whole time?"

She sat down and Torf filled her in. Then, when asked, I answered her about my time since joining the Federation and what I was up to. Knowing what I said would get back to the Alliance, I told her about our capturing the two quantum bombs from Eridani, and that I was going to use one of them against Earth if the Alliance didn't pursue peace. I told her that my second target was going to be Alpha Centauri. When she asked me why I was disarming the bomb from her base, I told her that I had enough of the bombs, and that I wanted to be certain it couldn't be used against me at a later date. I told her my next attack would be on bases that I thought might be storing them, *that way the Alliance would keep their fleets close to their bases and not out patrolling.* Then if the Alliance hadn't sued for peace by the end of the year, then that's when I'd drop the bomb. Once I did that the other Federation fleets armed with the bombs from our supply, were going to bomb every planet of the Alliance wiping them out completely. So, my advice to her was to get away from any Alliance homeworld if peace talks hadn't started by my deadline of the end of the year. I think my lies were convincing enough for her to believe what I had said. And I knew that my words would be relayed to Fleet command if not the council.

The next morning, I escorted her to the ship that was going to convey her and her base personnel back to Earth. Maharia had done a good job of destroying the communication systems and removing the warp drives.

On our way, I said, "Erin, there's just one more thing you should know before I send you on your way. The warp engines of this ship have been removed, so you only have impulse drive. Sorry about that, but I need to replace an engine in one of my ships and I like having a spare. Anyway, take care of yourself and be away from Earth come the new year."

After all my fleet personnel had returned to their ships, the base charges were set off, completely destroying the base, ships, and equipment we hadn't already commandeered. All that was left was rubble. My fleet lifted off and I gave Arras the con. I went to make a video call to Mark Kalashian. He came online smiling, "Hello my boy, your last report certainly, caused quite a stir in Fleet and Council commands. So, what have you been up to since then?"

"Yes, I thought it would. Threatening the Alliance like that should have rattled them. Since then I have destroyed another fleet and their base on Xi Bootis. We found another quantum bomb on the base and disarmed it. I kept the casing, because I plan to use it later. I'm uploading a video, recorded yesterday, of me talking to an old academy friend. I think she is convinced I will bomb Earth. I fed her quite a lot of disinformation that I know will definitely get to Fleet Command. How are things going in the other theatres sir?"

"At present we're winning every engagement. But as yet there have been no calls from the Alliance about making a peace, why?"

I smiled, "I've been thinking about a rather audacious move of attacking enemy bases while still in orbit before sending in my fighters. But, for that I'll need access to the military information held by the Federation sir."

"I applaud your idea and I'll get you the access you require. How are your ships and crews, morale wise?"

"The ships are in fine shape sir, considering how close we were to that blast, and morale is high.

I just need to keep up the momentum. So far, we have been lucky, but I will have to move further into Alliance territory. That's why I need that access sir."

He smiled, "Don't worry Hunter, I'll get it for you. That file you sent is here, so I'll have a look at it, Deadbeat out."

During the next couple of weeks, we patrolled around the edges of Alliance territory looking for prey. Luck, or our previous efforts, were against us, and we didn't find anything. Now that I had access to our data on all Alliance bases and locations, I was beginning to form a plan. I had two possible targets, both would be hard to smash, but one of them had high propaganda value. The combined military base on Prociyon was the newest Alliance base, opened just before the war, it's opening had been covered by the media from all worlds. Completely destroying it that would cause a media frenzy.

I had Mary call a senior officers conference that day at thirteen thirty hours. Looking at Arras, "That means you too, Arras, and you, Sirtis."

That afternoon, after lunch, Karen and I walked to my office ahead of the meeting at thirteen hundred. We sat down to drinks and relax a bit when she asked, "What's on your mind, dear?"

I told her that the crews were becoming restless. I

thought it was the inactivity and it was beginning to have an effect on morale.

"Hmm, yeah, it's getting everyone down."

After everyone was seated, some with drinks and others without, I said that the lack of action was beginning to show on the crew, "We've pulled off some pretty audacious things lately, so let's do another, just as audacious, how about we attack another base? I have picked two targets of about the same value to the Alliance, but one stands out as a juicer one to me due to its publicity. First off, let's talk over whether we want to risk another base attack."

Arras said, "I'm for it! However, I am also concerned about the possibility there could be a quantum bomb on the base."

Sirtis jumped in, "That would not be a problem Captain, I have added a new feature to our scanners so that they are now able to pick up the presence of solafarise and dimetramangante, which are the two major fissionable elements in a quantum bomb. If our scanners detect their presence, we simply don't attack that particular fleet or base."

I looked at him just as stunned as the people in the room, "You're telling me that we can now know if a fleet or base has a quantum bomb present?"

"Yes Clay."

Staring at him incredulously, "Since when? ...and when were you going to let me know about this little gem?"

"Since lunch, Sir. I finished the recalibration while you were having lunch; and I'm telling you now, Sir."

Karen started laughing. Sirtis had delivered his reply deadpan. His face remained totally expressionless throughout. The laughter was infectious, and everyone started laughing, me amongst them.

"Well done Sirtis! In that case, does anyone have any qualms about attacking another base?"

There were answers of no, all for it, and let's do it.

"Alright then, I have selected two targets: Sirius or the juicier one, Prociyon. Which one will it be?"

Prociyon was the unanimous choice. I had the aerial view of the base put up on the screens, and we got down to making up our attack plan. Two hours later, everyone knew their role in the attack and where to position their ships. Everyone returned to their ships, and while Karen and Bucket returned to the flight deck to make their plans, Arras and I returned to the bridge. I sat down and pointed up. Mary nodded and opened the comms, "Flagship to fleet, make course for Prociyon, warp 20, engage."

Stardate 2515.08.19:
Four days later, we were orbiting the planet above the Prociyon Combined Forces Base. Sirtis had scanned the base and it showed no trace of the elements used in quantum bombs. With that all done, I ordered the fighters launched. Viewing the rear screen, I saw all the fighters launch out of the tubes and form up in their attack formations.
I tapped my comms pin, "Hunter to KD, just hang in here until I call for you, over."

"KD to Hunter, will do boss, KD out."

Then the fleet headed for Prociyon and took their aerial positions, a thousand feet above the base. They each called in, one by one, announcing their ship name, and "In position and ready to open fire." Each section of the base was going to receive broadsides from the ship designated to that section. When Defiant was in position, I gave the order "Fire!"

Chapter 24.

At my command, all ships opened fire at previously determined buildings. Defiant's first salvo was directed at the communications building. Firing an SK torpedo into the building completely levelled it and all the buildings surrounding it. After the initial salvo was over, I ordered all ships to decloak. Then I called to the fighters "Hunter to KD, time to have some fun, bring them in Sweetie."

"KD to Hunter, on our way. KD to all pilots, you know your targets, let's go."

The fighters came in under our ships, and broke into two groups, the smaller one, took on any enemy fighters that had launched, while the other started strafing any opportune targets.

Fifteen minutes after unleashing the firestorm, I observed that the main guns of the destroyers were only firing occasionally and called for a status report. The incoming reports convinced me that enough damage had been done, and I called for all ships to ceasefire. My fighters kept circling over the base looking for any opposition, but no opportunities presented themselves. I heard Karen say, "KD to all fighters, ceasefire and return to your pads, KD out."

Once the smoke cleared and our guns fell silent, I

saw someone waving a white flag. I watched as others crawled out of the rubble that had once been buildings. "Arras you have the con. Tark, I want a security team. We'll beam down."

"Yes sir."

I went to my office, retrieved my phaser and followed Tark to the transporters. When we materialized, Tark stayed beside me and the rest of the ten-man security detail fanned out around us with rifles at the ready. I strode forward to the man holding up the white flag, "Who's in charge here?"

The Major holding the makeshift flag dropped it and came to face me, "I think I may be the last officer sir, I'm Major Will Talbot," and saluted.

I returned his salute, "Admiral Clayton Davis, Major. Can you give me some sort of status report please?"

He looked around and replied, "Sir, I think I'm the last admin officer left alive. You gave us a hammering. There's not a building left standing as far as I can see. You came out of nowhere. How did you do it? This area is always scanned; You caught us completely unawares."

"You should know by now Major, nothing about being at war is fair. I think we've done enough damage for now. You won't be using this base for a long time, and it'll take a lot of rebuilding. I am going to withdraw my fleet and leave you to gather your people and move out of here. I suggest you call on your superiors to send help. Seeing your comms are down, it's a long walk to the nearest town, so I'll leave you to it." We saluted each other, and my detail walked away to be beamed aboard ship.

Back on the bridge, I ordered all ships back into orbit, where we cloaked again. I said to all ships, "We'll wait here. The Alliance is bound to send help; and when they do, we will greet them in our own, very special, way. We will take out their flagships and escorts only. We will not fire on any transports or medical ships. Hunter out."

Later that day I sent a complete report of our action to Kalashian. The next morning after breakfast, I summoned Torf to my office. "Torf, now that all the ships sensors have been recalibrated by Sirtis, I think we best take a look at our next move. Sirius is going to be our next base to hit. I want you to send one of your ships ahead to reconnoitre the base. See if there are any quantum bombs onsite. Let me know what you find. If you find any, we will move on to another target."

"I'll send Jantine, it's only a day away from here, and she could be back before our ambush, that way we'll be at full strength for any fight."

"Alright, but if there are no quantum bombs on Sirius, I don't want her to come back. She is to remain in orbit and cloaked gathering intel until we join her there. Being one destroyer down, won't affect the outcome of the ambush, you know that. Any questions?"

"Yes Sir. As you say Sir, being a ship short won't affect the outcome of the ambush, but why are we now attacking bases?"

"Well look at it this way Torf. If we destroy a base, the Alliance has to send help. Which means that we know where a fleet will be. So, after we attack a base, we wait for them to send help and ambush the incoming fleet instead of just patrolling around hoping to catch a fleet somewhere. See what I mean?"

He smiled that notorious cragoid smile of theirs, that resembled a half smile and half sneer, "Yes sir, a very sound tactic. If that's all sir, I'll get Triton on its way."

I smiled, "Yes that is all Torf, away you go."

The morning of the fourth day, Triton returned and Jantine requested permission to come aboard the Defiant, which I granted, then had her join me in my office. She wasted no time in giving me her report about the base on Sirius. Her scanners had detected the presence of a quantum bomb, so she had descended closer to the base, and was able to detect which building on the base held the emanating source the scanners had picked up. I put the aerial view of the base on screens and she pointed out the building and gave me its co-ordinates.

A thought jumped into my mind as she was giving details that caused me to smile, "Thanks Rose, all of this is of tremendous value. You've done a great job. Now when you get back to the Triton, get her ready for battle, I think we'll have a fight coming before the day is out."

"Thank you, Admiral, I'll do that." Then we both got up and she made for the transporters.

It was just after coming back onto the bridge, that Gort announced, "Admiral a fleet, no **two** fleets have just come out of hyperspace. Their heading is toward the planet, sir."

"Thank you Gort. Battle stations! Mary, all ships on speaker please. Hunter to all ships, two fleets have arrived and making their way toward us. Snake this time we are well and truly outnumbered. No niceties your ships are to target the destroyers with SK's; and remember, no firing on unarmed ships, Defiant will target the flagships, Hunter out."

To the Defiant's bridge I said, "Jonas, move us

closer to the flagships. Theta, target both of those flag carriers amidships." I pointed up, "All ships, Fire!"

Both flagships were blown to bits by our SK's. Ten destroyers were obliterated with the first salvo of torpedoes and another twelve were destroyed with our second. I called for all my ships to ceasefire, then tapped my comms pin, "Hunter to KD, send two squadrons to kill those last two destroyers, Hunter out," and watched the fighters launch on the screens.

The last two destroyers didn't stand much of a chance against our fighters, though they did put up a fair fight. After the fighters had caused severe damage, crippling both of their remaining destroyers, I ordered them to ceasefire and return to the Defiant.

Once the fighters were back on board, I told all ships to set course for Sirius at full impulse and called for a senior officers conference in an hour.

At the meeting, and after everyone was seated, I asked Rose Jantine to give everyone the report she gave me earlier in the day. When she finished, I said, "I know what you are all thinking, if there is a quantum bomb on Sirius, why are we going there? The answer is quite simple, because we are going to destroy the whole planet!"

My words caused a stir with everyone. I turned to Sirtis, "If the bomb explodes, will our shields protect our ships if we are in orbit?"

"Yes, and from the resultant shockwave as well. You saw and felt the last time one exploded; we were much closer then. If you fire from orbit the shockwave will be less fierce and shorter in duration, Sir."

"Thank you Sirtis, Now here's what we are going to do boys and girls, we are going to play the Alliance against itself. We will spread out in orbit around the planet. Once there, you are to lay in a course for Beta Australis. At a given time, I'll order us to decloak. Every one of us will fire an SK at this building on my order. We will immediately go into warp, before the shockwave hits, and head for Beta Australis. This will do two things; one, it destroys the entire planet, and two, if anyone sees us, they'll think we were destroyed in the blast. While everyone thinks we're dust, we'll be having a two-week furlough back at homebase, before we go out again to continue our mission. Any questions?"

Karen remarked, "I don't suppose you'll be using my fighters for this one."

Everyone laughed as I replied, "No dear, not this time."

I gave the coordinates of the target building to my destroyer captains and ended the conference.

Stardate 2515.08.25:
At full impulse, it only took four days to get to Sirius. During the trip to the planet, I created an addendum to the Prociyon report, I had already sent to Mark. I filled him in on the destruction of two more Alliance fleets and advised him of my plan for Sirius.

When we reached Sirius, each ship took up their assigned orbital position, and awaited my command. I walked over to Guns' workstation and gave Theta the co-ordinates, "Load an SK and this is where we're sending it," When I passed Mary, I pointed up, "All ships, load your torpedoes!" I waited until everyone had confirmed, and then, in rapid succession, I ordered, "Decloak! Fire! ...now get out of here, warp 20, go!"

We didn't know the results of what happened at Sirius until we came out of hyperspace two weeks later. We slowed to half impulse near the outer planet marker. Mary called Akron Base Command for landing clearance. We came in low over the base and used our vertical thrusters to land in our bunker hangars. We were home, and I granted two weeks shore leave for all crews.

Karen and I were glad to be back in our quarters. She turned on the screens and selected the news channel and asked it for the day after we hit Sirius. We sat down, drink in hand, snuggled a little, and leaned back on the sofa ready to see what we had done.

We heard the reporter say, "And now, more news is coming in on the rumour that a quantum bomb may have been responsible for the destruction of Sirius yesterday. What we do know is, the Federation's so-called Ghost Fleet, led by Admiral Clayton Davis, was attacking the military base on the planet just before the planet exploded. It was also confirmed that the so-called ghost fleet was obliterated in the resultant shockwave. What isn't known is whether there was a Q bomb on the base at the time. There have been persistent rumours that the military has been keeping Q bombs there for some time. At present, Alliance Fleet Command has been unwilling to comment. However, a spokesman for the Fleet Command, has suddenly scheduled a media conference for eleven am today. We will be following this story from Fleet Command at the conference today."

Karen and I were laughing, "Well we must be ghosts then. How are you enjoying your death my dear?"

"I'll show you how much," she said with a twinkle in her eye, "Later, …much later."   Then she added,

"After we've seen what the Alliance Fleet Command had to say."

"Oh, that's easy," and directed the computer, "Fast forward to eleven hundred."

The image flickered while the computer jumped to eleven hundred. Following an exterior shot of Alliance Command Headquarters, it switched to a shot of an auditorium, then zoomed in at someone speaking from a lectern, "It is with profound grief that we announce that, at the time of the attack on Sirius, a team of our scientists were studying a quantum bomb, that had been delivered there only the day before. We believe the attack on the planet may have triggered the bomb's explosion, destroying Sirius and the attacking fleet. That is all, thank you."

Chapter 25.

As soon as we finished our reports and submitted them, Karen and I took the Serenity back to our favourite spot on Nu Indi for the rest of our leave. We wanted to get away from work, but due to our ranks, we had to leave our communications open. We had a few days enjoying the peace and solitude of the crystal lakes before a video message appeared on the Serenity's main comms screen.

Stardate 2515.09.13:
The video was from Mark, summoning both of us to his office at Federation Fleet Command HQ on Zeta Australis. He had arranged our same quarters and landing port for Serenity. Packing up in disappointment, we left Nu Indi, and were landing at the rooftop port an hour later.

"Wow," Karen said as were getting out of the ship, "That trip took us the whole day the last time."

"Those engine upgrades that Maharia did are fantastic," I added.

We dumped our bags in the apartment and went down to Mark's office, where we were shown into his office the moment we arrived. He stood and greeted us, then directed us to sit, "Sorry to interrupt your furlough, but a few things have come up that need both of you here."

I leaned back in my chair, "Does this have anything to do with the fallout from what happened at Sirius?"

He looked at me, nodding, "Yes, in a way it does. This next part is unofficial, but you need to know what has happened. We have received secret communiques from certain ambassadors of planets within the Alliance, wanting to know if it might be possible for the Alliance to engage in secret peace talks with the Federation. So far, members of the Council are holding out for the Alliance not to make the talks secret, but to announce openly that they are willing to commence peace negotiations with us."

I thought for a minute considering his answer before replying, "I think they're stalling for time and need more incentive to come to the table. I have an idea about how we can encourage them, and I'd like outline it for a Fleet Command vote.

Chuckling, he replied, "Well you're going to get your chance at zero nine hundred tomorrow. You, Karen, myself, and the rest of the senior council of Fleet Command will be meeting in my briefing room to discuss that and other matters."

Karen asked, "So why am I going to be there tomorrow Mark? All I can do is back up everything Clay has to say."

Mark smiled, "Well, the two women on the Fleet Council value your opinion and would like to hear your thoughts on some of the actions taken by Clay recently; and probably on what he proposes to them."

It was my turn to laugh, "In other words Dear, they want *you* to judge *me*. Which is quite alright by me."

She looked at Mark, then at me, then back at Mark, "Really?"

By then, both Mark and I were smiling too. He mustered the most serious expression he could, nodded, "Really!"

The following morning, we were both in our dress uniforms when we entered the briefing room and took seats beside each other at the foot of the table facing the Chairman of the Fleet Council. There were four Fleet Council members, one of which was Mark. Also, in attendance by invitation was the Chairman of the Federation Council and four members from the Federation Council. When we were all seated introductions were made.

The Fleet Chairman began, "I would like express a thank you to all present at this extraordinary meeting for their attendance. It seems that the leader of our ghost fleet, Admiral Davis, is not the ghost that the Alliance would have us believe."

After some laughter and a bit of chuckling at his attempted humour, the Chairman went on, "I for one, would like to hear the Admiral's own account of what happened at Sirius. So, let's actually start with that shall we? Admiral if you please!"

I explained the attack on Sirius, starting when we were waiting to ambush the Alliance fleets at Prociyon. After the Prociyon attack, I sent the Triton off to reconnoitre Sirius, because I had already chosen it as my next target. When I started relaying the part about giving the order into hyperspace before the explosion, the Chairman started laughing. His laughter was contagious, and soon others at the table were as well. He said, "Hah! No wonder the Alliance thinks you and your fleet are dead!"

Karen was asked a couple of questions by one of the female admirals on the Council, which she answered to their satisfaction. Then the chairman told us officially, the news that Mark had given us earlier unofficially. He concluded his remarks with, "The Alliance is moving too slowly, and I am afraid they may not even eventuate. I hear from Admiral Kalashian that you have your own thoughts on this, and an idea of how to force the issue. So Admiral, tell us your idea; in detail please.

I took a drink of water, and began, "Very well Sir. Like you, I think they're stalling or waiting for something. Now my idea to force the issue is for the Ghost Fleet to get ruthless, constantly attacking their bases and ambushing any rescue fleets. Also, I wish to strike at their homeland by leaving them a present at their Fleet Academy…" and went onto explain what I had in mind. By the time I finished, everyone in the room was laughing, including Karen. This was the first she heard of my idea.

The other female admiral turned to Karen, "And what do you think of your husband's idea Wing Commander? I gather this is the first you've heard of it."

Karen was quick to respond, "Yes ma'am, it is, and I think Clay's idea will rock the Alliance to its very core. Even if they spend time trying to a way to defuse all the anti-tampering devices and remote-control triggers, they will not succeed. We have used brand new technology they have never seen before. It is time their best people aren't engaged on other projects to give them the upper hand in the war. Imagine their surprise and fury at finding an empty threat. Plus, it's a way of forcing them into peace talks, which they will have to do in case the threat is real, by then, however, we'll be in another galaxy attacking bases. Only you and the Council will know if it works. I believe in my husband I think it will work."

When Karen finished, the chairman adjourned the

meeting for a lunch break. He set our meeting to reconvene at thirteen hundred. We all stood, made our way out and went to the senior officers' mess. Mark didn't join us, because he and the other fleet admirals entertained the five Federation Council Members.

At thirteen hundred the chairman reconvened the meeting. After a short discussion and vote, I was given permission to keep attacking the enemy bases and to try my trick on the Alliance on Earth. I was to continue my harassment of the enemy as I saw fit, or when I was ordered to desist by Fleet Command. We were then informed that the Federation was going to openly move against the Alliance and invade their territory early in the new year. The plan was to attack and hold Alliance planets and establish large fighting forces on each planet taken.

The first three worlds to be attacked were going to be Gamma Virginnis, Beta Hydra, and Zeta Tuscanus. I was told to make the bases on those worlds the first thing I did after depositing my gift for the Alliance on Earth. I said I would, and requested that I be kept informed as to the targets, one by one, before invasion. I was tasked with softening up the bases on those planets prior to Federation invasion. The Council agreed to my strategy and designated Mark Kalashian to keep me informed prior to all planned invasions. Once all the business of the meeting was concluded, I was asked to stand. The chairman announced that I was being promoted and raised me in rank to a Three-Star Admiral, jumping over the two-star ranking. During the seemingly impromptu ceremony he changed my shoulder bars to the three-star bars. The chairman then asked Karen to stand and promoted her to Air Marshal. That wasn't the end of our surprises though.

The Federation Council Chairman stood and walked directly in front of us, "It is with great pleasure that I am able to present to each of you, Admiral Clayton Davis and Air Marshal Karen Davis, the Federation Medal of Honour and Bar. He then proceeded to pin a medal on each of us. When he finished, he remarked, "You two had better slow down. We're running out of medals." At the conclusion of all the presentations, drinks were served, and everyone began to socialize.

After breakfast the next morning, Karen and I paid a return visit to the supply quartermaster. We hadn't even gotten all the way in before we heard, "Not you two again!" It was the quartermaster giving us a hard time, "What have you done this time?" He tried to look stern, but the crinkle around his eyes and the upturned corners of his mouth gave him away. We told him about the surprise promotions and Medals of Honour. He said, "I suppose you want me to update your medal and ribbon bars, don't you?" Then he added, "…and you wanted them yesterday but are willing to take them later today. Am I right?" Neither of us could stop laughing, telling him he was spot-on, and asked if it was possible. He told us it might be tomorrow but to come back later today to check in.

With that task completed, we went up to Mark's office. After we sat down, he addressed Karen, "Karen, you better head down to supply for new uniforms. I've just heard from Fighter Command that your promotion has been confirmed. Congratulations Air Marshal Davis!" He shook her hand; and then, breaking with decorum, leaned over and gave her a kiss on the cheek.

Turning to me he said, "Your promotion is also confirmed. Congratulations Admiral Davis." He shook my hand and started to lean over toward me, stopped, and then burst into a giant smile. When we all stopped laughing, he said, "You know Clay, that if you are promoted any more, that you will lose ship commands, and be transferred to an office job?"

Half in shock at that thought, "In that case, I won't accept any more promotions. I'm a *Battle Commander,* Mark. That's where I can do the most good. I belong on the bridge of a ship, not behind some bloody desk. Make a note; no more promotions! Please, no more promotions!"

He laughed, nodding his head, "Noted, Admiral

Davis!" then added, "Now, what are your plans after you leave here?"

"Well, we've got a few little things to do here in the capital, then we'll head back to Beta Australis. By that time our leave will be almost over. When we get back, the Ghost Fleet will make for Earth, deliver our present, and then do some mischief before we leave. I'll find time to do some research on next year's target planets and start developing attack plans.

He nodded, "That sounds good to me. You need to remember; you are your own boss. If you feel that your crews need a break, then give them one, ok?"

"Understood Sir."

As we were leaving Mark's office, we promised to stop in and say our goodbyes before we left the planet. And now it was time to head back down to see the quartermaster, again. We could hear him laughing inside before we even touched the door. He started as soon as the door opened, "You couldn't stay away, could you? No, your medals aren't ready; it will be tomorrow afternoon."

Karen said, "Actually, we're not here for the medal and ribbon bars; this time. We both need to get new uniforms. Karen requisitioned her new air marshal daily uniforms, which were white like mine, and a new dress uniform. I asked for a dozen shirts with my new three-star ranking plus a new dress jacket and promised to come in the following afternoon to pick up the medal and ribbon bars.

The next afternoon, we went down to supply and collected our medal and ribbon bars. We pinned on our new ribbons in the turbo lift on our way up to the senior officers' mess for drinks and dinner. There we met Mark and told him we would be leaving in the morning after breakfast, so we said our goodbyes that night in the mess. We left early the next morning. On the way back to Akron Base, we spent two more days at Nu Indi, using up what was left of our leave.

Back on Akron Base, we landed in the hangar on the Defiant. We didn't get far into the ship before running into Sirtis and Maharia. Sirtis was all business, "Ah Clay, just to let you know that my new AI nav unit has been wired into all ships. Oh, and I had that dummy Q bomb loaded into one of the Alliance transports we 'acquired'. It's all rigged and ready to go, but I suggest you take me with you when you place it."

I smiled, "Thanks Sirtis. We have the go ahead from Fleet Command to place it. Anything else I need to know about?"

"Yes Clay, there is. Karen, you'll love this too!

Maharia and I have perfected a cloaking device for the fighters! While you were away, we used the spare fighters to test the cloaking. Our results prove that fighters fitted with the device can now be cloaked, and at full speed, without the cloaking being damaged; the first twenty are ready to go into action."

Maharia said, "I plan to make the changes while we travel in hyperspace. I can do it while the fighters are in the turbo tubes. That keeps them ready for combat all the time. I'll need a week to make the changes and I suggest I do one side of the Defiant at a time. Which side do you want done first?"

Karen thought for a minute, "Make a start on the portside tubes please Maharia. If I need my fighters, I'll use the fighters in the starboard tubes. Thank you both, I can't wait to use them."

I asked, "Maharia, if we were to stay here for another week, how long would it take to have all the fighters ready with cloaking?"

She smiled, "With Sirtis helping, and my full work crew, they can all be finished and ready by next Friday Clay."

Karen was beaming when I agreed. "Alright, that's what we'll do. If you're finished by next Friday, I can give everyone a couple days leave and we'll launch after that on the Monday morning."

Karen interjected, "Sirtis, first thing Monday morning, at zero nine hundred, I want you to brief all my pilots as to what they can and cannot do while cloaked, and where the switching is. You can help Maharia after that, but remember I want you to start on the portside."

Chapter 26.

On the following Monday all my ships reported that all crew compliments were at one hundred percent, no one was back late from leave. At zero nine hundred all fleet pilots were briefed by Sirtis on the new cloaking device for the fighters; how it operated, when it could be operated, and where the cloaking switch is on the fighter panel. Located within reach, he wanted everyone to memorize the location so that they did not have to take their eyes away from what they were doing.

For the rest of the day, Maharia, Sirtis, and their crew installed the cloaking devices on the fighters on Defiant. The completed fighters were then swapped out to a destroyer. This allowed the crew to work continuously without having to move from ship to ship. Once all the swapping was done, all of the fighters on all of the destroyers were outfitted with the cloaking device, and all of the fighters that still needed outfitting were safely aboard the Defiant. This would permit Maharia and company to work on the fighters while in transit, and have the job completed before the fleet arrived on location.

The following day, I selected the away team that would take the dummy Q bomb to the Fleet Academy and cement it into the parade ground. Arras would lead the mission using the cloaked Alliance transport. Sirtis and Tark, along with a ten-man security team, and four maintenance workers who would do the actual installation.

I created a sign, actually four copies of the sign, to be placed and fixed to the bomb on all sides, so that it couldn't be missed.

> **DO NOT TOUCH ME!**
> **I AM A QUANTUM BOMB!**
> **I have been placed here by Admiral Clayton Davis of the Federation of Outer Rim Planets.**
> My casing has been fitted with the latest tamper-proof security measures and trembler devices.
> **If any attempt is made to move me – I will EXPLODE.**
> **If any attempt is made to disarm my remote trigger – I will EXPLODE.**
>
> **DO NOT TOUCH ME!**

I then recorded a video message, "To Admiral McManus, this is Admiral Clayton Davis from the Federation of Outer Rim Planets, I have left you, the members of Fleet Command, and the Council of the Alliance, a little present that now sits anchored to the ground in the parade square. I would suggest that it is not touched! It is one of the quantum bombs I captured at Eridani. It has been rigged with extremely sophisticated security measures. Should any attempts be made to remove the remote detonator or move the bomb itself, it will explode.

Now I say to members of the Alliance Council, if you do not sue for peace with the Federation before stardate 2515.12.25, I WILL EXPLODE THE BOMB. I have the ability to set off the bomb remotely. If you comply with this request, I will send you instructions how to disarm the security measures. The choice is yours: MAKE PEACE or Die!

As you can tell, reports of my death by your Fleet Command have been greatly overstated. Up to now I have been easy on the Alliance, but from this point on, all that changes. I am going to start giving you an idea of what total war means, Admiral Clayton Davis out."

The next day, at a meeting of my senior officers, I told them all about the meeting Karen and I attended at Fleet headquarters. We discussed the new AI nav system that Sirtis installed in all of our ships. I told them the status of the fighter cloaking device installation was excellent. Maharia and her team have been able to install cloaking in every fighter on the destroyers and are now working to complete the install in the remaining fighters on the Defiant. This created a lot of discussion about the fighters and their new cloaking abilities. Then we moved to the briefing of the mission on Earth. After explaining the plan, a lot of assumptions were verbalized and joked about.

I let them go for a while, then smiled and got everyone back on task, "Now don't think we are going to leave that present and depart. It may look that way to the Alliance; I hope it does. After the fake device is in place, we are going to attack the Skyring, particularly the military half of it. The fighters will attack all ships that are docked, while we fire on the ring itself. By the time we leave, I want the military part of that ring totally destroyed. That will set the Alliance back years before a new one can be built.

I told Command we were going to get ruthless, and this will be the beginning. When we leave, it will be at half impulse, until all the fighters are back aboard. Then we'll make the jump into hyperspace and head for Gamma Virginnis at warp 20."

We leave the base here at ten hundred hours next Monday for Jupiter in the sol system. Once there, we'll reduce to full impulse and cloak, then onto Earth, any questions? ...Good; dismissed."

Stardate 2515.10.19:
Defiant and the rest of the fleet are in orbit above the north pole of Earth as the away team, led by Arras, gets ready for its mission. They were sitting in the transport with all of their equipment, ready to go. I reminded them, "Remember, you only have four hours to complete the job. You must leave the Academy by zero five hundred. Ok, set your phasers

to stun, and good luck."

After I left the transport, Arras lifted the rear doors, and using thrusters, launched from the hangar deck of Defiant. I watch them depart through the shields and cloaks and headed back up to the bridge.

On the bridge we were able to hear every word said by the away team while they were on their mission. The only people moving around were stunned, secured, and held by the security team until after the mission was completed.

The maintenance team dug the huge hole needed for the concrete, and a chain that would secure the 'Bomb.' This was the part of the mission that would take the longest. When the clock showed the halfway mark of mission time, I sent Torf and my destroyers to reconnoitre the Skyring and keep station until Defiant's arrival on site.

By zero four thirty, the mission clock indicated that they had thirty minutes left to complete the mission. Meanwhile, Arras reported the away team was finished and leaving the planet.

"Well done Arras, you're away with half an hour to spare. Mary send the video file," she nodded as I tapped my comms pin, "Hunter to KD, launch your fighters."

"KD to Hunter, copy that, fighters away!" Shortly thereafter, the speakers crackled, "Arras to bridge, we are safely back aboard sir."

"Thank you, Arras. You, Tark, and Sirtis, please resume your places on the bridge. When they arrived, I said to them, "Each of you is now on my senior staff and will answer to all senior officer calls. Mary, keep monitoring Alliance comms, I want to know what's happening with our present."

"Aye sir,"

"Alright Jonas, let's head for the Skyring."

"Aye sir," he acknowledged.

At the Skyring, Defiant moved into position. "Everyone in place?" I called.

I waited for all replies to come back affirmative, "Alright, it's zero four fifty-five, let's wake them up, decloak and Fire!"

We decloaked and opened up with phaser and photon cannon. I had Defiant launch an SK at the communications centre beside the fleet command office. The resulting blast wiped out both buildings.

The fighters did their jobs and accounted for five flagship carriers, two transports, dozens of destroyers, and were still going. I watched the Skyring start to crumble and break apart under our sustained fire. Jantine's Triton hit the engineering section that kept the Skyring's gravity stable. As the gravity engines went out, the Skyring began to wobble. The wobble grew stronger, the whole structure started twisting, and pieces began to break off and tumble toward Earth. If there had been any survivors, they were certainly doomed.

I called a cease fire and ordered the fighters to return to base.

Looking at the mass destruction, I did some quick mental calculations and put the death toll at nearly two thousand. With a sickened feeling in the pit of my stomach, I turned away from the screen, and quietly ordered, "Cloak, and follow the plan. Go to warp at the galaxy outer marker, mister Major if you please."

"Aye sir," he replied and Defiant started to turn.

As we were making for the outer marker beacon, Mary picked up one of the early news broadcasts and put it on the screen, "It seems that the Alliance outlaw Clayton Davis hasn't died; earlier today he left a Q bomb on the grounds of the Fleet Academy. We take you now to our reporter on site. Morning folks, he said, "As you can see behind me and a ring of security guards, is a Q bomb, anchored in place.

Here is a picture our cameraman was able to get earlier."

A wide shot of the Parade Ground slowly zoomed in on the Q bomb and continued to zoom in until only the bomb and the message were visible. Then the image cut back to the news anchor in the studio, "Well, there you have it folks…" There was a brief interruption as a technician, wearing a headset, dashed into the image and handed the anchor a sheet of paper. "I'm sorry for the interruption folks, but there is breaking news. Just coming in now are unconfirmed reports that the Skyring is under attack, possibly by the outlaw Davis." The technician came on set and interrupted again. "Ladies and gentlemen, it is with great sadness I have to report that the Skyring has been destroyed. All persons on board are feared dead. I repeat, these are only unconfirmed reports, and we will give further updates as they come to hand. In another story…"

I had Mary shut off the broadcast with a slashing notion across my neck, and the screen reverted to our forward view.

Three hours later we came out of hyperspace, reduced to quarter impulse, cloaked, and moved toward the planet's outer markers. After we took up orbit above Gamma Virginnis, I summoned all captains aboard. Arras and I went to my office. All scans of the planet confirmed there was no presence of any Q bombs and that there were, in fact, three military bases on the planet.

While we waited for the other captains to assemble, I wondered if it would be possible to attack all three bases simultaneously and proposed the idea to Arras. She and I were discussing the problems and possibilities as the other ship captains began to arrive. The first thing they saw when they came into the office were images of the three bases on the screens. Once everyone was present, I posed the same question to the group: would it be possible to attack the three bases simultaneously? Some were for the idea, particularly John Hammer, and some were against dividing our forces. After an hour of debate, the discussion was going around in circles, without any consensus of opinion.

"Alright, this is getting us nowhere, what if I send one of the transports down to reconnoitre all three bases, to see if it is, at least, feasible; and in that case, who do we send?"

Eventually it was decided that Arras would go, because her tactical knowledge was almost as good as mine, even though she didn't get to exercise it that much with me being present. Torf would accompany her, due to his battle skills in deciding when to fight, and when not to. They would leave after lunch to reconnoitre and assess if it was possible for a smaller force to destroy each of the bases.

Once Arras and Torf returned, I would reconvene the meeting. Each of them would report what was found at all three locations, and then the assembled group of captains could determine a course of action based upon the latest intel. The meeting was adjourned, Torf stayed aboard Defiant for lunch, while the other captains returned to their ships.

The transport ship was made ready, and food and drink supplies for an additional three days were added as cargo, in case their mission took longer than expected. As it turned out, this addition was a good idea. They didn't return for two days but kept me fully appraised throughout their mission.

When I reconvened the captains' meeting the next day, Arras and Torf reported that the naval base could easily be destroyed by a small force with fighter support. The other two bases were mobile infantry. They reported that while they were observing one of the infantry bases, there seemed to be a lot of refortifying going on. So, after some discussion, they waited until nightfall and Arras, who could pass for human, infiltrated the base. She found that the soldiers were building deep, underground bunkers and passages.

Taking a risk, Arras remained at the base, and joined a work detail, knowing that soldiers often complain while working. At one point she made sure her face was hidden, and then grumbled, "What the hell are we doing this for anyway?"

The answers she relayed sent shivers down my spine. She repeated some of the things she heard, "Some general has stated that this was going to be one of the first bases attacked when the Federation invaded, and he wanted the base made bomb and mortar proofed; so we can fight and move around when the shelling starts."

They both said they saw the same thing going on at the third base. The personnel count was too high and everyone they saw appeared to be very busy; too busy. Arras said she did not infiltrate the third base however, to confirm.

After this disturbing news, I ordered, "Torf, you and Arras stay here. The rest of you, back to your ships, we'll reconvene later, dismissed!"

Chapter 27.

After everyone left, except Torf and Arras, I asked Mary for a secure encrypted video line to Admiral Kalashian's office.

A couple of minutes later, Mark's smiling face came on screen. As he about to speak, I interrupted. "Admiral, I have something here of importance that you need to hear. Captain Arras and Commander Torf, have returned from reconnoitring the three bases on Gamma Virginnis and I want them to share what they discovered with you."

The viewer switched showing them to Kalashian. When they appeared on his screen, he said, "I can see you both, go ahead please."

Arras presented to Kalashian all of the information she had shared with me. Her report was backed up by Torf, and he added details from his observations of the third base. Kalashian peppered them with questions throughout their reports. His final question was directed to Arras, "So captain Arras, you didn't infiltrate this last base?"

"No sir, I thought it prudent not to tempt fate. Commander Torf and I decided to return to the Defiant to give our report sir."

Mark responded, "Well done to both of you. Now

can you please leave so I can speak with Admiral Davis."

"Aye sir," they both responded and left my office. The viewer switched back to him, "Hmm, this is not good news Clay, not good at all. You know what this means don't you?"

"Yes Mark, I do. Apart from all our wasted work. It means there's a spy amongst the hierarchy, and I wouldn't like to be in your place right now."

"Yes granted, that *is* some use to me, but it also means anything you said you were going to do during that particular meeting is also compromised. You could be heading into a trap, and the Alliance knows that your present is a fake. Luckily you did not say anything about the Skyring, otherwise you could have been ambushed there.

His face showed the distress and anger he felt caused by this revelation. I watched his expression change while he was processing what he was going to do. "Alright, here's what I want you to do: total those three bases, then get out; go back to Beta Australis; and then put your people on end-of-the-year leave until the middle of January. I will be in touch with you before then. I want to know where you are at all times but contact me only when I am alone. No one, and I mean no one, is to know where you are or what you are doing except me... Now, I have to do some mole hunting. Good luck son, Deadbeat out."

"Hunter out," and I tapped my comms pin, "Hunter to Snake, are you still aboard Defiant?"

"Aye sir."

"Good, get your captains back on board. We're going to finish that conference. Mary, switch me through to KD, Bucket, Arras, Brains, and Tark please. The conference is resuming, in my office now everyone, Hunter out."

When everyone was assembled in my office and seated, I filled them in on the report from Arras, and my orders from Kalashian. I told them we will all work together to destroy the naval base. While we were doing that, the fighters will hit the first infantry base hard. Our goal is to drive them underground into their new bunkers. Then, when Defiant and the destroyers arrive, we will destroy everything on site. While we're totalling the first infantry base, the fighters are to move onto the last one and do the same thing; drive them underground. When the fleet arrives, the fighters will return to their tubes.

I turned to Sirtis, "Now, will our cannon and phasers be enough to take out the underground bunkers?"

Sirtis turned to Arras, "How deep down were the

passageways and bunkers captain?"

Arras thought for a minute, "Hmm, about fifteen maybe twenty feet at most."

He turned back to me, "No sir, they won't. But, if you fired SK's into the ground, they will compress the earth and force the dirt downward, filling any cavity and collapsing everything."

"Good, thank you Sirtis." I turned to address the group, "You heard the man. Once we destroy the buildings, we'll hit them again with SK's set to penetrate the earth to a depth of 20 feet. We will use the SK's on all three bases. I want all of this done *without* cloaking; even the move between bases. Then, after the job is done, and we are back in space, we will jump into hyperspace at warp 15 making our way back to homebase. I do not care if we go back without any SK's, they will be replenished with the rest of our stores. Once home, we will stand down and everyone will be granted end-of-the-year shore leave. The crews are to report back aboard their ships on January fifteen…Any questions?"

Torf stood, "That's certainly a long leave sir, are we allowed off planet?"

I smiled, "What you do, or where you go with your leave time is entirely up to you; as long as everyone is back, ready to go, on January fifteen. Any other questions? …No, very well, you all know what to do. First base attack in an hour, dismissed!"

The naval base attack was carried out on time, by my destroyers. The Defiant was not needed and did not engage. I just watched my destroyer flotilla completely destroy the base and the ships on the ground. While the flotilla was doing its job, Karen called in that the fighters had commenced the attack on the second base.

All three bases were totally destroyed, and the fighters were back in their launch tubes three hours later. We hit both infantry bases with SK torpedoes to the point where they looked like pieces of Swiss cheese, with giant holes everywhere. When our work was done, we used our upward thrusters to make space. Once in space, we turned toward Beta Australis, and all ships made the jump into hyperspace. Jonas dialled up warp 15 and we headed home.

Karen and I stayed on base for the first few days back, until everyone had left their ships. The first thing I did back on base was to contact Mark and filled him in with details of the mission. We spent the next couple of days trying to decide where to go for our leave. Karen was torn between going back to our tranquil spot at the crystal lakes on Nu Indi or going further afield to the pristine beaches on Altair.

In the end we flipped an old coin I had, and we settled for our favourite spot on Nu Indi, vowing to have a look at Altair the next time.

Before we could take off for Nu Indi, Karen had to replenish the food and drink supplies on the Serenity. The base store expedited her order, and soon the Serenity was fully stocked and ready to go. I sent a message to Mark telling him where we'd be and headed for the hangar. I opened the bunker roof and Karen flew the Serenity out. She parked her at the admin office of our secure, restricted area to wait for me. I closed the bunker rooftop doors, left the hangar, and headed over to admin to join Karen onboard. We didn't need to plot our course. I just pulled it up from the nav log and laid it in.

With her new engines, Serenity was a dream to fly… and quick. We were landing on Nu Indi in no time. The first thing we did when we landed was to undress and make our way to the shore naked. We dove into the peaceful, calm lake and swam side by side, letting all our cares and worries wash away. We reverted back to being two newlywed lovers without a care in the world, except for each other.

For the next two months, we ate and drank, made love and slept, whenever we wished. It was glorious! It all came to an end in the middle of December however, when a ship landed within walking distance of the Serenity. We were glad we had been in the Serenity when the visitor arrived and quickly put on some clothes. I grabbed my phaser pistol, set it to stun, and was getting ready to leave the ship to investigate the new arrival, when I saw Mark Kalashian, standing at the bottom of the stairs, smiling up at me, "Good evening Clay, sorry to interrupt. Let's leave this until the morning; I need some sleep."

"Copy that Mark, breakfast at eight onboard Serenity."

Mark smiled, "Love to. See you then, goodnight," turned, and headed back to his ship.

I never did make it to the bottom of the stairs, so I turned around, went back up, and secured the ship's door. I let Karen know who it was and that he would be joining us for breakfast at eight Her only response was, "Damn! We just can't get any peace Darling. I suppose we're back to wearing clothes again."

I couldn't hide the lecherous grin that popped up, "Well not just yet," and shrugged out of my clothes. She giggled when I gave her a tap on her behind, and we headed back into the bedroom together.

Just before eight, Mark came aboard the Serenity and I showed him into the combined kitchen and dining room. Karen said, "Good morning," over her shoulder as she continued her cooking. I waved him to a seat at the table, which was already set with coffee and Gianna juice. As he took sips of coffee, he remarked on the beautiful spot we'd found.

"Tell me, what sort of fish are in that terrific lake; or do you just swim in it?"

I laughed, "Mainly we just swim here but sometimes I do throw a line in for some different food. There are some really big Tarpon in there."

He laughed, "Hmm, I should try to get away more often, Tarpon you say, a good fighting fish. I must give it a try, maybe after this war is over and done."

Karen set plates of hot food in front of each of us, then grabbed her own and came to sit beside me, "Rule number one, no business while we're eating Mark, wait until after."

He nodded with a mouthful of food and made some kind of sound acknowledging her but waited until swallowing before complimenting her on her cooking. We continued with small talk over breakfast, then moved outside to our lounge chairs and savoured a second mug of coffee.

Once we were settled in, I asked, "Alright Mark, this isn't, a you-were-in-the-neighbourhood visit. *What is going on?*"

He laughed, "Too true Clay, though this is a lovely spot. Ok, to business it is," and went on to tell us he was able to identify the spy. He then filled in the details of how he did it. The spy was one of the Federation Council members. When outed, he suddenly became very cooperative. That is, until he had a sudden, unfortunate accident. It happened in the senate building one afternoon. It seems he tripped and fell over a balcony; a high balcony, a very high balcony. After his 'unfortunate' death, plans had to be changed. The invasion of Gamma Virginnis would still go ahead, but only as a decoy. The main target would now be Delta Pavonnis, followed by Kappa Phoenics, with the third being Tau Bootis.

Knowing Mark as well as I do, I knew he was holding something back, so I asked, "My role in the invasion is *what*?"

He cleared his throat and paused. He contemplated his coffee, and then put it down. Finally, he leaned forward and answered me, "Nothing. You will have nothing to do with these three. I have three other missions for the Ghost Fleet, all dangerous, but something you can handle. The third of which is the most dangerous. First, I want you to hit and destroy the Fleet Academy on Earth, and if you can, Fleet Command as well. Secondly, do the same thing to Fighter Command and Academy on Alpha Centauri. Thirdly, your fleet will rendezvous with Admiral

Tau's number five fleet near the edge of Alliance space and from there, find the ambush we know that will be set and do unto them what they would do to us. Once the feint invasion of Gamma Virginnis is progressing, you will scout the original other two target worlds, and ambush the ambushers, any questions?"

I wanted to know, "What will be we facing on Alpha Centauri?"

Karen responded to that one, "That's where I come in dear, I can tell you everything about those targets. Remember, I graduated from there as did most of my pilots; and don't forget that Command and the Academy are all one. I'll get together with Reece and come up with a plan for you."

I nodded acknowledgement to Karen and turned toward Mark, "Mark, make our rendezvous with Admiral Tau for January thirty. By then we will have found his reception committee, and perhaps destroyed them. As for the rest, I'll play that as I see it. Is that alright?"

"Perfectly!" he replied and then smiled, "Now, while I'm here, I might try for one of those Tarpon, before I head back, if you don't mind me being around."

We both laughed. Karen quickly retorted, "If you

catch one, I've got the perfect recipe for cooking it."

He excused himself and went back to his ship. A little later we saw him on some rocks above the shore of the lake.

Chapter 28.

Stardate 2516.01.15:
The day before Karen and I returned to Akron, we contacted Command and requested permission to fly directly into the hangar. We spent the last night of our leave, wrapped in each other's arms... in bed... on the Serenity. When we arrived at Akron, Command had the roof doors open for us, so we were able to fly directly into the hangar.

Dressed in our uniforms, we went to the wardroom for breakfast. When we finished, Karen went to her office, and I headed for the bridge. I walked onto the bridge and greeted everyone, "I hope you all had a good leave." I was heading across to my seat when I spotted Arras, "Status report Captain."

"All crew present and correct Admiral, and the loading of supplies has commenced."

"Good, I want everything completed by tomorrow night."

I had information for everyone, I directed it at nav specifically, "Mister Major, we launch for Earth at zero eight hundred on Wednesday."

He replied in the usual manner, I gave Mary the up signal, "Hunter to all captains, briefing aboard the

Defiant in fifteen, Hunter out." I glanced at Sirtis, "That includes you chief."

Sirtis turned to me, "Aye sir."

"Mary, inform Karen and Reece that I want them there too," and left the bridge for my office. In my office I put the Alliance Academy up on one screen, Fleet Headquarters on the second screen, and the Fighter Command and Academy on Alpha Centauri on a third.

When everyone was assembled and sitting down, I called for status reports from each captain. They, in turn, answered that all crew members were present and correct, and that supply loading was underway. Jill Torrence was the only exception. She reported that she was missing an engineer, but loading had begun and was on schedule.

"Hmm, ok after such a long leave we all know that's to be expected. Give him until tomorrow morning before replacing him from base personnel."

Then I addressed the group, "We launch on Wednesday at zero eight hundred. Our first mission is to go back to Earth and total the Alliance Fleet Academy, and Fleet Command itself! Our second mission is to do the same to Fighter Command and Academy on Alpha Centauri. The plan of attack for Alpha Centauri is being drawn up as I speak, and I'll update you when it's ready. Mission three is much different from the other two missions. It is, quite possibly, the most dangerous. It is believed that the Alliance is planning to ambush us at Gamma Virginnis. Our third mission is to ambush the ambushers. We are to search for, and destroy, any Alliance forces waiting to ambush our invasion fleet headed for Gamma Virginnis. Then we will rendezvous with Admiral Tau's number five fleet and escort them to the planet. Any questions at this point?"

I continued, "As soon as the invasion is underway, and Admiral Tau tells me they have a handle on it, we will make for Beta Hydra and begin mission four. We have been tasked with scouting out and destroying any and all Alliance reception committees prior to the Federation invasion there. Mission five is exactly the same thing on planet Zeta Tuscanus.

After that, we'll return here and re-arm. No doubt, by then, Command will probably have something else up their sleeves for us. As you can see, it's a pretty full agenda that will take us into early February. The first two target locations and layouts are on the screens, take time to study the details before you return to your ships. Are there any questions?"

There were none. Now it was Karen's turn, so I

directed the next question to her, "Air Marshal, do you have an attack plan worked out for Target Two yet?"

Karen replied, "Not fully worked out yet Admiral, but by this time tomorrow it will be finished and ready to present."

"Very well, we'll all reconvene here at eleven hundred tomorrow, thank you. You are dismissed."

Just before I was ready to leave my office later that morning, Mary paged me, "Admiral, I have the captain of the Oberon on the line for you. Shall I patch her through?"

"Yes please, Mary. What can I do for you Jill?"

She said that her missing engineer had just reported in, "He told me that there had been a delay with his transport ship."

"Very well but tell him he needs to make allowances for those sorts of things. Put him on notice that if it happens again, he will be charged."

"That has already been done Admiral. I read the riot act to him just a while ago, sir. Oberon out."

"Hunter out."

Stardate 2516.01.23:
The meeting reconvened the following day so that I could present the finalized attack plans. "I know that you all have been waiting to hear the finalized plan, so here we go… Mission One: Destruction of the Academy and Fleet Command on Earth - The fighters will attack first. After the fighters engage, the destroyers open fire on the Academy. Defiant moves directly above the Fleet Command building and drops an SK downward through the roof, before moving back into space and recovering the fighters.

Mission Two: Destruction of the Fighter Command and Academy on Alpha Centauri – Because Alpha Centauri is only an hour's jump away in hyperspace, we will attack the same day as the mission on Earth.

We will use the same plan with the fighters beginning the attack and the destroyers following up. Defiant will stay in space to provide protection and will only enter combat if needed. Any questions? Good luck and good hunting, dismissed."

We launched the following day timed to get us to Earth by midnight. As soon as we came out of hyperspace, we cloaked, went to half-impulse and established Earth orbit. The attack began at zero one hundred, to help minimize casualties.

My attack on the fleet headquarters building went

better than expected. The blast from the SK levelled the entire building, instantly turning it rubble. I moved Defiant back into space, and soon the fighters began returning. I watched the demolition of the Academy on the viewer with feelings of great personal sadness. After all, it had been my home for five years.

When the rest of the fleet joined us in space, we jumped into hyperspace. An hour and ten minutes later were in orbit above Alpha Centauri.

Karen led her fighters into the attack on Fighter Command. As the first shots were fired, Torf moved his destroyers into position ready to commence phase two. Karen's fighters destroyed all the fighters on the open ground and were entering each hangar with guns blazing, creating untold devastation inside. Her team made a real mess of the place.

"KD to all fighters, time to leave boys and girls. KD to Snake, we're bugging out, it's all yours, KD out."

We watched the fighters climb out, headed to Defiant, while the destroyers headed in and started demolishing the base and command centre. Nothing was left standing when the flotilla ceased fire and came back up into space.

Four hours later, we cloaked and entered the Gamma Virginnis system. After establishing an orbit, everyone involved in the overnight action was given time off to rest, recuperate, and catch up on lost sleep. The long-range scanners were set to continuously sweep the system for enemy ships.

After breakfast the following morning, we went back to normal rotation. It was Gort who broke the reverie, "Admiral, the scanners are picking up two large formations of enemy ships. There are two fleets hiding behind each moon sir,"

"On screen please Gort, magnify. Can you magnify anymore Gort?"

"Not until we're closer sir."

I pointed up and Mary tied me into comms, "Hunter to all ships, we will move in between the two moons where our scanners indicate there are two large fleets hiding, behind each moon. We cannot make out if there are any transport carriers from this distance. When we are on station, all senior officers aboard the flagship please, Hunter out."

Arras, Sirtis and I were waiting when Karen and Tuckett arrived, closely followed by all the other captains. The viewers were set to maximum magnification and yet there was still no sighting of the transport carriers. I tapped my comms and ordered Gort to run another sweep of the planet, while we worked on the plan of attack. It wasn't long before Gort called me back, "Found them Admiral; on screen now."

We all looked up at the screens and saw eight infantry carriers all in a row; but very little activity on the ground. Torf suggested that they were parked there, ready to move troops to wherever they were needed, on very short notice. Most of the others agreed with his assumption as did I. This new information didn't alter the attack plan at all. It did, however, give the fighters a chance to enter the battle.

The plan was to attack the large fleets by moving in behind the first fleet while cloaked. Defiant would destroy the two flagships using SK's one from each side, while Torf would have his flotilla attack their destroyers, obliterating them with SK's. We would attack the group hiding behind the first moon first, then move onto the second group at point-blank range. I would launch all my fighters, prior to our first attack. They would strike at the carriers on the surface, "Do you think your fighters can disable or kill those carriers?"

Looking at the screen, Karen said, "If they stay like that, and we stay cloaked until the first salvo, it'll be like fishing with a net, sir!"

"Good! Don't leave the planet until they are all dead. If you run into difficulties, call in an SK strike. Understood?"

"Aye sir."

"Ok, you two go brief your pilots. We'll move into attack position behind the first battle group. Arras, we fire on my mark, dismissed!"

I was watching the enemy fleets on the viewer when my comms chirped, "KD to Hunter, all pilots briefed and ready for launch."

"Thank you KD. All pilots; be careful down there. Launch! Hunter out."

A couple of minutes later, Karen's voice came through the speakers, "KD to Defiant, all fighters clear of the ship and heading for the ground, KD out."

Theta announced, "Within torpedo range Admiral. We have an SK locked on each of their flagships, sir."

I ordered, "All ships Fire! Independent action, Defiant out. Theta, target some of those destroyers as well. Jonas, move to the next battle group. Theta, fire the SK's as we come into range, also target some of those escorts."

"Aye sir."

The speakers suddenly barked, "KD to Defiant, we could do with some help down here!"

"Defiant to KD, help is on the way."

Every ship that Theta targeted, blew up. It didn't matter if their shields were up or down, they just disappeared.

"Defiant to Titan, over."

Torf answered, "Titan to Defiant, over."

"The rest of the escorts are all yours Torf, I'm making for the planet to help the fighters, over."

Torf replied, "Copy that Defiant, happy hunting, Titan out."

"Jonas, to the planet, max impulse please. Theta, get ready to target some more torpedoes. Defiant to KD, co-ords please."

"Sending!"

I smiled, "Get your people clear, firing now, transmit results."

Theta fired when I pointed and then nodded that the SK's were on the way. In less than twelve seconds Karen was on comms, "Bang on target Defiant.

thank you! Now we'll mop up. KD out."

Still smiling, I said, "Defiant to KD, above the
planet when you've had your fun, Hunter out."
An hour later my fleet had re-formed, the fighters
were decloaked, and back in their tubes. There was
nothing left of the enemy except some space debris
and the remains of eight transports on the surface.

"Mister Torf," I called, "Status report please."

"All enemy ships destroyed Admiral. We only
found six survivors and have them locked up aboard
Titan. No damage to any of our ships or personnel
in the flotilla."

"Copy that Snake, well done to all. All ships will
remain decloaked and make course for the
rendezvous with Admiral Tau's fleet at warp 10,
Defiant out."

"Copy that Admiral, Titan out."

I pointed ahead, and Jonas who had been watching
me, nodded and the ship started to move.

"KD and Reece, my office. Arras, you have the
con."

With a concerned look on his face, Sirtis asked,
"May I join you also please Admiral. I may be of

help." Wondering what he was about, I nodded, and he accompanied me to my office.

Karen and Reece entered and were waved to seats. I asked for their status report. They reported the troop ships were apparently caught unawares and no infantry personnel were able to exit the carriers. Initially, the fighters were not able to inflict much damage because of the defensive fire.

That's when Karen called for the SK strike; and because the carriers were all side by side, the two SK's sent down from Defiant blew all of them apart. The fighters remained in the area to make sure no one survived before they left the planet.

After their report ended, Sirtis said, "Sir, I may have a way of strengthening the fighters' firepower, but I would need your permission to proceed. I will also have to consult with both of these officers for a time."

I smiled, "Permission granted. The Air Marshal and Group Captain will be at your command. Thank you all, dismissed."

Chapter 29.

Stardate 2516.01.30:
While we waited, uncloaked, for Admiral Tau's fleet to arrive, we were taking no chances and kept our shields up. I prepared and sent a battle report to Kalashian giving a full accounting of the actions taken against the Alliance Fleet Headquarters and Academy, the destruction of Fighter Command and academy, and the smashing into oblivion of four entire fleets and eight troop carriers. I also asked that Tuckett be promoted to Wing Commander.

I haven't seen Sirtis, Karen or Reece since they gave their reports at the captains' meeting. Obviously, they're working on Sirtis' ideas for more firepower for the fighters.

The next morning, comms received a coded message from Tau's fleet. Mary decoded it and reported to me that they would be at the rendezvous by zero nine hundred. She said the message included an invitation for me and my captains aboard his flagship as soon as he arrived.

"Copy that Mary. Say we look forward to his arrival and will join him there; now put me on speakers please. Defiant to all ships, captains to my ship please."

I signalled Mary to cut the speakers, "Mary, forward

this message to the chief engineer, air marshal, and group captain, please."

"Jonas, you have the con. Arras, Tark, with me. Mary, we will be in my office. Let me know when Tau's fleet has arrived."

Karen and Reece arrived; closely followed by Sirtis. They all stood there, grinning at me. I looked at Karen, "I missed you at breakfast, what have the three of you been cooking up?"

"Not all that much Admiral," she was still grinning, "Sirtis has come up with a way for the fighters to carry and launch two SK torpedoes. At present, Maharia is fitting out one of our spares with a couple of SK's for testing."

Sirtis continued where Karen left off, "At present we only have twelve torpedo tubes aboard Admiral, but when we have our next leave, I'll remedy that with enough to equip all the fighters with them if the trial flights work out."

Smiling was contagious, and now it was my turn to smile, "Alright, keep me informed please."

The captains had been arriving one by one while I was learning about the fighters' new torpedo capabilities. When all were assembled, I told them

about our invite aboard Tau's flagship when it
arrived.

Only minutes later, Mary was on speaker, "Sir,
Admiral Tau's fleet has arrived. I sent the co-ords
for his flagship to our transporters."

"Copy Mary, we will beam over, thank you."

The meeting was adjourned, and we all went to the
transporters. When we materialized on the
reception pads aboard Tau's flagship, an escort was
waiting to take us to Tau's conference room. Tau
was Zetian, but a bit shorter than most. After
introducing my officers to him, the formality was
reciprocated, and we all sat at the conference table.

Tau began, "Well, you're earning quite a reputation
Admiral Davis." A Zetian smile is very broad,
unique, and engaging, "Looking at your battle
ribbons and those of your captains, I know all of you
have seen a lot of action; though why you're called
the Ghost Fleet is beyond me!"

I returned his smile, "Admiral, I noticed that your
screens are focused on my ships. Keep watching the
Defiant for a minute please."

I tapped my comms, "Theta, go to ghost protocol,"
and then sat back and watched everyone's reaction.
As Defiant disappeared, two distinct, and quite

different expressions appeared on the faces of those assembled. Half of the people began to smile with a feeling of pride, while the other half displayed shock, surprise, and amazement.

"Admiral, please try to scan for my ship!"

Tau ordered it done, but the reply came back that my ship was gone, it just wasn't there anymore, and he exclaimed, "Beta's balls, what the hell!"

I couldn't stop the smile, even when I ordered Theta to stand down from ghost protocol and Defiant came back on screen. "Davis, how the blue blazes was that done? Beta's balls *that's incredible!*"

"Sorry Tau, that's eyes-only top secret." The smile that I couldn't hide before burst openly on my face at this point.

All eyes looked toward my officers in amazement and wonder; along with a good deal of respect. It was nearly five minutes before we were able to return to the business in hand. Finally, the group settled down and Tau was able to continue, "Right, now back to business. That scoundrel Kalashian told me you are here to protect my fleet and the invasion, before you disappear elsewhere. After your little demonstration, I can well believe him. So, what would you like to suggest?"

"I don't need to suggest much Admiral, except that we move into position, and you carry out your mission. You *did* have a reception committee, but we've already taken care of that."

I went on to give him my action report, which again amazed him. I also told him that we had half a dozen survivors that we'd like to beam aboard his ship.

He accepted and told us to beam them aboard. His security captain tapped his coms pin and alerted their security team. I nodded to Torf and he tapped his, ordering the prisoners beamed to Tau's flagship.

The prisoner transfer taken care of, Tau asked Karen about her ground action. He was given a detailed description of what his forces could expect based upon what we had just experienced. I warned him about the underground bunkering we encountered as well. The briefing continued for another hour to completely fill in Tau and his captains. At the conclusion Tau gave the order to move the combined fleets into position above Gamma Virginnis.

A day later, his infantry had control of the planet. I broached the fact that I had other missions to fulfil. He thanked us for our support and said his fleet could take it from that point and gave me permission to carry on with my objectives.

By the end of the week, we had destroyed the Alliance reception committee at Beta Hydra and the one at Zeta Tuscanus. Including the fleet's, we destroyed supporting Tau at Gamma Virginnis, we accounted for sending a dozen enemy fleets to oblivion. I contacted Admiral Tau to tell him of our success and ask if he was willing to accept an additional thirty survivors from our latest encounters. He accepted the prisoners and told me he would 'take good care of them.'

I filed my report to Admiral Kalashian and told him that we were returning to Beta Australia to give my crews two weeks furlough. I added that Karen and I would be staying at Akron base during that leave period.

Kalashian contacted me at one point on our way back, to tell me that had Reece's promotion to Wing Commander had been approved.

Stardate 2516.02.07:
It was good to be home, if only for a week or two. I assumed correctly, that Karen wanted to start flight testing the modified fighter. The first thing I did, once we were home, was to contact Command for permission to leave our overhead bunker doors open for a period of three days. I specified unless, of course, the base was attacked.

Karen said the team wanted to start test flights on

the newly modified fighter ASAP. With the doors open they could fly in and out without having to request permission every time.

During our time at Akron base, I rarely saw Sirtis on the bridge, and sometimes I was lucky to see him and Maharia at regular mealtimes. Karen would disappear for hours on end as well.

In our quarters I programmed the screen to replay the news for the morning after our attacks on Earth and Alpha Centauri. I sat down on the lounge, leaned back, and relaxed, ready to see how the news broadcasts portrayed what the Ghost Fleet had done.

The Broadcast from the Alliance media was time stamped 2516:01:23:0600. The news anchor began with a greeting, "Good morning to all of our early risers. This is the Morning News. Parts of the Alliance capital were awakened early this morning by the sounds of gun and cannon fire in another cowardly attack by the rebel outlaw Admiral Clayton Davis, and his so-called 'Ghost Fleet'. In this latest atrocity, the Alliance Fleet Academy and the Fleet Command buildings were completely destroyed with great loss of life. Though Alliance forces battled greatly with the outlaw fleet they could not prevent the destruction.
In news just to hand, it appears that the murderous Davis, struck again during the early morning after leaving Earth. He has reportedly demolished Fighter

Command on Alpha Centauri. This catastrophic loss is yet to be confirmed. It's difficult to believe that both attacks, light years apart, could be the work of just **one** fleet. Due to the distances involved, it does not seem possible. We'll give you more news as it comes in throughout the morning…in other news."

Laughing, I muted the sound and made a coffee. Fast forwarding, I looked for pictures of the destruction. When I found them, I slowed the player to normal speed so that I could hear the narration, "These are the first pictures available of the Fleet Academy as it appears today. On the left side of the screen is a photograph of the Fleet Academy taken yesterday. On the right is the way the Flight Academy is today. This total destruction is purportedly at the hands of Clayton Davis, the Admiral of the Ghost Fleet. These pictures of the carnage were taken earlier today of what was once The Fighter Command building. We have been able to attain cell phone video taken by a civilian of the actual attack. As you can see by the carnage all around, he is lucky to be alive today."

The footage showed my fighters blowing up the Alliance fighters on the tarmac and then going inside the hangars to cause more destruction. The image started bouncing up and down, like the photographer was running, and then the video showed the cannon and phaser fire hitting the command building. In the background you could hear the news anchor, "It still remains a mystery how both of these attacks could be attributed to one ghost fleet. The two attacks occurred in one morning only hours apart, in two different solar systems light years apart. Yet, both are being attributed to one ghost fleet. Still chuckling, I turned off the broadcast from the day of the attack and set the screen's date to display today. I was just settling in with today's news when Karen came bouncing into our quarters. She was so excited to share her news she could hardly contain herself. She hurried over, wrapped her arms around me, and gave me a huge kiss, "We have two of the fighters finished. They are now both fitted with dual SK torpedo tubes. We're going to test them after lunch, over on the base bombing range. We test flew them this morning without the ordinance loaded, and they handle *perfectly*. I can't wait for the tests this afternoon.

Maharia has gone ahead and requisitioned the entire base stock of torpedo tubes, fittings, and firing mechanisms. We were able to get enough to outfit one hundred and forty fighters. We can do every one of our fighters *and* have some spares as well. I'm so deliriously happy Darling."

After we had lunch together in the officers' mess, I went to my base office, and Karen went for a joy ride in an SK equipped fighter. It's hard to believe that testing out a high-speed fighter on low altitude bombing runs, and then high-altitude bombing couldn't be boring... but it was. Everything worked as expected. The new SK tubes did not change any of the flight characteristics. They did not lower the top speed of the craft. They didn't change handling. The 'new' fighter was exactly the same as the 'old' fighter in every aspect except one. It was now carrying two of the most powerful torpedoes in the known universe; and every fighter in the Ghost Fleet would have them.

In my office, I received notice there was a video call waiting. I contacted dispatch and had them patch it through. The screen activated and quickly displayed Mark Kalashian's smiling face. "Clay, how you going son? Just thought I'd update you; and before you ask, the answer is 'No,' I don't have anything for you to get your teeth into just yet. Our invasion forces now hold six worlds, without any counterattacks. Gamma Virginnis you know about, but we've also taken; Tau Bootis, Eta Bootis, Arcturus, Xi Bootis, and Fomalhaut. At present plans are being made to invade Barnard's Star and Beta Baranicus. The push is on my boy and gathering momentum.

We've also heard from the Alliance Council asking for peace negotiations. They have requested that the peace talks take place on Epsilon Indi. It's a halfway point and neutral territory for envoys from both sides.

The talks are scheduled to begin at the same time an armistice will go into effect. All of this is scheduled for March one at ten hundred hours. Unofficially, I heard from one of our informants that the destruction of both their Fleet Academy and Headquarters buildings started them thinking. The Fighter Command carnage the same day made them realize that they do not have the ability to stop what you are doing, and that a ceasefire and peace negotiations are the only way. So, well done my boy! I want you to be present with me at the peace talks. What do you say Clay, will you attend?"

Thinking it over, "Yes sir, as long as I can have my cloaked fleet in orbit in case anything goes wrong. Remember they've still got Q bombs available. However, the Defiant's scanners can detect them. What's a juicer target than most of our council hierarchy?"

"You're right I suppose, in that respect; and it *is* better to be safe than sorry. All right you have my permission to station your fleet there. Now all I have to do is come up with an excuse to have you there."

"That's easy Mark. Call me a representative of Vega 13 survivors."

He laughed an evil laugh, "Oh that will be positively a delicious and deliberate insult to them, considering your homeworld was the first bombed. I like it, we'll do it! Now, I'll leave you to get some work done, Deadbeat out."

Not that I am one for politics, but I did like the idea of being present at the peace talks; especially with my fleet in orbit as the only one present.

Chapter 30.

Stardate 2516.02.21:
While the crews were on leave, there was only a small handful of maintenance men around. Sirtis, Maharia, Karen, and Reece were only able to complete ten additional fighters, but that was about to change. This morning all crews and pilots report back from leave. I gave my captains time to check their crews in and then summoned them to the large briefing room on base. Sirtis, Maharia, Karen, and Reece were also told to report.

After finding that all ships' crews were present and correct, I addressed the captains while they were still standing, "Ok sit and let's get down to business. Alright now, there's a lot to get through and a lot to do, so listen up.

One: I want all engineering personnel from every ship to assemble in the Defiant hangar at 0915 today. Arras will move Defiant to the outside runway at 0900.

Two: The pilots on your ships are to fly their fighters to that hangar at ten hundred.

Three: Air Marshal Davis and Wing Commander Tuckett, at 0900 you are to brief ALL pilots on the modifications to be made to the fighters. Have the destroyer pilots made aware when their fighters have to be in Defiant's hangar."

Following a quick sip of water, I continued, "Four: Chief Engineer Sirtis and engineer Maharia, will sort the assembled engineers into work crews, assign one or your own engineers as team leader, and begin the fighter modifications. I want all modifications to all fighters completed by the end of the week. You two are not to do the work yourselves; supervise your people as they do the work. You are only to help if there's a problem. Remember, we will be loading supplies of food and munitions at the same time on all ships.

Five: There will be a senior officers conference every morning at zero nine hundred to sort out any problems. Now you know what needs to be done, get to it, dismissed!"

At each morning's conference, the list of fighters still to be completed grew smaller and smaller. As fighters became available, one of the pilots was tasked with flight testing it. During the flight testing the new tubes were loaded with photon rather than SK torpedos. This process served two purposes; it confirmed the integrity of the installation, and it gave each of the pilots' hands-on experience with the newly configured craft.

By the end of the first day, the five teams had outfitted fifteen of the fighters. A couple of the teams were able to get three fighters completed a little earlier than the other teams, so they pitched in to help the others to finish up. The engineers felt it was critical that a ship was completed the same day it was started. They said they didn't want to have to remember where they left off.

The second day, work went faster. The engineers said the gain was something to do with a learning curve. Today, each team was able to complete four fighters.

With their skills refined, the teams were more accurate and worked quicker on the third day than they were the day before and accomplished outfitting 25 fighters. The amount of time it took to modify a fighter with two new SK torpedoes continued to go down. The teams set Thursday's goal at thirty fighters. By Friday there were only twenty fighters left. Every one of the teams had cut their times so drastically that they were completely outfitting a fighter in about an hour. They had become so efficient that they finished the last ship before thirteen hundred hours.

The Friday morning briefing was different from the others. Maharia had reported there were only twenty-fighters remaining to be outfitted. She also reported that the crews were working more efficiently and said she wouldn't be surprised if they finished early.

After congratulating everyone on a job well done, I said, "If your teams finish early Maharia, you have permission to give them the rest of the day off; but tell them we will be launching tomorrow. Tell them to report back to their ships tomorrow at 0600. Captains, when you get back to your ships, tell your pilots to come back and pick up their fighters.

When all fighters are back onboard, have your crew load each of them with two SK torpedoes in addition to their normal armament. Consider tomorrow to be our pre-launch briefing, because we'll be lifting off shortly after. That's all, unless there's something else."

John Hammer raised his hand, "Sir, there is scuttlebutt going around that a peace is coming. Do you have any news on that front?"

I smiled, "John, you should know not to listen to scuttlebutt (everyone laughed). I have nothing official yet, but unofficially, an armistice has been proposed. As I said, it is not official yet, and until it is, we will not take it for granted. The proposed effective date is March one, but again, it is not official. Anything else? No, alright dismissed."

Later that day, Mark Kalashian was put through to my screen. This time I was able to greet him first, "Hello Mark, I'll be briefing my captains tomorrow morning about our launch for Epsilon Indi and the security mission. That is, unless it's been called off."

He smiled, "No, not in the least Clay. It's now official; the peace conference will go ahead. Tonight, we start broadcasting the news of an armistice on March one. I will arrive on Epsilon Indi the day before the talks are to begin and will transmit the co-ords for you and Karen to beam down. Dress uniforms and no phasers, Deadbeat out."

That night Karen and I were having dinner in the mess when the first of the Federation armistice broadcasts went to air. As expected, it caused a bit of an uproar. It was hard to hear yourself think when everyone started talking at the same time.

Karen's reaction surprised me. "Damn it, I've been busting a gut to get my fighters ready, and now this? Bloody unbelievable!"

I couldn't help but laugh. That was, until she turned on me, "Is that all you can do, laugh?"

"No, I'm sorry. But there's more." I looked around the room to see if anyone could hear us before continuing, "I'll tell you the rest back in our quarters."

Later, when we were back in our quarters, I filled

her in on all that I knew. I told her what Mark passed on to me and about how I forced him to agree to have our fleet in orbit around Epsilon Indi. "So, if something does happen, we will be the only ones guarding the planet. Our scanners can pick up any trace of a Q-bomb, and if the fighters have to launch, Reece can take care of it. You and I, in the meantime, are down on the planet, ok?"

She nodded her head agreeing with me.

At the briefing the next morning, the captains were told where we were going, what we would be doing, and when we would launch. I added, "Admiral Kalashian has requested Karen and me to be part of the delegation, and we have accepted.

While we are down on the planet, I expect you people to be checking the scanners continuously, and challenge any inbound ship heading for the planet. If you think it's something major, let us know immediately. If these peace talks are to progress successfully there can be no disturbances. We do not want anyone to walk away from the table because of an incident. Remember, stay spread out and cloaked. Keep in contact with each other. Arras will be in charge while I'm on the planet. We launch for Epsilon Indi in an hour. You know where we are going. Speed will be warp 10, and standard SOP when we come out of hyperspace at the outer marker, dismissed."

Stardate 2516.03.01:

All my ships are in place ringing the planet, and all last-minute details taken care of when Karen and I stepped onto the bridge in our dress uniforms.

Mary gave a low whistle when she saw us in our dress uniforms, "Admiral, the co-ords have been received and forwarded to the transporter room. Admiral Kalashian is waiting your arrival."

"Thank you, Mary. Arras you know what to do, we'll be back aboard later."

"Aye sir, and good luck." Then Karen and I headed to the transporter.

When we materialized, Kalashian was waiting. After shaking my hand, he gave Karen a kiss on the cheek, "Good to see you both. Well, let's join the circus."

Our credentials were checked at the main entrance and then we had to pass through the body scanner before we were cleared for entry. From there we were directed to the main conference hall where we had to wait to be announced. Somehow Mark had contrived to make us the last to enter the room. Inside we could see delegates from all of the Alliance and Federation planets and systems sitting around a huge table; large enough to seat all fifty representatives.

A few people noticed that Admiral Kalashian had arrived, but it wasn't until we were announced that all eyes turned our way. Mark was announced as the chief representative of Federation Fleet Command, then Karen and I were announced, "The representative of Vega13, Admiral Clayton Davis, and his assistant, Air Marshal Karen Davis."

The stares from the Alliance representatives became openly hostile. Mutters of discontent and calls for my imprisonment began to circulate. We expected this to happen, so Karen and I walked to our seats with neutral expressions and very little eye contact with the other delegates.

We sat next to Mark, made eye contact, and nodded. Shortly thereafter the chairman banged his gavel to start the proceedings. "Welcome representatives. Let me introduce myself. I am Tal Bercan from Epsilon, and currently serve as Counsellor to the Alliance Council. During these talks, I have nothing to gain or lose, and therefore will remain neutral. However, should a deadlock be reached, I will have the casting vote. You have all been introduced. As you can see, the delegations sit on opposite sides of the table. This is by design so that each of you can see your counterparts when you are addressing the group, and they are able to see you. All questions are to be addressed to me first. As Chairman, I may, then call on the appropriate person to answer said query. Are we all agreed?"

As all heads nodded, Bercan banged his gavel and announced, "Let the record show that all representatives are in agreement. Before these talks began, each party was asked to write up a set of propositions in the interest of peace between the parties. The agenda for this meeting will be based upon these propositions. I will first read a proposition put forward by the Alliance, without comment. I will then read a proposition from the Federation, again without comment. There will then be a period for discussion. At the end of the discussion period, there will be a vote on the issue under discussion. The meeting will progress in this manner, voting on an issue before moving on to the next proposition. Do I have agreement?"

Again, all heads nodded. Bercan again banged his gavel and announced for the record, "Let the record show that all representatives have agreed to the format." He banged the gavel one more time to start the discussions, "Very well then, we will move to the first item.

Item One: The Alliance proposes that each side lay down arms and return to the status quo that existed before the war was declared. The Federation proposes that both factions integrate to form one large body of worlds, expanded to include all Outer Rim systems."

He paused to take a sip of water before continuing,

"There it is; now you have the two proposals. Before I open the period for discussion, I wish to remind everyone, you have agreed that all questions and all comments are to be directed through the chair. There will be no side discussions or argument permitted. Now, who would like to begin the discussion?"

The discussion was slow to get going. The delegates were hesitant to say what they were actually thinking. It helped when one member of the Federation delegation elaborated on their proposal by adding details, "The proposed one body of worlds would grant to everyone the same rights and protections that the Alliance was first formed upon. It would also keep in place all elements stated in the original Alliance charter."

This seemed to release some of the tension and wariness and discussion, real discussion began to flow. The idea that all worlds within the new federation would freely exchange knowledge and technologies with each other quickly gathered momentum. Delegates easily agreed to free trade of goods and services to all worlds within the new Federation.

Eventually the discussion came around to defence. It was suggested that both parties would join forces to create one combine military responsible for defending and protecting all planets and systems in the new Federation. This would include all branches; naval, air, and infantry. New military academies would be established for each of the branches, with locations to be determined at a later date.

Time was also a topic of discussion. Delegates quickly realized that both parties were using the same system, so agreement was swift. They agreed that all federated planets and systems would retain the universal Earth calendar for the telling of time.

Provisions for unallied systems and planets to join the new Federation were discussed. Delegates seemed to agree that membership would be by invitation. They felt that the planet or system needed to demonstrate intellectual maturity and technology on a par with existing members of the new federation. They felt it was critical that the potential member agree to adhere to all rules and regulations of the new Federation.

While the main discussion was going on, two Alliance delegates began a sidebar conversation. There was quite a bit of whispering before it ended.

"Those are the proposals," Chairman Bercan said, "you will now vote upon them individually. Item One: Structure for Peace. Each of you has only one vote. You will vote **for** the Alliance proposal of status quo, or you will vote **for** the Federation proposal of combining worlds. There will be no votes against; you are only to vote **for** the plan of your choice. Those are the proposals; first the Alliance proposal, a show of hands please."

I counted only thirty hands raised.

Bercan continued, "…And now for the Federation proposal."

Seventy hands went up; all of the Federation representatives, plus twenty of the Alliance representatives.

"Let the record show that the Federation proposal has been adopted by a vote of seventy to thirty." Bercan wrote down the final vote on the document and then looked up, "We now move to Item Two… At this point I must state that the Alliance has no further proposals. Therefore, all proposals from this point on are from the Federation. Each will be presented, discussed, and debated before being voted upon. Item Two is a name for this new, combined union. It is proposed that the new name be 'The Combined Federation of Planets.' Is there need for debate from the Alliance representatives?"

Their head representative, Council Chairman Bortov, replied, "No, mister Chairman."

Bercan nodded, "Alright, a vote on the new name

please. Those for?"

We all raised our hands as did one delegate on the Alliance side. The lone Alliance vote in favour of the new-name came from the Zetian councillor. Bortov was scowling at him for having his hand raised.

Bercan declared, "The Combined Federation of Planets passes with a vote of fifty-one to forty-nine," and banged his gavel.

"Item Three: Quantum Bombs. It is proposed that all Q-bomb technology data be destroyed, with witnesses in attendance; that all Quantum Bombs be outlawed; and that all types and varieties of Q-bombs held by the Alliance be destroyed, with witnesses in attendance. Does this require debate Councillor Bortov?"

"Yes, it does mister Chairman. These bombs should be kept as deterrents in case this new combined federation will require them as deterrents."

My hand shot up. After being acknowledged by chairman Bercan, I responded, "Mister Bortov, even though you've ordered the use of these bombs, *you* have never seen them used! *I have,* and let me tell you, the death and destruction the Q-bomb causes is **horrific**. They *must **never*** be used again! I made my objections to your fleet command as you well know. Do not talk to me about the need for them, they have only one purpose, the murder of innocents!"

Arguments went back and forth for half an hour before the proposal was put to a vote. The proposal to outlaw Q-bombs passed with a vote of sixty to forty.

Chapter 31.

After the Q bomb vote, Councillor Bercan adjourned the meeting for a lunch break and told everyone to reconvene at thirteen hundred.

When the talks reconvened, Alliance councillor Bortov asked for the floor and was acknowledged, "Mister Chairman, the Alliance would like to add one additional proposal for consideration. I have submitted printed copies of the text but, with your permission, will paraphrase to the body. It states that if these recommendations for peace are accepted by the Alliance Council, the first order of business of the new council will be to arrest Clayton Davis for war crimes; his ships confiscated and destroyed; and their technology become shared knowledge."

I jumped to my feet, and yelled, "WAR CRIMES, you're a good one to talk! You're the one who authorized the use of Q bombs on the four Charbois Quasar system worlds and untold number of additional worlds. You are a BLOODY HYPOCRITE!"

My statement received murmurs and nods from all the Federation representatives. At the same time Bercan was banging his gavel for order, Mark was pulling me into my seat. He whispered, "Shut up! Don't you think we saw this coming? We have something planned just for this occasion, now play along."

The chancellor of the Federation Council stood, asked for the floor, and was granted permission to address the body by Chairman Bercan.

The chancellor said, "My opposite number from the Alliance has proposed a motion which we will soon vote on, however his proposal is one for debate. We will oppose his motion, because our worlds will not stand for the arrest of Admiral Davis. He is a Federation hero, not by fear or the use of Q bombs like my opposite councillor, but by sheer audacity and courage. Even the Charbois people looked on him as their saviour and showed him loyalty, but the Alliance certainly took care of that.

I wonder how many Q bombs will be used by councillor Bortov if these talks aren't accepted by our councils. Certainly more than the twelve the Alliance says they have left. We have it on good authority that Bortov had another seventy moved to underground bunkers on various Alliance worlds, thinking we wouldn't find out about them… I wonder if his own Council knows how many Q bombs, he has stockpiled. My answer to you Bortov, arrest Clayton Davis? Not going to happen!"

Chairman Bercan called for the vote, and Bortov's proposal was defeated sixty-five to thirty-five. Not to be outdone, Bortov proposed that my ships be destroyed, and technology shared as a separate issue.

The chairman said, "There will be no further proposals made from the floor Councillor Bortov; you had your chance for tabling proposals. I will allow this one, but no more! I think this a fleet matter and as the fleet representative, Admiral Kalashian, please make your debated response to this proposal by councillor Bortov."

Mark got to his feet, "Certainly chairman Bercan. In all good conscience, I cannot allow this to happen. Admiral Davis' ships are not Fleet property; let me explain please. Clayton came to me with a proposal, he offered to build, design, man, and equip his own ships in exchange for permission to fight for the Federation, a place to build his ships, and command of a Federation fleet while his ships were being built. Now that sounded like a good idea to me, but I had to follow the chain of command. Clayton's proposal went all the way up to the Chancellor of the Council, who can verify this."

The chancellor nodded as Mark continued, "Eventually permission was granted, and his ships were built; but as to their advanced technology, Clayton assures me all that was lost when the chief scientist overseeing the project was killed. He was home visiting his family on Charbois One and was a victim of Councillor Bortov's use of the Q bomb on the Charbois System worlds. He had a habit of taking all of his work with him wherever he went, so he, his family, and all of his work was vaporized when the Q bomb exploded. No one, not even Clayton, has any copies.

Now, regarding his Ghost Fleet... The ships in Clayton's fleet are unlike any other Federation vessel. They bare no Federation markings. ...and his fighters are like no others. As far as we are concerned, they are his own property, and as such, not subject to seizure by Fleet Command. A man's property is his own to do with as he sees fit, but obviously in this case, it has worked out quite well for the Federation. That is my case against the proposal Mister Chairman."

Bercan said, "Hmm yes, I don't suppose you'd be willing to have your ships seized Admiral Davis?"

Standing, I defiantly said, "No sir, I would *not*. If that were to happen, it would have to be over my dead body!"

Bercan turned to the group, "A motion is on the floor ladies and gentlemen, those for seizure?" Only twenty hands were raised. Mark had swung the vote his way and Bortov's proposal was defeated again.

Bercan announced, "Now that there are no more

proposals from the floor, we continue to item four on the agenda…"

The peace talks continued the following morning, as items on the agenda were discussed and then voted on. Most were accepted, but there were a few that were deadlocked, even after a second round of discussion. Bercan, having the casting vote, voted against three, and for the rest. All in all, the Federation had had a resounding win at the conference but whether the terms would be agreed upon by the respective councils was yet to be determined.

After all items were individually discussed and voted on, the peace talks concluded. In closing Bercan announced, "I think we have all made progress during these talks, it is now up to you to present our results to your respective councils. I further suggest that the armistice stay in place until the terms of these peace talks are voted on by your councils. If they are agreed upon, I further suggest that each of you, the delegates to these peace talks, return here with your current council leaders in three months to attend the official signing of the peace accords. Thank you all for attending, and may peace be with you."

As Mark, Karen and I walked outside, I casually said, "Well that's done. Now we wait to see if the Alliance will accept the terms. If they do, we may be out of a job."

Mark laughed, "Don't you believe it. There'll be plenty to do, what with all the usual outlawry going on and taking advantage of the situation; and you, my boy, will be in the thick of it."

"Alright, we're supposedly at peace, what do you want me to do?"

"Well for the time being, stand down. Give it a month or so; take some leave. Give your crews some well-deserved furlough time. By that time, I'm sure I'll have something for you."

"Copy that! I know my crews will enjoy the furlough, and Karen and I will too." We shook hands, and then Karen got a kiss on the cheek. I tapped my comms, "Two to beam up."

Stardate 2516.06.13:
After returning to Akron, the fleet stood down for six weeks. Karen and I stayed on base for a couple of nights, just long enough to prepare the Serenity for our trip to Altair.

After leaving the base, the flight to Altair flew by (pun intended) entering Altair's atmosphere we did a fly-over exploring the planet. We found one place that appealed to us both and set up camp on the beach of one of the many freshwater lakes. It was much like the crystal lakes we love so much back on Nu Indi. The best part being was that it was secluded and since we had no one nearby, we were able to resort to our favourite wear of nothing.

All too quickly our time away ended and we had to prepare for the ten-day return to Beta Australis where we would have to return to work. I must say that I did find it a bit disconcerting that I hadn't heard from Mark during our time away. No doubt he didn't want to intrude into our leave the way he did the last time.

Once Serenity was in space, Karen programmed in the return course and I jumped the ship into hyperspace at warp15. Once the autopilot was set, we moved from the bridge into our living quarters to enjoy the final ten days of our leave.

Arriving back on base the day before our leave was scheduled to end, we flew the Serenity directly into its place on Defiant's hangar deck. Once Serenity was secure, we made our way to our quarters. I never made it through the living area before I headed for my desk to check for any communication from Fleet Command. Nothing! There was still nothing from Kalashian, and I voiced my thoughts to Karen as we showered and changed into fleet uniforms.

That evening we had dinner in the officers' mess

and most of the fleet's officers were already there. As soon as we entered, I saw Sirtis getting drinks at the bar. When he saw us, he called us over and invited us to join the two of them. He asked what we wanted to drink and placed the order. Karen made her way to the table where Maharia was sitting while I helped Sirtis with the drinks. When Sirtis and I arrived at the table, Karen was asking Maharia about the new AI nav system. Maharia smiled and demurred, suggesting that Sirtis was the one to talk to about that. As he sat down, he said, "Karen, I couldn't help but hear Maharia's answer. What would you like to see me about?"

Karen smiled, "Sirtis, I was just asking your wife if it would be possible to get one of your new AI nav systems fitted into the Serenity?"

He laughed, "But of course Karen. I have a couple of spare units and can fit one into Serenity first thing tomorrow; if that's alright with you Clay."

I laughed, "Sirtis you always amaze me. I dare say you won't be required on the bridge tomorrow. I think I can order you to spend tomorrow fitting a new AI nav unit into Serenity, besides, as the saying goes, a happy wife makes for a happy life." They all joined in with laughter.

After the laughter had subsided, Sirtis wanted to talk business, "There is one thing Clay that I've wanted to talk to you about. I think I have come up with a new engine system, based on the theory of bending time and space, that could give you the ability to jump backwards and forwards through time itself." Then he added, "...I was wondering if you would let me spend some time developing the engine?"

"Absolutely!" came quickly, but then I qualified my enthusiastic response, "As long as you can make it out of the supply stock that we have on hand. Of course, you know if one works, all ships have to have them fitted. We're supposedly at peace now, so you can have as much *time* as you need. *That* is not a pun... to my way of thinking."

He sat back with a small look of satisfaction that would normally go unnoticed, but I picked up the subtle change. Probably because we have been working so closely together over these many months.

"Thank you, Clay, I won't let you down."

The following morning, I stepped onto the bridge at zero eight hundred and asked for a status report from Arras as I sat down.

"Crew are all present and correct Admiral, and all systems are working perfectly. The loading of torpedoes will commence in ten minutes along with food supplies sir."

I nodded, "Thank you captain. Mary, the other ships please."

"Aye sir."

"Hunter to Titan, status report please Commander Torf."

Torf's voice came over the speakers, "Admiral, all ships have reported all crews present and correct, with supply loading to commence in five minutes sir."

"Thank you Snake, Hunter out."

Just after zero nine hundred, Mary said, "Sir, I have an incoming video link for you from Admiral Kalashian."

I smiled, "Very well Mary, I'll take it in my office," and got up and made for my office.

The screen shimmered as I sat down. I was looking at Mark with a big smile on his face, "Well Clay, it looks as if the peace is holding both the Alliance council and ours have passed the resolutions from the talks on Epsilon Indi. The current council leaders from each side will meet there on June Thirteen to sign the peace accords.

Now there's going to be plenty of ships in orbit around Epsilon Indi. I want your fleet there too, same as last time. You'll accompany me to the signing and the talks afterward, which will determine how the new Fleet Command will work and who has what position. The way it looks right now, I and a few others will be making for Earth, where we'll be the senior ranking fleet commanders.

Also on the agenda, will be to establish interim heads of state until the new council takes control the first of December. I want your fleet in place a week before anyone else gets there. Let me know when you arrive. I'll already be on the planet, any questions?"

I shook my head, and Mark said, "Very well, Deadbeat out."

Chapter 32.

Beaming down to the planet, I met Mark and we made our way into the council chambers. As we entered Councillor Makrova, the Chancellor of the Federation Council, came over to greet us.

Using a private conversation voice he said, "If the meeting after the signing goes our way Mark, you'll have to get your bags packed because I'll be proposing you as head of the AFP Fleet Command. I'm also proposing Marco and Crenellen as your juniors to oversee the restructuring of Fleet Command and making Clay your number one fleet commander. Bortov knows that our numbers far outweigh his, so I think we'll get everything we want until the new council is decided. But even then, our representatives should give us majority numbers in the senate council. I should be able to out-manoeuvre him here. However, on Earth it will be touch and go, if our representatives don't back me up. Clay, I'll need you to get me to Earth ahead of Bortov, as soon as we're finished here."

"That won't be a problem councillor as long as you don't mind travelling on a warship. I will make arrangements for you and your staff to have quarters, how many in your party sir?"

He smiled, "Six Clay, and don't worry about discomfort, I've travelled on warships before. Now let's get all this media circus finished first before we move into the important back room stuff. Thank you both."

The ceremony was the media circus that Makrova had predicted and took nearly two hours for the signing of the peace accords before the backroom meetings could begin. The first meeting determined the composition of the interim ruling council for everyday business. Markova was selected as the interim Chancellor and Bortov was relegated to an assistant's role.

The meeting about the administration of Fleet Command went the way that Makrov wanted and Mark became the Chairman and Fleet Commander of the new Combined Federation of Planets Fleet Command. I was introduced to the new fleet high command personnel and named Senior Fleet Admiral of Operations.

My first assignment was to deliver the new Chancellor and his staff to Earth. Then I was assigned the job of patrolling the new and old planets in Federation precincts and dealing with lawlessness and profiteering. During this transition period I was to impose sentences for said crimes as I saw fit until the new Federation policing and law courts directorate was formed, or I was relieved of the task.

After the meeting, I was approached by an Admiral Yeager who introduced himself to me and shook my hand, "I've kept my eye on your exploits ever since you beat the Do or Die scenario back at the Academy. I knew you'd go a long way in your career during the war with the Zytrons and then along came the civil war which split us into two factions. You've gone from strength to strength. I must congratulate you Admiral."

I thanked him, though one part of my mind was wondering: *who is this person? How does he know so much about me, and I didn't even know he existed? Is this a genuine attempt at friendship, or am I being set up for a fall?*

Then Yeager said in a conspiratorial whisper, "I might be able to help you with your new job. Have a close look into the Pavoni Corporation. I've heard from different sources, that their business face is just that, a face that covers piracy of the first order, illicit trade, murder, and corruption. I must say, to my mind, some of their dealings with the old administration were somewhat suspicious."

"Please, tell me more Admiral."

He smiled, "Make it Grant, and I'll call you Clay. Now it seems that the board of directors of Pavoni Corp all come from Pollux. As you know Pollux is still a lawless planet, though we tried many times to quell the crime rate there. I suspect that they are trying to infiltrate the current Federation to become one of the biggest crime conglomerates of our time. They have already brought two other criminal gangs under the thumb and control them!"

Without showing any emotion on my face I was amazed at the amount of knowledge this man had gleaned and wondered how he knew so much.

"This is certainly a lot of information that just happened to have come your way. Do you mind if I ask how you came by all this?"

He smiled, "Of course my boy, I was, and according to your Admiral Kalashian still am, Head of Fleet Intelligence. So, you see we'll be working together quite a bit."

I nodded acknowledgement and smiled slightly. *Well, you certainly walked into that one Clay Davis. At least I'll have help doing this new job instead of poking around looking for trouble.*

Yeager continued, "Now, I know you're taking the new Chancellor to Earth, and I'll be going with you. Thankfully my own headquarters was never in the Fleet HQ building that you blew up. After you drop off the new chancellor, who I for one think is an excellent choice, I'll take you and your main officers to my offices. So, my boy, when do we leave?"

An hour later, everyone going to Earth was aboard the Defiant. After our course was locked in and we made the jump into hyperspace, Mark and I conferred in my office. The chat was mainly centred around Yeager and the information he could provide me to help with keeping order and enforcing the law. The trip to Earth was short, but during that time I informed all my captains and senior staff they would be accompanying me to the planet surface when we arrived.

Stardate 2516.06.15:
We escorted Chancellor Makrova to his new office at the Council chambers and provided security for him there and his new residence until the Chamber's Security Department were able to take over. At that point the Chancellor relieved me and my crew to carry on with our other duties.

Since I bombed the Fleet HQ building and the Fleet Academy, restoration work had gone ahead quickly. Both sites had been cleared of rubble and new replacement buildings were under construction in their places.

Because the Fleet HQ building was still under construction, Admiral Kalashian had taken over the Academy Shuttle Port as temporary Fleet Headquarters. The shuttle port was a four-story structure. He turned the bottom floor into a recruitment station and offices for the Academy and the top floor into temporary quarters for himself and his junior admin admirals Marco and Crenellen. The middle two floors became offices, conference rooms, and briefing rooms.

My officers and I were sitting around Mark's new conference table in one of the briefing rooms listening to Admiral Yeager's report on the activities to date of the Pavoni Corporation. Mark and I heard all of this yesterday when Yeager took us to his intelligence headquarters, but my officers hadn't. Intelligence HQ is situated underneath a concrete office tower in city central. It's a bomb-proof bunker thirty feet underground and can only be accessed through very stringent security protocols.

After Yeager finished bringing my officers up to speed, Mark turned to me and said, "Clay, this group will be your first target. If you can stop their activities, it will go a long way in reducing the crime within the Federation. I have no wish to hear details, only results. How you do it is between you and your personnel. Remember you have carte blanche on how you handle it, any questions?"

"Yes sir. Who do I report to directly sir?"

"This isn't a fleet issue, but a peacekeeping one, and will come under command of Fleet Intelligence. Therefore, you report to Admiral Yeager. Now I have work to do but I'll leave you all with Admiral

Yeager to work out a plan of action."

With that, he and his two assistants, Marco and Crenellen, walked out of the room, and my officers, Yeager, and I got down to business developing a plan of action against the Pavoni Corp. The first of those actions went into force that very afternoon. Thanks to Yeager's connections, every one of Pavoni's authority to trade licenses were revoked. The Pavoni Corporation was very quickly, and very suddenly, unable to do business anywhere in the Federation.

The next morning, wearing civilian attire, I beamed down to the front of the Pavoni building, where I went in telling them I had an appointment with their chairman and board. After reception checked, Mr. Balance did indeed have an appointment and I was escorted to the boardroom one hundred floors up. Entering the room, I noted that each board member looked at odds with their station in life and more akin to criminals, which in fact they were.

I strode to the end of the conference table, scanned the room, and made sure to make eye contact with each and every one of them sitting at the board table. "Gentlemen, I doubt any of you have heard of me. My name is Balance, and you have earned my attention. You are out of balance with the universe we live in through your illegal activities. Therefore, I'm here to announce to you all that you have a choice, cease your operations now, or see them destroyed one by one. You have until the close of business Friday for this to happen. If it does not stop, I'll be forced to eradicate the offender. You will stop your illegal activities, or I will. The choice is in your hands. I thank you for listening, and Good Day."

With that remark, I turned and left the room while they were all too stunned to react. I had myself beamed aboard the Defiant before any action to prevent me from leaving. On the bridge, everyone was smiling as I made my way to my seat.

The following morning Karen and I were in my office, when Mary hailed me, "Sir, Admiral Yeager is on video for you."

"Thank you, Mary, patch him through please."

He was smiling as he came on screen, "A good morning to you Clay, I've just received confirmation that Pavoni's ships are going to attack Fleet supply ships in the Psi Capricorni region two weeks from now. By my calculations I've pinpointed where the attack will probably take place. Here's what I came up with…" The screen then displayed Yeager's calculations and a star map with the location circled. He closed with, "Go get 'em Clay!

With a wicked smile, I cut the video and looked at

Karen, "Time to do our thing darling. I think this maybe an opportunity for your pilots to blow off some steam."

Karen said nothing, but her body language and expression said it all. I could see the excitement and anticipation in her eyes. She couldn't wait! I had Jonas calculate a course to the co-ordinates Yeager had given us and then determine an ETA using only warp 10. Satisfied that we could make the co-ords in ten days and still have time to plan an ambush of the Pavoni vessels, I ordered my fleet to break orbit and make for the co-ords at warp10.

Crew members throughout the fleet knew that going into hyperspace meant there was a good possibility of going into action in the near future. You could feel the excitement in the air and morale went up. There was a lot more smiling going on, and there was a bounce in everyone's step.

When we reached the co-ordinates, we came out of warp, cloaked, and went to impulse drive. We stayed cloaked and waited; but while we waited, we made attack plans. Our attack would be made by the fighters only, all of my destroyers and Defiant were to remained cloaked and not engaged; unless, of course, we were needed.

In a flare for the dramatic, I had myself recorded dressed in civilian clothing, against a backdrop of the local stars. Looking straight into the camera, I said, "Tell your bosses that you have been attacked by Mr. Balance. They know my terms! I will let one of your vessels survive, but which one that will be? That, I haven't quite decided yet, so make sure you heed my words all of you. The end of Pavoni is fast approaching; you have the word of Mr. Balance."

While we were recording the video, Mary received a video message from admiral Yeager. After watching it, I decided to call him back, and had Mary do so. After the call was established, I told him about our plan for the ambush. He reiterated that he had made sure the transports were empty and not carrying anything. He had rechecked the co-ordinates and was certain we would all be in the same area at the same time.

Stardate 2516.06.30.1415:
All of the fighters are out of their launch tubes, cloaked, and standing on station around the Defiant; waiting. Waiting for the supply ships. Waiting for the pirates. Waiting for them to converge. Waiting was the hard part; but the anticipation...The anticipation of action yet to come; that was the best part.

Chapter 33.

As the two fleets converged, the supply ships tried to make a run for it back to the planet they had just left. They also issued a mayday call for help. Watching on the viewer, I calmly ordered, "KD, intercept the pirates! Keep them away from the fleet supply ships and keep all your fighters cloaked!"

"Copy that Hunter! You heard the boss, girls and boys. Go get 'em and stay cloaked!"

I smiled at her remarks, she was starting to copy some of my sayings when giving her orders. "Mary, jam the pirate comms and override them with my video broadcast please. Oh, and record what we see."

"Aye sir."

I turned to Arras and remarked, "That should confuse the bastards, being fired upon from nowhere, and a floating apparition talking to them from space."

Arras was laughing, "It would sure as hell would make me shit myself boss," and we both continued to laugh.

Half an hour later, I called off the attack when most of the pirate ships were floating ruins. I pointed overhead, and when Mary nodded, I ordered, "Snake, have one of your ships follow them to their base, and we'll pay them a visit."

Torf replied, "Aye sir. Oberon, you heard the Admiral, Snake out."

Then I heard, "KD to Hunter, all birds are back in the nest and I'll join you after our debriefing."

"Copy that KD, Hunter out." I signalled Mary to kill the comms. "Mary it's time to send the second video please."

"Aye sir, sending now sir."

I smiled, because the second video I referred to was one to the Pavoni Corp. I had recorded after the one to the pirate captains using the same techniques. I appeared to be floating in space for this one as well, but the message was different, "I warned you what would happen should you defy me. You can now consider your corporation at war with the universe itself. This will be my last communication and your final warning! Prepare to reap the solar flares. You are all considered to be part of an illegal organization... and as such, will be punished. Mr. Balance, out."

That night we stayed in the vicinity of the battle and waited for word from the Oberon. I was hoping the

Oberon was able to follow the pirate ship to their base and send the co-ordinates back. When I made my report to Grant Yeager, he had a laughing fit when I told him about the messages, I sent to Pavoni.

He replied, "Okay… that explains it! I received reports that all of their senior directors were seen leaving the Pavoni building in a rush. They boarded their private ship at the Spaceport and left Earth for parts unknown… at least, for the moment. One of my agents was able to attach a tracker to their craft and we're waiting to see where it ends up."

I got a video call from Mark Kalashian the following morning. It was good to see him. His first question, though, caught me by surprise, "Hunter, glad to see you. You must be getting ready for some shore leave for your crews. How would you like to have your own base here on Earth?"

I was stunned, but quickly recovered. "That would be wonderful Mark…but building a base for my fleet would require a whole lot of space. We would need bunkers for my ships; a supply depot; and quarters for the crews. In fact, we would need everything available on a fleet base: quarters, mess halls, workshops, space to manufacture SK's and other arms, and so on. Why?"

He was laughing, "Yes, I'm aware of that. In fact, I

found an area that will suit all your needs just over the Rockies in part of the Mojave Desert. The complex is just about complete and been manned by special high clearance ground personnel. The base commander is Admiral McManus, an old friend of yours I believe, Clay. I have made it clear to him that you have the final say on all base matters. Besides, you outrank him now. I've assigned you and Karen the entire top floor of the quarters and mess building as your luxurious quarters while you're here on Earth. So, back to my question: How long before you take some leave? I want you to give the base the once-over. If you like it, it's yours. The base is called Vega 13 by the way, and I hope you like it."

I told him that leave for my crews had been on my mind of late, and I was just waiting to finish my first lot of business with the Pavoni Corp. "We should be back on Earth within two weeks if things go well."

"Good, I'll make sure things are ready for your return, Deadbeat out."

I was walking onto the bridge from my office when Mary called out, "Sir, Flotilla Commander Torf is asking permission for a captains' briefing."

"Granted. Also summon my wife and Tuckett please. Arras, with me."

Arras and I made our way to my office where we waited for the others to arrive. Ten minutes later all were sitting around the conference table while Jill, the Oberon captain, gave her report. She said she followed the pirates to a large base on the fourth planet of the Gleiss 229 system. She said the base was huge and had counted almost a hundred ships sitting on the tarmac. She checked the room for reactions before continuing, "Because our wartime protocols are still in effect, I scanned the base. My scanners picked up the presence of a Q bomb. I took scanner readings from all corners of the base, and using a triangulation algorithm, have determined its precise location. Here are the co-ords for the Q bomb sir."

I was as stunned as everyone else in the room. I recovered and tapped my comms pin, "Sirtis, Tark, to my office immediately! " To the group, "We will have no discussion about this until they join us."

It was only a couple of minutes before Sirtis and Tark joined us and we began discussing the presence of the Q bomb and how to destroy it. "Jill, did you scan the rest of the planet?"

"Yes sir, I did. After I discovered the Q bomb's presence and pinpointed its location, I scanned the entire planet. I did not find any other Q bombs on the planet and the only life I found is on the pirate base."

"Sirtis, would it be possible to beam the bomb out of the base and onto our own ship?"

He was shaking his head, "No, the destabilizing streams in the transporter would react with one of the explosive materials in the bomb. It may not explode, but I would prefer not to find out if I'm right or wrong."

I sat back for a minute to think, "Alright we have a Q Bomb on this planet that we can't transport out, and we can't explode it with an SK like on Sirius, because there are too many buildings in the way for a direct shot, so how do we destroy it? Any ideas?"

Tark stood to present his idea, "With a ground attack. We infiltrate into the base well after midnight, attach explosives with timers to the bomb, and make our escape. Then we move the fleet a safe distance away from the planet and wait for the bomb to explode."

I turned to Sirtis, "What do we need to trigger the bomb; and do you have any handheld detectors Sirtis?"

"Yes, I have two handheld detection devices. The charge out of an SK will suffice to trigger the Q bomb. We won't need the whole SK, just the charge, but it must be attached to the Q bomb in the right area. I will need to be onsite since I am the only one who can determine exactly where that spot is.

"I'd rather you didn't go Sirtis. Can't you give Tark the directions as to where to place it?"

"I'm afraid not Admiral., There are a lot of variations to bomb casings and I can tell the most favourable spot on most of them, so I will need to be included on the away team."

I nodded in acceptance, then asked, "Jill, how far is it to the planet?"

She replied, "It's two days away at three quarter impulse power sir."

I looked at Tark, "How many men Tark?"

He replied quickly, "Fifteen sir, all heavily armed."

Karen jumped into the discussion, "I'll fly them down in the shuttle and have one of my pilots as an escort should things go south."

"Alright, sounds like a plan, do what you have to, to get ready boys and girls, we will make for the planet at half impulse cloaked, thank you all, dismissed."

We reached the planet at dusk of the second day, at midnight. The shuttle was ready for loading. Beside it sat the fighter, with Needle as pilot, that would act as escort. I had come down from the bridge to watch the loading and told Tark to make sure that Sirtis was a priority.

After the launch, I returned to the bridge to watch the viewer and listen to the operational comms.

Comms suddenly squawked, "KD to Defiant, this crowd is certainly sure of itself. There are no sentries! I'm parked beside the target building and waiting for our team to return, KD out."

Then, "Needle to Defiant, after half a dozen flyovers, I see no sign of any activity, Needle out."

Comms went silent. Almost five minutes went by before there was any activity. Then we heard, "Tark to KD, we have made our way to the package without any opposition. Brains is working on it as we speak and says he needs fifteen minutes. I will call when we are ready to come out, over."

"KD to Tark, copy that, still no activity here, KD out."

Suddenly Gort announced, "Admiral, I have a ship on scanners that just came out of hyperspace and is making toward the planet!"
I swung my head to look at him when he started

speaking. As soon as he had finished, "Thank you Gort. On screen!"

Arras and I studied the inbound ship intently. It was a perfect match to the description Grant Yeager had given us. We were looking at the ship the Pavoni directors used to escape Earth!

Mary announced, "Sir, I'm picking up a tracker signal. It's on the same frequency that Admiral Yeager passed to us!"

Arras and I looked at each other and smiled, as I thought to myself, *Perfect! We can end this whole thing right here, take the lot of them out in one foul swoop. Gentlemen, you just flew into your own judgement ha-ha. Oh shit, the away team!*

"Mary, patch me into the assault team. Hunter to away team; there is an inbound ship coming your way! The roosters are coming home to roost. You have ten minutes at most to complete the mission. They're probably calling their base right now - Get out of there!"

Tark's response was immediate, "Tark to Hunter, copy that. Brains has finished his work. KD, we are heading to you now, out."

"Copy that Tark, lights are out, and ramp is down, KD out."

A feeling of relief flooded through me as I watched their ship as it approached and prepared to descend to the surface.

Then Jonas spoke into his comms, "Defiant to away team, target will be approaching you from the southwest, over."

"KD to Defiant copy that, mother has all her chicks onboard and lifting off now to the north, Needle form up, KD out."

Squadron Leader Matra replied, "Copy that KD, on your portside, Needle out."

"Hunter to away team, well done everyone, no debriefing required, but Tark and Brains to your bridge stations when you land please, Hunter out."

Ten minutes later, Tark and Sirtis were on the bridge. I asked Sirtis how long they had.

"Two hours Admiral. Now, if you intend to watch the explosion, that is a very large device, I would suggest that we move position, even a high orbit will be too close."

"Jonas, move the fleet back one hundred thousand miles from the planet." While I was giving directions to Jonas, I saw Sirtis holding up two fingers and nodded, "…no, make that two hundred."

Jonas replied, "Aye sir moving now."

Two hours later we watched as the planet exploded into dust. Even at the distance of two hundred thousand miles we felt a severe shockwave, but nowhere near what it would have been if we'd been in a high orbit.

After watching the destruction, I gave orders, "All ships, make course for Earth at warp15, Defiant out!"

Chapter 34.

Stardate 2516.07.10:
We arrived back in Earth orbit and Mary contacted our new base, "Defiant to Vega13 Base, please acknowledge, over."

"Vega13 to Ghost Fleet copy you, over."

"Ghost fleet to Vega13, the Ghost Fleet requests permission to land, over."

"Permission granted Ghost Fleet. Pad one is for Defiant only, your destroyers can use any other pad. Alert your captains that they must land within the pad boundaries because the pads lower into the subterranean hangars, over.

"Roger that vega13 ETA five minutes."

As Defiant flew over the base headed to her pad, I surveyed our new base on the viewer. There were quite a few out-buildings, but not nearly enough for a large base. I assumed that most of the base was underground. As soon as we landed the pad began to lower underground. Based upon what I was able to see as the Defiant went down into her new hangar, I could see the walls were made of steel reinforced concrete and about three feet thick. The upper blast doors of the hangar appeared to be the same construction. They were massive but opened and closed quite quickly.

All crews had already been informed they had a month's shore leave beginning Friday at 0600 hours. Between now and then there would be a base orientation. The first order of business was for crew members to move into their new base quarters; followed quite closely by finding where the mess halls and clubs were. The total base orientation would take two days.

While the crew were moving into their new quarters, my senior officers, destroyer captains, and I were escorted to a conference room, where we met base commander Admiral Neil McManus. Saluting, he welcomed me and the Ghost Fleet to our new base. "It is an honour to have you home Sir. These yeomen," he said as he waved his arm at all the yeomen standing around the room, "are here to show your people their quarters and the mess areas."

Looking at my destroyer captains and my command crew, "Alright, all the usual routine with a new base. Get yourselves acquainted with it before you go on leave boys and girls."

Turning back to McManus, "It's nice to see you again Neil, after so long. I'll need an aircar in the morning. I have to go San Francisco."

"Good to see you too young Davis." Now McManus

was smiling as well. "There's one always available to you whenever you're on base Admiral. If you'll allow me, I'll show you around."

He escorted my captains and me to our first stop; my new office when I was on base and my conference room. From there we toured the officers' mess. At this point, I released my captains to get settled into their new quarters, and McManus took Karen and me to our immense quarters overlooking the Mojave Desert and the base itself. The base was well set up, with each building connected by covered walkways. The ends of each building faced toward the main group of runways for ground operations. Our quarters had floor to ceiling double glazed glass windows with electric controlled drapes for privacy and to control the desert sun in the late afternoon. As we moved through the quarters, there were four large couches in the lounge in front of and around the communication and media screens. The dining area was large enough for twelve people at the table. McManus left us to explore further and stow our gear, which we did after he left.

After breakfast the following morning, I gathered the reports and tapes I wanted to give to Grant Yeager as soon as we got to Fleet Intelligence. Finding our aircar was easy; it was exactly where McManus said it would be. We boarded and our trip to Grant's office in the Fleet Intelligence building only took a half hour.

His yeoman secretary must have announced us, because he met us outside the door to his office, where we shook hands and exchanged small talk. He invited us in and took us to a side table where he had hot drinks and snacks waiting. He gestured for us to sit, relax, and enjoy the drinks and snacks. I passed him the reports, which he started reading while still standing and Karen and I sat down to enjoy the coffee and rolls. He eventually sat at the table with us but didn't say much until he had finished reading my reports. Then we got down to the business of reviewing the video files and voice recordings.

Over the next couple of hours, we worked our way through all of them; playing a portion of the recording, pausing to ask questions, then playing again. He sought out clarification of what he saw and heard for his own peace of mind. Up unto this point he was only asking questions, but when he got to the arrival of the executives, he commented, "Yes, we tracked them to that point, but I was waiting to see if it was going any further before sending you a message."

He wasn't happy to find out that the Pavoni Corp had a Q bomb; but he liked my solution.

"Using their Q bomb to destroy their own base? Holy shit, at least there were only pirates on the planet! …and it means the end of the Pavoni Corp for good, so I don't have to worry about them anymore."

"I thought you might like my solution. Now there is no more problem; they're gone." I sat back with a smile of satisfaction, "...along with that planet."

Next, we talked about my new base in the desert. I filled him in with details about the base and discussed how my crew was adapting to desert life.

"They adjusted very quickly, when I gave them a month's leave."

"I think I could adjust too, with a month's leave," he laughed. Then he took a moment before changing the topic, "Alright Clay, at present I don't have anything for you to get your teeth into. If you don't hear from me before you return from leave, make plans to start a patrol of the Alphecca Hold Galaxies toward the Coreward Reach, but don't cross into the Reach itself. There have been some suspicious transmissions coming from that area, and I'd like to have you nearby should something solid come from my agents in the area."

Karen asked, "What sort of suspicious transmissions? Can you give us an idea?"

"I can't," he looked anguished, "I wish I could. What we've been getting is gibberish. I have two teams of experts working on it. They're still trying to figure out where the transmissions are coming from, much less what they are saying. Once I have something solid, I'll send in one of my agents to investigate, and relay everything to you enroute. Plan on staying in the area for six months; that is, of course, if you can. Make protocol visits to all the known civilized planets, and some of the lesser ones too. I'll leave that for you to figure out. Oh, and send me all your away team data, for my department and the Council, please."

I acknowledged the order and followed up, "Are there any dangers for us to be aware of?"

He nodded, "Yes, at one stage the Zytrons were using a few of the planets in that quadrant for bases. But since the purging of their forces, none of them have been investigated closely except for the major two galaxies. That's where all my agents are based. It will pay to do complete scans of the worlds you plan to visit; and send back your data."

I smiled, "That's SOP for the Ghost Fleet, so no problem on that score. Alright, if that's all, we'll head back to base and go on leave."

We all stood and shook hands before we made our way out of his office and the building. In the car on our way back to Vega13 Karen and I talked about where we would spend our leave and decided to visit the South Pacific Islands, where we could do some diving.

Back on base, we researched some of the area resorts and booked ourselves into a rustic resort in the South Pacific. I had McManus write out a couple of Fleet Command vouchers for our stay.

The following morning Karen piloted the Serenity out of the flight deck hangar on the Defiant and we headed off on our leave. It only took us an hour at impulse power to reach the resort. After landing on one of the resort's pads, we checked in and went up to our suite. The view of the ocean from our suite was spectacular. Sunset had not yet begun, but the colours of the low-angled sunlight bouncing off the shimmering ocean were vibrant and intense. It looked like sunset would be a perfect time for the first swim of our leave.

We quickly stowed our gear and headed down for dinner. We didn't want to miss our sunset swim. Over dinner we discussed the difference between our diving respirators that fitted into the palm of our hand, and all the equipment that divers a couple hundred years ago had to use. We only needed swimming masks and fins, along with the pencil thin respirators that fit into our mouths.

After dinner we went back to the room and got our diving gear. The resort supplied us with a fast water skimmer that had the locations of the good dive spots entered into its navigation system. Once we were above the site I had chosen, we discarded our clothing and went diving and swimming in our usual manner. The water was invigorating and the diving superb. We explored the wreck of a ship that had gone down in the early part of the twentieth century.

The next three weeks went by quickly. We were diving and swimming every day and made love every night. As usual, our time together was all too short, and we had to make our way back to base. We flew back the day before our leave expired and re-housed Serenity in her flight deck home aboard Defiant.

That night we had dinner with Sirtis and Maharia. They told us all about their leave in Norway and then Karen told them all about ours in the South Pacific. Small talk with Sirtis never lasts very long, and he was soon talking about work. He told us that he had completed work on his time and relative dimension space engine. He said that all of his preliminary testing had been successful and was ready to install it into the drive engines of Defiant for final testing.

I had to smile, "Brains, you are amazing! You may get your chance to do just that. We're going into a six-month patrol when we launch and testing this engine may break the boredom a bit."

Nodding and smiling, he said he would start the installation after we launched.

I called a captains' meeting for ten hundred hours the following morning. That would give the destroyer captains time to check in their crew, determine if any members were still missing and the state of their ship. It also gave my senior flight officers time to check the status and condition of their pilots and fighters.

At ten hundred all captains and senior flight officers were in my briefing room. I asked each captain for their ship's status. Every one of them reported all crews at full strength and armament was in the process of being loaded.

Once everyone had reported, I told them the details of our next mission; what it was, expected duration, inherent risks involved, and the possibility of encountering remnant Zytron troops. I told those assembled that I had ordered the quartermaster to load all ships with enough supplies to last eight months, should the mission be extended. After that, we got down to the business of determining what planets, in which galaxies, and in what order we would visit them. Then we plotted all the courses based upon where we would start and where I wanted to finish our patrol.

"Ok, that's done! Great," and then a wry smile

spread across my face, "but you realize of course, that everything could change on a moment's notice, should Admiral Yeager contact us. If any of his agents find out something is going on in our mission quadrant, all plans are off; but we'll face that if it happens, any questions? No…, good, we launch in three days, once the loading of supplies is complete. Zeta Margon in the Margon galaxy is our first stop. We'll go to warp 20, once we're in hyperspace. Alright, everyone back to their duties, dismissed."

Stardate 2516.09.12:
We launched on time and spent twenty-five days in hyperspace before we arrived above Zeta Margon. We came out of hyperdrive, cloaked, and established a high orbit. Once in orbit, I had Torf send three of his destroyers to do a reconnaissance of the remaining three worlds in the system while Karen, Arras, and I beamed down, to the planet to meet with the president of the system Council. We met with him in his office for over an hour, but he couldn't shine any light on the strange transmissions we all had received, coming from somewhere deep in the Alphecca Hold Galaxies. He did say that they had been monitoring them too.

Back aboard the Defiant I asked, "Gort, have you completed your deep scans of Zeta Margon?"

"Aye sir," he replied, "Everything is normal, and no abnormalities were found during the scans sir."

I nodded and thanked him, then caught Mary's eye and pointed up, "Snake, any report from your scout ships yet?"

"Yes Admiral, all three have reported in that they did not encounter anything unusual. They report no activity or any sign of life on any of the three worlds, and I've ordered them to return, Snake out."

"Thank you Snake, understood, Hunter out."

We remained in orbit above Zeta Margon for three days. I allowed an eight-hour shore leave, for all crew which also gave the officers time for a conference on our next port of call.

It was decided that we would move onto Alphecca Major, where Yeager's top agent resided. I decided that once we were there, I would invite him aboard to attend our officer's conference, in the hope that he would be able to provide us additional information on the transmissions coming from the area.

A week later, in orbit above Alphecca Major, Yeager's agent Quantrez, an Arcalian, was on board Defiant and sitting in my office with my command officers discussing the latest news he brought.

The news came from Grant Yeager, via Quantrez, that the source of the comms came from Cirlillian

Three, a small planetoid on the very edge of the Coreward Reach.

Even though we were ordered not to go into the Reach, Yeager had left the decision to investigate to my discretion. We were not, however, to proceed any further into the Reach than Cirlillian Three, unless ordered otherwise by him.

I ordered Rose Jantine of Triton to go ahead as a scout ship and reconnoitre the planet under cloaked conditions, and to stay in direct contact with Defiant at all times. The rest of my fleet would remain cloaked and proceed to the planet at half impulse power.

Chapter 35.

Stardate 2516.09.27:
During our journey to Cirlillian Three, Triton kept me informed on her progress and investigation of the planet. Jantine had scanned the planet and found life signs as well as a Zytron presence. When she reached the planet, she stayed cloaked and sent her cloaked fighters to sweep the planet. They found three Zytron bases before returning to the ship with their reports. Curious about what was really happening in regard the planet population, she sent an away team to infiltrate one of the major cities to investigate. They spent three days investigating before beaming back aboard the Triton to deliver their report.

Apparently the Zytrons that colonized the planet years ago were unaware their homeworld had been destroyed and were desperately trying to re-establish some form of communication with others of their kind. I assumed that this accounted for the garbled gibberish that Fleet Command was receiving from the sector.

Halfway into our journey to Cirlillian Three, Sirtis asked me for a private meeting. In my office he revealed that he had finished his work on the time drive engine, and it was ready for testing I was elated, and couldn't wait to test it out. I already had a plan of how we could use it in our current situation; if everything checked out.

I called a senior personnel conference when the fleet was back together orbiting Cirlillian Three. After everyone was seated in my office, Jantine presented her reconnaissance report. As she finished, I said, "Now there's a way we can check what happened while the fleet ships cleared this planet prior to the destruction of Zytronos. I want a detailed account of when fleet ships engaged with this planet during the offensive. Arras, that is for you to research please."

She nodded, and then asked, "How are you going to be able to check that information Admiral?"

I smiled, "What you really meant to ask was how are we going to check out the information you find, isn't it? Well girls and boys, Sirtis has developed a time engine. It is now fitted to our main drive and ready for testing. I intend to use it to find what we want. But first, Sirtis please tell everyone about the engine and what it will do."

When he was finished, there were a lot of questions, which he handled easily. There were a lot of comments between those assembled as well. When the questions began to taper off, Torf stood and faced me, "Admiral, I must protest. This experiment you are intent on making has dire consequences associated with failure. You're our commander! What happens if you fail to return; or the experiment doesn't work at all. The Defiant and all aboard could be blown to atoms! Please reconsider your decision."

I looked around at the faces of all my captains and crew, everyone showed concern and apprehension.

"Torf, you're my Flotilla Commander. Should what I intend to do fails, you will carry out the task of freeing this world from Zytron influence. Those are my orders. I have faith in Sirtis. Should I not return an hour from my departure, you will complete the mission, and return to our base on Earth. You will inform Admiral Kalashian of the loss of the Defiant and all her crew, that is an order! Am I understood?"

He looked around pleadingly at his Captains and then at me, "Aye sir, you are understood, and I will obey your orders."

"Thank you," I replied, then continued, "Arras, you have a job to do please attend to it. Sirtis, at your console make our return time an hour from now. Please go to your station; the rest of you please wait as I make the ship wide announcement before you are dismissed!"

I tapped my comms for Mary and asked her to turn on all ship's speakers. "This is Admiral Davis to all ship's crew, we are about to make a leap of faith that we may or may not survive. We are about to attempt time travel, something that has never been attempted before, so please all pray to whatever gods you have that we are able to succeed in our mission. Helm, take us to the edge of the galaxy, Admiral Davis out!"

Everyone filed out of the office looking at each other as if they would never see each other and us again. Karen accompanied me to the bridge and sat beside me as I took my command seat. Arras sat on my other side, and remarked, "Sirtis has all the required information sir."

Jonas had just announced we were at the edge of the galaxy when Sirtis ordered, "Warp10 now!"

There was no blinding flash, Defiant didn't explode. We just reduced to slow impulse power above the target planet without any sort of transition. Karen was still holding my hand as I stared in awe. Then I ordered, "Status report Sirtis."

Sirtis replied, "Admiral, the Tadis engine worked perfectly, we're at slow impulse and cloaked, moving to station keeping above the planet's north pole. All we have to do is wait to see what happens next."

"Thank you Sirtis. Jonas go to station keeping when we are above the pole but stay in a high orbit. Mary, I want views from all angles, and put me on internal speakers please."

"Aye sir."

"Admiral Davis to all crew members; we have successfully transitioned our ship in time, and as such have become the first space cruiser to ever have done so. My congratulations to all personnel, Davis out."

Gort announced, "Sir scans of the planet are complete, I have located four enemy bases, three of them coincide with Captain Jantine's recon, the fourth is the largest and also houses Zytron flyers."

I thought to myself, *Jantine only found three. How in the world could she miss the largest base in her scans?* Before replying, "Very well, thank you Gort. I just wonder if…"

That's as far as my pondering got, Gort interrupted exclaiming, "Sir! An Alliance battle group is coming out of hyperspace, and the enemy are launching vessels!"

Immediately I ordered, "Battle stations, all pilots to their fighters, Karen take charge of your fight…"

Again, I was interrupted, this time by Sirtis, "Admiral! You cannot alter the timeline, or you'll change our future!"

I realized immediately what he said was true and ordered, "Belay my last order! No action is to be taken; all we can do is watch what happens."

Karen sat back down beside me again, the command crew and I turned our attention to the viewers. As we watched, Alliance fighters were launched to intercept the enemy flyers coming up from the planet. Fifteen minutes later all the enemy flyers had been destroyed and we watched as the first wave of Alliance fighters headed down to the enemy base followed by troop boats launched from the infantry carrier. The attack by Alliance forces concentrated on the enemy base that launched the fighters. Our long-range view displayed the entire attack. We watched the first flight of Alliance fighters that had attacked make for space and back to their ship. They were immediately replaced by another wave sent down from the battleship. Between the air attacks and the infantry, the enemy base was destroyed; nothing was left standing. All enemy soldiers were killed ruthlessly by the Alliance infantry and the battle was over in less than an hour.

Gort announced, "The battle group is going into hyperspace and leaving the sector sir."

I sat back in my seat with an understanding, a sigh of relief, and a question, "If we decloak, will we be seen from the planet?"

Gort replied, "No sir, that base had the only deep space tracking system, there are no others on the planet."

I nodded and said to everyone within earshot, "Alright, well now we know why the other bases survived, they weren't attacked, just this one. That's why Jantine only found three bases in her scan. There *were* only three bases when she did her scans! Theta, decloak us. Sirtis, adjust your return calculations so we arrive only half an hour after we left, everyone get ready to re-enter our own time, Sirtis, you have control."

"Aye sir, calculations adjusted and going to warp10 now."

As we arrived back in our own time, Sirtis handed control over to Jonas. I ordered Mary to put us in contact with Torf's ship Titan.

When Titan answered our hail, I said, "Hunter to Snake, our mission was a complete success. Have all your captains join me in my office as soon as we re-join the fleet, Hunter out."

Torf replied, "Glad to see you're back sir, and to hear the mission was a success. My men will comply with your orders, Snake out."

One hour later, all the destroyer captains and my

senior staff were assembled in my office looking at the views of the enemy bases still in operation on Cirlillian Three. Then we watched the recordings we made of the attack so many years ago.

"So, now that we know that Tadis works, Sirtis has assured me he has all the parts he requires to build five more engines, and will be assembling them ready for installation into your ships as soon as he can. Once installed, all the Tadis units will be linked together and he will be the only one with control over all time jumps. Now, turning to the matter at hand, we need to discuss how we will attack and destroy all three of these bases simultaneously; and in the process, hunt down the remaining Zytron soldiers and kill them on sight. So, let's get to it!"

We worked together to develop an attack plan. Three of Karen's fighter squadrons were assigned destroyer protection for Hammer's Callista, Meeker's Europa, and Torrence's Oberon. This also included leading the air attack and providing ground cover for the security soldiers from each destroyer as they attacked the bases. The rest of the fighters would protect Defiant, Titan and Triton as we lowered ourselves into the atmosphere to assist our attack force if required. After the main attacks, all ships would withdraw into space. Then we will scan the entire planet for enemy combatants, find them, and kill them. Once that is accomplished, Tark and I, along with a strong security detachment, will beam to every town and settlement on the planet, to inform the local inhabitants of their freedom from Zytron rule.

"Alright, it seems we have a plan of action ready. Now you can all join us for lunch before making your way back to your ships. After lunch, I'll send our plan to Admiral Yeager, along with what we have uncovered and confirmed by Quantrez. All, we have to do then, is wait for permission from the Admiral. It's time for lunch, dismissed."

After lunch, I left Arras with the con, and spent my time compiling two video reports to be transmitted; one to Grant Yeager, and the other to Mark Kalashian. The one to Mark was to be marked with security classification 'Above Eyes Only', while the one to Yeager was marked 'Eyes Only'.

I started with the one to Yeager, telling him everything that had occurred since we picked up agent Quantrez on Alphecca Major. I edited out all references to Sirtis's Tadis engine before attaching the video files of the captains' conference and our plans to retake the planet. I finished by saying that I would await his confirmation before any of the plans were undertaken, then had Mary encrypt and send it to him at his office.

The one to Mark Kalashian took longer to compile. In addition to everything I sent to Grant Yeager, I attached quite a few video logs of my conversations with Sirtis, and some of Sirtis's personal logs which I, as captain, had access to. In the reference box of the communique I stated that it was For His Eyes Only. I put TADIS in the subject line, without any other reference. In the body of the text I explained that TADIS refers to a new type of engine, the Time and Dimension in Space (TADIS) engine. I then went on to explain the new engine in detail.

Because I marked it Above Eyes Only, the security classification meant that I had to encrypt it myself before Mary could transmit it to him.

Chapter 36.

Stardate 2516.10.01.0900:
I was in my office after breakfast, while Arras had the con, when Mary called me to say, "Sir, I have Admiral Yeager on video link and he's asking to speak to you."

I smiled, "Thank you Mary, patch him through please," and turned to face the viewer.

The screen shimmered and Grant's face replaced what I already had on screen, although he was smiling, I noticed the look of concern on his face, "Looks like I sent you into an ugly situation Clay, sorry about that. I've looked at everything you sent me and consulted with Fleet Command. Your situation was taken all the way up to the Fleet Commander. To say Kalashian wasn't impressed is an understatement; he's livid! But I've been told to pass onto you that you are to go ahead with your attacks and post battle visits to the settlements. Then in his words, 'you get your ass back here.' To save you sometime, when you drop Quantrez back on Alphecca Major, let him have all your data and he can transmit it to me instead of you sending it from Cirlillian Three, and I can review it before your return. Good luck Clay."

I smiled, "Well I really didn't think you needed to go to Mark for the ok. I intend to launch the attack in a couple of hours. If all goes well, we should be clearing here in about a week."

He smiled, "Not bad my friend, your estimation agrees with mine. The real reason behind going to fleet was that this has stirred up a gorgon's nest because quite a few planets were never properly cleared of those bloody robots. It's just one more thing that stupid Bortov was responsible for, and now we're going to have to clean up his messes while he was chancellor. Anyway, see you when you get back Clay, Yeager out."

After our video exchange, I had Mary call a senior officers briefing in fifteen minutes time. I finished what I was doing and then got ready for the briefing.

When all of my senior officers were gathered in my conference room, I asked Karen, "According to our attack plan, have you selected which squadrons will be going with Callista, Europa, and Oberon yet?"

She replied, "Certainly have, and they will all answer to Bucket who'll lead them, while I command the others."

"Good, thanks dear," I replied. "Reece don't forget that those ships will have to land so that their troops get on the ground before rising again for the attack."

Tuckett smiled, "I'm on it boss, they'll be well

covered while on the ground."

I nodded before saying, "Good, in that case everyone can deliver their briefings to their crews. You all know what you're doing, and which bases your hitting. Hammer I'll be your support, Torf will be Oberon's, and Rose you've got Europa," Looking at the clock, I continued, "We attack at eleven hundred, so there's plenty of time to prepare, good luck all, dismissed."

As our ships dispersed from formation to orbit above their target bases, the fighters launched. Arras on the con ordered Defiant to follow Hammer's ship Callista down into the atmosphere. While I listened to the radio chatter of our group, Mary was listening to the other two groups. The normally mundane chatter changed quite suddenly. You could hear the excitement in Reece's voice, "Bucket to Callista, attacking now, you are clear to land and disembark over."

Hammer was quick to reply with a crisp, precise, and short response, "Hammer to Bucket, copy that landing now. Hammer out."

As I looked to Mary, she had one hand thumbs up, and then... the second thumb came up, meaning that both other attack groups had landed. Watching the viewer, I ordered, "Theta, take out that tall building where all the main defensive fire is coming from, it's concentrating too much fire on Callista."

As Theta was replying, I saw the SK hit the building I was talking about. When the smoke of the explosion cleared, there was nothing to see. The building had been vaporized.

The Callista was quick to respond, "Hammer to Hunter, thanks, that was starting to piss me off! I don't know how many shooters there were in that building before you hit it with the SK, but I know there are zero now. All my troops are out now and moving, and I'm coming up to one thousand feet. Callista out."

Since none of the fire from the base was coming anywhere near Defiant, I ordered, "Hunter to KD, take your fighters and give Bucket a hand down there."

"KD to Hunter copy that, come on ladies let's join the fun, KD out."

Fifteen minutes into the attacks Mary announced, "Admiral, group three has taken their objective, and asking if they can be of help to anyone."

Thinking quickly, "No, get them to gather their troops, make for space, and remain on standby."

"Aye sir."

Quantrez, who had been standing off to the side observing, piped up, "Why do that Admiral, we could use some help here don't you think?"

I turned to locate the voice. When I spotted Quantrez, a small smile was beginning to spread across my face. "Oh, I don't think so... ," and my voice trailed off. I pointed toward the screen. It was a tiny gesture, but Quantrez saw it and turned his head to watch the action.

Just then the speakers came alive, "Callista to Defiant objective neutralised, ground troops are just doing the mopping up, have sent the fighters to help group two, over."

I couldn't help but smile when I looked back over my shoulder at Quantrez; then I replied to Hammer, "Defiant to Callista, well done John, thank you. Go ahead and land to retrieve your troops, Defiant out."

Then we heard a call from Karen, "KD to Hunter, all fighters returning home, not much more we can do now all bases have been taken."

I replied, "Hunter to KD, well done, and thank you all, Hunter out." Then I turned to Quantrez, trying to hide, without much success, the smile that was spreading across my face, "So...I hate to say I told you so, but..."

He was laughing and bowed saying, "I bow to your better wisdom Admiral. Job well done!"

Signing to Mary, I said, "Defiant to all ships, well done all. When you've finished, we'll rendezvous in orbit above the north pole and you can all decloak, Defiant out."

Two hours later, the debriefing session with celebratory drinks was in full swing in my office. I told them all that we were going home after the planet sweep the following day, and my visits to every city and settlement. To Quantrez I said, "I'll be giving you all the data so you can transmit it to Yeager when we drop you at home. He's already expecting it to come from you."

He smiled, "Thank you Admiral, can you please tell me honestly if we actually did travel back in time?"

I laughed, "No, of course not, that's just a trick we were playing on you, and the footage you saw was taken from the archive's on Earth of Battle Group One's footage. No ship has been able to time travel yet, but it would be interesting if we could though, wouldn't it?"

"You know you almost had me convinced I was shitting myself as the jump was attempted. Well played sir."

I hoped that my lie about the time jump had put Yeager's agents mind at ease. The last thing I wanted was our time jump capability being made public.

That evening, I had a video call from Mark Kalashian concerning that very thing, and we talked at some length about it. He was all in favour of the Tadis engines being installed into all of my fleet and wanted to know how soon the rest of my ships could be ready. I told him that while I was doing my planetary visits on Cirlillian Three, Sirtis was going to install the five that were ready into the rest of my ships. That way all my ships would have the same capability by the time we got back to Vega13 base on Earth. This then turned the talk to the reason I was being recalled home.

He told me that he'd finally got hold of the complete list of planets that had been invaded by the Zytrons, as well as a list of ones that had supposedly been cleared of them. It was going to be my job to investigate each one in turn and clear every one of them that Battle Groups One and Two had supposedly cleared, but still had Zytrons remaining on them.

Battle Group Three which had been commanded by Kalashian himself, had been meticulous in clearing every planet we came across during the counter offensive.

After I told him that it was going to be a tall order for just my fleet, he said that we'd talk further once I got back to Earth. That brought his call to an end and we said our good-byes. After that, I ordered the lights out and went to join Karen in our quarters... where we had drinks together before going to bed.

The following morning, I had the fleet spread out around the planet and had them all independently scan the entire surface for any Zytron presence. After three separate intense sweeps covering the whole planet, no Zytrons were detected. Therefore, it was time for me, Tark, and a security detail to start our visits of goodwill.

I placed Arras in charge, strapped on my phaser pistol, and was about to head down to the flight deck when Gort handed me a tablet with the locations of all present hamlets, villages, and cities loaded into it. I joined Tark and the security detail in the shuttle and saw that Karen was already at the controls. I nodded to her, meaning we could go and noticed that she and the co-pilot were also armed. We descended down to our first hamlet, without our cloaking in operation. I ordered everyone to set their weapons to stun.

We landed in plain sight on the outskirts of the first village. As the rear loading ramp was opening, Karen joined the group. The co-pilot powered down the shuttle and would remain on the craft, we exited down the loading ramp. I decided we should wait near our ship to demonstrate that we meant no harm to the villagers. While we waited, I saw a group of men begin to gather on the edge of the hamlet. Since we made no moves of aggression, the group began to approach our ship. When they were close enough to hear us, I asked to speak to the headman of the hamlet.

The person I had asked, was about six-foot tall with black hair and pointed ears, he was carrying a makeshift rifle that fired old fashioned bullets, and had a pistol strapped to his thigh, much like our own holsters, but again, the gun looked old fashioned.

He spoke up and introduced himself, "My name is York, and I am what you call the headman here in Yabba. These are all members of our council." He waved his arm to encompass the men behind him, then continued, "Who are you and what do you want, Stranger?"

I smiled and took a couple of small steps closer to him. Responding immediately in a warm, friendly tone I said, "My name is Admiral Clayton Davis of the Combined Federation of Planets. My companions and I are here to do something for you and your village York. We have defeated all the Zytrons on your world. All I need you and your council to do, is just hear what I have to say. Would that be acceptable York? May I address a council meeting?

He thought over what I had said, then nodded his approval, "That is acceptable Admiral, as long as you're willing to hand over your weapons until we have heard what you have to say."

"In the interest of peace, I accept." Then I turned to my group and ordered, "Lower and hand over your weapons people."

I carefully took my phaser from its holster and handed it to York. The men with him had moved forward and were handed the away team weapons. York said, "Come Admiral, you and your friends may follow me and have no fear. I will have all the council meet us in our meeting house."

As we followed York, the councilmen carrying our weapons followed. York called a youngster to him and said something to the boy before the boy rushed off. We were led inside a large building and invited to take seats. Not long after we were seated, six women emerged from a door in the centre of the back wall carrying trays full of a piping hot beverage. It smelled wonderful, like a cup of freshly roasted coffee does in the morning… but it wasn't coffee. The reddish-brown liquid was inherently sweet and smelled of vanilla and cocoa. While we were enjoying the beverage, the meeting room began to fill with villagers. As the villagers took their seats, I realized that we were at the head table.

York stood up and raised both outstretched arms in a gesture that quieted everyone. He reached down with his right hand, picked up his gavel, and raised it back up for everyone to see. Then he banged it on the table one time, "Alright now, we all saw these people land outside our village, and their leader assures me that they mean us no harm. He has asked to speak to our council, but this involves our whole village, that is why you have all been called here. I will now call on their leader, Admiral Clayton Davis of the Combined Federation of Planets, so we can hear what he has to say. Let any questions be kept until after the Admiral has had his say, Admiral please."

Gathering my thoughts, I stood and moved to the centre of the room, "To York, your council and to all of you; you have all heard who I am. Along with me is my wife, my senior security chief and a small security detachment. We have come here today to inform you of the latest news regarding your planet. That is finally after all these years, been freed of all the Zytron invaders.

Ever since our first counter-offensive against the Zytron invaders, years and years ago, our forces have been locked in a civil war. That has now been resolved. My recent orders are to investigate all of the known planets that were invaded by the Zytrons. We discovered their presence not long after we arrived here and have been in battle with them at their bases for the last couple of days. Those battles ended yesterday when we destroyed their final base. We have scanned your planet again for any more sign of them and did not find any. I am presently informing all communities of this world that they have all been eradicated. There are no Zytrons alive on this world anymore. Your planet has been freed of their presence!"

Chapter 37.

Stardate 2516.10.30:
After my speech to the inhabitants of Yabba village, our weapons were returned, and we were treated like heroes. The village celebration lasted more than three hours before we were able to head back to the ship. The whole village went with us to see our liftoff as we continued on our tour to the next community.

We used the Defiant to travel between communities, carrying the good news to each of them. We were able to complete our circuit by noon on the sixth day. Everywhere we went we were treated like heroes after hearing our news. Sometimes during our tour, the initial meeting was strained, as was the case with York at Yabba, and in other cases, quite friendly. We only had to surrender our weapons three more times after the Yabba meeting, but because we surrendered them quickly, our hosts gave us the benefit of the doubt. Many friendships were established, and I believe that future Federation ships will be welcome, should they lay over on Cirlillian Three.

The morning after we completed our goodwill tour, we left the planetoid and set course for Alphecca Major so that we could take Quantrez home before we headed home ourselves.
We dropped him off there, along with copies of all

the data relating to our mission on Cirlillian Three. He promised to transmit them to Yeager when he got back home and settled in. As soon as he was on his way, I had my fleet set course for our home base on Earth.

Sirtis began the Tadis engine installations as soon as we achieved warp and had them up and running in every ship the week before we arrived back home. The final step was to link all of the Tadis controls to his console on Defiant. As soon as we landed at Vega 13 base, I gave all crews a three-month furlough.

Karen and I stayed on base because of all the administrative paperwork that needed my attention…and then there was the two-hour conference with Neil McManus about the base administration. I wanted him to understand what he could sign off on, and what would require my personal authorization. This would allow him to go ahead with any changes to base personnel, up to, and including any re-construction or new construction he deemed necessary, when I was away on fleet operations.

Then we had to report to Yeager's office in San Francisco. There we spent another three hours going through the mission reports that Quantrez had sent to him. We also discussed the good relations I had established with the local inhabitants of Cirlillion

Three.

After that he suddenly asked, out of the blue, "Now what's this I hear about your ship being capable of moving through time?" Grant wanted to know.

I laughed to cover my consternation at the fact that my lie to Quantrez hadn't worked, but I continued the lie with Grant, "Well, all that was a joke we played on Quantrez to make him think we had that capability. Obviously, it must have worked Grant. Later I admitted to him that it had all been an elaborate joke."

He started to laugh, "Well you certainly had him convinced, so much so he made it a part of his report. So, the Defiant isn't capable of time travel?"

Looking him in the eye, I replied, "No, no ship is."

He looked at me seriously, "Clay, you're a good liar, but not good enough. I **know** you're lying to me. You see, Mark Kalashian and I have spent a good deal of time together lately, and he already told me all about your fleet's time travel capabilities. Nice try!"

I looked downward and apologized. He laughed and said, "Thank you for the apology, but if I hadn't known already, your statement to me would have been believed. That is a compliment my boy! You almost had me convinced, and I knew better. Keep that up if it ever comes to light. Now we have to meet Mark, the three of us are expected at Fleet Headquarters, let's go."

We left our aircar just outside the intelligence building and joined Grant in his limousine to fly the rest of the way to Fleet Headquarters.

During time we were away, they completed construction on the Fleet HQ building. Now that it's finished, we noticed how similar it was to the fleet building on Zeta Australis. We landed on the roof port and headed for the turbo lift. On the way down Grant explained that the building was one hundred and fifty floors high. The first fifty were normal fleet offices and floors fifty-one to fifty-four were offices for Kalashian's junior fleet officers. Kalashian himself, as Fleet Commander, had the entire fifty-fifth floor for his office, briefing rooms, large conference room, and living quarters.

The sixtieth floor was the senior officers' wet and dry mess, while floors fifty-six to fifty-nine were wet and dry messes for all other ranks. Floors sixty-one to ninety-nine were living quarters, while one hundred and one to one forty-nine were quarters reserved for visiting officers' and visiting dignitaries. Floor one hundred was the restaurant floor, with numerous restaurants ranging from fast food to fine dining. Floor one fifty was reserved for

security ops and access to the roof hangar.
The turbo lift in the new building was even faster
than the one I remember from the old building. In
seconds we were stopping on the fifty-fifth floor.
When the doors opened, we were facing a reception
area with one male and female fleet receptionist at a
huge, long desk. After giving our names, we were
escorted into Kalashian's secretarial captain's office.
The captain then escorted us into Mark's new office.

The first thing I noticed when we walked it was how
big it was. My eyes darted all over, trying to take it
all in at one time, but without much success. The
first thing I focused on was Mark's desk. It was
massive; and the top was conspicuously empty,
except for the built-in control devices and a couple
of hand-held remotes. There were four comfortable,
executive chairs gathered in front with room to
spare. The wall behind the desk was entirely glass
from floor to ceiling. I didn't see any privacy
drapes, but Mark later explained that none were
needed because the glass was self-tinting, controlled
by one of those devices on the desk. The wall to
Mark's right were a myriad of video display screens.
On closer inspection, I realized it was actually one
giant screen that could be sub-divided into as many
smaller screens as necessary. Grant, Karen, and I
were still standing and looking around when Mark
spoke up and invited us to sit in the lounge area to
our right and came to join us.
Almost immediately, Mark got down to business,

"Well Clay, I've been going over all the communiques and reports from your last mission, and for that reason, I had you ordered back. Because of what was in your report, I believe the situation has changed. Therefore, I'm taking you back from Grant, because this is not only an intelligence operation, it has become a fleet problem as well.

Your next mission is going to be long and involved. I've split the list of planets into two parts; the first part of the list will be looked after by conventional fleets and infantry. Each fleet will have carriers as normal and will be assigned specific targets. The second part is yours. Your part of the list includes all planets and systems beyond Cirlillian Three in the Coreward Reach and extends all the way to where the Zytronos homeworld was. From there you'll continue to investigate worlds and systems beyond that point for the following six months, unless you receive information that will take you further, any questions?"

"Yes sir, Just a couple. My fleet has all of the same needs as all of the other fleets, yet we don't have adequate troop personnel for a mission of this magnitude. This mission will require the services of a mobile infantry carrier, and therein lies the problem. There's not a carrier built that can travel at the speed my fleet does, nor do they have any of the other refinements my fleet possesses. Is there anything that can be done about that? Secondly, this mission will mean a long time in deep space; it could be years before we return. My crews will need rest and relaxation from time to time. What's to be done about that?"

Mark looked at me gravely while I outlined my concerns, and then thought for a few minutes before responding, "Alright Clay, I've heard you; now let's tackle your second problem first shall we. Here's my solution to it: You take advantage of the worlds you clear. Land and have down time after it's cleared and give your crews a week or two of shore leave whenever you feel it's necessary before moving on. Then after six months, have a month of R and R along the way. Do you agree with my proposal for leave?"

Mark's solution to the problem was perfect, so I was able to answer him straight away. "Yes, that would work, but there's still the problem of infantry."

He smiled, "Yes, I'm aware of that, and have been mulling it over since you first brought up. I've come up with an idea that I think you both will appreciate. I sent a personal request to Chief Sirtis, while you were on your way back to Vega 13, asking if he thought it possible to design an infantry carrier with all the capabilities of the ships in your fleet. When he replied in the affirmative, I ordered him to start working on the design. After you dismissed everyone for leave, he and his wife brought the plans to me. I told him that his designs were approved on my order and that he was to go to Beta Australis to start construction of the new troop carrier."

Recognizing how significant this would bc to thc fleet and the missions, Karen unfolded her legs, sat up straight, and leaned in. Thinking about all of the possibilities, I could hardly contain my excitement, "Well, don't stop there! Keep going, I want to hear more."

Both he and Yeager started laughing, and Mark kept smiling as he continued, "That carrier will have all the capabilities of your ships. It will have its own armament capable of holding off any attack. It will carry two thousand mobile infantry troops and their boats, as well as fifty Javelin-class fighters. This will give your fleet the infantry capability that you have longed for. Oh, and you'll also get another destroyer to join your fleet. As usual, you'll have your pick of personnel and pilots. He paused briefly to pass me a computer flashdrive before continuing, "Here are the personnel records of all fleet personnel and all pilots."

Taking the flashdrive, I said, "I won't need it, but Karen will, for the pilots. I'd like Tor Wensall for captain of the carrier. I want to stay with the moon theme and would like it to be named Ganymede. Also, I'd like the destroyer named Phobos, with

Guy Anderson or Julia Morris as its captain and let them pick their own command crews."

He replied, "Alright, I'll see what I can do. I thought you'd like my proposals; now let's all go get some drinks and have dinner. Oh, by the way, I have assigned the entire 101st floor to you as your permanent home away from home. I think you'll find your quarters, office space, and briefing rooms to your liking. The door pads are already programmed to accept both of you, and if Grant was doing his job properly, your aircar should be in the skyport."

"Yes Admiral," responded Grant, "That's already taken care of; bay twenty Clay."

With that, Mark stood up, "Come on everyone. Let's go get something to celebrate with." We all stood and followed him out to the turbo lift and rode it up to the senior officers' wet mess on the sixtieth floor.

In the bar, we easily found a table for four. Mark ordered a bottle of scotch, four glasses, and a bucket of ice. Once the drinks were poured, he raised his glass. "A toast," he proclaimed, "To the Ghost Fleet's newest members… to Ganymede and Phobos."

We all raised our glasses and repeated, nearly in

unison, "to Ganymede and Phobos."

While we finished the bottle of scotch, Karen and I filled Mark and Grant in on our exploits from the latest mission.

The following day, after Karen had completed picking the fifty-five pilots she wanted for the new ships, we went down to see Mark in his office. We presented ourselves to his secretary and were immediately escorted in and directed to the chairs in front of his desk.

After we sat down, but before we had settled into the plush chairs, Mark got right down to business, "Clay, I can give you Wensall for Ganymede, but can only give you Julie Morris for Phobos… Anderson was killed during the war after you let him live, but Morris has destroyer experience."

I nodded, "That's fine Mark. I can work with that. Morris will be a great addition. Believe it or not, Karen has finished her list, so I'll let her talk."

Karen leaned across the desk to return Mark the flashdrive he'd given us the day before, which now included her list of pilots. As soon as Karen had finished her list, I made a copy of the flashdrive for future use. Then Karen leaned back and began, "Even though this is already on the list, I'd like Squadron Leader Matra, callsign Needle, promoted to Wing Commander for the new carrier. That is the only change I am requesting; the rest is per the list."

Mark replied with a smile, "Alright Karen, I can almost guarantee you'll get who you want, and also the promotion for Matra you've asked for. Now what are you two up to for the rest of your leave?"

"Well, first off, we have to find a physicist at the university. I wish to pose a hypothetical question and need to talk to someone that works solely in that field who may be able to give me an informed answer. Then we're off to Akron Base to visit Sirtis. I want to see his plans and get an estimate of when the ships will be available. After that, we may go to our favourite spot on Nu Indi before returning to Vega13."

He smiled, "Ah you lucky people, I can still remember that tarpon I landed there. It's a lovely spot. First, I'll order construction started on the additions to your base. After that, I'll have your new personnel transferred to the base to report there the day after you return from leave. Your new quarters on the 101st floor will always be available for when you need to come and go, especially seeing there will be a lot of that in the future. Now, if that's all, I've got work to do. Get out of here and enjoy your leave."

After being dismissed, we returned to our new

quarters on the 101st floor. Karen gathered what we needed for our leave, while I contacted the university to tell them what I required and ask if there were any faculty members who could help me. Then we left the skyport at headquarters and flew to the university, where we met a panel of three physicists.

Chapter 38.

Stardate 2517.01.18:
Standing in front of the panel of scientists I stated my query, "Gentlemen I've been told that you are the top physicists in your field of time manipulation and travel. Now we all know that time travel is theoretical, but what happens should certain events happen whilst one travels in time? That has yet to be answered, as a layman I know that rules apply to time manipulation, and my query to you is, though hypothetical, if a person was to enact actions in his future, and then travelled back through time say ten years, would the events that were enacted in his future still be unaltered if he did nothing to change his past?"

The scientist in the middle of the panel spoke, "Admiral, you pose an interesting question. We do know that events made in the past will influence our future timeline. What you have asked however, is the complete reverse of past to future. Instead, we must contemplate and theorize about future to past realities. We and others theorize about time manipulation and is a point worth study for physicists like ourselves. Though certainly at this juncture we could not give you a quick answer, this could take months between ourselves and others in our field before we would be able to attempt any sort of definitive answer; if you can wait that long. I would suggest you inform us how to contact you when we come up with a consensus of opinion to answer your question. Is that at all possible sir?"

I told them to contact Mark Kalashian, the present Fleet Commander at Fleet Headquarters, and he would see that the information got to me. I thanked them for taking on this challenge and told them I looked forward to hearing from them. With that, Karen and I left the university and returned to Vega13. On the way back, I called Neil McManus to set up a meeting for later that day.

At the meeting I told Neil about the base extension work that Kalashian had ordered and why. Neil said that if the ships were ready prior to the work being finished, they will have to sit out in the open on the main runway, and I agreed. The extra quartering will have to take precedence due to the influx of the new personnel. I reminded him that we will need enough command Ghost Fleet comm pins and normal crewmen pins for the incoming personnel, as well as more than enough uniform cloth patches for all the infantry troops. He said that we had more than enough comms pins, and that the patches were already on order and will be on base before the mobile infantry battalion arrives.

Using the speaker on Neil's desk, I contacted Mark and filled him in on our decisions about the base extensions and how the buildings for quartering would have to take priority. He agreed with us and said the first of the four thousand construction personnel would arrive the following morning. I told him I'd call him later for Serenity and the call ended.

While Neil and I were in conference, Karen went to our quarters and packed everything we would need for our trip. She also requisitioned stores from the quartermaster and had them loaded aboard Serenity. Karen took her out of the bunker and parked near the admin building.

After my meeting with Neil ended, I made my way from my office to join Karen aboard Serenity. She said that we were good to go as we settled into our command module seats. Receiving permission from base control for our liftoff, Karen piloted Serenity into the sky.

When Serenity was in space, I called fleet comms and had them patch me through to Kalashian. When he came on the viewer, I told him about the question I had posed to the scientists, and that they would be contacting him to pass on their theories to me. He asked me why I needed that answer, "My ships will all have time jump ability, and I was thinking I'm likely to be away on this mission a long time, so I was contemplating if when the mission was done, we could Time Jump back to earth, so that we arrived back say a year after we departed."

He started to laugh, then went into a thoughtful mode, "This time jump thing is sort of mind boggling, but if altering the future doesn't alter after you've done it, then jumping back would certainly be worthwhile. Now I see why you posed that query to them; anyway, yes if I get anything from them, I'll pass it on Clay, what's next?"

"Right now, Karen and I are aboard Serenity bound for Beta Australis. I may contact you from there."

"Good boy Clay," he replied, "Be safe, and have fun both of you, Deadbeat out."

As we approached Akron base, we were given the co-ords for the new ship building offices and hangar area and granted permission to land. Taking in the site view of the new works as we descended, we could clearly see were Ganymede was being constructed out in the open and also Phobos. We saw a large hangar next to the admin building when we landed. We looked inside before heading to admin. and were amazed to see row upon row of new Javelin class fighters all painted with the ghost fleet insignia and colouring.

While we were looking at all of the Javelins, I saw Maharia out the corner of my eye. She was inspecting a fighter and making notes on her tablet. We called to her as we approached. She was overjoyed to see us, and with a sweep of her hands,

"What do you think, fifty-five brand new fighters, ready to go, and waiting for their parent ships to be finished, in the next hangar the infantry boats are being made, all with our normal refinements."

I remarked, "Absolutely wonderful! How have you been able to accomplish all of this in such a short amount of time?"

She blushed, "Well, we've got over ten thousand work crews here and thirty thousand more working on the two ships. Come, let me take you over to admin to see Sirtis. I was just headed that way myself, now that all my inspections are complete."

With her in the middle, she linked her arms into ours and walked us into the admin building. Taking the turbo lift to the third floor we found Sirtis sitting behind a desk. As soon as she saw him, she announced, "Look who I just found husband!"

He looked up, then jumped out of his seat, a giant expression of joy spreading across his face. "Clay, Karen, I'm so happy to see you both!" He ran, or almost ran, over to us so he could shake my hand and give Karen a kiss on the cheek.

When all of the pleasantries were over, we sat, and the conversation turned to business. It was me who began, "I couldn't believe it when Admiral Kalashian told me that he asked you to design an infantry carrier for the Ghost Fleet. He filled me in on all of the details and then said he had sent you to Beta Australis to begin work immediately. I was certainly happy, but it's not the sort of leave I was expecting you both to take."

Maharia answered, "Oh don't worry, we both prefer to work. Holidays are so boring or disappointing."

I smiled, "Well, yes they are sometimes, but I'm a great one to talk. Karen and I are here, but my excuse is that an Admiral's work is never done. Sirtis, we've already seen the new fighters; how about you show us your plans and drawings of our new carrier?"

He couldn't have been happier and brought up the carrier's finished design on screen. "This is what the carrier will look like. What do you think Clay?"

As we looked at it, I whistled, "It's shaped much like the Defiant, only bigger. It's incredible Sirtis, truly incredible! Will it be capable of the Ghost Fleet speeds? What about cloaking? What about time travel? What about all of our other refinements?" I found myself talking faster and faster.

The words came rushing out; all the while Sirtis was using that satisfied smile again. He nodded at each of my questions and continued to nod as he filled us in with details, "Yes sir, it will have a top speed of warp 28, but cruise at 20, just like every ship in your fleet. It will have the same cloaking capabilities. Yes, it will be able to time travel with the rest of the fleet.

Both of your new ships will have every refinement the rest of the fleet has. If you'll look at the monitor, I want to point out the other features: the fighter launchers are here and here." He used a screen pen on his computer to show and mark in red the areas he was showing us, "…and there are twenty-five torpedo launchers here and here each side, Phaser arrays here and here. Phaser and Photon cannon, here, here, here, and here. The infantry boats will all come out here on both sides. Like Defiant, this is the bridge and it's layout will be exactly same as yours. The new destroyer will be identical to our present ones. The Tadis Engines will be installed the same time as all the others and all I will have to do is tie them remotely into the control on Defiant. That part is only an hour's work. Then, all we have to do is paint on the Ghost Fleet emblems and colouring, and the name of course, which I hear is Ganymede for the carrier and Phobos for the destroyer."

I nodded, "Those are their names. This is truly incredible Sirtis, and I like the shape… I love your designs Sirtis; and Wensall is going to love them too. Now the big question; how long before they're ready?"

Before replying he looked Karen and me in the eyes, and then paused, "Sir, with our current work force, working three shifts per day, both ships will be ready for battle four months from today.

Following his statement, Karen exclaimed, "What!"

I was flabbergasted, "Belar's balls! Four months! If you can do all this in four months, I'll let you do nothing for the first month on our next mission except eat, drink, and sleep."

We spent the rest of the day going over every last detail with Sirtis. I told him to contact me at Vega13 base when the ships are ready and loaded with enough food and SK's to go on a mission of untold duration, "Plan on three years, but I don't think it will be that long. Let's supply for four years, just to be safe". It was at that moment I decided all of my ships would only use SK torpedoes; all standard photon torpedoes would be removed.

That evening we had drinks and dinner with Sirtis and Maharia. We spent the night on Serenity and took off early the next morning for Nu Indi, where we spent the rest of our leave. It was far too short… again, and we had to head back to earth. As usual, we arrived back the day before our leave was scheduled to end.

The first day back from leave, I was so busy that I spent the entire day in my shore office. I didn't even have time to board the Defiant. I did take time however, to ask Arras for the status report.

She reported, "All crew are NOT present and correct sir. We're missing both senior chief Sirtis and chief Maharia. All other ships have reported all present and correct."

"Very well Arras, don't worry about Sirtis and Maharia, they're away on a special mission. Now pass along to all ships that I request all captains and all my senior staff outside on the base parade ground *now*, that includes you and Tark, copy?

"Copy that Hunter, Defiant out."

I contacted McManus and ordered him to muster all new fleet arrivals on the outside parade ground, then I made my way there as well. I stood beside McManus, before tapping my comms pin twice, which connected me to the parade ground loudspeakers, and directed all senior command crew stand with their captains and another group of the new pilots. Once that was done, I turned to face everyone assembled, "Welcome to you all. I'm Admiral Clay Davis; and **welcome to the Ghost**

Fleet!

After allowing the surprise murmurs to die down, I continued, "At the present time, the ships you will be joining are still being built, so you won't have much to do for a while, except a lot of training, especially for the pilots and command crews.

Your new ships have capabilities you've never heard of before... and won't believe, once you see them in action. I want each of you to become exceptionally proficient with your new ship. Your life depends on it; as does the life of every other crew member on your ship.

Every one of you will receive a new comms pin today. The pin is easily recognizable by its special shape and colour. It's very special and does everything your old comms pin did, and a whole lot more. To get your Ghost Fleet comms pin, you will have to turn in your old comms pin. The old ones will go into the bucket. While the command crews will be issued their gold Ghost Fleet comms pin by me, pilots will get theirs from Air Marshall Davis. After this muster and you all have your new pins, you may return to your quarters for the time being, while the senior staff and I go over a few things. Pilots, however, are to remain on standby. Somehow, I think some of your training will start today. When I, or my comms officer, call for a senior staff meeting, it means I want captains, wing commanders, and above unless otherwise invited. I am calling a senior staff meeting in my conference room for right after this muster. Thank you to each and every one of you. Welcome Aboard!"

Karen took a box of regular Ghost Fleet pins from the stage, as did McManus, while Needle and an aide each grabbed a bucket. Before Needle moved off, I had her put her bucket down and I passed her a gold comms pin and shook her hand with a smile. Then I grabbed the box of gold pins and we moved to our different groups. Torf joined me and followed with a bucket, to both the new captains and their command crews groups.

Every member of the command crews was given a gold comms pin. As I gave Wensall his, I smiled, "Just wait until you see your ship, you'll wet yourself, you old goat."

"Ah, that's yet to be seen laddie, what a pretty looking pin."

When I got to Morris, I gave her a big smile too, "Welcome to Ghost Fleet Julie."

She responded, "It's a pleasure Clay, I see you got Torf here too. Hello Torf."

"Hello Julie," Torf replied, "Glad to see you."

Chapter 39.

Stardate 2518.01.18. 2245:
I was the last person to enter the conference room and everyone stood while I made my way to the head of the table, "Everyone be seated please, and we'll get down to business."

I glanced at all present before I began, "Now this meeting has new members present, and tomorrow we have the mobile infantry arriving on base, so their commanding officer and second officer will be joining you in the call for senior officers. When we are in space, all calls will be held in my conference room aboard Defiant because my office isn't big enough." All the older hands laughed at my comment. I smiled, then continued, "You will now stand and introduce yourselves so that you all know each other before the jarheads arrive. Julie, you're up please."

Julie stood, "I'm Captain Julie Morris, callsign Jools, I will captain the Phobos destroyer. Way back in the old Alliance, I was the Captain that married the Admiral to his wife Karen, the Air Marshal."

All present had a short laugh as Julie sat down. Then Wensall stood, "Well, most of you already know me from previous battles. I'm Tor Wensall, callsign Windy, and I'll be the captain of the troop carrier Ganymede."

Next in line was Needle, "I'm Wing Commander Jane Matra, callsign Needle, I will command the fighter pilots aboard Ganymede."

After her updated introduction, the rest of the old and new hands continued introducing themselves to each other.

Once all the introductions were made I said, "Now for the older hands, a couple of things; I want you all to unload your supply of Photon torpedoes, that goes for the fighters also. From now on, all ships in the fleet will only arm with SK's. Torf, I need you to have your ship ready for training purposes. Your command crew will be replaced by Captain Morris and her command crew. Your regular crew stays onboard and shadows the new people to offer advice if needed, so they get to know how we operate. You will stay onboard to offer insights to Julie about our methods, and to observe her command crew."

I continued, "Captain Arras, that goes for you too aboard the Defiant; you'll be doing the same with Captain Wensall and his crew. The bridge on Ganymede will be identical to ours on Defiant."

She nodded her acknowledgement as I continued, "Air Marshal Davis, Wing Commander Tuckett, Wing Commander Matra; you and your senior officers will use the fighters from Defiant and start checking out the new pilots. Acquaint them with the refinements to our Ghost Fleet fighters. For the live fire and torpedo runs use up all the photon torpedoes presently on base and the old ships supply. Start your training today please, get them used to our launch pads. This needs to be accomplished ASAP because after tomorrow Defiant won't be here. When Defiant departs you will have to use the standard runway."

Without getting up Karen replied, "Aye sir, we'll have an early lunch and commence at thirteen hundred."

I nodded my approval, then turned to Wensall and Morris, "Hopefully you two were given manuals on your new ships (they both nodded). Good. If there's anything you need to brush up on, do it this afternoon; tomorrow it's for real, Torf, Arras, your command crews are to stand down until further notice, but they aren't to leave base."

They both acknowledged in the usual manner. Before I dismissed everyone, I told them there would likely be a senior officers' meeting the next day, "I will know for certain after I talk to the incoming infantry commander and would make the call on short notice. Defiant and Titan are not to start crew training until after that."

After everyone had gone, I called McManus to my office for a meeting. He told me the infantry troops would arrive at zero eight hundred the next morning. I told him that I'd be available to greet them on the parade ground for a short briefing.

Changing topics, "Neil, at present all ships are unloading their stores of Photon torpedoes. Use them for training purposes until all stocks are gone. As of now, all ships are to be loaded only with SK's, make sure you keep plenty in stock. Now, how many uniform patches for the infantry did you get hold of?"

He replied, "What I did was allowed each man seven combat uniforms, one for each day. Then I multiplied that by the number of troops, then tripled the initial order. We now have forty-five thousand on hand, each in bundles of seven. Their own Q store was finished last week and supplies to it have been arriving ever since. Why I say this is because leftover patches will be kept there after our initial handout.

I smiled and nodded, "I think that should be enough then. Alright, anything else?"

He smiled, "Yes Clay, I know that you'll launch on a mission soon. Now that all the quarters and required buildings are completed, I have postponed all heavy construction of the hangar bunkers and the ancillaries until after you launch. That way no ship is here to be looked at during construction, and it'll keep the runway clear of any machinery as well."

I laughed, "Neil, I can always trust in you to think of those incidental details. I wholeheartedly agree with You. Well done, now let's head off to lunch."

After lunch, training had begun and the Photon torpedoes were being removed from all of the ships, I made a video call to Mark. When he came on the screen, I said, "Hunter to Deadbeat, sorry I didn't catch up with you while I was at Akron, but there wasn't much news. Today has been the first back from leave. All the new fleet personnel arrived this morning and their training is already underway. Tomorrow the infantry contingent arrives at zero eight hundred. All the light construction has been completed and the heavy construction on the bunkers and the ancillaries is postponed until my fleet launches so that construction workers won't be able to see them, then McManus will have them start."

"Good Clay, concise report as usual. When will you be likely to launch, so I can coordinate all the fleet launches for the same day?"

I smiled, "Sirtis told me the ships would be battle ready four months from the day I was there. That gives him another three weeks. Then he has to travel to Akron and back here, so add another two weeks, say roughly six weeks."

He laughed, "Well that's a bonus, I was thinking at least two months. Alright my boy, keep me informed, Deadbeat out."

The following morning our mobile infantry detachment arrived. As I addressed them, platoon commanders distributed the new uniform patches; then the troops were marched off to their quarters. Their leader and his senior officers joined me and Neil in my conference room where I met them individually.

After the meeting, I asked them to remain and called a senior officers call. When everyone was present, I said, "Alright boys and girls, allow me to introduce to you General Wade Daxer, callsign Dax, and his 2IC Colonel John Muckins, callsign Bull. I see from your smiles you all think he's got the right surname to be mobile infantry."

My joke went over well and was even laughed at by Muckins himself, I continued, "As we discussed yesterday, every one of you now present in this room are to report whenever a senior officers call comes; so its's fair that Dax and Bull know you all and what you do in the fleet that their attached to, so around the table please, you know what's required."

Each person stood and announced their name and role, then welcomed them to the Ghost Fleet. Then I said, "Alright Dax, Bull please take your seats, now the training: Luckily, I know what's happening with the pilots because of my inside knowledge (all laughed quickly). They will practice using the launch tubes before Defiant and Titan leave, after that will be target practice and getting used to their cloaking.

Tomorrow Wensall, you and Morris will launch Defiant and Titan respectively for a week's training in deep space. Arras, Torf, let them see our warp speeds as well as some gunnery practice, and keep me informed of your status, alright any questions? …No, then dismissed!"

Two weeks later, all the deep space training was complete, Defiant and Titan had returned a week earlier, and Karen's fighters were back aboard Defiant. All ships had been loaded to the brim with SK's and were ready to go. The only thing my fleet needed now was full provisioning prior to launch.

I placed all fleet personnel on stand-down, but to remain on standby, which meant they weren't allowed off base, but they didn't have to man their workstations and could relax.

Stardate 2518.02.04. 0900:
Karen was relaxing on the lounge chair in my office, going through things on her tablet, while I was working at my desk. We were planning to go for a walk around the base when my comms pin chirped,

announcing a call from Akron base. Since we were still inside, I said, "Comms, please patch the call to my office screen. Hunter out."

My screen shimmered and I looked at both Sirtis and Maharia, "Hello to you two, is this call what I think it is?"

It was Sirtis who replied, "Brains to Hunter, it certainly is sir. The birds have been flight tested and are ready to go; also, we both would like to come home."

I laughed, "In that case, wait for me to come and get you and I'll bring the bird handlers with me. We'll depart today and should be there in a week. Thank you, my friends, see you soon. Hunter out."

I contacted the communication room, requested a senior officers call, and asked for Admiral McManus to attend as well. Then I said to Karen, "Ok dear, the walk is off. How about a trip to Beta Australis instead? Come on, let's go over to the conference room."

She put away her tablet, got up and headed toward the door. When she joined me, gave me a kiss, and whispered in my ear, "Yes boss."

I waited until everyone was present and seated before I began. "I've called you to inform you that one hour from now, Defiant will launch, bound for Akron base on Beta Australis. This being desk bound is driving me up the wall, so I will be in command of the trip. I want the command and engineering crews for Ganymede and Phobos on board in addition to the regular Defiant crew. They will be doing all of the work while the Defiant personnel will be shadowing and coaching. Tark, you'll have to find everyone quarters. The rest of you will remain on base, with Admiral McManus in charge while I'm gone, any questions?"

General Daxer spoke up, "Can Colonel Muckins and I come along. I'd like to get to know our new ship on the way back Admiral."

I nodded, "Granted Wade, alright anything else?... dismissed."

Shortly thereafter, I heard the loudspeakers announcing, "Defiant pilots and crew, man your workstations! Ganymede and Phobos command and engineering crews please board the Defiant, launch in forty-five!" This was repeated every five minutes, until fifteen minutes before we launched.

As soon as Jonas informed me were in space and the course was laid in, I ordered, "Warp twenty-five, engage."

At Akron we loaded Sirtis's ship into its hangar on

the Defiant. After requesting take off clearance, all three ships lifted off for our return to Earth at warp twenty.

We arrived back at Vega13 a week later, Ganymede and Phobos landed on the runway, while Defiant landed on its pad and lowered into the bunker. All personnel were outside and looking over the two new ships, with Ganymede drawing the most interest. Both ships looked spectacular sitting there with their Ghost Fleet markings.

When Karen and I went over to check out the new ships ourselves, General Daxer joined us. While we were looking them over, "Wade, you and Bull already know where your quarters are, so you can start your men's quarters assignments anytime. Did you have a good look around while we were coming home?"

He replied, "Yes sir Clay, and it's the best ship I've ever travelled on. Your chief is quite a guy for inventing this… and all the other refinements too! I can't wait to see them in action."

Chapter 40

I knew that Mark would want to know that Ganymede and Phobos were finished, battle ready, and home at Vega13. Sirtis had completed linking their Tadis engine remotes into his console on the Defiant. I went to my office to make a video call to Mark. He didn't look like he was in a good mood when he answered, but he smiled after seeing me, "Well hello Clay, what can I do for you?"

I smiled, "It's the other way around Admiral, it's what I can do for you. This call is to let you know that my new ships are here and parked on the runway. My fleet can be ready to launch after three days for victualling."

He started laughing, "Clay my boy, you've made my day, three days, noted, I'll get back to you. Talk soon, Deadbeat out."

The next morning, the crew and mobile infantry troops started to prepare their quarters for when travelling, as did the crew of Phobos. By the end of the day all Ghost Fleet ships were ready for instant launch. Knowing Mark and using my own intuition, I ordered the loading of food and drink supplies to commence on all my ships.

To save time later, Karen and I then moved what we required for the next mission from our base quarters, to our quarters aboard Defiant. Leaving the rest of the stuff that we didn't need, behind in our base quarters.

The following day, I was working at my desk when a call was patched through and I found myself looking at Professor Harrelson, the university physicist, "Good morning professor, what can I do for you?"

"Good morning Admiral, and it's a case of what I can do for you. Since you approached us with your hypothetical enquiry about time travel, my colleagues and I have been pondering your wonderful question. No one has ever posed your question and we were delighted to work on it. If a person from the future returned in time to the present, would what he did in the future remain if he was present in the past. This was the first time this question had been asked, so I put out a call for all scientists in the Federation working in our field to ponder this. After all our data was processed, the consensus of opinion amongst our community is that as long as said person doesn't do anything to upset that timeline, that future would be unaffected, therefore it would remain intact as altered."

"Well thank you very much professor for getting back to me so quickly. I must admit that I had doubts about whether you and your colleagues would be able to form an opinion on this matter."

"Nonsense my boy," he laughed, "What you hypothetically posed was, as I said at the time, a question no one had bothered to ask. This spurred all the scientists in our field into immediate action. I have prepared a copy of all our empirical data for you and a final report, would you like to download this as well?"

"Yes please professor."

"Very well, here comes the file now Admiral, and thank you for the opportunity to help you in this regard."

As I watched, the file appeared in my computer in-tray, "On the contrary professor, thank you very much for doing this for me."

"Well, I hope this helps you. If there's anything else, please don't hesitate to call. Goodbye Admiral, Harrelson out."

After he was gone, I transferred the file to my personal flashdrive, then looked at it. Most of it was beyond my mathematical knowledge, but the final report, I copied again and sent it to Mark Kalashian.

The results of my enquiry lifted my spirits high, *if my mission took longer than three years duration, I could now use the Tadis Engine to return a lot sooner… if the scientific consensus is right, but I'll*

make that judgement when it's time to face it. I
started to read the professor's final report again,
mentally weighing up the risks without prior testing.
Then Karen came in to take me to lunch. As I was
getting up to join her, comms paged me. They told
me that Admiral Kalashian was on a video call for
me, so I had them patch it through.

After he came online, he said, "Glad to see you
working hard Clay. The reason I'm calling is that
I'm sending you a file I want you to look at later.
It'll make your mission briefing easier and gives you
your launch date and time.

I have looked over the final report of the scientists
you sent over. They appear to confirm your idea,
although there are no guarantees that it's correct
until it's tested, and only you have that ability at this
time."

"That's right Mark, at least the scientific assessment
gives me something to think about before we make
the jump."

"Good I'll leave you to look at it, Deadbeat out."

Karen asked, "What was that conversation about?"

"On the way to lunch sweetheart, let's go."

On our way to the mess, I told her all about the

report. She said, "That's good news for you darling. They were actually able to come up with an answer to your question, I did have doubts though."

In my office that afternoon I pulled up the video file and smiled while watching it. After it finished, I tapped my comms pin, "Hunter to Lt Major, please report to my office, Hunter out." Jonas answered immediately to tell me he was on his way.

It was not long before he knocked on my office door. I called for him to enter and to have a seat, "Jonas, I want you to plot two courses for me: Vertrillion One and Vertrillion Two. Then calculate how long it will take to travel to each of them from here using warp 20. They're the closest planets after Cirlillian Three in the Coreward Reach."

"Aye sir," he replied.

"Tell no one what you're up to and return to me when you're done, dismissed."

I was just about to call it a day when Jonas returned to my office. I gestured for him to have a seat while I looked over his calculations. In addition to the calculations I had asked for, he had also plotted the course between the two planets as well as calculated the time using a number of warp speeds. When I had finished studying his work, I looked up and smiled, "Fine work Jonas! Now, remember to forget that I ever asked you to do this, dismissed."

"Forget what sir?" is what he said, but you could tell by the smile on his face what he knew only too well.

The following morning at zero nine hundred, I had comms announce a senior officers call. It wasn't long before I heard the base speakers announce, "Now hear this, now hear this all senior officers to Admiral Davis's office immediately!" which was repeated twice more.

Ten minutes later, everyone was seated in the conference room when I entered, "Good morning all, please be seated. Now some of you already know this but some don't. For those that do, make note of time and date."

Then I played Marks video file. "Good morning Ghost Fleet. A number of mistakes were made a few years ago during the Alliance counter offensive against the Zytron invaders. It has been brought to my attention that it is possible that not all planets and systems were cleared of their presence. Luckily, today all Federation fleet vessels have upgrades to their scanners. Thanks to a chief scientist and engineer from the Federation, we can now scan and detect any Zytron presence on any given planet without having to land." Everyone turned and applauded Sirtis's recognition and he bowed eloquently. "With this ability some fleets are going to make a better sweep of our Federation and beyond in a two-part offensive to rid ourselves of the Zytron menace once and for all time.

Ghost Fleet you are going to be the second part of our offensive, which will be a long and at times, arduous mission. You will start from the closest planet in the Coreward Reach and go all the way to where the Zytronos homeworld used to be, then travel even further for a period of six months. Be prepared to spend years in deep space during this mission, after it ends you will all return to your base on Earth and have a year's stand down time for your efforts. All fleets will launch at zero nine hundred on stardate 2518.02.22. Good luck and happy hunting, I'll now pass you back to your Fleet Commander, Deadbeat out."

The file ended and I turned off the screen, "Now apart from which planet we start from, that I'll tell you soon… are there any questions?"

Wensall raised his hand, "Clay me boyo, can ye be telling me how long we could be gone, because I'd rather die on me own homeworld drunk and wit a woman, than with them ugly soldier types in deep space!"

His question made everyone laugh; me included.

I knew Wensall had deliberately made his joke to

ease the built-up tension in the room, the smart shifty bugger, so I replied, "Well Tor, as you know I took part in that campaign, and it took us three years to get anywhere close to Zytronos, but that was because fleets had to land troops to hunt and engage the bastards and sometimes, we didn't move for over a month. This time we've got a lot of things in our favour, we can move anywhere undetected, and we can scan for any presence and pinpoint them. So, at the outside I would have to say we could be away for up to three years."

He replied with a smile, "That be fine by me boyo."

Then I asked, "Any other questions?"

All hands stayed down, and everyone was silent, so I said, "Alright moving on, there is much of a muchness with our first target, both Vertrillion one and Vertrillion two are the same distance and there's only an hour's difference in arrival time, so I flipped a coin and made Vertrillion One our first target. We'll slow to half impulse at the outer marker and cloak, then all ships will spread out and make three intense scans of the planet except for you Tor, you'll stay in orbit at the north pole. Then once the scans have been done, captains, we'll compare results onboard Defiant. Should we detect any presence, Ganymede will be informed, and the troops released. Needle, your fighters will cover the boat landings and be ready to assist the ground troops with attack runs, or whatever they require."

Jane Matra replied, "Aye sir."

Then I continued, "Dax, remember your boats can go in cloaked, and that each fighter has two SK's available if needed."

"Aye Admiral, my boat pilots are all used to the cloaking device now, Hoorah!"

I smiled, "Alright any questions? Good, you all know when we launch, and our first target, lay in your courses and we'll enter hyperspace at warp 20. Get your ships provisioned, Dismissed!"

As they all filed out everyone had a smile and were joking with each other.

Stardate 2518.02.22.
Monday, the twenty-second, at zero eight hundred I strode onto the bridge, and asked Arras for the status report as I sat down.

She replied, "All crew present and correct, our course is laid in, docking clamps are released and we will elevate to above ground level in five Sir."

"Copy that Arras, thank you."

Then Mary said, "Admiral, all ships report all crews

present and correct, courses laid in and each will elevate the same time as us, except for Ganymede and Phobos on the runway."

Watching the clock, at zero nine hundred on the dot, I ordered, "Launch!"

Looking at the viewers, all ships were in space and in formation, I pointed, and Mary nodded, as I ordered, "All ships warp 20, engage!"

After we were in hyperspace, I smiled and thought to myself, *Well, here we go again, galloping across the cosmos on our way to who knows what, but I certainly thank my lucky stars for all my fleet crew members and their extraordinary spaceships, along with my superbly built ship the Space Cruiser Defiant!*

Author's Note:

Well that brings us to the end of this story, but it's merely the beginning saga of the Space Cruiser Defiant, and its crew.

As always, any comments you have, or book enquiries can be expressed through my website http://timothydiamond.net

I can only hope you look forward to more Timothy Diamond novels in the future, as to what they will be, well I'm not quite sure yet, but I do have a couple of projects in mind and will keep you informed through the blog page of the website. Until we meet again with my next novel my thanks for reading, and do take care, cheers.
Timothy Diamond.

All Other Books Written by Timothy Diamond and available direct from Tony at tony@tonytolcher.ws or his website: http://timothydiamond.net

Playing With Fire is the 1st book in the Catalyst Series.

It introduces Tom Davis, our main character and explores his early life.

Chasing the Sun, tells the tale of travelling to and back from the Nullarbor Plain. And playing golf on the Worlds Longest Golf Course. From Ceduna SA to Kalgoorlie WA.

Devine Retribution: book 2 of the Catalyst Series.

Sees Tom back in action this time in S. E. Asia and other secret warzones.

Kingdoms Bounty is set amid the backdrop of the life and times of William the Conqueror of England and his boyhood friend and ally Walter Tolchard, born into the nobility of French Normandy.

Book 3 of the Catalyst Series.

Tom's role has changed, and after thirty years of playing the game, it's time to quit...or is it? What will Tom do?

The Ultimate Gamble centres around Admiral Nelson and two members of the Fox-Davis Clan. How they rose to prominence in the naval battles alongside their beloved leader Horatio Nelson.

Book 4 in the Catalyst Series. The other Side of the Coin

Focuses on Tom's business and personal life during a time of upheaval.

Grievously wounded in one of the last battles of the American War. Our hero stays in America to carve out a new life. Through war and peace his family become counted one of the few rich and powerful law-making families of Texas.

Timothy Diamond's new action adventure, introduces Andy Fox Davis another member of the Fox-Davis Clan. And the eventual quest to go after what his cousin had found.

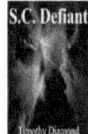

Timothy Diamond's latest epic takes into the realm of deep space, as he turns his hand to science fiction.

Where we will follow the Captain and crew of the battle cruiser Defiant through war and peace.

450

www.ingramcontent.com/pod-product-compliance
Lightning Source LLC
Chambersburg PA
CBHW060805030726
47503CB00002B/349